"Intense pacing . . . . searing emotions, and explosive sexual tension! Once I started reading *Shoot to Thrill*, I couldn't stop! This is high-action suspense at its very best!"
—Debra Webb, bestselling author *Find Me*

Praise for the novels of
Nina Bruhns

"Shocking discoveries, revenge, humor, and passion fill the pages . . . An interesting and exciting story with twists and turns." —*Joyfully Reviewed*

"[A] delightfully whimsical tale that enchants the reader from beginning to end. Yo ho ho and a bottle of fun!"
—Deborah MacGillivray

"This is one you will definitely not want to miss!"
—*In the Library Reviews*

"Nina Bruhns . . . imbues complex characters with a great sense of setting in a fast-paced suspense story overlaid with steamy sex." —*The Romance Reader*

"Gifted new author Nina Bruhns makes quite a splash in her debut . . . Ms. Bruhns's keen eye for vivid, unforgettable scenes and a wonderful romantic sensibility bode well for a long and successful career." —*Romantic Times* (4 stars)

"The intricate and believable plots crafted by Nina Bruhns prove she is a master of any genre. Her talent shines from every word of her books." —*CataRomance.com*

"The kind of story that really gets your adrenaline flowing. It's action-packed and sizzling hot, with some intensely emotional moments." —*Romance Junkies*

"Nina Bruhns writes beautifully and poetically and made me a complete believer." —*OnceUponARomance.net*

"Tells a very rich tale of love . . . A book you are going to want to add to your collection." —*Romance at Heart*

Shoot to THRILL

NINA BRUHNS

BERKLEY SENSATION, NEW YORK

THE BERKLEY PUBLISHING GROUP
Published by the Penguin Group
Penguin Group (USA) Inc.
375 Hudson Street, New York, New York 10014, USA
Penguin Group (Canada), 90 Eglinton Avenue East, Suite 700, Toronto, Ontario M4P 2Y3, Canada
(a division of Pearson Penguin Canada Inc.)
Penguin Books Ltd., 80 Strand, London WC2R 0RL, England
Penguin Group Ireland, 25 St. Stephen's Green, Dublin 2, Ireland (a division of Penguin Books Ltd.)
Penguin Group (Australia), 250 Camberwell Road, Camberwell, Victoria 3124, Australia
(a division of Pearson Australia Group Pty. Ltd.)
Penguin Books India Pvt. Ltd., 11 Community Centre, Panchsheel Park, New Delhi—110 017, India
Penguin Group (NZ), 67 Apollo Drive, Rosedale, North Shore 0632, New Zealand
(a division of Pearson New Zealand Ltd.)
Penguin Books (South Africa) (Pty.) Ltd., 24 Sturdee Avenue, Rosebank, Johannesburg 2196,
South Africa

Penguin Books Ltd., Registered Offices: 80 Strand, London WC2R 0RL, England

This is a work of fiction. Names, characters, places, and incidents either are the product of the author's imagination or are used fictitiously, and any resemblance to actual persons, living or dead, business establishments, events, or locales is entirely coincidental. The publisher does not have any control over and does not assume any responsibility for author or third-party websites or their content.

SHOOT TO THRILL

A Berkley Sensation Book / published by arrangement with the author

PRINTING HISTORY
Berkley Sensation mass-market edition / August 2009

Copyright © 2009 by Nina Bruhns.
Excerpt from *If Looks Could Chill* copyright © 2009 by Nina Bruhns.
Cover art by Craig White.
Cover design by Rita Frangie.
Interior text design by Kristin del Rosario.

ISBN: 978-0-425-22905-7

BERKLEY® SENSATION
Berkley Sensation Books are published by The Berkley Publishing Group,
a division of Penguin Group (USA) Inc.,
375 Hudson Street, New York, New York 10014.
BERKLEY® SENSATION and the "B" design are trademarks of Penguin Group (USA) Inc.

PRINTED IN THE UNITED STATES OF AMERICA

10 9 8 7 6 5 4 3 2 1

This book is lovingly dedicated to my children,
Gordon, Spencer, and Natalie.
Dream big, kids, and never lose sight of them.
I love you always.

Acknowledgments

My heartfelt thanks to Brian Kissinger and CJ Lyons for their invaluable help with the intricacies of airplanes and diseases. And to my beloved critique partners, especially Dorothy McFalls, for keeping me on the straight and narrow. Thanks, guys!

And naturally a huge thanks goes to my wonderful editor, Kate Seaver, and my fabulous agent, Natasha Kern, for believing in me. Don't know what I'd do without you, ladies!

ONE

IT was their shoes that gave them away.

The bastards.

Kick Jackson glanced at the three suits walking into the greasy New York diner where he ate lunch more days than not. He hoped against hope he'd been wrong and it was actually Jimmy Tang coming with his stuff.

It wasn't.

Kick had known the respite was too good to be true. That one day his former life would come rushing back at him with weapons drawn. Wanting him to do another of their dirty missions somewhere in the fetid underbelly of the world, so they could keep their own lily-white hands clean.

What part of *go fuck yourself* didn't they get?

Kick sighed in annoyance as the blue-haired waitress, Doris, shoved the burger plate with extra fries he'd ordered over the counter at him, and wordlessly refilled his chipped cup of coffee. Of all the days for them to show up. He *really* needed his stuff.

And hell, he'd already told anyone who'd listen that he was done with his old life. For good. No more. *Finito.* He didn't give a fucking goddamn that the national security waiver he'd signed when he was young and foolish said they could pull him back whenever they wanted for the rest of his life. Getting blown to hell had just been the last straw in a long list of reasons he didn't want any more to do with that gig. Ever.

But Zero Unit, his former CIA NOC-ops outfit, wasn't known for taking no for an answer. They'd tracked him down officially—well, as officially as it got with a Non-Official Cover unit, meaning top secret and highly covert—at least half a dozen times over the sixteen months since his release from the hospital, making it clear they wanted him back. Last time they'd even tried threats. Obviously they'd forgotten he had nothing to lose. Hard to threaten a man who didn't care what happened to him—as long as it happened here in the good ol' US of A.

He might be in a bad way, but he still had his pride. Which was why he'd shot the last guy they'd sent with orders to bring him in to Zero Unit—not so affectionately known as the ZU—headquarters by force if necessary. Like that was going to happen. The moron had actually tried to take him down. Kick'd had no choice but to shoot him. And he'd even been nice and aimed for the leg. Maybe a permanent limp would teach the kid not to mess with the big boys. Kick's own mangled leg had certainly taught him a lesson or two. . . .

But today his former unit commander had added insult to injury by sending a team of rank amateurs after him. *I mean, really.* Who wore sneakers and combat boots with suits and ties? Kick barely resisted snorting out loud as they approached his back in an oh-so-subtle fan formation.

Whatever.

"Hello, Kyle," said the big one who seemed to be the lead clown. To be fair, he wore appropriate black dress shoes with his blue pinstripes . . . unlike the jarhead standing to his right in combat boots with an ill-fitting brown suit or the Amazon to his left looking uncomfortable in an ugly business skirt and formerly white sneakers. "How's the leg?"

Kick ground his jaw. "The name's Kick, and the leg's fine; thanks for asking." No sense starting out on the wrong foot. As it were. The two goons had their hands within quick reach of their concealed weapons. And, well, he *had* shot that other guy. They were probably feeling twitchy. He could relate.

Pinstripes eased a hip onto the stool next to his, hooking his heel on the crossbar. "The boss would like to have a little chat with you, Kyle."

"It's Kick, and I'm getting bored with this ritual, Mr. . . ."

"Call me Al," Pinstripes helpfully supplied with a fake smile that didn't make it past the taut muscles of his cheeks. He didn't offer his hand. Smart guy.

"Seems to me, Al," Kick said, sparing the man a casual glance—*Large-caliber sidearm in left shoulder-holster; creds in left breast jacket pocket and right hand positioned close to calf, therefore right-handed, and probably a knife strapped to right ankle*—"that the boss would have gotten the hint by now. I'm not. Interested."

Pinstripes gave him a raised brow. "Haven't you been watching the news? I'd think that al Sayika incident two days ago would make you interested."

"You mean the three-second spot on CNN about al Sayika terrorists moving from Afghanistan to the Sudan?" *As if.* Fuck al Sayika, and double fuck Afghanistan. Scene of the worst betrayal in a lifetime filled with betrayals: the place where Kick had left more blood and body parts than he cared to remember—and where he'd lost his best friend. Hell, those were the *last* fuckers on earth he'd be interested in. "Then you'd think wrong," he said, managing to hold his face neutral despite the acid churning in his gut at the reminder of everything he'd been trying so hard to forget for over a year.

"The deal is," Pinstripes said, "NSA intercepted some very disturbing chatter regarding your old friend Jal—"

"Don't wanna know." Kick held up his hand like a stop sign. "Do. Not. Wanna. Know."

Pinstripes sighed. "You're not going to be . . . difficult again, are you, Kyle?"

Kick did a half turn on his stool to face him, and brought his fingertips to his chest in a gesture of Who, me? innocence.

Instantly the goons behind him went for their weapons, but before they could pull them out, Pinstripes patted the air, signaling them to stand down. "Listen, I don't want to have to get rough, Jackson," he said, dropping all pretense of friendliness. "But the situation out in the big, bad world is getting very serious and the boss wants you, simple as that. This time there's three of us and one of you. No way are you getting the drop on us. I've got my orders, and you're coming in."

Just then, Doris walked up with her crisp apron and stooped gait, coffeepot in hand, and gave the others a gimlet eye. "You three eatin' or just taking up airspace?" she demanded with a classic New Yorker scowl.

"They'll have coffee," Kick told her, eyeing his burger regretfully. He really was hungry. *Damn* Jimmy Tang for not showing up on time.

"*Hmph*," Doris muttered, smacking a cup down on the counter in front of Pinstripes and filling it. She shoved it over to him. Too fast. He tried to catch it, missed, and scalding hot liquid flew all over his hands. He yowled in pain and jumped to his feet, shaking them furiously.

Thank you, Doris. Kick vaulted over the counter, seized the coffeepot from her, and sprayed it at the goons with one hand and grabbed her wrist with the other. He flung the pot, pulled his SIG Navy automatic from the back of his waistband, and shoved it at her temple, grateful his hand only shook a little.

Doris screamed over the sound of the coffeepot shattering on the floor, her aged vocal cords cracking pitifully.

"Move and the old lady gets it in the head," Kick growled at his would-be captors, shoving her unceremoniously toward the door to the kitchen. "I told you, I'm not coming in."

She screamed again as he dragged her through the padded swinging door and kept screaming as it flapped closed and he lowered the SIG and let her go.

"Sorry about the mess," he muttered, digging in his pocket for the roll of twenties he always kept there for emergencies. He pressed two into her hand as she crossed her arms and calmly continued to scream.

The grizzled short-order cook, Manny, glanced over with a frown, flicking a worried gaze between Kick and the door as he tossed strips of bacon onto the grill. He jerked his head toward the back exit that led to an alley behind the diner. "Better make tracks, son. We'll hold 'em off."

Kick could hear the goons yelling out front and dishes breaking as they scrabbled over the counter to give chase.

"Thanks, sweetheart," he told Doris, and gave her a parting peck on the cheek, wincing at the scream in his ear. "I owe ya."

"What are you gonna do now?" Manny called after him.

"Disappear."

Doris's scratchy voice floated through the chaos. "Got to face them down someday, boy."

"Running's safer," he yelled back, a twinge already starting in his leg. "And tell Jimmy Tang he's fired!"

"**MY** God. Cheer up! It's not like we're going to a funeral or something, Rain."

Lorraine Martin's best friend, Gina Cappozi, rolled her eyes and gave her a firm push through the doors of the venerable Park Avenue hotel located several blocks from Bellevue Hospital, where they both worked. They had arrived punctually at eight PM, thanks to Gina's showing up at Rainie's apartment two hours early to nag and prod her into the slinky blue strapless Versace cocktail dress Gina had made her buy—under vehement protest—at Filene's on their day off. And give them time to walk to the hotel.

Rainie tugged at the hem, which ended a good bit above her knees, but had to tug it right back up by the bodice when the low décolletage threatened to expose her. *Great.*

They joined a small herd of smiling and preening single medical professionals, and were swept along through the chic Art Deco–style lobby and up the escalator to the mezzanine check-in desk. Everyone was all dressed up and reeked of anticipation. Gina glowed excitedly. Rainie just felt nauseous.

Speed dating.

Good grief. How had she *ever* let herself be talked into this?

Rainie had pretty much given up dating over the past couple of years. Who had the energy to get romantic after a long day or night in the emergency room dealing with blood, drugs, violence, and senseless death? Gina insisted that was exactly why she *should* get romantic at every possible opportunity. Sort of self-medication for the overwhelming stress of the job.

Easy for Gina to say. A medical doctor as well as a tenured professor, she headed a genetics research project at Columbia University, and did a stint in pediatrics at Bellevue once a week, dealing with cute little babies. Major stress there.

Well, at least Rainie wouldn't have to worry about staving off an actual relationship with anyone she met here. One thing about medical professionals, most were as driven as she was, totally married to their work. That's why these speed dating events were so popular with the staff of Bellevue. Just pick your flavor and head upstairs. *Yikes.* Which was also why Rainie had avoided them thus far. Just too embarrassingly obvious what was going on. Sure, it had been a while since she'd felt that mindless flutter of physical attraction to a man, and even longer since she'd done anything about it, but had she really missed sex that much? Not really.

"Wow, look at the muscles on that guy," Gina murmured, indicating a grinning blond surfer-dude type flexing his biceps for a bevy of female admirers as they waited in line at the registration table.

"Please. He can't be a day over twenty-five," Rainie muttered, semiappalled. She and Gina had both turned thirty several moons ago.

"Then he could use a nice pediatrician," Gina said with a wink.

Camera flashes lit up the foyer as the kid showed off for one of several photographers recording the event. By morning, pages of pictures and video clips would be loaded onto the dating organization's website. Yet another reason Rainie had refused Gina's previous invitations to accompany her. Who needed their embarrassment recorded for posterity?

"He doesn't look like he has a brain in his head," she muttered, praying her friend was kidding. Gina was smart as a whip, but had an out-there sense of humor. "Probably emp-ties bedpans all day," she added for good measure.

"And your point is?" Gina said cheekily.

Apparently, hormones trumped intelligence.

Oh, brother.

"Okay, I get it," Rainie responded with a dry smile. "You have to leave your standards and good sense at the door at these things."

"Now you're catching on."

They smacked name tags to their chests, and Rainie reluc-tantly followed Gina into the overcrowded ballroom. Sets of tables with two chairs, each labeled with a number, were packed into half the room, while the attendees sipped drinks and chatted in the other half waiting for the proceedings to start. The noise was deafening.

Rainie's pulse crept up. She hated chaos and disorder, situations she couldn't control.

"So, who do you fancy?" Gina asked, leaning in close to her ear, visually sizing up the male prospects like she was scanning the sale racks at Macy's.

Rainie sighed and nervously glanced over the crowd, try-ing to spot a man, any man, whose looks intrigued her enough to make her want to take a chance. But all she saw were the familiar doctors, residents, interns, and admin staff she saw every single day at the hospital. Oh, maybe not the exact same people, but they might as well be. The men circling around the room like well-dressed sharks had the same polished, professional appearance; the same polished, professional smiles; and undoubtedly the same polished, professional come-on lines that were eventually used on every nurse in the hospital under the age of forty.

Okay, fifty.

Seriously contemplating an escape strategy, she skimmed her gaze back to the entry door. Where a man was just walk-ing in.

Whoa.

Rainie's exit survey stopped dead in its tracks.

Well, maybe not *that* man. He didn't look the least bit polished. And he was *well* over twenty-five. His rumpled navy suit and dark five-o'clock shadow looked more like they belonged to a burned-out police detective than a doctor—she knew the type well from dealing with cops daily in the ER. He looked hard. Jaded. No-nonsense. *Dangerous.*

And intriguing as hell.

Her pulse started doing the Snoopy dance. Not a good thing. This was exactly the kind of man a control freak such as herself should avoid. But just like her high-risk job, the type also held a kind of fatal attraction.

What was a man like that doing at a medical professionals singles night? And yet he wore a name tag, and you had to have a hospital ID to get in. Police liaison maybe? Military field medic?

Towering over the rest of the crowd by a good six inches, the man had thick, sable brown hair that still bore evidence of a recent wet-combing, which hadn't done much to tame its waves or unruly length. Not military, then. She couldn't see much below his shoulders, but they were broad enough to fill out his bad suit to capacity and then some.

Interestingly, he seemed even more uncomfortable than she felt.

His hooded eyes roamed over the room like he was looking for something, or someone, specific. And caught her staring. Her pulse did a few more dance steps. *Oh, no.* She wanted to look away. Knew instinctively she *should* look away. But for the life of her, she couldn't.

Instead of continuing his survey, he stared back until she felt her face flush.

That's when he started walking. Toward her.

Oh, Lord.

All this time Gina had been chatting away, pointing out this man or that. Finally she noticed she was being ignored.

"You're not being very—" Her friend's words halted with a small gasp.

"Ho-boy. I think I'm in trouble," Rainie muttered, watching with rising trepidation as the man came closer and closer. Or was that excitement she felt thrumming low in her belly?

What on earth was she dreaming of? Unfortunately, she had a pretty good idea.

Gina read her illicit thoughts and her jaw dropped. "You

have got to be kidding," she hissed in her ear, scandalized. "*That* guy? He looks like a serial killer!"

"I think he's sexy as hell," Rainie murmured without thinking, then glanced at her friend in consternation. Had she really said that aloud?

"Do *not* take him home, Lorraine Martin."

Apparently she had. "You know me better than that, Geen. But maybe a drink . . . here at the bar."

"But," Gina protested, "that wasn't the idea, either, Rain. You need *more* than just a drink, girl. This is your chance to find someone safe and take him upstairs. Someone like a nice—"

"Boring doctor?" She shook her head. Not a chance. She might be a lonely chickenshit, but she wasn't desperate. "No, thanks. Besides, so what if I have a drink with him? You know I can take care of myself," Rainie reminded her. It was true. After dealing with the crazies who populated the experimental drug program she was in charge of in the ER and seven years of studying self-defense, she was more than capable of fending off unwanted advances of any variety. She did so frequently.

"I know, but—"

"I'll be fine, Gina. Go. Before I change my mind again and run screaming for the exit."

After a short hesitation her friend murmured, "Fine. Take your walk on the wild side, sweetie. But call me first thing in the morning or I'm sending the police." Then she melted into the crowd.

By now the stranger had threaded his way through the crush, and he came to a stop directly in front of Rainie. Her heart was beating like a bass drum.

His gaze drifted slowly down her too short, too tight, and too revealing dress, then drifted back up again, pausing at her breasts. Her nipples zinged in response, tightening to hard points. Which of course he noticed. He didn't smile, but his blue eyes darkened to a stormy grey as he watched them.

Her flush deepened, along with her consternation. "Look, I—"

"Would you like a drink?" he interrupted, the query amazingly calm and civilized, considering *she* felt like she was about to faint.

This was definitely not a good idea.

"Have we met?" she asked, playing for time, because she knew damned well they hadn't. She glanced down at his navy blue lapel. His name tag read Dr. Nathan Daneby.

Her eyes popped—*Nathan Daneby?*—and rocketed back up to his face. Astonishment plowed through her. "*You're* Dr. Nathan Daneby? From Doctors for Peace?"

A shadow of alarm skittered across his features. "You know me?"

"Yes! Well, no. I mean, not personally, but everyone knows your name. Okay, maybe not everyone, but I do." All the nervousness *whooshed* out of her, replaced by excitement. "I've been an admirer for years. I've followed your career ever since the war, when you saved those villagers in Afghanistan. That was so amaz—" She halted in midsentence, wincing in embarrassment. "Sorry, Dr. Daneby. I'm babbling. I'm sure you didn't come here to meet groupies."

His alarm morphed into something else she couldn't quite pin down. He made a choking noise. Putting a finger between the knot of his striped tie and the collar of his white shirt, he tugged like it was strangling him. "Actually, I'm seldom recognized in the States. In fact, never. This is a first."

She cleared her throat. God, she was *so* blowing it. He was going to walk away any second. And amazingly, for the first time in living memory, she didn't want the man to leave.

"S-so, *um*," she stammered. "Then why *are* you here? In New York, I mean. And, *um*. Here. At this"—she gestured vaguely, mortification creeping back up her neck—"*um*, thing."

Surely, he wasn't here to find a *date*. Dr. Nathan Daneby was famous! Well, sort of. In certain circles. Like among nurses who read *National Geographic* in the lounge and daydreamed about having the courage to venture outside a ten-block radius of home without being paralyzed by fear.

What would it be like to have Nathan Daneby's daring adventures? She couldn't even imagine.

He stepped closer and lifted his hand toward her. It was large, strong, and unmanicured. A hand that obviously wasn't afraid of hard work. For some reason that made him even more attractive.

She could smell him, too. Musky, dark, and exquisitely masculine. All him; no cologne, no shampoo, no minty breath. Just pure man.

Would he notice if she leaned in just a little and inhaled?

Extending his forefinger, he lightly tapped the name tag stuck on the minuscule bodice of her strapless dress, then traced the pad of his finger slowly, *God* so provocatively, along her name and profession. The pebbled tip of her breast sang with a long jolt of electricity that streaked straight to her center.

"I imagine I'm here for the same reason as you, Lorraine Martin, nurse practitioner." He bent down close to her hair. "But I'd prefer to stay under the radar, if that's all right with you."

His finger lingered on the slope of her breast. Suddenly she ached for him to slide it down under her dress and touch her nipple. Cup her naked—

Good Lord! What was going on with her? She hadn't reacted this strongly to a man in years. *If ever.* Her face was on fire.

"Absolutely," she said, striving to keep her voice steady despite the wildly inappropriate thoughts skidding through her mind.

"So about that drink . . . ?"

Don't do it! her good sense yelled inside her head.

"Sure," she said aloud.

"Here?"

His low-spoken query was rife with meaning. Her pulse went crazy in her throat.

Could she? Should she?

My God, she couldn't believe she was even *considering* leaving the hotel with him. She who was always so careful. So aware of her personal safety. So cognizant of the many perils out there waiting to snuff out your life at any second without rhyme or reason. This man was a virtual stranger. One who fairly vibrated with danger. A man who belonged to a world so different from her own that it gave her vertigo just thinking about it.

No! No! No! Don't do it!

Still, the refusal wouldn't come out. Which was so totally out of character she wondered if some alien being had taken over her body.

Talk about hormones trumping intelligence.

But Nathan Daneby *wasn't* a stranger, she argued with herself. Not really. And she'd love to ask him about his exciting work. To talk about his amazing travels and adventures. And maybe . . . yes, maybe even more than talk, if she could get up the nerve to accept what his stormy eyes were blatantly promising.

More breathtaking excitement than she'd ever experienced in her life.

After all, when would a woman like Lorraine Martin ever get another chance to know a man like him?

So, with a thundering heart, she took that last step off the cliff of uncontrolled madness. And said, "Why don't we get out of here?"

NATHAN Daneby's storm blue eyes took on an unmistakable glitter. The harsh angles of his face seemed to grow sharper, the rough shadow on his jaw darker. He still wasn't exactly smiling, but there was no doubt that he was pleased with her response. For a split second he looked as though he was going to lower his mouth to hers and kiss her.

But he didn't. "Let's," he murmured.

Taking her hand firmly in his, he led her through the throng to the coat-check to fetch her wrap. When a photographer stopped them at the ballroom exit to snap their picture together, he bowed over her hand and pressed his lips lingeringly to her palm.

She almost melted.

"I'll get a cab," he said when they emerged from the lobby into the warm August night.

"No!" She blushed when he gave her an inquiring look. "No need. I know a nice place a couple blocks away," she said, and shook off the irrational tingle of fear that snaked over her arms at the thought of getting into a taxi.

His look narrowed. "Are you afraid? Of me?"

She swallowed. "I, *um*, I don't like cars," she explained, feeling a bit foolish, and turned to continue walking.

Around her, the sounds and smells of the city filled her senses with the comfort of familiarity. The waiters and bartender at the Green Man bistro were also familiar, so she'd feel safe there. Perhaps it was a false security, but she refused to let the irrational fear take over her life completely.

"Which didn't answer my question."

She smiled gamely over at him, took in the concerned look on his face, and shook her head. "No. I'm not afraid of you, Dr. Daneby. I wouldn't have come if I were."

"Please, call me Kick."

"Kick?" She'd never heard him referred to by that nickname before.

He shot her a lopsided smile. "Don't ask." He slid his arm around her shoulders as they walked. "I'm glad you're not afraid. I promise there's no reason to be. I only want . . ."

She glanced up when his words trailed off. "Want what?"

All at once he turned and pulled her into his arms. "This."

She gasped in surprise as he lifted her into a kiss.

"Oh!"

But her gasp melted into a low moan as his tongue took advantage and slid past her lips. He tasted so incredibly good! He deepened the kiss, taking away her ability to think.

She put her arms around his neck and leaned into him. He stumbled a little, and without lifting his mouth, turned and pressed her against the smooth marble of the hotel wall they were walking past.

"Open more for me, baby."

A groan rumbled through his chest when she willingly obeyed. His kiss was hot and hard and thoroughly sinful. He kissed like a man used to taking what he wanted. A man who wasn't afraid of anything. A man strong enough to banish her own fears just through the sheer strength of his presence.

Suddenly, a nearby door smacked open with a loud bang.

In a single, lightning-fast motion he tore his lips from hers, jumped away, and whirled. Whipping a large gun from the back of his waistband, he aimed it at the door. A giggling couple spilled out through it. Just as quickly, the gun disappeared again under his jacket. If she'd blinked, she might have missed the whole thing.

But she hadn't.

She stared at him, confusion welling through her.

He had a gun!

But Dr. Nathan Daneby hated guns. He always made a big deal about that in all the magazine articles. A ban on weapons of any kind was also one of the main tenets of Doctors for Peace, the organization he worked for. They forbade their members from carrying them. Ever.

Which meant . . .

This man—couldn't be Dr. Nathan Daneby.

But . . . But . . .

Oh, shit. Rainie's knees threatened to buckle. She reached behind her, fingers scrabbling against the cold marble of the wall, searching for purchase. *Oh, shit.*

Seven years of martial arts were no match for a bullet.

The man—whoever the hell he was—swore low and harsh, cursing at the sidewalk as the couple hurried off down the street without even seeing them.

Real fear started to trickle through Rainie's limbs.

She tried to sidle away from him, but her high heel caught on a grate in the pavement. In a blur, he spun back to her. She froze.

For a long second he regarded her in taut silence.

"You aren't Nathan Daneby," she managed to croak. Her voice broke on the false name.

He didn't move. Not a muscle. But there was a light sheen of sweat forming on his brow. It wasn't *that* warm out. "No," he finally said.

A whimper came from her throat, sounding a lot like desperation. "Then who are you?"

"Seriously, you don't want to know."

Now, there was the truth. "You're right," she said, and straightened away from the wall, forcing steel into her spine. "And I've changed my mind about that dri—"

"I don't think so."

She blinked. Panic dissolved the steel. "Please move aside," she bluffed. When he didn't, she lurched sideways. "I'm leaving now."

He swiftly closed the gap between them and grasped her upper arm. His grip was like iron. "I'm afraid I can't let you do that."

Dread swirled through her veins. *Oh, God.* This was really and truly happening. "Let go of me, or I'll scream!" She yanked frantically at her arm.

"No," he calmly said, banding his arm around her shoulders and pulling her flush to his side. A second later, the barrel of his gun dug painfully into her ribs. "You won't."

She squeezed her eyes shut. Willed herself not to scream anyway. *She would not panic. Panic would not help.*

Deep breath, let it out slowly. Deep breath, let it out slowly.

"Please don't hurt me," she pleaded, the words thready with blind terror. "I'll do whatever you want. Just please don't—"

"Follow my orders," he said, "and nothing will happen to you. Understand?" The gun retreated a fraction from her ribs.

A trickle of hope warred with the deluge of terror. *Deep breath.*

I will be fine.

I will be calm.

I will be safe.

She looked up at the imposter, trying desperately to judge his sincerity. Was it just a trick to lull her into compliance? His pupils were black and dilated, and the sable hair falling over his forehead was dark with sweat. Almost as though—

A wave of shocked recognition coursed through her. *My God!* He was . . . Suddenly, she understood. She was a nurse, with free access to the hospital supplies.

She should have known.

"You want drugs, don't you?"

His brows flared. "No!" A breath jetted out and he scowled fiercely, making her jump. "*No.* That's not what I need from you."

His storm blue eyes bored into hers, and panic reared up anew, stronger than ever. *She'd been so sure.* If not drugs, then . . . "What *do* you want from me?"

She felt the cold caress of the gun barrel under her breast.

"Just one thing," he growled. "Take me to your apartment."

TWO

THE man called Pig woke up with a start.

The redhead had come to him again. She was a real red-head, you know. Not one of those bottle-job wannabes. He knew for sure, because she was naked.

She was always naked in the dreams.

That's what was so damn frustrating. She was always na-ked, but she only ever wanted to talk. Just talk. Jesus help him. All this time. Endless days and nights—at least he as-sumed they were days and nights—and she had yet to let him touch her. It had to be years now. At least a year. Two. Maybe even three. Who knew? When everything around you was black, black, black, time ran together into one long, fucking stretch of limitless pain and suffering.

The least she could do was freaking touch him.

Pig banked his frustration. Again.

At least she talked to him. Talking wasn't so bad. Even if it was a dream. Nobody else did. Nothing he wanted to hear, anyway. "Get up, Pig." "Eat your slop, Pig." "Bend over so we can beat you, Pig." Thank Christ they weren't into rape. Not men, anyway. He'd heard the muffled women's screams, though. Real ones. Just girls, from what he could tell. *They* hadn't been so lucky.

And they called *him* a pig.

The naked redhead held out her hand to him. "Hi. I'm H—"

He strained to hear her name. Like he did every time. But he never caught it. Something with an *H*. He'd tried to guess endlessly. Holly. Helen. Hope. Hallie. Hanna. Heather. Helga? Nothing sounded familiar. Though her face and body were as familiar to him as his own.

Okay, that wasn't true. He had no idea what his own face looked like. It had disappeared. Gone completely. All but the long, filthy beard he could touch. And the bruises he could feel. They were all too familiar. As for his body, well, he was happy not to see it, thank you very much. He couldn't afford to lose what little he had in his belly.

"What's your name?" she asked him, smiling sweetly. So damn sweetly it made his eyes hurt just looking at her pretty smile. Or maybe they just hurt, period. They'd hurt for fucking ever.

She waited patiently. Oh, yeah. His name.

Whatever. He had no fucking idea.

No, not true. It was Pig. That's it. "I'm Pig," he said.

She blinked. He could tell she didn't believe him. But she smiled again anyway. That blinding smile. No, he was already blind. That wasn't her fault.

"I hate that name," she said, her eyes soft and sad as she watched him.

"Me, too."

"Then don't use it. I'll call you . . . James." Every time she appeared, she tested out a different name on him. Like she was trying to get him to remember. A hopeless cause. "What would you like to talk about today, James?"

Yesterday—or had it been last week?—he'd been Fredrick, and they'd talked about music. She liked country and classical. He was more of a jazz fan.

"Ice cream," he said today. Damn, he really missed ice cream. Almost as much as he missed sex. Some days more. Hell, most days more. Which said a lot. Because he really loved sex. At least, he had . . . before. Not so sure anymore. But he was pretty damn sure he still loved ice cream. They couldn't take that away from him.

Whoever the fuck *they* were. . . .

* * *

NATURALLY, she *would* live on the fifth floor of a six-floor walk-up. The stairs were fucking endless.

Kick grimaced at the pain throbbing in his left leg and kept his arm tightly around Nurse Practitioner Lorraine Martin, leaning on her as much as he dared. The SIG dug discreetly into her ribs, keeping her honest.

She had to sense his leg's weakness, and he wouldn't put it past her to jerk away and shove him down the stairs before they made it up the five flights. Not that he blamed her. He was messing with the woman big-time. But he just didn't have a choice here. He needed her. And he needed a place to hide for a day or two. He couldn't chance anyone else finding out where he was. Because if someone else knew, *they* would know.

Could you *believe* the woman had actually heard of his friend Nathan Daneby? And admired him. How perfect would that have been?

Damn the fucking painkillers that had screwed with his finely honed reflexes, and damn the fucking door slam that had sounded way too much like a gunshot, throwing him briefly straight into his past and causing him to break cover and blow the whole sweet deal.

Damn it to hell. He had been so fucking close to talking her into sharing her bed with him, with no need for guns or threats. So close he could still taste her on his tongue. Feel the shape of her lush breast on his palm. And the uncomfortable tightness of his pants.

Jesus, God.

They made it upstairs to her apartment door and she pulled out her key, but Kick stopped her before she could insert it into the lock.

He'd already checked her driver's license to be sure she was taking him to the right address, and he'd asked if she had a roommate. She'd denied it. But, then, so would he under the circumstances.

"Is anybody home?" he asked again.

"I told you. I live alone," she said stiffly.

He nodded, and pressed the buzzer anyway. Before she could react, he pulled her to him, stabbed his fingers in her hair, and covered her mouth with his. He wouldn't exactly call it a kiss since she was struggling against him. But anyone looking on would just think she was moving around because she was excited. She tried to bite his lip. He bit her back. Not hard enough to break the skin, but hard enough to elicit a gasp of pain . . . or perhaps outrage because he sucked her lip into his mouth and tongued the spot. After that she went rigid and didn't try anything else.

When a full minute had gone by with their lips crushed together and without anyone answering the buzzer, he released her. They were both breathing hard.

He took the key and opened the door, herded her inside, then closed and locked it, depositing the key in his pants pocket. Yeah, the one with the hard-on under it.

She watched the key disappear, then glared up at him. "If you think—"

He lifted the gun to silence her while he sized up the place, grateful when she actually took the hint.

It was a typical older Manhattan apartment, compact and efficient. Antique furniture and pastel paint, with the minimal clutter of an occupant who spent most of her time elsewhere. In the case of a nurse, probably at work. Incongruously, the walls were covered by colorful travel posters. The kitchen was galley-style, accessed through a wide opening by the front door. Kick made sure no one was lurking in it, then turned his attention to the living room's alley-side wall, which was punctuated by two windows with a steam radiator between. And more posters.

"Do the windows open?"

She hesitated, obviously surprised by the question. "Yes."

"Open one."

Her eyes widened in fear. "What are you—"

"Not pushing you out," he assured her with a shade of exasperation, reminding himself she had no way of knowing he truly had no intention of hurting her. "I need to check the fire escape."

"Why?"

Nosy little thing. He prodded her none-too-gently in the shoulder. With his hand, not the gun. "Just open the damn window."

She did. Reluctantly. He wondered whether it was raising the window or obeying his orders that she didn't care
for. Not that it mattered. He was in charge whether she
liked it or not.

He followed. Keeping a hand firmly on her wrist, he stuck
his head outside the window. The fire escape was located
between this apartment and the next one—about a five-foot
stretch from where he stood. No doubt there had once been a
balcony that connected it all, but it was long gone. The good
news was, unless she was an Olympic gymnast she couldn't
escape that way. Not without risking a five-story fall and
being smashed on the street below like a bug on a wind-
shield.

The bad news was, neither could he. Not in his present
state of fitness. Sixteen months ago, he could have. In his
sleep. With one hand tied behind him. But no longer.

He left the window up, lowered the blinds over it and the
other one, then turned to her. "All right, show me the bedroom. You first."

She stiffened, but after a glance at the SIG she didn't argue. She was learning. She led him to the open door of the
only other room in the place. He reached in, flipped on the
light, and did a quick once-over before he put his hand to
the small of her back and made her go in.

It was a soft room, the color of old butter. The subtle scent
of a flowery perfume—her perfume—lingered intimately in
the air, making him acutely aware that he was invading
her most personal space. His eyes were naturally drawn to
the bed. It was large but not huge, covered with lots of pillows and a quilt of the type he'd seen in antique stores. Like
the furniture. *Dresser, bookshelf, a carved wooden armoire
that took the place of a closet.* None of it really seemed her
style. He would have pegged her for more of a modern-
contemporary type. Still, what did he know?

"I inherited the apartment from my grandmother," she
said, reading his mind. Her chin lifted slightly. "I like old
things."

He didn't comment, just pointed to the bed while he
checked the bathroom. "Sit down." Again, the walls were
covered by bright travel posters. Greece. Portugal. Iceland.

Egypt. No wonder she'd been attracted by Nathan Daneby, world traveler extraordinaire. Of course, he was, too.

He came out and she had not moved. He pointed to the bed again. "Sit. Down."

Her eyes were wide with fear. "Please, no!" She backed away from him, pulling her flimsy wrap protectively around her body. For all the good *that* would do if—

He pushed out an impatient breath. "I told you, obey my orders and nothing will happen to you. I *mean* that."

She shook her head at him accusingly. "You're lying."

"No, I'm n—"

"You kissed me," she blurted out. Her teeth worried her bottom lip where it was still red and swollen from his love bite. Or whatever the hell it had been.

For some totally illogical reason, her outrage irritated him. "I kissed you before that and you didn't object," he reminded her tersely. "In fact, I could have sworn you enjoyed it."

"That was before I knew you were a—" She snapped her mouth shut.

"A what?" he demanded. Now he was really getting annoyed.

Her throat worked. "A . . . a kidnapper!"

Kidnapper? He almost laughed. Was that the best she could do? On the grand scale of the many colorful things he'd been called in his lifetime, *kidnapper* was just about the least insulting.

"Okay, fine. You don't kiss kidnappers. Just sit the hell down."

She opened her mouth to object again.

"*Now.* Before I change my mind."

Thankfully, she crossed her arms over her abdomen and stalked wordlessly to the bed. She was still wearing her high heels so her shapely backside twitched enticingly back and forth in her short, sexy dress.

Which almost made him careless. She was about to sit down by the pillows. And the nightstand.

"Wait! Not there," he barked. He pointed again at the foot of the bed. "There."

She hesitated and her nostrils flared just enough to confirm his suspicion before she primly sat where he'd directed.

"All right, where is it?" he asked.

"Where's what?"

"The weapon."

Her chin lifted. "I don't know what you're talking about." But her eyes told a different story. They flicked ever so briefly toward the upper end of the bed.

Nice try. With grim efficiency he searched the contents of the nightstand. He didn't find any guns, knives, or mace in the cubby or the small drawer.

He did, however, find a box of condoms. And a bottle of mint-flavored massage oil.

Fuck. He *really* did not want to know that.

He gritted his teeth and slammed the drawer shut with a spike of angry regret for what he might have been enjoying had the stars been aligned differently and he weren't such an unlucky son of a bitch. And kept searching.

There was a loaded Beretta between the mattress and box spring. And a stiletto in a sheath that had been taped to the back of the headboard.

Okay, then. Not as harmless as she looked.

He hiked his brows at her.

Her cheeks glowed bright scarlet but her chin rose even higher. "A woman has a right to defend herself. No telling what kind of pervert will push his way into her bedroom."

He gave her a strained smile. "True enough."

Putting both the Beretta and stiletto in his jacket pocket, he slipped it off and folded it before setting it on the nightstand. He kept the SIG in its holster under his arm, but unbuttoned and slowly rolled up his sleeves. She watched him nervously. Then he pulled a pair of handcuffs from his back pants pocket.

She sucked in a breath when she saw them. And in a flash scrambled across the bed to get away. He caught her by the ankle, narrowly avoiding a vicious kick in the face from her other high heel, which he swiftly ripped off and threw to the floor along with its mate.

"Goddamn it!" he growled, using all his strength to flip her and pull her back to the center of the bed. By now she was using fists, too.

"Let me *go*!"

Jesus. The woman had some excellent defense moves.

"Then stop hitting me!"

With difficulty, he released her ankles and grabbed her wrists between kicks and punches, launched himself on top of her, and pinned her down with his body. With her arms held above her head, she could only wriggle ineffectually under him.

"Better?" he ground out.

"No!"

He quickly realized he'd made a tactical error. A *big* one.

Her shawl had come off in the struggle, and her strapless bodice had shifted down to the brink of being . . . way too distracting. Her already short hem had crept high up her thighs.

She was wearing stockings. Silky ones. The kind with lace tops that stayed up by themselves.

He stifled a groan and took a deep, cleansing breath. "How many times do I have to tell you, I'm *not* going to hurt you?"

She didn't look convinced. In truth, she looked plain terrified. And about to cry. Tears swam in her eyes, threatening to spill out the corners. Which did the trick, yanking him back from the verge of doing something really stupid.

Like trying to kiss her again.

God, what was *wrong* with him?

He did not *do* teary-eyed women. Hell, he did not do women at *all*. And *this* was exactly why. They turned him all inside out and totally robbed him of his brain cells.

Clamping his jaw tightly, he reached down to retrieve the handcuffs and snapped one cuff onto her wrist. The other cuff he fastened with a *snick* to his own.

Giving her a warning glare, he rolled off and lay panting on the bed by her side, scowling at the ceiling.

Apparently that surprised her, too. Hell, he was just full of surprises.

Turning her head on the pillow, she stared at him anxiously. He kept his eyes firmly on the plaster overhead.

It was crisscrossed with cracks. Like the scars on his leg and back. There was a spiderweb wafting back and forth in one corner.

At length, she finally asked, her voice a thready murmur, "You're not going to rape me?"

He tried really hard to be angry that she could believe that of him, but couldn't quite muster the will. He gritted his teeth. "I. *Don't*. Rape. Women." He emphasized each word so she'd get it once and for all.

After a few seconds she said, "Are you going to rob me?"

He counted to ten. Twice. "No."

There was another pause before she whispered, "Kill me?"

God*damn* it!

"*No!*" He wanted to scream it at her, but managed to contain himself to a low roar.

There was an even longer pause. "Then why are you doing this to me?"

There you go. Another reason he didn't do women. It was *aaallways* about them.

He squeezed his eyes shut and took another deep, calming breath. "I just wanted to fuck you, okay? *Willingly.* Is that so hard to understand? And in the process, find a place to lie low for a day or two. That's it. Sex and a bed. Nothing sinister."

She sniffed and he heard her swallow. "Why?"

"Why do you think? Jesus freaking Christ, woman, you're a walking hard-on in that dress. And frankly, you seemed more than interested."

She swallowed again, this time more heavily. "I, *um*, meant . . . why do you need to lie low for a day or two?" He could swear there was embarrassment in her voice.

He cracked his eyelids and turned to look at her. Sure enough, her cheeks were bright red again. Hell, maybe she didn't like crude language. Or maybe she was truly clueless and in denial about where that kiss had been leading.

At least she wasn't crying anymore.

"You're holding me against my will," she said archly when he didn't answer right away. "I think I deserve an explanation."

Possibly. Especially if he wanted her on his side before he lost control of himself and the situation. He glanced at the clock and briefly debated what to tell her. How much of the truth. Not about him, but the other thing. Because too much truth could put her in danger. Which was the last thing he wanted.

"All right. It's not real complicated. There are some people after me. I don't want them to find me."

She worried her lip again. He really wished she'd stop doing that. He *so* didn't need the reminder of—

"What kind of people? What did you do?"

He sighed. Damn, she really *was* nosy.

"I quit my job. They didn't like that. They want me back, but I don't want to go back. I need a few days to get some stuff done before I disappear again."

She turned onto her side to face him, her expression solemn as she digested that. "Again?"

He willed himself not to look below her chin. "It's not the first time," he admitted. But he hadn't taken them seriously enough, and they'd found him again. He'd learned his lesson. One reason he was here tonight.

"They must really want you back."

"Yeah. They do."

"And they must be really dangerous people if you want to disappear."

"Yeah. They are."

"It's, like, the mob, or something?"

He let out a humorless laugh. "Yeah. Or something."

She studied him for a long moment. "When I first saw you, I thought you were a cop. Are you undercover?"

He studied her back. "Why would you think that?"

Her shoulder lifted. "You sure as hell aren't a doctor. The only reason I fell for that Dr. Nathan Daneby ruse was because he's usually described as being handsome but scruffy. Living in primitive Third World countries does that to you, I guess. Anyway, it seemed to fit, and—"

But he wasn't listening. He'd snagged back on the "handsome" comment. Yeah, and the fact that when she'd shrugged, her dress had slipped even farther down her breast, exposing a rosy sliver of areola.

The temperature in the room spiked up. Among other things. He started to sweat again.

Fuck.

Fisting his fingers into a tight ball to prevent them from reaching out to touch her, he forced his gaze back up.

She'd been watching him stare at her breasts. She was blushing again, this time all the way from her delectable décolletage to the tips of her ears. But she made no move to cover herself.

She didn't look scared anymore.

"Who are you, really?" she whispered.

Uncertain, tentative, guarded, yes. Frightened, no.

Uh-oh. He backpedaled fast. "Lorraine—"

"Rainie."

"What?"

"My name. Call me Rainie."

He wiped his free hand over his mouth. "Okay, look, Rainie, I don't think—"

"Do your friends really call you Kick?" she interrupted again.

She hadn't asked his actual name, he noted. He searched her eyes for a sign. Of what, he wasn't exactly sure. But what he *was* sure of was that the one-eighty this conversation had suddenly taken was probably not a good idea. *Definitely* not a good idea. The whole kidnapping/held-against-her-will thing put a very different spin on having any kind of physical relations with Lorraine Martin. Legal-wise.

And also blackmail-wise. His old unit, the ZU, was very good at blackmail. Not that they used the term. But the consequences would be just as real, for both of them.

"Well?"

He pushed back stomach-churning memories. "Yes. They really call me Kick."

"Okay," she said carefully. "Kick. So, are you?"

For the life of him, he couldn't remember what she was talking about. "Am I what?"

"Undercover?"

Lying had been part of his professional life for so long that he almost let another one slide off his tongue without thinking. But he was done with all that. Another of the myriad reasons he'd wanted out. He'd always hated the lies and deception. And was trying his damnedest to put it all behind him now. Which meant telling the truth. As far as he could.

"No. I'm not a cop."

An emotion he couldn't identify flitted through her eyes, which were suddenly pooling again. *Damn.* Now what?

She licked her lips, raised her hand, and pressed it haltingly to his chest. "Kick?"

"Yeah?"

"I really need you to tell me the truth about something."

"What's that?"

Her fingers bunched the fabric of his shirt. "Are you a good guy or a bad guy?"

He felt the corner of his mouth curl up sardonically. *Now, there was the five-million-dollar question.*

Tentatively he felt inside himself, searched his shadowed soul. Good or bad?

For him, despite it all, despite everything he'd seen in his life of betrayal, lies, and deception, and everything he'd done in his bloody and violent world, in his own heart he knew the answer.

He lifted his fingers and traced them along her jaw, feeling the creamy softness of her skin, and the impressive strength beneath it. He felt the fine trembling of her body's desire for him, lurking just below the surface. And saw the desperate need in her eyes for it to be okay to want him. That he wasn't a monster.

He wanted to reassure her. To tell her without reservation he was one of the good guys. But would that be another lie? On the final day of reckoning, would he be judged good or bad? He just didn't know. Not for sure.

So he did the only thing he could. He told the truth.

"I wish I knew, Rainie," he murmured softly. "I really wish I knew."

THREE

RAINIE felt like she'd been dragged down a rabbit hole.

She didn't know what to think. Or do. She tightened her fingers in the front of Kick's white shirt. Then abruptly pushed him away.

"What kind of an answer is that?" She couldn't help the sob that escaped with the words. Or the visceral reaction. She wanted to pound her fists against his chest but he grasped and held them in his steely grip.

"An honest one."

Angry disappointment welled up like a storm surge. Why was this happening to *her*? Why not to Gina? Or someone else? She was so attracted to this man! God, she wanted him. More than any other man she'd ever met. Why did he have to be a—

Her frustration spilled over and her body began to tremble uncontrollably. Her pulse pounded.

"What if I don't *want* an honest answer?"

"I'm sorry," he murmured, jetting out a breath. "You have no idea how sorry."

"Kick, please . . ." Her voice caught. She couldn't understand what was happening to her, the strange chaotic emotions roiling within her.

He let loose a swear word, and pulled her against his chest. "Come here." He kissed her forehead and tried to put his arms around her but one was stopped by the handcuff. With an impatient jerk at the metal, he soothed his free hand over the bare skin of her neck and shoulders as though to comfort her.

She wanted to writhe and scream against the comfort. Against the unfairness of it all.

Because that wasn't where she wanted his hand.

With a mewl of anguish, she rolled onto her back, pulling him down over her.

"Please lie," she choked out. With shaking fingers she guided his palm to her breast. "Pretend you're a good guy. Just for tonight."

Shocked, he locked his gaze with hers. At first he didn't move a muscle. Then slowly, hesitantly, he rubbed his thumb over the taut, aching nipple. "Sweetheart, a genuine good guy would roll out of this bed and run like hell straight out of your life."

His blue eyes were tempest dark, his skin an inferno of heat. *Like the devil's.* A tempting, handsome devil. One she knew instinctively would demand her soul for even a taste of what he offered.

But right now she didn't care.

"In that case," she whispered, "pretend you're a bad man. A very, very bad man."

Two heartbeats later his mouth crashed down on hers. His hand tightened around her breast and she moaned in anticipation of the inevitable. Deep down she'd known this would happen from the first moment she laid eyes on him across that crowded ballroom at the hotel. She just hadn't known how complicated things would get first.

But she didn't want to think about that now. All she wanted in this moment was to melt to his touch. And experience everything a man like him could give her.

She felt the silk of her dress jerk down over her body along with her panties, and gasped at the sensation of suddenly being naked beneath him. The caress of his hands and his lips on her bare skin and the rough brush of his suit against her sensitive inner thighs made her flesh ripple and convulse with excitement.

Amazingly, she had no fear of his superior size and strength, nor of his obvious mastery over her body. She only wanted to feel more. *More.*

She reached for his belt but the handcuff brought her up short. "Your clothes," she urged, breaking the kiss, her voice breathless. She was literally dizzy with need.

"Later." His mouth trailed wetly down her throat and kept going lower, until it latched onto her breast. He pulled hotly on her nipple, sending an agonizing ribbon of pleasure zinging through her center. His fingers pinched and rolled the other one, bringing her up off the bed. She cried out, grabbing at his hair, and nearly came.

He growled low in his throat. "Oh, sweetheart." He ripped her drawer open and grabbed a fistful of condoms, spilling them onto the bed. The next second he slid down between her legs and spread her thighs wide apart. Then his tongue and his lips were on her, working and circling her need. Almost at once bringing her to the brink of a sharp, thrillingly brilliant crest.

It must be the residual adrenaline rush from her earlier terror, but she'd never felt anything so incredibly— *Oh, God!*

She exploded over the edge, screaming her pleasure as white-hot sensation ripped through her, over and over.

He gave her no respite, no chance to refill her lungs with precious air before he rose, his clothes half on, half off, and mounted her, plunging into her deep and hard. She gasped, her legs tightening instinctively around his waist as she again gave herself over to the blinding pleasure.

He was hard and huge, and he made it last. Lacing his fingers with hers, he held them fast over her head as he pounded into her, groaning her name with each powerful thrust.

There was no finesse, no subtlety. Just good hard sex. It was exactly what she needed. He made her forget everything. Her work, her past, her fears; her dismal future. There was just the here and now. Just Kick and Rainie, the two of them together as they hurtled full-speed into a shattering, body-ravaging climax in each other's arms.

After quickly releasing the handcuffs and peeling off his disheveled clothes, he held her close as they gasped for breath, recovering from the tumult, hearts beating out of control and bodies slick with sweet-smelling sweat.

She never wanted to let him go. Ever.

"Damn, Rainie," he groaned. "What the hell was that?"

She laughed through an answering moan, light-headed with pleasure. "You're pretty amazing yourself."

But it was more than pleasure. Much more. She felt an extraordinary, almost frightening connection with this man, one that was sure and strong and flowed through her veins like a powerful elixir of nurture and . . . safety. As she held him tight and breathed in the earthy scent of his skin and their lovemaking, she wondered what in the world was happening to make her feel this way. And also wondered . . .

Did *he* feel it, too?

After all, it was *her* name he'd been calling, *her* pleasure he'd been bestowing. This wasn't some anonymous hookup. He'd been making love to *her*, Rainie Martin, not to anyone else.

The thought was incredible, really.

And also . . . impossible.

She had to be imagining it all.

These feelings couldn't be real. They *couldn't* be. She was a nurse. She knew very well that the body's chemical reaction to acute fear felt identical to a rush of sexual desire. She *knew* that.

In her mind.

So why did it feel so different in her body . . . and her heart?

It couldn't, that's what. The very idea was ludicrous. *Can you say Stockholm Syndrome?*

Not that the sex hadn't been fantastic. It *so* was. It just wasn't . . . imbued with some miraculous, magical bond. Because that sort of thing only happened in fairy tales. Not real life. Especially when the man rolling on top of you didn't even come close to being Prince Charming, but far more resembled the Big Bad Wolf. . . .

But before she could accept the logic of her own argument, his mouth found hers and plied her with a long, slow, bone-melting kiss. His cock leisurely thickened and lengthened again, gradually finding and filling her with its iron-hard hunger.

And she decided that, after all, princes . . . and logic . . . were highly overrated.

HE *wasn't* bad.

How could a man so generous with his body and so tender with his emotions possibly be a bad guy?

Rainie lay back on the bed with a silly smile, twirling the handcuffs around and around on her forefinger while Kick was in the bathroom. The whole situation—and her uncharacteristic reaction to it—was so bizarre she had no clue what to make of it all. The only thing she knew with any certainty was that she did not regret a single moment with him.

Well. Okay, maybe *some* of the moments she regretted. Like when he'd first held her at gunpoint and she'd been sure she would die any second. That moment had been absolutely terrifying. So then . . . how had he ultimately succeeded in making her feel so . . . *safe*? Something was just not right about this whole picture.

She needed to find out more.

"What's the deal with the travel posters?" he called. "Have you been all these places?"

She almost choked. "*Um*. Not exactly." The day she got on a plane—or any other mode of transportation for that matter—would be the day . . . well, hell froze over. "I just like dreaming about different places."

"Why not go? Don't they give nurses vacation time?"

"I, *uh* . . . don't like to fly." She didn't talk about this. The only person who really knew about her . . . problem . . . was Gina. Rainie was not about to discuss it with this man, who oozed peril and adventure from every pore of his body. Even if he wasn't Nathan Daneby.

"Tell me about these people," she called back instead, tossing the handcuffs on top of his jacket, which was still on the nightstand. "The ones threatening you."

He popped his head out of the bathroom and drilled her with a frown. "No way. It's too dangerous."

There. See? He *was* a good guy. Trying to protect her.

"But don't you think I should know something about them?" she reasoned. "Just in case."

His frown deepened. "In case what? Forget it. These are not people you want to mess with."

A frisson of gooseflesh sifted over her arms at the distinct warning tone in his voice. "I don't plan to mess with them, Kick," she assured him. "But what if something really happens to you? Someone should know what's going on. To report it."

He made a derisive noise. "Report it to whom?"

"The police?"

"Trust me, that wouldn't help," he said, sliding back into bed, wincing as he did. He tugged her into his arms.

His skin was scorching hot. She pulled back a fraction and looked up at his face. His pupils were dilated and his face flushed. But not in a sexual way. More like, a fever way. Or . . . an anxiety attack way. Surely, not . . .

"Are you okay?" she asked, concerned.

He gave a deep yawn, his body shivering a little at the end of it. Then he yawned again, squeezed his eyes shut, and grimaced. Cursing under his breath, his expression was suddenly filled with . . . guilt?

"Kick?"

"I'm sorry, baby. I really wish . . ."

He looked so miserable, a tremor of unease went through her. "What's going on?"

He swallowed, swiped an unsteady hand over his sweaty brow. "There's no easy way to tell you this, so I'm just going to blurt it out."

Her pulse inched up. *Now what?* "Okay . . ."

"You were right about me. I denied it, of course, but you hit it right on the head."

"I— I don't understand."

"About the drugs."

"But . . ." Suddenly she remembered that first thought when he'd pointed the gun at her outside the hotel. And her chest squeezed. "My God!" she gasped, scrambling backward across the bed, out of his embrace. "*That's* what this was all about? You're after *drugs*?"

Her heart felt like it had been run over by a truck. How could she have been so wrong about him? So totally fooled?

"You *bastard*!"

"No." He shook his head with another wince. "Trust me, I'm not after drugs. But"—he swallowed again—"I am . . . an addict." His face screwed into a portrait of angry frustration. "And I'm about to go into withdrawal."

He leaned forward and reached for her, but she backed safely out of range. *Trust?* She didn't think so. She stared at him in numb disbelief. Had he deliberately stalked her? Somehow found out that she was the go-to person in the ER when it came to drug overdoses and withdrawals? "What exactly do you want from me?"

"Help."

"*Help?*"

"To get through it."

Hurt seeped from her heart through her whole body as the awful truth dawned on her. So he *had* stalked her. "You planned this all along! You came to the hospital's speed dating night specifically to find me! Deliberately set out to seduce me and then use me. Didn't you?"

"Rainie, no—"

"*Didn't you?*" She almost spat the words. She didn't know whom she was most mad at, him, or herself for all those naïve, idiotic things she'd been feeling about him just moments before. What a romantic, delusional fool!

He shuddered out a pained breath, flopping back onto the bed. "No! Not you. Not specifically. But yes. That was the plan. To find someone with medical knowledge to help me through these next couple of days. But I never thought I'd meet someone who—"

She thinned her lips. "*Save it.*" She'd worked with hundreds of drug addicts in the ER. She knew all about their manipulation and lies. "Give me one good reason I *should* help you."

She tried not to think about the gun lying right next to him on the nightstand. Or the fact that even hurt as she was, she doubted she could turn down a genuine plea for help. It was how they'd talked her into heading the most hazardous program in the ER. She was too damn gullible for her own good.

"I'm sorry. Believe me, if there'd been any other way—"

"There is," she gritted out. "It's called a rehab center."

"Too public. The people after me would know where I was within an hour of checking in. I need to be completely off-grid for the three days it takes to get clean."

"Three days?" It was her turn to snort. "What are you addicted to, caffeine?"

"Oxycontin."

Hell. She did a small mental backpedal. Oxycontin was a painkiller. A notoriously and severely addictive one. And to be fair, a lot of innocent people got hooked on it before they even knew what was happening.

Which didn't excuse Kick's actions last night. But . . . at least he wasn't talking about cocaine, heroin, or eX. Something disgusting like that.

She sat up Indian style on the bed, drawing the sheet over her nakedness. "You were injured?"

"You could say that." He sat up also, and stretched out his left leg so she could get a good look. Her stomach clenched. The skin was riddled with scars. He extended his left forearm, also scarred. Then turned his back a half turn to her. Thin scars crisscrossed the tanned expanse of his left shoulder. She vaguely remembered feeling them last night, but because of what she saw every day at the hospital they hadn't really registered as unusual. Or maybe she'd blocked them from her consciousness, afraid of what thinking about them might trigger within her. Like it was now.

She fought down a sick wave of nausea. "It must have been a terrible accident."

"Tell me about it."

When she opened her mouth to ask more, he raised a hand to stop her. "The point is, I've been lazy. I left the hospital well over a year ago but it was easier to buy the painkillers on the street than to go through withdrawal."

"Your doctor cut you off?"

He sighed. "A few months ago. I was supposed to be gradually weaning myself off them. Then a guy I knew, Jimmy Tang, offered to supply me. I didn't see a reason to stress out getting clean."

"But now you do."

"Yeah." He looked directly into her eyes. "Imminent death has a way of setting one's priorities straight."

Okaaay. "What are you talking about?"

"If those people I told you about catch me . . . where they're planning to send me, I'm as good as dead if I start going through withdrawal."

Surely he couldn't *really* mean—"Dead? As in . . ."

"A doornail. Seriously, permanently dead."

She swallowed. Who the hell was after him? And how could anyone send him somewhere he didn't want to go?

More importantly, did she believe him? Though it was obvious he certainly believed it himself.

"Just so you know," she said, "three days isn't going to do it. It'll take at least—"

"Three days will get me through the worst," he countered. "If they come for me, at least I won't be curled up in a fetal position puking my brains out. And if I'm running from them, I won't be worrying about where to find my next bottle of pills."

She studied his face, the horror of what he was actually saying barely registering on his all-but-neutral expression.

How could a person live like that? It was inconceivable to her. Rainie had battled a constant, gnawing fear of random violence ever since she was twelve, when her parents had died senselessly at the hands of a carjacker. But to have someone deliberately hunting you down was different. That was downright terrifying.

Or . . .

Or was this all a drug-induced delusion?

Oxycontin didn't usually cause paranoia, but every user was unique, and individual reactions were always possible. . . .

"Who are these people, and why are they after you?" she asked. "What makes you think they want to send you anywhere?"

He eased back against the headboard and closed his eyes, the corner of his lip lifting in a grim parody of a smile. One that told her he knew she doubted him. "Because I used to work for them, and that was my job. Getting sent places to do things nobody else would do. Now they want to send me back. To a place just like the one where all this happened." He waved a hand over his scarred limbs.

A shiver went down her spine. She really didn't want to know. It was probably better she *didn't* know. But she couldn't help asking. "And where is that?"

"Hell," he said without hesitation.

Ho-boy.

Opening his eyes, he gazed at her with wide black pupils and red-rimmed lids. "So, Lorraine Martin, nurse practitioner. Are you going to help me? Or are you going to help them send me straight back to hell?"

RAINIE took a deep, calming breath. What was she supposed to say to that?

Obviously this man was deep in some very serious shit.

She was furious with Kick about deceiving her, and still couldn't decide whether he was a good guy or a bad guy, but she could never turn away a person in real need. That wasn't in her nature. It was the reason she had chosen to work in the ER, a place that pumped her anxiety higher for every minute she spent there. But despite her irrational fear—or perhaps because of it—she had a deep, ingrained need to help people get through their worst nightmares, like when the ugly, unpredictable world out there left them bleeding, helpless, and dying. As it had her parents.

"Of course I'll help you," she told Kick.

But that didn't mean she had to like it.

"Thank you," he said, holding out his hand to her.

Or sleep with him again.

She ignored his hand and his searching eyes and slid out of bed. "How long do we have?"

"We don't. It's already started."

She felt his gaze on her as she padded to her dresser and got out jeans and a T-shirt. "I've seen the fever sweats and the yawning. What about nausea?"

"Not so far."

"Pain?"

"Yup. My leg is hurting pretty bad."

"It'll get worse. Soon you'll be hurting all over. Are you sure you're ready for this?"

"Do I have a choice?"

She pulled the T-shirt over her head. "If you went with me to the hospital, there's an experimental—"

"I told you, no hospital."

"Okay. Then *I* could go there and get you a prescription of Buprenorphine. That would help with some of the withdrawal symptoms, anyway."

He was standing behind her before she even knew he'd moved off the bed. His fingers tightened around her shoulders. "You wouldn't by any chance be thinking of turning me in?" he asked softly.

She held herself perfectly stiff. "No. I said I'd help you and I will."

"You don't sound very happy about it."

"Funny thing, I don't like being lied to and used."

He forcibly turned her around to face him. "I know. And I'm truly sorry about everything . . . before. But, Rainie, you have to know what happened in that bed, that wasn't a lie. That was real."

Pain zinged through her again. How could he *say* that?

She shook her head, keeping her gaze riveted on the floor. "It doesn't matter. It's over and done. You can stay in my apartment to detox, and I'll help you as much as I can. But then you're out of here, and I don't ever want to see you again."

There was no place in her world for a crazy wild card like Kick. Aside from anything else, she was all about order, and he was the very definition of havoc.

"I understand."

His fingertips touched her cheek, then brushed lightly along her jawline. His knuckle caught her chin and lifted her face to his. But before his lips could reach hers, she turned her head.

"Please don't," she whispered.

He let out a breath that soughed warmly over her temple. Then he let her go.

Before she could change her mind, she strode out of the bedroom and went to the sofa where she'd left her purse. She grabbed it, slipped on her shoes, and headed for the front door.

"I'll go pick up the prescription and a few other things you'll need."

"Like what?" he asked from the bedroom door. He was still naked, leaning a hip against the frame, arms crossed. He didn't look happy. Good. She wasn't happy, either.

"Electrolyte fluid. Maalox. Ginger ale. You should try to get some sleep while I'm gone. I doubt you'll get much during the next few days."

"When will you be back?"

The words were quietly spoken, but the tension behind them was palpable. *He didn't trust her.* Didn't trust that she would return to help him, but instead thought maybe she intended to call the cops.

She gazed back at him, still feeling the sensation of his powerful body on hers, of his hard length filling her; she could taste the flavor of his tongue in her mouth.

He didn't trust *her*?

"An hour," she said, stifling the urge to scream with bitterness. "Maybe an hour and a half."

"Okay."

"Will you still be here?" she asked. She figured there was just as good a chance he would bolt as soon as she was gone. *Because he didn't trust her.*

He hesitated infinitesimally. Then said, "Unless they find me first."

She did her best not to feel resentful. "If they do, it won't be because of me."

His lips curved up but his eyes were empty. "Won't matter. They have their ways. I just hope I can keep one step ahead of them this time."

There was nothing she could say to that. So she just nodded, unlocked the door, and swung it open.

She froze. Standing in a semicircle around her door were five men wearing black ski masks. All holding guns.

Really *big* guns.

And every one was aimed at her.

Oh, shit.

The metallic *snick* of bolts sliding and bullets chambering filled the hall.

The last thing she remembered was screaming, as she crumbled to the floor.

FOUR

AS soon as he heard Rainie's scream, Kick lunged back into the bedroom, beelining it for a weapon.

How the *fuck* had they found him so quickly?

He fumbled the SIG off the nightstand and it went skittering, so he grabbed the Beretta from his jacket pocket, then rolled onto the floor toward his discarded clothes. Face it, the only thing worse than being caught unawares was being caught unawares with your pants down. By sliding in right next to the bed he was able to pull his discarded suit trousers on as the intruders stormed the room. Not that it mattered in the grand scheme of things. He was fucked either way. Five of them and no egress. Even he knew when to yield the moment and live to fight another day.

He tucked the Beretta under the mattress, raised his hands above the level of the bed, and carefully poked his head up. Instantly he was staring down the barrels of four M-4s. But he wasn't looking at them. He was scanning the eyes behind the ski masks.

Well, well. If it wasn't Mr. Pinstripes, sans the suit. This time the team all wore break-in black—with appropriate footwear. Someone must have given them a lecture.

"Hello, Al," he said with disgust, wiping the gathering sweat from his brow.

He was manhandled to his feet.

Pulling off his ski mask, Al *tsked*. "You've been a naughty boy, Kyle." He tossed a glance over his shoulder at Rainie, who was lying limp on the floor being fussed over by a fifth man. Al aimed a knowing smirk at Kick's state of undress, then glanced at the scatter of condom wrappers on the floor. "A *very* naughty boy, by the look of things."

"Bite me," Kick said wearily, shaking the goons off and zipping up his pants. He had to make two passes at the zipper tab because his hands had started shaking. "And leave the woman alone."

"Kyle, Kyle, Kyle. Did you really think you could avoid us using an old-school maneuver like this?" He *tsked* again.

Kick grabbed his shirt from the foot of the bed where it had ended up bunched into a ball. "Hell, it worked for Robert Redford."

Al snarked. "*Three Days of the Condor*? Daaamn. We have been bored, haven't we?"

Kick shook out the shirt. "Speak for yourself. I've been highly entertained leading you assholes on a chase for the past year. By the way, how's the kid with the bullet in his leg?"

Al's humor faded. "Walking again. No thanks to you."

"Please. Spare me the violins. It was a flesh wound. But nice try. How'd you find me?" he asked neutrally. Professional curiosity. Be nice to know where he'd slipped up.

"We had a real interesting talk with a guy named Jimmy Tang. Showed up at the diner after you bolted. A veritable pharmacopeia. Told us all about your little secret. Shame on you, buddy."

"Fuck you. Next time you're blown up by a land mine you can throw shade my way."

"Anyway, figured you'd want to get clean fast, under the circumstances. Thought you might head for the nearest clinic or hospital." He wagged a finger. "The speed dating nurse thing, though. *That* was clever."

Obviously not clever enough.

In the living room Rainie moaned, drawing his attention.

"What the hell did your apes do to her?" he demanded, attempting to break through the wall of muscle to get to her.

"Ain't done nuthin'," the guy kneeling over her said defensively. "She just folded. Been out like a light since."

The goons held him back forcibly. Al raised his M-4 again. "Cuff him, boys. Make sure to do up the FlexiCuffs nice and tight."

"Wait." Kick jerked away, holding his hands up to show he wasn't going to pull anything. "Let me check on Rainie first. Please."

"No fucking way."

Her eyes fluttered open, unfocused. He could see the split second when she remembered what had happened. They widened, and her throat let out an awful sound, like a wounded animal.

How many times had he heard that sound . . . when the person you had in your sights knew they were going to die?

With a heartrending "No!" she compressed into a fetal position and wove her fingers together behind her neck, shaking like a leaf. "No. No. No," she whimpered over and over.

"What the hell," the goon kneeling next to her muttered, looking to Al for guidance.

"Can't you see she's terrified?" Kick snapped. "Let me go to her."

After a maddening pause, Al nodded. "He tries anything, shoot the woman."

Jesus. How had he ever have worked for these people? He'd gotten a whole new perspective on their methods since jumping over the fence.

He slid to his knees next to her, stifling a grimace of pain from his leg, and put a gentle hand on her shoulder. He pushed back the hair that hung like a curtain around her downcast face. "Rainie, sweetheart, it's okay. They're only after me. They won't hurt you. I promise."

She just curled tighter and shook her head.

He bent over and kissed her temple. "We'll leave you alone now. Thanks for trying to help me. Thanks for . . . everything."

Grunting from the flash of fire in his leg as he stood, he turned to limp for the door.

"Not so fast, Jackson," Al ordered. "Pick her up."

He froze. *What?* "Hell, no."

"She's coming with us."

He couldn't believe this. "Why?"

"Because she's seen too much. Can't have her calling the cops, now, can we? At least not until you disappear."

Kick clenched his jaw in fury. He should have fucking known this would happen.

"You are the scum of the earth, you know that?" he growled. "She's an innocent bystander. Let her go."

Al punched a forefinger at him. "*You're* the one who brought her into this mess, Jackson. Cooperate, and she'll be fine. Now, pick her up. That way you can't try any funny stuff."

He ground his teeth. They were so *fucking* going to pay for this. Somehow, someday, he'd make them pay.

"Fine." He took a deep breath and stooped down, trying to slip his arms around her. "Rainie, I'm so sorry about this."

She finally turned her face toward him, her eyes filled with fear. "Please don't take me," she whispered.

He glanced at Al, who just made a sign to hurry up. The rest of the goons stood watching impassively, weapons at the ready. Jesus, what was *wrong* with these people?

"I've got no choice, baby." He tried to gather her in his arms, but her defensive position along with the stiffness of his leg made it too awkward to lift her. "Rainie, can you stand up for me?"

She just stared up at him, her eyes wild. He could feel the pounding of her heart and the trembling of her limbs, see the flush of terror in her face.

"You're going to have to help me, sweetheart. I can't do this alone." He was afraid if he didn't move her soon they'd hurt him. Or worse, her. "Help me," he said firmly. "I really need your help, Nurse Martin."

That finally cracked through to her. She swallowed, and hesitantly, so hesitantly, unfolded her body and reached up to slide her arms round his neck. Together they managed to stumble to their feet.

"I said carry her," Al commanded, striding to the door. "Masks off and conceal your weapons, people. Let's roll."

Kick inhaled deeply and flexed his leg in preparation, then went to do as he was told.

"No."

At the softly spoken word, everyone in the room turned to Rainie. "What did you say?" Al barked at her.

"No," she said, her voice a little stronger.

Al narrowed his eyes. "You are in no position to bargain, sister. Pick her up!"

"He can't," she argued, sounding more like the little troublemaker he'd come to know. "His leg—"

"I don't give a rat's ass about his damned—"

"*And* he's starting to go through drug withdrawal. You may as well shoot me now as make him carry me down five flights of stairs. Look at him! He'll never make it. And I won't be much of a hostage if I'm dead from a broken neck." By the end of the speech, she sounded almost like her old self.

"You're not a hostage," Al said, looking really irritated. But after an assessing glance at Kick's sweaty face and shaking hands, apparently he saw her point. "All right, fine. Cuff her, too," he growled at the man with the FlexiCuffs, then glared at her. "I'm warning you, one false move from either of you and you'll both be sorry."

If Kick hadn't been so relieved, he might have cheered at her. But just then a wave of dizziness swept over him, making him stumble. Four guns were instantly pointed at them.

Rainie froze like a deer in headlights. He grabbed her for balance and kept pulling until her face was buried against his chest. "Put the goddamn weapons away. You *have* me, okay? I'll go wherever you want. Just stop scaring the shit out of the lady."

Al smiled triumphantly. "Okay, then. That's better. Let's go see the boss."

THE only thing keeping Rainie from dissolving into a puddle of blind panic was the fact that Kick really needed her. By the time they were down the stairs and out in front of her building it was obvious he was hurting badly.

"How you doing?" she asked as she helped him lean back against the rough brick to catch his breath.

He gritted his teeth and moved close to her ear. "Run," he urged under his breath. "Now, while you have the chance."

She shook her head. She might be terrified to the bone, but she wasn't stupid. Those guys meant business. Besides, he needed her. "You're about to collapse."

"I'll be okay. They'll—"

But the rest of his sentence was lost as just then an unmarked black SUV screeched to a halt at the curb.

Oh, shit. Her insides quailed. Please not—

"All right, you two, let's move," Al ordered, and they were hustled over to it.

"No!" The panic she'd barely been holding at bay swamped over her like a barrel of acid. "No, I can't— Please don't make me—"

But before she could blink they'd been shoved into the middle seat. Their captors swarmed in after them, the door banged, and the engine gunned.

Trapping her.

In a *car.*

She should have run when he'd told her to. She slammed her eyes shut and doubled over, fighting to breathe. Ripples of light danced at the edges of her vision.

Deep breath, let it out slowly. Deep breath, let it out slowly. Deep breath—

"Rainie?"

"I'm okay," she gasped, banding her arms around her middle, fighting the dizziness. *I'm okay. I'm okay. I'm okay.*

Deep breath.

I will be fine.

I will be calm.

I will be safe.

She would not panic. Panic would not help. She must stay calm. *It is just a car.* Cars couldn't hurt you.

Let it out slowly.

But people did. And these people were very bad. *Oh, God! If she didn't get hold of herself, they might—*

No!

Her fingers tingled; her mind floated toward blackness.

She felt Kick's arms slide over her head and around her, urging her closer to his body. She struggled against his hold. He felt hot and shaky, but determined to hang on to her.

"Breathe, sweetheart," he told her from far, far away. "Even breaths. That's right."

Calm and reassuring, his rumbling voice called her back from the edge of the abyss.

Suddenly she was freezing, her teeth chattering. Reluctantly, she gave in and let him hold her tight. Actually, there was nothing she could do to stop him, she was shivering so badly. The heat of his body did feel good. Unwelcomely good. Like it had earlier, when they'd made love. Or had sex. Or whatever the hell it was they'd done. Back when he'd made her feel so safe and secure. What a joke.

She cut off the thought and just breathed, concentrating on the sound of his voice as he murmured encouragements in her ear. The smell of his body filled her, already uncomfortably familiar. Almost against her will, a tiny bud of calmness slowly blossomed in the chaos of her anxiety. Because of him.

She'd never had help taming her fits of panic before. Not since a school counselor had tried showing her how to control the panic attacks that had grown out of the trauma of witnessing her parents' violent deaths. The psychobabble exercises hadn't actually helped the attacks, but she had learned how to hide them pretty effectively. And to build a life predicated on doing everything in her power to avoid setting them off. *That* had been effective.

And now, somehow, having Kick's arms around her was also helping her cope.

Being in a moving car.

God, she hadn't been in a vehicle of any kind since the funeral limo. And even then she'd refused to ride in it home to her aunt and uncle's, where she was going to live until college. She'd walked all fourteen miles back from the cemetery, with the limo tagging along behind, blocking traffic.

"Feeling better?" he asked, jerking her out of the memory.

"A little."

She eased out a final steadying breath. The whole attack had lasted maybe five minutes—about average—but as always afterward, she felt like she'd run a marathon. She looked up at his worried face. He was flushed and perspiring.

Damn. He was about to crash and burn. She ran her sleeve over his brow. "Some nurse, huh? I'm supposed to be taking care of *you*."

A tremor went through his hands. "Don't worry. I'll soon have the best care our tax dollars can buy."

Her brain was apparently still muzzy. "Tax dollars?" What did taxes have to do with anything?

He sighed and laid his head back against the headrest. "Never mind."

"What do they really want from us, Kick?"

"Not us. *Me.* When we get to where we're going, and they have me where they want me, they'll no doubt separate us," he told her quietly. "They'll tell you it was all a big misunderstanding. Tell you bad stuff about me. Very bad stuff. If you cooperate and go along with that, they'll smile and apologize, and let you go."

She was just stubborn enough to be outraged on his behalf. Not that she wasn't still mad as hell at him. "And if I refuse?"

"Don't," he warned. "Don't fight them, Rainie. I've been trying for a year and a half. You can't win."

His body jerked in reminder of what he was starting to go through. And of her promise to him.

"I really hate being told what to do," she said, wiping his brow again.

He sent her a smile through pain-gritted teeth. "Yeah. I've noticed." His smile curved, and he added softly, "Except in bed."

Their eyes met and an unwilling lick of heat wound through her body. Memories of the amazing pleasure he'd given her nearly crowded out everything else, including the hurt of being used by him.

Nearly.

She looked away. Earlier, she'd been certain she could never forgive him for that. Now she wasn't quite so sure. But it still hurt like hell.

Because she'd been so damn attracted to him.

He groaned and she glanced back. His face was etched in

misery and now he'd started shivering. The withdrawal was
kicking in, in earnest.

"Nauseous?" she asked. He nodded.

Great.

In the front passenger seat, the man Kick had called Al
was on the phone talking in clipped tones. Behind them,
Larry, Moe, and Curly were engaged in their own snickering
conversation, apparently having decided she and Kick didn't
need watching.

"Hey," she said, extracting herself from Kick's arms and
waving her hand at them. "This man needs medical attention."

"Then do something. You're the nurse," Moe pointed out
rudely.

"Yeah, well, he's going to start throwing up any minute,
and there's nothing I can do about that without proper medication."

They all made disgusted faces. Larry picked up a discarded McDonald's bag, emptied the used wrappers onto the
floor, and handed it to her.

Pressing it into Kick's hands, she turned back and demanded, "Where are you taking us?"

They ignored her and returned to their conversation.

Freaking stooges.

She could barely see out the SUV's windows because
they were so dark-tinted, almost black. But even if she could,
she'd have no idea where they were, since she'd never driven
in the city. Or been outside a ten-block radius of her apartment. Not since she moved in.

Suddenly they pulled into an alley. Graffiti covered the walls
and trash littered the rutted ground. *Okay, not a good sign.*

The metallic ring of seat belts *snicking* open shot through
the vehicle, followed by the sound of gun bolts being pulled.
Definitely a worse sign. Because at the end of the alley was
the solid brick wall of a warehouse. No doors. No openings.
No other exit.

End of the line.

Her pulse jumped out of control. She shot a desperate
glance at Kick. He closed his eyes and swore.

Oh, God.

They were both going to die.

FIVE

"WHO are they?" Pig asked her. His beautiful naked redhead.

They'd already gone through the Name Ritual. Hers was something with an *H*. Like Heavenly Angel.

His was still Pig.

Except she didn't like that name. So today he was Charles.

She gazed at him with her pretty green eyes that were the exact color of a spring meadow on a cool, sunny day. God, he loved her eyes. Not that he didn't love the rest of her. Her nude body was pale and perfect. Not a mark or a blemish on it. Just acres of gorgeous, silky skin. Miles of lush, soft curves. Curves a man could lose himself in completely. And her breasts. Fucking perfection. Plump and round. Nipples petite and rosy red, just made for a man's mouth.

"Who do *you* think they are, Charles?" she asked, tilting her head, bringing him out of the fantasy with a disappointed jolt.

"They're bad guys," he answered.

Ya think? What was your first clue, dipshit? The wrists rubbed raw from restraints? Or his clothes—what was left of them—stinking of dirt and sweat and God knew what other body fluids? Maybe the scars and the bruises . . . Oh, yeah. Or the blindness.

"Why are they doing this to you?" she asked.

He battled back his anger because anger only got you more scars and bruises. He huffed. "Because they're sadists?"

"But why *you*?"

Yeah. That was the fucking gazillion-dollar question. The question he'd asked himself over and over and over. "They must think I know something. Or they did. Back when."

"Back when . . . ?"

"When they . . . When I . . . Fuck. I don't know. They used to ask me questions when they beat me. They've stopped doing that." The questions anyway.

"*Do* you know something?"

He sighed painfully. "You can't be serious."

He didn't know shit. Not where he was, not who they were, nothing. Hell, he didn't even know his own freaking name.

Okay, again, not true. He did know *some* stuff. He knew enough to keep his damn mouth shut and his eyes shut tighter when a dim glow had suddenly begun to light the edges of his world of darkness a while back. Days? Weeks? Months? God knew. But he was slowly getting back his ability to see faint, fuzzy shapes in the perpetual darkness. Not a lot. Just outlines. Movement. But still dangerous.

"If they find out I can see, they'll kill me," he whispered to his red-haired Angel.

"Can you see *me*?" she whispered back.

Christ, yes. Every sweet, tempting, luscious inch of her.

"Let me touch you," he begged softly, aching to feel the smooth silkiness of her perfect skin beneath his cracked and battered hands. He reached for her. But she just laughed and rolled away.

"*Pig!*"

He froze. Didn't dare move.

"*Get up!*"

God help him.

Not again.

* * *

KICK didn't think his day could get any more fucked.

He was wrong.

He'd hoped like hell they were being taken to a legit downtown CIA office. One with analysts and secretaries, copy machines and coffeemakers. No such luck. They'd driven in the other direction. And as soon as he saw the ugly alley teeming with garbage and detritus, he knew exactly where they were.

ZU-NE. The northeastern headquarters of Zero Unit. His old stomping grounds.

ZU-NE had moved since he'd last bivouacked there. Moved to a different state, in fact. But that was normal. The ZU maintained five regional headquarters, which changed locations regularly. But every place had the same signature.

From innocuous condo buildings to sprawling farms, they all looked like the very last place on earth where one of the most sophisticated, well-funded, and top-secret government commando units in the world would be housed.

Filthy, abandoned, ringed by tall, dilapidated buildings, this dump looked like the back alley of hell. How appropriate.

Kick grabbed Rainie's hand before her imagination could run wild. "Don't worry; it's okay," he assured her, even though the three humps behind them had their weapons aimed at his back. *Just a little paranoid?*

A square section of the grimy building at the end of the alley suddenly began to rise like a garage door, exposing a gaping maw of blackness beyond. The SUV glided forward through the opening.

Kick fought down a sickening wave of nausea that may have been from the withdrawal, but more probably was revulsion at being pulled back into this world. Was a normal life without violence, betrayal, and death too much to ask for? Apparently for him, it was.

And the fact they'd brought Rainie here did not bode well for her, either.

"W-what is this place . . . ?" she stammered.

"This," he said past the bile, "is where I used to work. Zero Unit." He squeezed her hand. "Welcome to hell."

* * *

THE outer door glided down again, cutting them off from the outside world. Kick knew it would be steel-reinforced and impenetrable without some major explosive power. As they climbed out of the SUV into the vacant warehouse bay where it had come to a halt, two more armed guards ran up to them.

No need. Even if he'd had the means, he wasn't going anywhere. By now his rubbery legs could barely support his weight.

"You okay?" Rainie asked, grabbing his arm as he stumbled.

"I'll live." *Maybe.*

Escorted by an entire phalanx of trigger-happy guards, they were marched out of the bay and down a long hallway Kick knew would end in an interrogation room. It was absurd. Did they really have such a high opinion of his ability to escape? More likely, this was just one of ZU-COM's usual unsubtle displays of power, intended to scare him. Sorry to disappoint, but he was beyond feeling much of anything but queasy. Before he'd walked more than a few feet he was sick on the floor.

Their guards cursed at the mess, grabbed him under the arms, and practically dragged him the rest of the way. Rainie yelled at them in outrage the whole time. She was amazing.

They pushed him into a chair and thrust a wastebasket from the corner at him. He puked again.

A moment later, bootfalls thumped up from behind them and a harsh, commanding voice that was all too familiar snapped, "A *drug* addict? No wonder you didn't want to come back to the unit."

His fucked-up day was complete. Colonel Frank Blair. His former commander. Ex-uniformed special ops and fanatically conservative, the old boy was pure piss and iron. Hated anything that smacked of weakness. Kick had respected him as a leader, but never liked him. He didn't waste his breath with a retort. Good and bad alike ricocheted off Blair like solid granite. The man was impenetrable.

"Good God, soldier. What the fuck happened to you?"

"This unit happened to me," Kick muttered, looking around for Rainie. At the perimeter of the room, her arm was being firmly held by one of the guards. So far Kick hadn't recognized anyone but Blair. His old division mates must be on a mission somewhere. Maybe they'd even been rotated OCONUS on purpose, so he wouldn't have any friends here to help him. Not that they would have anyway. Unquestioning obedience was de rigueur in the ZU. Another reason he'd had to get out. He'd finally started asking questions.

"Listen, Colonel, let the woman go," he said as forcefully as he could muster. "She's no part of this. You've got me where you want me."

"Where I want you is the Sudan," Blair barked. "And until you're at least in Egyptian airspace, she stays."

Rather than objecting to her own kidnapping, Rainie surprised them both by protesting, "You can't possibly send him anywhere in that condition! Look at him. He needs medication and to stay in bed for at least a week."

The colonel scrutinized her with a cold stare. "They tell me you're a nurse."

She huffed up like an indignant bird. "Yes, and—"

"Good. We weren't expecting this complication. We'll be counting on you to help him through the treatment."

"*What?*"

"What treatment?" Kick asked suspiciously. "There isn't any—"

Blair cut him off. "Doc says they can put you under and give you some drug to induce rapid detox."

"Not without a proper facility!" Rainie argued. "The method is dangerous, and still only experimental."

"But you've done it before, I take it?"

"Well, yes, but—"

"Don't worry. We have a sick bay."

Kick should have been worried by the look on her face, but he was starting to hurt too much to care much what happened to him.

"And if I refuse?"

Blair narrowed his eyes. "Jackson needs to be operational ASAP. Getting this drug business over with quickly is in his best interest. *And* yours." There was no mistaking the threat, but Rainie didn't seem to understand that.

"I don't see it that w—"

Kick grunted as a wave of sharp pain sliced through his

whole body. His vision rippled like a pebble in a lake, and his fingers lost muscle control. The wastebasket slipped from his grip with a crash on the cement floor.

"Get him the fuck out of here," Blair ordered. "He disgusts me."

Kick wanted to tell him the feeling was mutual. But his tongue wouldn't work any better than his fingers.

He was jerked to his feet. Blair leaned his ugly mug in at him. "I gave you every opportunity to prove you're a *real* soldier, Jackson. But you turned out to be a weakling. One setback and you fall apart. If I had a choice, I'd boot you back into the goddamn gutter where you belong."

Despite the ache in his body, the sudden pain that razored through Kick's soul was far worse. His former commander's loathing cut deep, reminding him of all those others he'd disappointed so badly in the past, starting with his father and ending with Alex Zane, the best friend who'd lost his life depending on him. After that fiasco, he'd given up trying not to disappoint. Was that weakness? Or the strength to accept reality . . .

"Unfortunately I don't have a choice," the colonel continued with a glower. "You are the only person in this country who knows Jallil abu Bakr by sight. Therefore, the only one who can take him out with certainty."

For a second, Kick was filled with pure, hot rage. *Jallil Abu Bakr.* The most notorious of the two leaders of the infamous al Sayika terrorist organization. And the fucker who'd killed Alex and the rest of his team. If he could, Kick would gladly torture the man to death, slowly and horribly, as he deserved. But Kick was in no shape to face abu Bakr or any other member of al Sayika. It would be pure suicide.

"Why would I want to help you?" he managed to croak.

"Besides your lady friend here?" An infuriating threat that had Kick seeing red. "Grow yourself some balls, soldier. Do it for your country. These motherfuckers are planning to blow up the US embassy in Khartoum, along with the British, the French, and the UN diplomatic mission. Innocent lives will be lost. Lots of them. Or doesn't that matter to you anymore, Jackson?"

Kick lunged at the bastard. And lost his balance. He fell to his hands and knees, head spinning. He heard Rainie cry out but he couldn't move to help her.

"You've got thirty-six hours to get clean," Colonel Blair said coldly. "Then I'm throwing your ass on a plane. Be ready."

IT was hard to stay angry with a man you've just seen so thoroughly humiliated trying to defend you. Or maybe even save your life. Rainie hadn't totally bought into his story earlier, about his former employers hunting him down so ruthlessly. Now she was a true believer. He'd said they were gangsters, but everything about this place screamed military. Or mercenary. That colonel had been just plain scary.

Worse, they expected her to help put Kick through a very dangerous medical procedure. One that could easily kill him.

Pressing her hand to her stomach to quell the gnawing fear, she deliberately ignored the many questions in her mind—foremost of which was whether or not they planned to kill *her* once they'd gotten what they wanted.

Her guard shoved her to follow the others, who half dragged Kick down a second hallway, then turned into what looked like a brightly lit hospital room.

They lifted him none too gently onto one of the two narrow, railed beds that occupied the white room. Gleaming monitors and instruments that Rainie immediately recognized from the ER lined one side wall, and a row of cupboards ran along the opposite.

"Doc'll be by in a few minutes," one of the guards said, cutting off her handcuffs, then they all left the room, slamming the door behind them. The lock *snicked* home. Leaving her alone with Kick.

He started to moan.

She was almost grateful for the distraction. She could ask him who they were later. This part, the medical stuff, she could deal with, and be in control.

Quickly, she went over and started opening cupboard doors, looking for the things he'd need to get through the coming hours. She was astonished by the range and number of pharmaceuticals and supplies she found packed into them.

Some "sick bay." The room was better stocked than many ERs she'd been in.

What kind of gangsters—or even mercenaries—had facilities this good located in skeevy neighborhoods like the one outside these walls?

"Good grief," she mumbled. "Who *are* these people?"

"Don't ask," Kick said on a groan. "The less you know about Zero Unit, the better."

Just then the lock clicked and the door swung open. A tall, rangy man wearing green camouflage pants with combat boots and a khaki T-shirt strode in. Great. *This* was the doctor?

He went right to the bed. "I've only got a few minutes. I was supposed to be wheels-up three hours ago, but they held me back when they found out about your addiction from your pusher last night."

Kick gave him a weary smile. "Don't hang around on my account, Doc."

"God*damn* it, Kick, I told you to get *off* those damn painkillers! What the devil were you thinking?"

"Sorry. Just didn't seem all that urgent at the time."

"Yeah, well, it was. Now you have to go through a potentially fatal treatment unnecessarily, you dickhead. But it'll definitely be fatal if they send you out into the field in this state."

"I'm dead anyway. Sudan is a suicide mission. You and I both know that."

Rainie gasped at the matter-of-fact pronouncement. "What do you mean, *suicide mission*?" She jumped up from crouching at a low cupboard where she'd been searching for a bag of saline to start an IV. "They can't just send you out to—"

The doctor spun. Apparently he hadn't seen her there. "Who the— Ah. You must be the nurse."

She didn't get the chance to answer, because two of the guards suddenly reappeared. "Ma'am, we'll have to ask you to come with us."

Instinctively she backed away, spilling boxes of supplies onto the floor. "No!" She scrambled behind the bed where Kick was lying curled in a ball. Oh, yeah, like he was in any shape to intervene, even if he wanted to. She really had to start fighting her own battles.

With an effort she straightened her spine and tried to appear brave on the outside, even though inside she was quaking like an aspen. "I'm not going anywhere."

Still handcuffed, Kick's hands reached out to take hers. "It's all right, Rainie. They just want to ask you some questions. Answer them and you'll be fine." She gave him a look of disbelief. "Baby, if they'd wanted you to disappear, you'd already be history."

Oh, swell. Now she was terrified again.

He pushed out a sigh. "You really don't get it, do you?"

She was too freaked out and exhausted to play games. "No. What are you trying to say?"

"These men are federal agents, Rainie. Zero Unit is run by the government."

She let out a soft noise of disbelief and leaned down toward his ear. The *government*? "You said it was the mob after you!" she muttered under her breath.

"*You* guessed it was the mob," he murmured back. "I was just trying to protect you. Because once these people sink their claws into you . . ." He shook his head.

She straightened. *Not gonna think about* that *part.*

But government agents. Right. Sure. Like spies? Or J. Edgar Hoover wannabes—

Abruptly, her jaw dropped as she realized. "But . . . But wait. That means *you* . . ."

A weary smile rolled over his lips. "Yup. Me."

"You work for the government?"

"Did. Past tense. Remember? No more. Thus the whole kidnapping thing."

She honestly didn't give a damn about the time frame. The point was— Hell, she didn't know what the point was. She was just shocked.

"*Our* government? You're sure?"

He chuckled wearily. "'Fraid so. Zero Unit is part of the Company."

Her disbelief morphed to incredulity. "The Company. As in . . ."

"Yeah. *That* Company. I used to work for CIA."

* * *

RAINIE'S mind was still reeling when she was ushered into a sparse but ordinary-looking office with a neat but ordinary-looking man sitting behind the cluttered but ordinary-looking desk.

CIA?

C-I-freaking-A?

Kick?

Wow. Okay. Maybe. But all that aside . . . Could an official US government agency really kidnap people? And threaten to kill them? Send them on suicide missions against their will?

She didn't think so. That would be—

Suddenly she was no longer terrified.

She was *furious*.

"Where the hell do you get off treating people like this?" she demanded of the mousy man behind the desk. "I want to see some identification. No. I want to see the person in charge of this outrage!"

"That would be me." He gave her a friendly smile and folded his hands in front of him. "My name is Jason Forsythe, Miss Martin, and I work for Central Intelligence Agency. I'm terribly sorry for any inconvenience you may have experienced."

She almost choked. "*Inconvenience?* Are you completely *insane*? I was abducted at *gunpoint* from my own apartment, by what I now find out is my own *government*? You call that *inconvenient*?"

"Please, sit down, Miss Martin. Yes, Doc mentioned you suffer from post-traumatic stress disorder. I truly apologize if our methods stirred up unpleasant memories for you. But—"

"*Excuse* me?" Her body stiffened and she dropped ramrod straight onto the edge of his uncomfortable wooden visitor's chair. "What makes your so-called doctor think I have PTSD? He's never even met me before two minutes ago."

Forsythe's shoulder lifted. "The men who brought you here described your behavior. But as I said—"

"He's wrong. I *don't* have PTSD," she said, her stomach clenching. She swallowed down the seething resentment at even having to talk about this subject. "I have event-specific emotional trauma, if you must know."

"*Hmmm.*" He nodded slowly. "From your parents' deaths?"

Again she was unpleasantly astounded. How much did they already know about her? *Can you say Big Brother?*

"Yes," she admitted before it dawned on her she should really just shut up. Which she finally did.

"Interesting distinction," he said when she didn't elaborate. "But hopefully irrelevant, now that you know we're on the same side."

This time she did choke. "You're kidding, right?"

He laughed softly, as though she'd made a joke, but his eyes remained humorless. "I assure you I'm not." He reached into his jacket pocket and extracted a small, thin wallet. "You asked for my credentials. Here they are. Now, if we can—"

"I have no way of knowing this isn't fake," she interrupted, scrutinizing the ID card that appeared legit, but who knew what real CIA creds looked like? She sure as heck didn't.

Although, get real, Kick had already told her these people were CIA, and he had no reason to lie. Some comfort.

Forsythe jetted out a breath. "You have a cell phone, I assume?" She nodded. "We mean you no harm, Miss Martin. Feel free to call the Agency and confirm my identity."

The offer surprised her, but she wasn't about to turn it down. She'd feel a lot better if someone on the outside knew where she was and whom she was with. She pulled out her cell and dialed Gina's number.

"Speakerphone, please," Forsythe said.

Reluctantly she pushed the button.

"It's about time!" Gina exclaimed before Rainie had finished saying hello. "I've been worried sick, calling you all morning. Where *are* you?"

"You wouldn't believe me if I told you. Listen—"

"So how was it?" Gina asked, her voice dropping to a conspiratorial hush. "How was he? Mr. Tall Dark and Dangerous."

Forsythe smiled blandly over the desk at her.

"Gina—"

"When you didn't call this morning, I was sure he'd kidnapped you and—"

"Gina—"

"—handcuffed you and did all sorts of—"

"*Gina*! Listen to me!"

"Sorry, got carried away. What is it, hon? You sound strange. He didn't—"

Rainie plunged in. "I'm being questioned by a man who claims to be with the CIA. I need you to check for me and find out if he's legit."

There was a long pause. "You're serious?"

"Yes. CIA. The name is Jason Forsythe. Can you check it out and call me back as soon as possible?"

"Should I be worried?" Gina asked carefully.

Rainie took a deep breath. She wanted to scream, "Yes! Please come rescue me!" but if Forsythe was who he said he was, she should be fine. *Hopefully*. If he wasn't, there was no way she wanted Gina involved in any of this. She was even starting to regret having called her at all.

"Don't worry," she told her best friend. "Mr. Tall Dark and Dangerous actually turned out to be Mr. Tall Dark and Addicted. There was fallout." She glared at the man across from her. "I just want to be sure the people I'm talking to aren't bad guys masquerading as law enforcement."

"Okaaay."

"Hurry. I'll be waiting."

She hung up knowing Gina would already be in a frenzied panic calling her former fiancé, Special Agent Wade Montana of the FBI, trying to confirm that Rainie wasn't being held by drug dealers or worse. Gina and Wade had an ugly breakup last year, and Rainie hoped he wouldn't hold out on Gina just to punish her for dumping him. He had no way of knowing Rainie had been his staunchest advocate in the relationship.

"Very smart," Forsythe said, almost approvingly. With one finger, he pushed a paper toward her on the desk. "While we wait, I'd like you to read this."

"What is it?"

He just nodded at the paper. It was a typical-looking no-nonsense government form, filled in and signed. By someone named Kyle Jackson. Jackson . . . Wasn't that the name the nasty old Marine had called Kick? Lord, how embarrassing, she'd never asked him his last name. At her inquiring glance, Forsythe nodded again.

She skimmed through the considerable verbiage. First came a short, strict confidentiality agreement, treasonous if broken. The gist of the rest was that by accepting employment with Zero Unit, Kick agreed he could be called back to duty at any time for any reason, even after he quit working for them, in the interest of national security. The form was initialed, signed, and dated 1993.

While she was reading it over a second time, more thoroughly, her cell rang.

"I called Wade," Gina told her, sounding totally unlike her usual lighthearted self. "I had to beg, but he relented and called a friend at Langley."

Rainie's heartbeat sped up. "And?"

"There is a Jason Forsythe working for CIA. They wouldn't get more specific than that, other than to tell me what his signal code is for today. Ask him."

Rainie raised her brow at Forsythe.

"Labrador," he said.

Gina exhaled audibly. "That's right. He's legit."

"Thanks, Geen. And tell Wade thanks for me."

Gina ignored the hint. It was an old argument. "You sure you're all right?"

"I'm fine. I'll call you later, okay?" She punched the Off button and eased out a breath she'd probably been holding ever since she opened her apartment door. "So what happens now?"

"You've finished reading the document?"

She glanced down at it and nodded. "What does this have to do with me?"

"I wanted you to know Kyle Jackson signed this agreement of his own free will. I'm showing it to you so you'll know we had every right to bring him in, using any means necessary, despite his protests."

"That may be so, but *I* never signed any such agreement."

Wordlessly, Forsythe pushed another form over to her. This time her own name and address were filled in at the top, along with her Social Security number and birth information.

A frisson of apprehension sizzled through her. She could

barely voice the unnerving question circling her mind like a vulture. "What exactly do you want from me?"

"Nothing you weren't willing to do before we showed up," Forsythe said with an air of soothing assurance.

She wasn't assured. "And what's that?"

"Take care of Mr. Jackson. Help him through his withdrawal."

"That's it?" The print on the paper danced in front of her eyes. Why didn't she believe him?

"Yes. We simply weren't aware of his problem until last night, so we weren't prepared to deal with it when we apprehended him. Luckily Doc has experience with this sort of thing, and could set things up for you. But his team has mobilized and he must join them immediately. I also happen to know you are in charge of a test program for a similar detox technique at the Bellevue ER, so don't bother pleading ignorance. We need you to put Mr. Jackson through the full regime before he goes on his mission."

Rainie shook her head. "No. Get someone else. I won't be a party to what you're forcing him to do."

Forsythe put his hands on the desk and leaned forward. "We don't have *time* to get anyone else." He sat back again and steepled his fingers. "In any case, Mr. Jackson has already been put under anesthesia, and Doc has already left to join his team."

"Without being closely monitored?" She gaped at him in outrage. "Kick could die!"

Forsythe's mouth thinned. "That would be up to you. Unless you want his death on your hands, I'm afraid you have no option but to help."

"Bastard," she whispered.

He regarded her for a long moment. "I'm sorry you feel that way, Miss Martin." He stood, unsmiling. "I trust you'll find everything you need for the duration in Mr. Jackson's room."

Anger filled every cell of her body as she rose, as well. "I'll need to contact my supervisor at the hospital and let her know I won't be in tomorrow."

"That's been taken care of."

Of course it had.

The door opened and her guard appeared. "Ma'am? If you'll follow me?"

Fuming, she returned to the Zero Unit sick bay. Kick was right. These people were used to getting their own way. One way or another. And she had the sinking feeling she wasn't getting the whole story. She couldn't shake the feeling she was about to get screwed.

And *so* not in a good way.

SIX

WHEN she got back to the room where she'd left Kick, as Forsythe had said, he was already under.

Stretched out on the bed with a white sheet pulled up to his chest, Kick looked strangely peaceful. A description she would never have used about the man before now. *Gritty. Burned out. Fiercely determined*, yes. But not even after a night of sex that had left them both exhausted and replete had the restless, hunted look disappeared from his eyes, for more than a few fleeting seconds.

"Oh, Kick, she murmured softly. "How on earth did you end up in a place like this?" And what was his former job with the CIA that made them want to send him, and no one else, halfway around the world to do it? Terrible visions of what a hard man like him might consider "hell" pulsed uneasily through her mind. Whatever it was, he'd called the situation exactly right. These people didn't give a damn. They were sending him on this mission whether he wanted to go or not.

And now it was up to her to make sure he had a fighting chance at survival.

She sighed, and went to examine him. He had a catheter line inserted along his collarbone, which led to a series of computerized IV pumps that emitted a low hum. A monitor beeped rhythmically above his head. Automatically, she adjusted the alarm parameters on the pulse ox; the heart rate and BP were all normal.

She spotted a hastily scribbled note on top of the monitor.

> Profolol drip running on pump one to keep him under, watch the TPN bag, you'll need to piggyback lipids to give him enough nutrition, and the oxynovine (detox med) needs to run at 12 cc/hr for 18 hrs, then discontinue all. After waking and alert, the oxorelin flush should run at 12 cc/hr for 6 hrs. Monitor closely for forty-eight hours.

She flipped over the paper. There was nothing more. Outrage zinged through her anew. *Oh, thanks ever so much for the great instructions.* She *knew* all that stuff. What she didn't know was how the hell she was supposed to do all of it single-handed. The procedure took twenty-four hours to complete, plus observation time. At least at Bellevue she'd had round-the-clock help.

God, did she ever hate this—having to run the experimental protocol without knowing all the variables and being able to plan for them. Especially when someone's life was at stake.

Someone who just happened to be her lover.

Seventy-two hours.

This was insane! Hadn't that colonel said something about being on a plane to Egypt in thirty-six? She had to talk them out of it. Kick wouldn't even be past the critical stage.

Unfortunately, no one came for her to talk to. As the hours ticked by, her outrage at Forsythe continued, but at least her nerves calmed a bit. As well as her anger at the man lying helpless in the bed. Kick moaned, his body twitching and jerking as it rid itself of the toxic drug, especially the leg with the scars.

She sponged his brow with cool water, held the bowl when he puked, pulled the blanket up again when he kicked it off, tenderly stroked the damp tendrils of hair from his forehead. During the worst, she took his hand and held it in hers. She might still be upset with him, but there was no way she could sit and watch a man in such pain and not be touched deep inside.

But seeing him unconscious and vulnerable, fighting his addiction, and having experienced the full brunt of his former employers, she had a hard time staying angry that he had tried to use her to escape all this. Hell, she would have done the same thing. But why couldn't he have just been honest, instead of pulling that gun on her?

The day had definitely been an emotional roller coaster. Panic attacks always left her drained, and ones involving guns or violence usually sent her straight under the covers into a long, troubled sleep. It happened at the ER every once in a while; over the years she'd learned to control and cover her reactions at work, holding the fatigue at bay until she got home. But today the threat had been all too personal. The reaction more vivid and exhausting.

All the more so because of last night with Kick. That had been personal, too. Draining in a whole different way. Especially the part in bed. Even without subsequent events, she would have been wiped out after a night like that.

But now wasn't the time to think about the night they'd spent together.

She *definitely* wasn't ready to face those memories yet, not even in her mind.

THAT night Rainie was barely able to stay awake. She drank about a million cups of coffee and forced herself to keep her eyes open and on the monitor. Because Kick needed her.

A couple of hours before dawn, Forsythe finally came to see her.

Wordlessly, he handed her the early edition of the *New York Times*, folded into thirds. With a buzzing head, she glanced at it.

At the top of the page, the column headline read:

**MILLION DOLLAR DRUG THEFT AT BELLEVUE
GENERAL: MISSING NURSE SUSPECTED**

She was so tired that the meaning didn't occur to her until she read the first paragraph of the story. There, her own name was prominently listed as a "person of interest" in the investigation.

That's when it hit her.

She gasped in indignation. "*Me*? I had nothing to do with any theft! I was *here* all last night! You have to tell them!"

Forsythe met her with a level look.

Then it dawned on her. "Oh, my God! *You* did this!"

His gaze chilled. "Just a little insurance. So you understand the stakes."

"What do you mean by that?" she demanded.

"Mr. Jackson's detox is nearly complete," he said. "This evening he'll be taken to New Jersey and put on a military transport to Egypt. And you along with him."

Rainie's pulse went into hyperspace. "*What*? You promised I could go home after this is over!"

"And you will. The doc said it'll be seventy-two hours before he's completely out of danger. It's only been eighteen."

She shook her head emphatically. "I can't go to Egypt."

Forsythe crossed his arms. "You'll never have to leave the plane. I promise."

Oh, God. "No, you don't understand. I'd be useless. I have severe panic attacks in any kind of vehicle. Ask your men. I freaked out completely in the SUV coming here. I can't even imagine how I'd react to being confined in an airplane over the ocean for hours on end. I'm hyperventilating just thinking about it."

"Here are your options, Miss Martin," Forsythe said evenly as he handed her the form she wouldn't sign the day before. "You can show your patriotism and see Mr. Jackson through his whole treatment as you promised. Or . . . you *could* go home to your apartment and never see us again."

She glanced back at the newspaper article. *And be arrested for stealing drugs and never work again*, was the clear subtext.

"You'll be generously compensated for your time," he told her. "And the police will be provided with evidence of your innocence in the drug robbery, of course."

"Of course," she said, *really* feeling like she was about to faint.

"I'm sorry about the emotional trauma, Miss Martin. But the plain truth is, you really have no choice. You *will* be accompanying Mr. Jackson to Egypt."

SHE could do this.

Rainie's best friend, Gina Cappozi, reached for the phone and picked it up determinedly. Hadn't she just spoken to Special Agent Wade Montana yesterday? Yes. She had. And it had gone very well, thankyouverymuch. They'd both been cordial, polite, and to the point. The fact that she'd been totally distracted over her friend's überstrange request to confirm the name of a freaking *CIA officer*, and had not exchanged a single personal word with Wade, was completely irrelevant. She'd begged for his help, and he'd given it. End of story.

No wounded silences. No angry recriminations. No heartfelt pleas. Just business.

See? They could be friends.

Why should today be any different?

Maybe because she'd spent the entire night agonizing alternately over Rainie's terrible choice in going off with that burnt-out druggie loser she'd met at the speed dating, and Gina's own choice last year of not quitting her job, marrying FBI super-agent Wade Montana, and following him to Washington, D.C., to live happily ever after in comfortable obscurity.

Was Wade still pissed off about that?

Courage failing her, she hung up the phone for the twentieth time.

He hadn't *sounded* pissed off. But voices could be deceiving. How well she knew. The whole time they'd gone out together *she'd* sounded perfectly normal, like a woman who wasn't completely terrified of falling in love and losing her whole identity because some man decided he didn't approve of his wife or girlfriend being smarter than he was.

She'd taken a chance on handsome, sociable Wade, and he'd proven to be everything she'd always feared and more.

So she'd told him where to stuff his two-carat diamond ring, and went back to dating younger men who couldn't care less about her career, because they were brainless studs only interested in one thing. It was an arrangement that worked well all around.

Though the ring had been really fine.

Ah, well. She could afford to buy herself a *four*-carat diamond now if she wanted to—thanks to a small but increasingly lucrative patent she owned—and not have the downside of being tied for life to a conservative, old-fashioned, opinionated, dictatorial, if handsome and sociable . . . Neanderthal.

She glanced at the clock. A Neanderthal who'd be leaving the office for lunch if she didn't stop being such a wimp. She picked up the phone and dialed.

"Montana."

"Wade, this is Gina again."

There was a short silence. "Twice in two days. Don't know if I can stand the excitement," he drawled. "Is this your cleverly disguised way of telling me you've changed your mind and can't live without me?" His tone said he knew very well changing her mind was the last thing she'd ever do, but he just couldn't help twisting the knife a little. *Nice guy.*

"No," she said crisply, striving for cheerful indifference to the nasty undercurrent. "That Forsythe guy I called you about this morning? The one for Rainie? I need you to give me his phone number."

Another pause. "You know I can't do that, Gina."

"It's important, Wade. It's been over a day and Rainie still hasn't come home. Or called. Or answered her cell."

"File a missing persons report."

"I have, but—"

"Then try letting NYPD do their job, babe."

She ignored the dripping sarcasm. "They called me a few minutes ago asking about her. Stupid me thought they'd taken my report seriously. But instead they started implying she could be responsible for a break-in at the hospital last night. A lot of drugs were taken."

"If they've got evidence, maybe she—"

"There's no *way* Rainie had anything to do with that

break-in. Please, Wade, I'm really scared. I'm afraid the CIA is trying to—"

Wade made a rude noise. "A *conspiracy* theory? Jesus, Gina, I thought you were supposed to be a fucking genius or something. Or has your obvious distaste for me colored your entire perception of federal law enf—"

"Oh, stop it and grow up!" she snapped. Then reined in her temper. "I'm sorry. I'm just so worried about Rainie. Why would she have disappeared like this?"

"Maybe she likes sex with a real man. Someone over the age of, oh, say, twenty-one. She's probably spent the last two nights with that guy you disapprove of so much, fucking his brains out."

Gina felt like she'd been slugged in the stomach. Tears stung her eyes. "Don't you *dare* give me that shit, Wade Montana. I liked *fucking* you fine. It was all your goddamn male chauvinist baggage I couldn't live with," she said between clenched teeth.

"Oh. Yeah. Because *you* have no baggage at all," he shot back. "Especially none of that goddamn *feminist* garbage."

She squeezed her eyes shut and counted to ten. Twenty. Thirty. Then she opened them again and said, very, very calmly, "Give me the phone number, Wade. Give me the damn phone number *now* or I swear I'll e-mail all your FBI buddies and tell them how much you like being tied up and spanked. And you *know* I'll do it."

There was another long silence. "You are such a fucking bitch," he finally said.

"Yeah, well, you used to like that about me. The number?"

"Hold on." A moment later he read it off to her. "And just for the record," he said, quiet fury ringing in his voice, "*you* liked it way more than I did." Then he slammed down the phone.

Slowly she let out the breath she'd been holding. *Okay, then.* Wasn't *that* a barrel of laughs.

But at least she'd gotten the damn phone number.

KICK woke up feeling like shit on a stick. If the stick had been made from glowing hot metal and shoved the long way through his bad leg and was lodged there like a spear. A glowing-hot, poison-tipped spear.

But all things considered, it could be a hell of a lot worse. A day of his life was gone. But then, so was his addiction. Well. Sort of. The cravings would still be there for a while. Okay, probably for the rest of his fucking life. But cravings Kick could handle. As long as the crippling physical need was gone. Which it was. Mostly.

A noise attracted his attention. He cracked his moist eyelids. And saw Rainie. Standing over him fussing with the sheet.

Hell. What was she still doing here? That worried him. He'd really hoped they'd let her go once they had him in their clutches. No good would come of her being anywhere close to him. He'd been down this road before and it hadn't been pretty.

But *she* sure was. Pretty, that was.

"Hey," he said, unreasonably glad to see her at his bedside. God, he was a selfish bastard.

"Welcome back," she said, and gave him a genuine, if tired, smile. "How are you feeling?"

"Better than I have a right to be. You okay?"

She nodded. She was holding his hand. He smiled back and passed out again.

But this time he remembered his dreams. Pretty Rainie was in every one. Smiling sweetly as he shot her in the head.

HE woke up several more times, until finally he was able to stay awake for over an hour. After changing his IV, Rainie gave him a cup of water with a straw in it, and fed him applesauce with a plastic spoon, and he was even able to keep it down.

"I feel like a baby," he said. It was kind of embarrassing. Big, macho commando man.

"Your second infancy," she teased. "Enjoy it."

"*Hmm.* I'm fairly certain I was breastfed," he said.

She gave him a sardonic grin. "You *are* feeling better."

"Yeah." He eased back on his pillow and looked up at her gratefully. And nervously. "Why are you still here?"

A shadow of unease flitted across her face. "They, *um*, persuaded me to stay."

He closed his eyes and sighed. So goddamned predictable. "What did they threaten you with?"

She handed him a folded-up newspaper. He read the headline and cursed under his breath. "Bastards."

"Yeah."

"I'm sorry," he said. They might be bastards, but Al was right. He was the bigger one for getting her involved in the first place. And he knew better. He *knew* better. "God, I'm so damned sorry I dragged you into this."

"Me, too." And yet, as he gazed into her tired green eyes, they softened. Her cheeks grew pink. "But the sex was really nice."

He couldn't believe she'd brought that up. A tingling spilled through him, his body suddenly remembering what pleasure was, rather than merely painful torture.

Nice? "More like amazing," he said. Was it possible she'd forgiven him for using her? "Look. Maybe . . . if I survive this thing and get back to New York, I could maybe look you up sometime?"

For a second, she looked surprised. Hell, he'd surprised himself. Since when did he make dates? Even when the sex was amazing . . .

But her deep, hesitant intake of breath as she looked deliberately down at the floor was more eloquent than words.

He held up a hand, actually shocked at the letdown he felt at her rejection. Not that he blamed her one damn bit. It wasn't like he'd shown her a real good time. Besides, that crazy emotional disappointment he was feeling? Probably just a residual influence of the drugs. "Never mind," he agreed. "You're right, not a good idea."

She gave him a bleak smile. "Different worlds" was all she said.

But that pretty much summed it up in a nutshell. She was a nurse, for crying out loud. He was . . . what he was. They came from diametrically opposed worlds, and wish as he might to dwell in hers, no sane, normal woman would ever knowingly accept the things he'd done, the person he'd become, in his. Not even for amazing sex.

In the end, it all came down to one thing.

She saved lives.

He took them.

LATE that night, they were driven to McGuire Air Force Base in New Jersey, and escorted out to where a huge, lumbering C-17 was being loaded with cargo bound for Cairo, Egypt. From there they'd transfer to a private transport south and over the border to the Sudan. Kick's ticket to hell.

He was still weak and shaky, but he'd completed the whole course of the detox treatment itself. Feeling better. Almost human. Okay, maybe not *that* good, but getting there.

At the sight of the plane, he stifled a groan. So much for feeling human. He wished he had a dollar for every time he'd had to strap himself onto one of those hard-as-rock, spine-cracking cargo seats that lined the walls of the giant flying warehouses, while headed out on a mission too covert to risk flying commercial. He'd be a rich man.

Even richer than he was now. Hazardous-duty pay wasn't bad, and he'd earned plenty of it. The numbers added up quickly when you were never home to dip into your portfolio.

Too bad he probably wouldn't be around to enjoy his nest egg now that he'd finally found something . . . someone . . . worth spending it on.

But despite the fragile hope he'd momentarily let slip to Rainie, this Sudan mission would be a bitch to survive. Realistically, he probably wouldn't.

Afghanistan had been bad enough, but at least that theater had been full of regular US military support. When his spec ops ZU team had been ambushed trying to take out the fanatical al Sayika leader Jallil abu Bakr, help was just a walkie-talkie hail away. That wasn't going to be the case in the Sudan. The closest thing to friendlies he'd find there would be the wandering Bedouin, and a few refugee camps scattered around the Sahara Desert, such as the Doctors for Peace camp that his buddy Nathan Daneby had started a hundred clicks or so south of the Egyptian border.

Kick wondered if Nate was still there at the DFP camp.

He doubted it. Last he'd heard, his tireless friend was helping the UN set up another field hospital somewhere down by the equator. The Sudan was a huge country—three and a half times the size of Texas—and it seemed every inch of it was being ravaged by some kind of pestilence, drought, or war. And now the virulent terrorist Jallil abu Bakr had come to add his sick agenda to the country's burden of problems.

Kick's mission was to rid the world of the scumbag once and for all. He'd failed last time. This time he wouldn't fail. So help him God, he wouldn't.

On the way to the airport, CIA weasel Jason Forsythe told Kick he would rip up his Zero Unit employment contract once and for all, if Kick completed this one last mission for them. Free at last, free at last. He could only pray Forsythe was telling the truth. But in all honesty, Kick really hadn't needed the extra motivation.

Somewhere in the fog of unconsciousness during the past twenty-four hours, fighting to save himself from the toxic drug that had been slowly ravaging his flesh as a consequence of that last failed mission in A-stan, he had finally realized he would never be truly healed, in body or in soul, until abu Bakr was dead and buried. Like his team and his best friend, whom abu Bakr had brutally murdered. On Kick's watch.

To get his self-respect back, to get his *life* back, he had to finish that ill-fated mission. Nothing else would help. If that meant going to the Sudan to face conditions that would test a healthy man, let alone one barely able to stand on his own, so be it.

Kick needed the closure.

No. What he really needed was . . . revenge.

THE SUV came to a halt beside the C-17 and Kick climbed out into the New Jersey night, followed by Rainie and the lone guard that had come along with them. Apparently the ZU trusted him now. Or maybe they knew he couldn't fight his way out of a paper bag at the moment.

Forsythe slid out of the front seat and waved the driver to the back of the vehicle, where he pulled out three backpacks and a couple of long duffel bags, depositing them on the tarmac. The burly guard picked up the whole lot and strode through the darkness toward the C-17.

Kick took a deep breath. This was the part he'd been dreading. Saying good-bye to Rainie. He sucked big-time at this stuff, especially when the person meant something to him. Which, maybe not so strangely, Rainie did. A lot. How had that happened so quickly? Him, the bitter war fighter, gone all soft and mushy.

He wished like hell it weren't such a classic *Casablanca* moment.

But instead of stopping by the car and turning bravely to him with tears in her eyes, spouting on about hills of beans, she just kept walking determinedly next to Forsythe, who was clearly headed for the C-17's rear cargo ramp. *Hello?*

"Hey. Where are you going?" he called, limping after her. For some unknown reason, his pulse quickened. Instinct?

Her feet stuttered to a stop, then her shoulders squared and she started walking again. "Same place you are," she said without turning, her voice strained.

"*What?*" Disbelief slammed through him. *Oh, no.* No, no, no. He grabbed Forsythe's shoulder and spun him around. "Goddamn it! What the hell have you done?" he growled. "I swear I'll—"

There was a thump, and the business end of the guard's MP-7 appeared in front of his face. Forsythe waved the goon off. Probably not the smartest move.

Kick wrapped his hand around the CIA jerk's throat. "She is *not* getting on that plane with us," he ground out, too angry to care when the MP-7 reappeared.

"Calm down, Jackson," Forsythe wheezed. "She's only coming along to administer the final meds for your detox. Doc said you need to be monitored for seventy-two. She volunteered."

"You're lying."

"She won't be in any danger. She'll never leave the plane."

Kick took another calming breath, shook off the top layer of fury, and let him go. He turned to Rainie. She was so damn beautiful. But her face looked pale, her skin clammy, her red-rimmed eyes wide and dilated. As in, scared to death but trying her damndest not to show it.

That newspaper article she'd shown him. It *hadn't* been just about the detox. He should have known.

"They're blackmailing you into coming along, aren't they?" he demanded.

Of all the unconscionable things they'd ever done to him, this was by far the worst. He didn't want her anywhere *near* this mission. *Any* mission. Didn't want to spoil the little good they'd shared together by having her find out what he really was, what he was about to do.

And they fucking well knew it.

A muscle ticked in her jaw, and she cleared her throat. "I believe the proper term is *extortion*. But I want you to know I have no problem taking care of you. It's the plane ride I'm afraid of."

Something clicked in his mind. Leaving the hotel that first night, she'd said she didn't like cars. Both times riding in the SUV she hadn't said a word, but sat curled up tight on the seat, trembling, her face pressed into his shoulder as he held her close. The first time he'd assumed she was terrified of what was happening, and tonight that she was vibrating from sheer exhaustion—he'd been that tired himself before. But now he didn't think exhaustion had anything to do with it. It was terror, all right. But not of the gun.

As if reading his mind, she said in a stiff voice, "My parents were killed in a car hijacking. I'm petrified of getting into a vehicle of any kind. I've never even been in a plane."

He finally understood what he should have seen that very first night. He stared at her for a long second, then turned on Forsythe, even angrier. "Let her go home. I'm *fine*. I don't need a goddamn nurse."

"It's okay," she intervened. "The panic attacks never last more than five or ten minutes. I should be okay then. Theoretically."

"Jesus," he muttered, slashing a hand through his hair. "And you're okay with that?"

"Do I have a choice?"

He ground his teeth in frustration. "This is completely out of control."

"Tell me about it. Still, I probably should have faced my fears a long time ago. Now I have a good reason." She tried to smile, but failed miserably. "Besides, I've always wanted to see Egypt."

He set his mouth in a grim line at her doggedness. And had to physically restrain himself from pounding Forsythe into the pavement. Instead, he turned and hit him where it really hurt. "You're sending her home commercial," he gritted out. "First class. Hotels, too."

Forsythe nodded a faux-nice concession. "The least we can do."

Kick did his best to make her comfortable on the transport, but there was really no such thing on a C-17 unless you were the pilot. He made himself hold her close when she started shaking and feeling dizzy, banded his arms around her when she balked and wanted to run, spoke soothing words to her as he coaxed her into a flip-down cargo seat and strapped her in, then held her twitching hands in an iron grip and made her breathe and count slowly backward from two hundred so she wouldn't unbuckle and run screaming into the cockpit to be let out.

He'd seen veterans come home from war, and operators come home from particularly bad missions, with similar symptoms. PTSD—post-traumatic stress disorder. ET—emotional trauma. CIS—critical incident stress. The list went on. None of it good.

Hell, he probably suffered from some form of psychoalphabet himself. His behavior over the past year hadn't been exactly rational, when examined objectively and without the justifying influence of painkillers. The ZU psych had tried to get him to deal with his repressed anger, or at least talk about it, but talk was useless.

Action. That's what *he* needed. He understood that now. Kick had to exorcise the devil who had done this to him and his dead team. *Abu Bakr.* Wipe the fucking bastard off the face of the earth. Nothing less would do. Then, if Kick survived, he would get out and stay out of this business forever. If he was killed, so be it. But better to die fixing the problem than to live like he'd been living for the past year.

But not Rainie. More death and destruction was not the

remedy for her fears. She needed to be safe. And back home where she belonged. As far away from Kick's violent world as she could get.

Forsythe could make all the promises he wanted. Kick wasn't about to trust the fucker.

He wouldn't rest easy until Rainie was wheels-up and oscar mike on a plane back to the States, and he knew for sure she'd be all right. Even though he had the growing feeling that when she left him, *he'd* be the furthest thing from all right, ever again.

SEVEN

ON the plane, Rainie finally succumbed to an exhausted sleep. She'd been a walking zombie. Kick hadn't realized she'd stayed awake through his whole detox procedure. Sweet Jesus, no wonder she'd fallen apart during takeoff, practically clawing at him to get away and escape the plane. After the worst was over, he'd made a thick nest of blankets on the narrow strip of uneven, grill-pocked metal floor between the cargo containers and the flip-up seats and compelled her to lie down. He'd ended up lying down with her, holding her under the warm covers as the panic attack subsided. Eventually the drone of the engines and motion of the plane worked their magic. And holding her had worked its magic on him. He was able to grab a bit more much-needed sleep himself.

"We need to talk," Forsythe said, waking Kick when they were about halfway over the Atlantic.

"Yup." He eased away from Rainie and got to his unsteady feet. Immediately he missed the comforting feel of her warm body snuggled in his arms. Jeez, when had he gotten to be such a wuss?

"I need to read you in on the mission," Forsythe said.

Kick frowned, switching gears in a flash. "Read me in? What the hell? I thought *I* was the mission."

"Not exactly." Forsythe motioned to the front of the plane, to two jump seats located in a clear space behind the pilots. "We can talk better up front. Less noise. I've got your info packet and your gear stowed there."

As Kick followed, a hard knot formed in his stomach . . . around the other one that was already there—the dull but incessant knot of craving for the drug that had been lodged in his gut since awakening from the detox. Reading him in on the mission meant there was a previously formed plan, involving other people. Which meant the objective had to be more complicated than simply him killing one terrorist.

He should have *known* he couldn't trust a word the bureaucrat said.

In the forward section he spotted the field packs the guard had carried up from the SUV. *Three* of them. Bingo. Why hadn't he put two and one together?

Seeing him look at the packs, Forsythe explained, "They contain MREs and water, extra clothes, a SATCOM, and a variety of tools and small weapons. In the duffel bags are sniper rifles you can choose from, a machine gun, and a shoulder-held RPG. Wasn't sure what-all you wanted to take with you."

Kick crossed his arms over his chest and pressed in on the sick ache roiling in his abdomen. "Who are the other two packs for?"

"Sit down, Jackson, before you fall over."

"I prefer to stand."

Forsythe shrugged. "Suit yourself." He dropped onto one of the jump seats, nodding to the pilot who waved over his shoulder. "Here's the deal. This is not a Company operation. For political reasons, it's being run by STORM Corps. Technically, you'll be working for them."

"STORM Corps."

Kick knew the STORM acronym stood for Strategic Technical Operations and Rescue Missions, a spec ops outfit similar to Zero Unit, except it was nongovernmental. Used mainly by private companies and individuals to recover and defend hostages and other assets, they were occasionally hired by governments—including the United States—to carry out ultra-sensitive or controversial special operations in locations where official government agencies couldn't or wouldn't go.

Kick's anger notched down a degree or two. He'd never worked with STORM, but he'd heard good things about them from friends who had. Their reputation was sterling.

Forsythe picked up a briefcase. "You're aware that ever since our investigations into September 11, CIA has had a special relationship with the Sudanese government in the war on terrorism. We can't afford to jeopardize those tenuous ties should you or your mission be compromised."

Kick barely stifled a snort of derision. "Yeah, I'm aware."

It had always made him furious. Nathan Daneby and the other Doctors for Peace had lobbied hard for US sanctions against the fundamentalist government that promoted genocide against its own people and whose soldiers systematically raped women as a weapon of terror. Kick was physically sickened by the thought of CIA turning a blind eye, let alone having close ties to them. It didn't surprise him at all that Jallil abu Bakr and his gang of al Sayika thugs had found safe haven there.

"It was our friends in the Sudanese government who tipped us off to abu Bakr's recent entry into the country," Forsythe said, sensing his harsh thoughts.

"Then undoubtedly they'll be the ones who kill me when I go after him," he said sardonically. His team had been betrayed in A-stan, so why not the Sudan, too? They'd never found the internal leak that had compromised the team on that last disastrous op. Which was why he was pretty sure this would be a suicide mission for him. Loose ends rarely lasted in his line of work.

But being under STORM Corps put a new spin on things. Maybe he had a fighting chance to get through this alive. Not that it mattered much . . .

For a split second his gaze veered to the woman sleeping aft in the cargo hold. *Don't even go there*, he told himself, and forced his attention back where it belonged.

At some point Forsythe had opened his briefcase, and now held a thin file folder. Kick tried to focus.

"As always," Forsythe was saying, "your specific task is

to neutralize the principal, in this case abu Bakr. When that's accomplished, the two STORM operatives you'll be with will coordinate and direct an air strike to raze the enemy camp."

"An air strike on foreign soil?" Kick whistled. "Ballsy. No wonder you brought in outside help."

"Not help. Deniability. It'll be made to look like a Sudanese government raid. Clamping down on terrorism and all."

"Yup. I'd buy that," Kick said.

Forsythe ignored the sarcasm. "There's a small plane standing by in Cairo, waiting to take us south to the border."

"Us?"

"You and me."

"And what happens with Rainie?" Kick asked.

"Miss Martin will have a room at the Hilton and an open ticket to JFK waiting for her. Yeah, yeah, all first class."

He wondered how she'd do in the infamous Cairo traffic, which was kind of like Rome on speed with no rules and five times more cars. He wished he could be there to help get her through it.

No. He didn't. She wouldn't want him there. She'd made that clear enough.

Different worlds.

And she was right.

Forsythe rose. "Why don't you check out the gear in the packs, make sure everything you need is there. Then get some more sleep. You'll need it."

"Yup." Kick reached down for the guns in the duffel.

"Oh. There's one more thing."

Naturally. He looked up as he unzipped the bag.

"There's been a new lead in the investigation into who might be responsible for getting your team ambushed in Afghanistan. We think we have our man. The evidence is fairly convincing."

Kick froze where he stood. His fingers spasmed around the assault rifle he held in his grip. "Who?" was all he could manage to squeeze past the sudden grenade lodged in his throat.

Could it be he'd finally learn the truth? He'd give anything to find out the identity of the person who had betrayed them. Had caused the deaths of five good men, including his best friend, Alex Zane.

Because that person was a walking dead man.

Wordlessly, Forsythe handed him the file, then strode away.

Opening up the cover, Kick's heart pounded so hard in his chest it was painful.

But that was nothing compared to how it thundered when he saw the eight-by-ten photo that stared back at him from inside. It was a telephoto shot of two men. One of them Kick recognized immediately from A-stan. White-haired Abbas Tawhid. An old-school fundamentalist and real scumbag, he was a known associate of abu Bakr ... was his right-hand man in al Sayika, in fact. But it was the other man in the photo, to whom Tawhid was passing a small packet, that made Kick's heart leap to his throat in agony.

It couldn't be. He felt even more sick to his stomach, like he'd swallowed knives.

But it was. Clear as day.

The second man was his own good friend.

Nathan Daneby.

THE *Sultan of Pain.*

Mary, Mother of God. What was he doing here?

Pig's insides turned to water as the sound of the hated voice came closer and closer.

The voice of his worst torturer.

A *real* torturer, not these other murdering, raping clowns who thought they knew what the word meant. And maybe they did, to some people.

Not to him. He knew better. He'd met the man. Abu Bakr, the guards called him. But to Pig, he'd always be the Sultan of Pain.

Hopeless despair filled his chest. The cold, vicious brute used to appear at camp regularly to interrogate the man he'd christened Pig, until he'd finally convinced him he didn't remember anything. Which he really didn't. Other than the bloody memories of excruciating pain the Sultan left behind.

After that, the bastard had stopped his visits. And then

had come the long blackout when they must have drugged and moved him because he'd woken up in a completely different camp. Nothing had been the same. Not the hovels, not the food, not the people. Not even the smell. But as fucked-up as things were here, he'd been grateful. Because the Sultan was gone.

But now it seemed his luck had run out.

He didn't resist when the guards came for him. It was useless to try. He was starving. His body was weaker than a baby's. What was the point?

They made him walk, as always. Step by painful, breathless, near-sightless step. When he reached the dark silhouette of a building he'd never been in before, they jerked him to a stop. Surreptitiously, he strained to see something. Anything. But his eyes refused to focus. It was all just light and shadow.

The Sultan approached, speaking in urgent tones to another man. Pig drew in on himself, prepared his body for the first blow. But the men swept into the solid structure without so much as a glance in his direction.

His guards shoved him inside, and when he fell they yanked him to his feet, only to toss him onto a hard metal table and strap him down.

Fear and anguish flooded through his veins.

Oh, God. Please, God, no.

The Sultan peered down into his face and smiled. "Are you ready to talk now, Pig?"

"MISS Martin?"

Rainie came awake, a gasp ready to burst from her lungs; she swallowed it ruthlessly down. Not a sound escaped. She'd trained herself to suppress those instinctive reactions. Not terribly professional to act like a scared rabbit when she was woken up from a nap, which sometimes happened during emergency double and triple shifts.

She took a deep breath, wondering why the sleeping room cot was so damn hard. "Yes?"

"It's Mr. Jackson. I think you should take a look at him."

With a *whoosh*, everything came back to her. *C-17. Kick.*

Withdrawal. No time to panic now. She was on her feet in a flash. "What's wrong? What are his symptoms?"

"He's sweating bullets and his pulse is through the roof."

Kick was sprawled awkwardly across several flip-seats, holding his chest and sucking down air. She ran to him and dropped to her knees. Someone handed her a first aid kit.

"Are you having chest pain?" she asked, wrenching open the kit and pulling out the blood pressure cuff and stethoscope.

"Maybe a little," he said. His face was flushed and bathed in sweat. He held out his arm to be cuffed. "The beat feels wonky."

"Your heartbeat? Wonky, how?"

"Double-time. Speeding up then slowing down."

Not good. She listened to his heart. Way too fast. Slightly erratic. Damn. She pumped up the blood pressure cuff and measured it twice. High. Way high.

"So, am I having a heart attack?" he asked with a half groan, half smirk, trying for humor. But his eyes weren't laughing.

"Not to worry. Just residual symptoms from the withdrawal."

"Is it life-threatening?" Forsythe interjected.

"No. But he needs to lie down and rest until they go away."

"Sorry, no can do," Forsythe said. "We're almost to Cairo, about to land. He and I will be transferring immediately to a small plane that'll take us south to—"

"Absolutely not. He needs a few hours of sleep before—"

"Not an option. We're on a tight schedule. He can rest on the plane to the drop-point."

"I'll be fine," Kick said, struggling to sit up. "Long as I'm not having a heart attack." One of the seats flipped up and whacked him in the elbow. "Ow! Goddamn piece of—" He jetted out a breath and smiled through his teeth. "See? Feeling better already."

"Like hell," she started to argue. Both men leveled looks at her like a pair of stubborn mules. So she saved her breath. And made a decision that shocked all three of them. Mostly herself. "Okay. Then I'm coming with you."

"No," the men said in unison. "No chance."

She got her own mule on. "Oh, really? Because I'm pretty sure the Egyptian authorities will be more than interested to hear how the CIA kidnapped an innocent woman and transported her in an official US military plane across international—"

"All right, fine!" Forsythe interrupted, holding up his hands in surrender. "You win."

"Fast learner, aren't you," Kick said to her through clenched teeth.

"Been taking a crash course."

He was not happy.

Tough. She wouldn't leave him in this kind of medical limbo. His symptoms themselves might not be life-threatening anymore, but if he didn't stabilize . . . It would be insanity to go on a dangerous mission in an unstable condition. And if that was the case, she'd be the only one standing between him and certain death.

Which was another thing. She couldn't believe he was being so cooperative with these horrible people. When he'd first talked about this mission, he'd fought it tooth and nail, saying his former employers wanted to send him to hell. Why the sudden change of heart? She had a sinking feeling they'd threatened to harm *her* if he didn't go along.

He was risking his life to protect her. It was the least she could do to stay with him for a few extra hours, to protect his. But *damn*, she resented being used as a pawn. It made her feel even more responsible for the man.

More respect, too.

And mad enough to get on another plane, just to spite them both.

"Good," she said, and tucked the first aid kit firmly under her arm. "I'll hang on to this. Just in case."

"WE'RE hitching a ride with FedEx?" Rainie asked in surprise when Forsythe pointed toward a small plane with the familiar logo splashed all over it.

They'd all been shuttled by a silent soldier in Air Force fatigues over to another section of the bustling Cairo airport that was used by small private and commercial planes.

She shielded her eyes for a better look. It was an hour before noon and the sun was high overhead. She'd never been in such intense heat, even in the worst New York summer. It had to be two hundred degrees out. The orange logo on the plane was actually wavering in the heat waves like a flag.

"Not exactly," Forsythe said. "That's a STORM Corps Cessna. They have an agreement with FedEx. Amazing where those guys fly packages. Nobody looks twice at their planes. Pretty damn good disguise if you ask me. Wish we'd thought of it."

Kick rolled his eyes, hefting his pack over his shoulder.

Rainie glanced at him, hand still shielding her eyes. With a frown he took off the desert-print cammie cap he was wearing, the one that matched the desert camouflage uniform pants—or DCUs as he called them—he'd changed into, and tugged it onto her head.

"What about you?" she asked.

In answer, he pulled a pair of gold-lensed aviator glasses from his pocket and wordlessly slid them on.

The sight of him standing there all inscrutable in his fatigues and boots, a fitted khaki T-shirt, and impenetrable glasses sent a shiver through her body. He looked so irrefutably male. So powerful. So . . . damn sexy.

Hard to imagine just twenty-four hours ago he'd been weak as a kitten, and so recently had that relapse. No sign of weakness now. He was still a little flushed, deep lines etched around his mouth, but that could be the heat and stress. And his heart rate had almost gone back to normal last time she'd checked. Pretty close, anyway.

Thank God. Because she really needed him healthy, so he could hold her hand during takeoff.

Okay, more like her whole self. Last liftoff she'd lost it in a major way. Hopefully, after spending eleven hours in the C-17, this time her panic attack wouldn't be so bad.

She glanced up at the FedEx plane. It was small. Really small.

Almost SUV small.

The substantial lunch they'd eaten on the C-17 roiled in her stomach.

Deep breath. Let it out slowly. Deep breath, let it out.

I will be fine.
I will be calm.
I will be safe.
You can do this, girl.

She was so busy breathing and clinging to Kick's stiff arm, she almost missed the trio of men that ambled up and stuck out their hands in greeting. Except, no one could possibly miss these guys. The STORM Corps team was . . . impressive.

"Hey. Bill Henning," the first man said by way of introduction. Built like a linebacker, his smile was infectious. "This here's Marc Lafayette, and that's our pilot, San Chenov." Lafayette was olive-skinned with long black hair and sparkling blue eyes, and Chenov looked like everyone's dream cowboy, hat and all.

"Good to meet you. Jason Forsythe and Kyle Jackson," Forsythe said.

"Call me Kick."

They shook hands all around, conspicuously skipping her in the rotation. But they eyed her curiously. "An' who's this *jolie fille*?" Marc Lafayette asked in an interesting French-ish accent.

"I'm Rainie," she supplied, clinging a bit harder to Kick. She didn't offer her hand. The men looked friendly, but there was something about them. An attitude of watchfulness. An edge of . . . something raw and uncivilized. Like Kick had had when he strode into that speed dating event looking so dark and dangerous.

Hell, like he looked now.

"So, Rainie, you oscar mike with us?" Bill asked, raising a brow.

"*Uh* . . . wh-what?" she stammered.

He and Marc exchanged a look.

"Military alphabet. O for oscar, M for mike. Means on the move," Kick explained. "And no, she's not."

"Well, only as far as the insertion," Forsythe supplied smoothly. "Rainie is a medic. Mr. Jackson has had some health issues recently."

"Nothin' serious, I hope," Marc said, glancing at him with mild concern.

"Nope." Kick smiled and started walking again. "Let's get this damn show on the road."

Oh, God. They were oscar mike.

GINA had been calling the phone number Wade had given her for the CIA all day. Trying desperately to find that Forsythe character, hoping against hope he could tell her what had happened to her best friend.

Rainie was gone. *Gone.* As in dropped-off-the-face-of-the-earth gone. No trace of where she was or what had happened to her. Other than that short, enigmatic phone call two days ago.

Unfortunately, Wade had only given her the general phone number to the New York City CIA field office, and according to them Jason Forsythe didn't work there. But as always, persistence eventually paid off. Gina must have called a couple dozen times, and each time she'd been routed to a different person in pursuit of the illusive Forsythe. She was sure she'd talked to everyone in the whole damn office.

Everyone *but* Jason Forsythe.

"You don't understand," Gina told the insufferably unhelpful woman on the other end of the line in sublime frustration. Some flunky CIA receptionist with nine-inch Passion Pink fingernails and a boob job, no doubt. Gina was normally a very patient person—you had to be to succeed with the kind of long-term research she was involved in—but by now her temper was hovering dangerously close to the red zone.

"*She. Has. Been. Kidnapped.*" She enunciated each word through her clenched jaw in an attempt to keep from yelling.

"Then I suggest you contact the poli—"

"Goddamn it, what is *with* you people? She was kidnapped by *you*! The *CIA*!" Gina was seriously close to a meltdown. "I am telling you I want to speak with Jason Forsythe and I won't stop calling until I do!"

"I don't think—"

She ground her jaw. And pulled out her trump card. "Do the words *New York Times* mean anything to you?"

There was a pregnant pause on the other end—*finally*

thank you Jesus she had the bimbo's attention—and what sounded like a muffled hand over the mouthpiece.

A few seconds later a man's deep voice came on the line. "Miss Cappozi, I'm—"

"That's *Dr.* Cappozi," she corrected, then demanded, "Are you Jason Forsythe?"

"No, I'm afra—"

"I do not *believe* this. No *wonder* the reputation of this country's intelligence service is in shreds. A bunch of *morons* are running it!"

His response was calm and unruffled, his voice modulated with reasonableness. "If you'll just hear me out, Miss—er, Dr. Cappozi. My name is Gregg van Halen." He paused for a nanosecond. "No relation." When that didn't even earn him a chuckle, he continued, just as calm and unruffled, "Mr. Forsythe is unavailable, but I assure you I will get to the bottom of whatever this situation is."

She let out a burst of hot steam. "Just like the other twenty-seven people I spoke with?"

"I'd very much like to hear what you think has happened."

Amazing. Miracles *did* happen. It was about time someone actually showed some genuine concern, if only because she'd threatened to go to the press. She chose to take it as a good sign.

"Okay," she began, quickly organizing her thoughts. "My friend Lorraine Martin called me two da—"

Van Halen interrupted, "Dr. Cappozi, I'd prefer not to do this over the phone. Can you come down to my office and give me a full—"

Oh, yeah, she was *so* sure. *Not.* "Do I *sound* stupid?" she demanded incredulously. "You want me to come down there so *I* can disappear, too? I seriously don't *think* so. The phone will do—"

"Fine. How about meeting in a public place?"

She took a steadying breath. "How public?"

"What do you say to a restaurant? Tonight, after your shift ends. We could eat and—"

She blinked. *Hello?* "Are you asking me to *dinner*?"

"Well, I can hear you're angry, and you've obviously gotten the runaround today. I figure you don't want to wait until tomorrow, and you do have to eat. What do you say? Government's treat."

She shook herself out of her frozen shock. She couldn't care less who paid. She was too upset to eat, anyway. She glanced at the clock. "I get off at eight. Where should we—"

"I'll be waiting for you out front."

Alarm spiked through her already frazzled nerves. "Wait. How do you know where I work?"

He chuckled. "Wouldn't be very good at my job if I didn't, now, would I? See you at eight."

EIGHT

IF the other men thought it was strange that Rainie sat as good as paralyzed with Kick's arms wrapped around her, doing deep breathing exercises for a good twenty minutes after they climbed into the no-seater Cessna and took off, they gave no indication other than the occasional exchange of amused male glances. Kick wasn't being exactly warm and fuzzy, but at least he was there for her. He seemed to know instinctively that she needed his strong physical presence to keep the panic under control.

So much for professional. She was just glad she was able to hold it together enough to sit still. They were all perched on the field packs because there were no seats. Not even jump seats. And no seat belts. Skydiver configuration, Kick had stated when she asked. That's when she'd noticed the parachutes.

Parachutes.

Oh, good Lord.

Kick was going to jump out of the plane.

Jump out.

She felt queasy at the very thought. And even queasier when she realized that in order for him to jump out, he'd need a hole to jump through. Like a door, or hatch, or whatever you called it on a plane, which they'd have to open up to the wide blue yonder.

Zooming over the Sahara Desert in a tiny plane with a gaping hole in the side and no seat belts was not her idea of a fun time.

Oh, *God*. What had she been *thinking* coming along this far?

Kick, she told herself determinedly. She had to think of her patient. He needed her. Even if he was doing better than she was at the moment.

"You doing okay?" he asked, startling her. He was peering into her face with a concerned look.

"Sure." She tried to smile but her cheeks seemed to be welded in place. "I'm good."

He nodded and went back to talking with the other men. Bill and Marc. They were comparing equipment and passing around maps and checking guns. When they did that, she closed her eyes. She didn't want to see guns. They reminded her of—

Too many things.

"I'll take the Heckler and Koch," she heard Kick say, followed by the jarring *smack* of him catching a rifle, and the *snick* of metal parts being checked.

She squeezed her eyes tighter. She *really* didn't want to know what this mission was all about. Didn't want to think that in the course of it he might have to kill a real person with that gun.

Her stomach roiled as a horrible thought seeped into her consciousness. The possibility that he'd actually been sent here *in order* to kill someone. Or even more than one person.

Kick . . . a paid killer? A mercenary? An *assassin*?

The man who'd held her so steadily when she was crazy with panic, who'd calmly soothed her nerves when she wanted to scream with terror? The man who, just a few nights ago, had caressed her body and made love to her, given her incredible pleasures that no other man ever had?

No. It wasn't possible he could be a hired killer.

Under that stern, unsmiling façade, he was a good person. He didn't have that kind of evil within him. Did he?

For some reason she couldn't shake the heinous thought. Because it made sense of so many puzzling things. Such as why he'd tried so hard to escape his old life. Why the CIA didn't want to let him go. Why they had such a hold over him. Why a strong man like him had slipped so easily into drug addiction.

Why, that first night when she'd asked if he was a good guy or a bad guy, he hadn't been able to answer.

The overhead speaker crackled and the pilot announced, "Just passed the Sudanese border. Stand ready, people. Landing zone in five."

"Time for me to harness up," Kick murmured. His lips subtly brushed against her hair as he slid his arm out from behind her. "You'll have to move," he said apologetically. "My pack."

Right. The one they'd been sitting on, sharing the small space for the hour-long—or had it been two hours?—flight down to the southern frontier between Egypt and the Sudan. That jerked her right out of her fantasy world.

"Sorry."

She moved off onto the floor, where she watched him attach a small parachute to the pack, then climb into a larger parachute harness himself. The two other men were doing likewise.

She was miserable. Torn between misery over watching him parachute out of her life, and misery over what he might be getting ready to do.

None of her business, she reminded herself.

And as for never seeing him again, that's what she *wanted*. In a few minutes he'd be out of her life, forever. She'd already told him they had no future, and after asking that one time, he hadn't asked again. Obviously, he'd only had the amazing sex on his mind. She was glad he hadn't pressed her on it. Truly. They had nothing in common. Were polar opposites.

So why did she still feel so damn miserable?

He clipped his parachute's bright red rip cord behind Marc's on the release hook above the door, which Forsythe was unlocking. Kick looked down at her. There was something in his eyes that almost took her breath away. Or maybe it was the torrent of hot air that rushed through the hollow cabin when the door *whooshed* open.

Like a switch had been flipped, the bright blue of the Egyptian sky filled the broad opening. Far, far below, the mottled browns of the desert landscape swept past, undulating like a mirage from the heat rising in a thick layer above the desolate sands.

She grabbed a handhold in the far wall, her heart standing still. But she could barely see the rushing landscape. She could only see those hard, expressive eyes.

This was it.

Good-bye.

Kick was still watching her, not paying any attention to the bustle of the other men around him. Reluctantly, he lifted his arms to her. How could she resist one last touch?

She stood up, taking careful, measured steps toward him, hanging on to the handholds. He came to her, as close as his parachute tether would allow. Enfolded her in his embrace.

"Damn, Rainie," was all he murmured. "Damn."

"Two minutes to—" The speaker crackled. "What the . . . *Fucking hell*. Tangos on the ground! Three o'clock!"

The pilot's curse was their only warning. Suddenly there was a flash, then a distant *rat-a-tat-tat* sound. Like . . . machine gun fire? The plane tipped crazily, throwing them all off balance, slamming Forsythe into the wall.

Kick's arms banded around her as they stumbled toward the open door. She screamed.

"We're hit!" the pilot yelled. "Bail out!"

"*Goddamn—*" Kick recovered his footing and briefly loosened his grip on her.

More machine gun fire. And a huge boom.

The right wing blew into pieces. The plane tilted hard. Forsythe cartwheeled out the door.

She screamed again. "Kick!"

"Number one, gone!" Marc yelled as he pushed something out of the plane, then jumped after it.

"Rainie! Hold on to me!" Kick ordered.

She grabbed him around the neck. A nylon strap suddenly

cut into her under the arms, cinching so tight she gasped. Something skidded past her legs and tumbled out the door as the remaining wing tipped wildly.

"Hang on! *Tight!*"

Then she was part of the sky.

Her stomach fell like a lead brick. Panic slammed into her. Air rushed past so fast she couldn't breathe. Her chest ached. Her back and sides hurt where the strap bit into her flesh.

Oh, shit. *Ohshit-ohshit-ohshit.*

Something whizzed past, and a nanosecond later an explosion shredded the sky. Kick's arms pulled her tight against him, pressed her nose into his jacket as they flew through the air, pivoting so she was under him. She wrapped her legs around his waist and clung to him for dear life.

Debris flew past. Kick swore again.

"*My God, the plane!*" she cried, peeking up and seeing only smoke.

He pivoted back upright, and suddenly they were yanked upward in a bone-rattling jerk. For a second it felt like she was being ripped apart, then everything slammed into slow motion.

"You all right?" Kick asked loudly as the parachute broke the speed of their descent, along with that of her heartbeat.

"Yes," she said, and miraculously, it was true.

They were alive.

That's when reality kicked her in the gut. What had happened to the others? She peered up over Kick's shoulder in horror. The plane really was gone. All that was left of it was a spiraling-downward trail of smoke. She wanted to be sick.

"I need my hands to control this thing. Okay?"

She nodded against his neck, sucking in a horrified breath when he let go. But she didn't fall.

She looked down, down, down to the ground. Flaming pieces of the plane were scattered over the stark landscape in patches.

Floating under them, a few hundred feet apart, she could just make out a shape, its colors blending into the desert sand below. A parachute! She prayed everyone had somehow gotten out. . . .

More staccato machine gun fire sounded. Followed closely by a guttural scream.

Kick swore even more harshly. "The fuckers are trying to pick us off. Hang on."

Like she wasn't already. He tugged on a cord and the chute veered off to the side. She battled back another scream. The last thing he needed to deal with was an hysterical woman. He tugged again, and they zipped in the other direction. She clenched her teeth, faint with fear.

More whizzing split the air where they'd just been.

Omigod! Bullets!

Twice more clusters of bullets whistled past them, and each time Kick managed to outmaneuver whoever was shooting.

Finally the machine gun went silent.

"Out of range," he muttered. "About freakin' time."

"Thank God."

"Too soon," he said.

"What?"

"To thank God. You can do that after we get away from these fucks."

"I thought we just did."

"I meant on the ground," he said grimly. "Do me a favor, sweetheart. Pray to God the tangos don't have Jeeps."

GODDAMN it. Goddamn it. God*damn* it.

It took all Kick's concentration to hit the ground and not break both legs, or smash Rainie under him. He managed to run a few steps despite her awkward weight in front, and position his roll so his own shoulder and back took the brunt rather than hers.

When they tumbled to a halt, he used a precious few moments to catch his breath, ungrit his teeth from the pain of the collision, and release the makeshift harness holding Rainie's body to his. This time he did thank God that he'd spotted the nylon strapping in time to save her life. He'd had to sacrifice one of the field packs, but he could live without food and a change of clothes.

He wouldn't have been able to go on if she'd died up there in the explosion.

And yet, when he really thought about it, that might have been preferable to this. For both of them. Now he was stuck with her. In the middle of a fucking combat zone.

Goddamn it.

He struggled to his feet, pulled his goggles down around his neck, and did a three-sixty recon of the plateau where he'd steered them to touch down.

No tangos. Yet.

The place was like a moonscape. Familiar from A-stan and a dozen other desert venues he'd worked in, and yet distinctively savage in a way all its own. The endless sea of brown orange sand was punctuated by outcroppings of darker rock and boulders, and scored on three sides by deep wadis, or steep, dry riverbeds filled with golden dunes. Rugged hills dotted the plateau in all directions, from close by to all the way out on the horizon. The midafternoon air was hotter than Hades, three digits easily, the sun beating down like the devil's furnace.

God, he loved the desert.

In an alternate universe.

"Anything broken?" he barked at Rainie, unharnessing himself and punching down the parachute.

After a short pause she answered shakily, "I'm in one piece."

For now, anyway, he thought uneasily.

She obviously had no clue of the danger they were in. Whoever had gone to the trouble of shooting down that plane would be coming after them, hell-bent for infidels. Judging by where the shooting had come from, they had roughly half an hour before the hostiles showed up. Maybe less. He had to get her hidden before that. A woman in the hands of those animals . . . The images it painted in his head made him dizzy with fear as nothing else could.

Shit.

He had to focus.

And so did she, if they were to make it. But she was still sitting on the ground, arms wrapped around her legs with her face buried in her knees. He wished he could do the same. His whole body was rebelling. Screaming to shut down. On fire for want of the drug it had been deprived of so recently.

Man up, Jackson. No time for weakness.

"Come on, we need to move fast," he ordered.

She didn't react.

"Rainie, come on."

She didn't seem to hear him.

He grabbed her shoulders and shook her a little. "Rainie! We're totally exposed here. I need you to get hold of yourself. Can you do that for me?"

She looked up and blinked several times.

"You have to be Nurse Martin now. Strong. Competent. Unafraid. I know you can do it."

She took a deep, shuddering breath, and her eyes slowly cleared. "Okay." She glanced around and tensed up again. "But wouldn't it be better if we stayed here? Waited for—"

"For what? For al Sayika to find us?"

She blinked again. "Who?"

"The tangos who shot down our plane."

"Tangos?"

"Terrorists."

She blanched.

"They'll be coming for us next. Trust me, you do not want to be caught by these scumbags." She swallowed heavily, glancing around again. He could tell she was utterly terrified. Didn't want to move. "Come on, baby. Stay with me, okay?" He barely resisted yanking her to her feet. But he needed to be calm for her. A steadying influence. If he freaked, she'd shut down like a stadium after the game. Lights out, no one home.

She took another deep breath and let it out. "Okay. I'll try."

"Good girl."

She seemed to rally. Glanced at him. "Are you hurt?"

"No more than I was."

"Where are the others?" There was only the slightest wobble left in her voice. "They may be injured and need help."

His chest squeezed. It wasn't good news, but now wasn't the time to start varnishing the facts. She needed to know she'd always get the truth from him. As fucked-up as it was. Her life could depend on her trusting his word. And his.

"Forsythe didn't make it. He was thrown out of the plane with no parachute when the wing was hit."

She gasped, her eyes filling. "My God."

Kick agreed. He didn't like the guy, but nobody deserved to go that way. "I don't know about the others." But he didn't think the pilot had made it. Or Bill Henning.

"I thought I saw a parachute below us," she said, dashing away the tears from her eyes.

"Lafayette. He jumped before us."

"So he must be alive."

"With any luck."

But he'd heard the screamed curse when the tangos had opened fire on them. If Marc Lafayette wasn't dead, he was hurting. Bad, by the sound of that swear word.

Or, there was an outside chance he could have been bluffing. Sound traveled a long way in the desert. His loud scream—the kind of giveaway that was drilled out of every rookie ZU NOC operator—may have been so the fuckers below would hear him, think he was injured, and go after him first. To draw the enemy off Kick and Rainie. To give him time to get her to safety. And hopefully locate the field pack with the SATCOM.

Best not waste that advantage.

He urged her to her feet and thrust the wadded-up parachute at her. "Hold this. I thought I saw one of the packs on the ground as we landed. Give me a minute to find it, then we need to make tracks."

"I'll help," she said, and turned in the opposite direction.

"Stay close!" he ordered brusquely, but she was already searching around a scatter of low boulders a few yards away.

"Here!" she called moments later.

She'd found the duffel bag of rifles. Quickly, he pulled out the weapons. With nothing to break the bag's fall, one rifle's wooden butt had cracked in half on impact; another had a bent barrel. But the third looked to be in good shape. The Heckler & Koch PSG-1 sniper. *Excellent.* The cleaning kit had made it unscathed as well.

Using the bent weapon as a spade, he swiftly dug a hole in the sand and, after removing the firing pins, buried the two useless guns. Then he took the parachute Rainie was holding and stuffed it along with the rifle and cleaning kit into the duffel and hoisted it over his shoulder.

"All right, we're oscar mike. Shout if I go too fast for you."

"But what about the other man?"

"We'll find him later. Right now we need to get ourselves a place to hide."

She didn't argue, though she sent a troubled glance in the direction the other parachutes had gone down, on a plateau on the other side of a wide wadi, a dozen or more miles away.

"Walk in my footprints," he told her, and took off across the rocky sand.

"Why?"

He glanced back and saw her frown as she tried to match her stride to his. He took shorter steps. "So we only leave one set of tracks." Mostly it didn't fool anyone, but sometimes it worked. If they were dealing with amateurs.

"Why?"

He grimaced and faced forward again as he walked, working past the pain in his leg. "That way, if they catch me, they won't be looking for you."

Obviously she didn't miss the implications on both ends of that statement. She stayed silent for many minutes after that. Not that he wanted to talk.

"Where exactly are we going?" she finally asked when he stopped to examine the terrain ahead.

Good fucking question. He was trying to stick to the rockier, more hard-packed sand where it would be difficult to track them. They had a good shot at finding a decent hiding place in the myriad rock formations and cliff walls of the wadi that plunged down on three sides of the plateau they were on. Hopefully they could escape detection from their pursuers in the short run. But after that?

"We'll figure that out later, too."

"Then how do you know this is the right direction?" she asked.

"I don't."

That shut her up for another quarter mile of power-hiking before she broke down, breathing hard, and asked, "Kick?"

He sighed. "Yup?"

"Do you have even the remotest idea where we are?"

The corner of his lip curved in a humorless smile. That one he could answer. Because there was no doubt in his mind exactly where they were.

"In deep fucking shit."

OF course, Kick actually *did* know from studying the maps on the plane where they were and what direction they were headed—in general terms. Navigating in unknown territory using only the sun and stars to guide him was pure instinct after being a NOC operator for over sixteen years.

And once they were able to stop and check the SAT photo he had tucked into his DCU jacket pocket, he'd know precisely where they were.

Oh, yeah, he'd come prepared. This was not the first time he'd been goatfucked on an insert. Far from it. And if there was one thing he was good at, it was learning from his mistakes.

In the same pocket as the photo he also had a geo-map of the area, a roll of American dollars, GPS finder, pocketknife, bubble-pack of chlorine tabs, and a couple of protein bars. Strapped to his ankle was his trusty SIG Navy—which they'd returned to him at the compound—and an extra clip. Never leave home without it.

What he *didn't* know was what the hell he was going to do about the woman. There was a ticking clock running on this gig. NSA had picked up chatter that the attack on the Western embassies in Khartoum was imminent, within the coming week it was believed. Kick had to take out abu Bakr before the terrorists made their move. He couldn't afford any delay.

But no way in flaming hell would he take a woman along.

Somehow, he had to find a place to stash her, locate Lafayette and find out if he was still alive, and then hunt down the damn field packs. Without the SATCOM he couldn't call in a request for someone to get the fuck down here and take her off his hands. Or to call in the STORM air strike once

abu Bakr was neutralized, for that matter. And if he managed
to make it though this mission alive, it was a hell of a long
hike back to Egypt. No radio, no ticket home . . . for anyone.

He also had to find water fairly soon, if he didn't retrieve
at least one of the packs. The human body didn't survive
long in this scorching heat without water.

Speaking of which . . . He turned to scrutinize what
Rainie was wearing. Forsythe must have scrounged her some
clothes at ZU headquarters. She had on men's jeans and
a white T-shirt under a long-sleeved khaki work shirt that
looked like military issue. Her sneakers weren't ideal, but
they'd do. She was still wearing his cap. Good.

"Here." He pulled his sunglasses from his outer pocket.
They were the flex kind, so the frames were unbent from his
roll on the ground, but one of the lenses had popped out. He
snapped it back in and slid them on her nose. "Did you put
on sunblock when we did on the plane?"

"Didn't think I'd need any," she said, looking bleak.

Damn. Her face would burn to a crisp in this sun.

"Hang on," he ordered, and fished a corner of the parachute out of the duffel. Silk was a bitch to rip, but he managed to tear off a large square, which he tied around her head
and neck, Bedouin-outlaw-style, with just the reflection of
the glasses showing beneath the brim of her cap.

She looked like a harem girl gone gangsta.

For the first time that day he smiled. *Sexy. Very sexy.*

The silk crinkled, like she was smiling back. And suddenly he was struck by the most inappropriate urge to lift her
makeshift veil and kiss her.

The sun must be frying his brain. The woman wanted
nothing to do with him, and he didn't blame her.

He looked away. "I'll get you home safe, Rainie. If it's the
last thing I do," he told the horizon.

"I know," she whispered.

And he would. He'd get her back to her comfy life without him in New York, or he'd die trying. That was a fucking
promise.

But that wasn't what had started his insides churning with
uneasiness. Or the drug cravings, either.

It was her utter faith in him that those two words—*I know*—conveyed, and the overwhelming trust in her voice as she'd said them.

That nearly broke him in two.

"SHOULDN'T we be heading for higher ground?"

Before answering, Kick approached the blunt drop-off of the rocky plateau they'd been hightailing it across for fifteen minutes. Though he'd never show it, he was getting very nervous. For the past little while now, carried on the desert wind, he'd picked up the whine of an engine. At first elusive as a ghost's whisper, now it was a small but steady hum, like a gnat circling his head. The louder it got, the more his blood pressure went up.

He lifted his goggles and peered down into the sprawling wadi below. The dry riverbed that thousands of years ago flowed with cool water now flowed with a river of hot, undulating sand. He didn't appreciate its breathtaking beauty, spread out before them in a kaleidoscope of yellows, oranges, and browns, shadows and light curving along the rippled, windblown surface like giant serpents, defining the shapes of the dunes. It was beautiful, but deadly.

"What about up on top of that?" Rainie pointed at a nearby low butte.

He finally glanced at her. "I see you've been reading your *Art of War*."

"No. Just watched a lot of Westerns when I was a kid."

He wished he could see her face. To glean a hint as to whether she'd had a good childhood, or a painful one. Not that it made a bit of difference. Not to the present situation.

"Higher is certainly more defensible," he agreed. "First thing any good cowboy, Indian, or war fighter learns."

She turned to head toward the butte. He laid a hand on her shoulder.

"Which is why we're going down there instead." He indicated the cliffs below their feet. "They won't be looking for us down there."

She peered over the edge and said a bad word.

He hiked a brow. "Afraid of heights?"

"Kick. In case you hadn't noticed, I'm afraid of pretty much everything."

Vivid, visual memories of that night in her apartment, in her bed, flooded through him for an ill-chosen instant. "Not everything," he said without thinking.

She made a little choking noise. Was she remembering, too? Damn, he *really* wanted to see her eyes.

He forced himself to look around instead of dragging off those stupid sunglasses. *No* time *for this crap.* He did a slow survey of the entire three-sixty of horizon, searching for a telltale dust devil.

There. There it was.

He looked closer. No. Three. There were three distinct plumes within one long cloud of dust. And the mothers were closing in. Five, maybe ten miles away—hard to tell in the limitless landscape of the desert. The good news was, a substantial wadi lay between the plateau where the tangos were and the one Kick had deliberately aimed his parachute at, for that very reason. Crossing would slow them down. Maybe their Jeeps would even get stuck. The shifting dunes that filled the wadi bottoms could be treacherous to drive across. Even walking on them could be a crapshoot. The rare patches of quicksand were virtually indistinguishable from regular sand.

He turned back to Rainie. "They're close," he said. "We have to hurry."

She nodded jerkily.

This time he was glad he couldn't see her frightened eyes.

"Stay low," he told her. "I'll look for a good spot to climb down."

He took off at a crouch-run along the very edge of the cliffs, scouting for a trail down easy enough for a woman to handle, that looked promising for possible hiding places. About a half mile away he found what he was looking for. Not a minute too soon. He waved at her to come to him, which she did, stepping on the rocks as he'd instructed so it would be impossible to tell where they'd gone over the side.

"Are you out of your mind?" she said when she saw where he intended to take her. It was a deep split in the cliff face, with a hundred-foot drop to the bottom. "I'll never—"

"Yes. You will," he told her firmly. "There are lots of big cracks and boulders and handholds. You'll be fine. I'll be right under you. I promise."

"I can think of better ways to have you under me," she muttered.

He darted her a shocked look. Then snapped his mouth shut. "Consider it an incentive," he said. "Once we're hidden, I'm all yours."

And on that note, he dropped over the edge.

NINE

IT took ten minutes of hard climbing to make it down to the one-quarter point from the bottom. Kick gauged they were still a good fifteen or twenty feet above the sandy surface of the wadi. Optimum cover. The whole time, the sound of the Jeeps got louder and louder. Unfortunately, they hadn't gotten stuck. By now his pulse was pounding in his ears and his hands were shaking. He *really* wanted a fix.

"Rest here while I look around," he ordered Rainie, guiding her under a large boulder. On the climb down he'd been watching for a likely hiding spot, but so far nothing. The sheer cliffs were pocked with wind-caves, but most were too shallow to be of any use. Those that were had been impossible to reach.

Edging along a precipice that led around a jutting cliff wall, a horizontal wedge-shaped crack in the rock with a relatively flat floor suddenly appeared before him. A relieved sigh *whooshed* from his lungs. *Finally.*

The engine noise was almost on top of them. But something about it sounded different.

He took a few seconds to sweep the cave out with an edge of the parachute and make sure there were no scorpions, vipers, or other unwelcome intruders sharing the space. Then he dropped the duffel and hurried back to fetch Rainie.

He could hear voices now, shouts in Arabic—above the whine of a single motor. *Damn.* That's why it had sounded different. One vehicle.

Which meant the tangos had split up before crossing the wadi. He was dead certain he'd had a visual on three vehicles earlier.

It was a safe bet one of them was now headed for the site of the plane crash, to see what could be scrounged from the wreckage. Kick doubted anything useful was left. The explosion had been thorough. A lucky bullet must have sparked the fuel tank.

"Come on." He grabbed Rainie and practically hauled her off the path and along the narrow precipice. Her arm trembled like crazy under his own shaking fingers, and once, he heard her whimper a soft prayer, but she didn't ever stop moving.

One brave lady. His admiration for her went up several notches.

They reached the crevice and he helped her crawl in as deep as she could get. He slid in after her.

As she collapsed onto the ground, winded and sweaty, it was all he could do not to take the sniper rifle and position himself to pick off the scumbags as they stuck their noses over the cliff edge. But killing them would only bring their asshole buddies running back. He couldn't risk giving away the hiding place. He didn't care what happened to him. But he knew only too well what would happen to Rainie.

Anger stabbed through him. *God* fucking *damn it.*

How the hell had terrorists on the Egyptian border out in the middle of nowhere known about the mission, and the well-disguised plane the STORM team used for the insertion? Even zealots didn't go shooting down random FedEx planes.

Except he knew very well how. No mystery there. The information had come from someone on the inside. A traitor. Had to have. There was no other possible explanation.

Just like in Afghanistan.

The photo of Nate and Abbas Tawhid that Forsythe had

shown him swept through his mind like an ill wind. Fury followed close on its tail. Fury over the betrayal of a man he'd considered a good friend.

He tamped it all back down, to the black recesses of his heart. He did not want to believe what the photo implied about his friend. *Would* not believe it. Not until he'd spoken to Nate personally, and heard his explanation.

He hoped to hell he wouldn't have to kill him.

But regardless of who the traitor was, this mission had been compromised. The enemy probably knew exactly who and how many men they were looking for.

But please, God, not the woman. Surely, there was no way anyone could have known about the last-minute change in plans regarding her.

She unwound the scarf from her face and pulled off the sunglasses, raking her hands fretfully through her blond hair. "How close are they?" she whispered, staring up at the ceiling of the cave like she wished she had X-ray vision.

"I'd guess half a mile or so."

"They're going to kill us, aren't they?" She looked like she wanted to burst into tears. But she didn't. Maybe he would, instead.

No time for weakness.

He yanked his goggles down around his neck, rolled to her, and took her face firmly in his hands. "Listen to me. I can easily take them out if I have to." Possibly a slight exaggeration—the *easily* part, certainly—but she needed reassurance. Before he gave her the next bad news. "But our best bet is to make them believe I'm long gone."

"Yes, but—" Suddenly she gasped. "Kick. Look." She was gaping over his shoulder.

He turned to see what she was looking at.

In the middle of the wadi, a yellow streamer fluttered in the breeze. Attached to one of the field packs.

Hallelujah. Now he had no choice. And she couldn't protest his plan.

Swiftly, he pulled his SIG from its ankle holster, chambered a round, and thrust it at her. "Take this. You've got fifteen shots. Make them count if you have to."

Her face mottled in alarm. "What are you talking about?"

"Squeeze yourself as far back into the cave as you can." He grabbed her arms and got right in her face. "Stay here," he ordered. "Do not move. *Do. Not. Move.* I'll come back for you."

"No! Please, Kick, my God, don't leave m—"

"Rainie, if those men don't see tracks leading across the wadi, they'll assume I'm hiding somewhere around here. They won't stop looking until they find me. *And* you. Do you want that?"

"No!" She hung on to him desperately. "But—"

"I have to do this. It's the only way to keep you safe."

Her eyes begged him. He almost weakened. "But what if you—"

"I won't." He drilled his gaze into hers. He had to do this. "It may be after dark, but I *will* be back for you." Hell, if he had to come back from the fucking grave, he'd find a way to do it. He caught her chin in his hand and kissed her on the mouth, hard and fast. "I swear it on my life."

She let out a sob, clinging to him. Then she inhaled shakily, and let him go. He'd never been so torn. Or so proud of anyone in his whole life.

Before he could look into those pleading green eyes and change his mind, he picked up the duffel bag and climbed out on the ledge.

Without turning back, he said, "I'm coming back. I promise."

And then he left her.

RAINIE had to work really hard not to launch herself out of the cave, run after Kick, and beg him to take her with him.

Or succumb to a full-out panic attack the second he disappeared from sight.

Deep breath. Let it out slowly.

I will be fine.

I will be calm.

I will be safe.

She kept repeating the mantra over and over in her head as the guttural male shouts above her grew stronger and louder. *Please, please, let it be true.*

Deep breath. Let it out slowly.

She just couldn't stop the bone-rattling shaking of her body. Tears of desperation pressed against her eyes. Not for herself. But for Kick.

He intended to cross the wide-open expanse of the valley of sand on foot, with nothing to shield him from their bullets but her prayers.

Oh, God. He was going to die. And then so would she.

This was worse than a nightmare. Far worse than a simple car hijacking by a couple of crackheads. Because if these men caught her, they would not just kill her. They would hurt her first. In ways she didn't want to imagine.

But even if she managed to elude the evil men, she would surely perish in this vast desert without Kick to take care of her. There was no doubt about that. She'd read somewhere that in the past, whole armies had gotten lost out here in the Sahara. Swallowed up by the harsh desert sands without a trace. If a whole army of trained men couldn't make it out of here, with all their equipment and expertise, what chance did *she* have?

Oh, God. Please save me!

How had she gotten herself into this unreal situation? She who had never once taken an unnecessary risk, who had structured her whole life so as to avoid a meaningless death like her parents'. And now she was staring down a fate that was far, far worse. It was so damn unfair!

Suddenly, Kick burst out from the rocks at the base of the cliff and ran full tilt across the dunes toward the backpack, his gait slightly drunken because of his leg. Except running across sand was like running through water. His progress was excruciatingly slow. Any second now they'd spot him and . . .

She pressed her knuckles against her mouth to keep from crying out, and held an agonized breath, waiting for the pursuers' gunfire to explode from above.

Deep breath. Let it out slowly.
I will be fine.
I will be calm.
He will be safe.

Up on the cliff, the voices didn't change. No gunfire came.

Thank God.

A half-hysterical laugh of relief caught in her lungs. He was going to be all right. He had to be.

She watched him scoop up the pack without stopping and toss it onto his back, wrapping the cammie-colored parachute around his body as he limp-sprinted slo-mo across the hills of sand. It helped disguise him, but not by much.

She squeezed her eyes shut, unable to watch any longer, dreading the inevitable moment when they saw him and cut him down in flying ribbons of scarlet.

She didn't have to wait long. Within moments, excited shouts in Arabic came from the plateau directly above her. She held her breath as the men argued. But still no guns were fired.

She dared to open her eyes. And saw obvious tracks that led right to the opposite cliff, then into a ragged split in the wall of rock where he must have climbed up. There were no tracks leading away.

No sign of him or the backpack, either.

Her heart leapt with hope.

All at once she heard a rockfall tumble down around the jutting boulders that separated her hiding place from the passage where she and Kick had hiked down. Heavy footsteps slipped and clattered, accompanied by harsh men's voices calling to each other. *Coming down the cliff.*

Rainie pressed herself deep into the cave, almost shocked when the men didn't pause but continued straight past her to the bottom. Blessed relief!

But it was short-lived, because she knew they were chasing Kick and were just minutes behind him. They were sure to catch up unless he ditched the pack and the duffel with his sniper rifle, and even then, his tall, imposing frame would be impossible to miss fleeing across the opposite plateau.

Unless he risked firing on them and bringing the others back, his only chance was to hide, as she was. And pray the bad guys gave up before finding him.

The vehicle above had taken off, spraying gravel over the edge, while the two men climbed down. No doubt off to seek a way around to the cliffs on the other side of the riverbed, to cut off Kick that way.

The two men below scrambled across the dunes, then sure-footedly started to climb up the steep passage after him, pausing to search every nook and cranny where he could be hiding. Half an hour later they were at the top, and in a flash, they disappeared beyond the rim and out of sight.

Leaving her safe in her hideaway.

Safe for now. But alone. So very alone.

She eased out a breath. Around her, a hot wind swirled, whispering through the cave like fiery tendrils of a ghostly presence. Shadows from the blazing sun had started to lengthen, painting long slashes of black on the darkening yellow sand. The silence of the desert was deafening, the solitude utterly complete.

It hit her then. Like a lead pipe to the gut.

She was absolutely and completely on her own in this savage, alien wilderness.

She blinked. And was suddenly more terrified than she had ever been before in her life.

AS he woke up, pain was all he could feel. Even more pain than usual. Pain in his chest, in his stomach and limbs, pain in his head.

Pig was lying down. On a thin, reeking mattress of straw. He could feel the hard stalks poking mercilessly into his bruises. Gouging into the open sores on his back.

His fingers still burned from the Sultan's torture, and a few slices from his flesh throbbed. But overall, he was better than expected. Surprisingly, after just a half hour of agonizing questioning, the Sultan had angrily waved his guards to cart his bloody body back to his hut. Maybe the bastard finally believed he remembered nothing.

But worse than the pain, his Angel with an *H* hadn't come last night. He always felt robbed when she didn't come to him. Especially on days like this. Jesus *God* he needed her. Like air and water he needed her. Needed her soothing voice in the night. Needed her to keep the fury at bay. To keep him from going fucking insane.

Okay, *more* fucking insane.

He took a deep breath and listened. They had just started

their afternoon prayers. He said his own silent prayer of thanks to Allah, for distracting the fuckers, and gingerly sat up. His head spun for several seconds, then settled down. He opened his eyes, testing how much more he could see today. Angry disappointment almost deflated him. Same as goddamn yesterday. Just fuzzy, wavering images swimming against a dismal grey background.

Stop feeling sorry for yourself, asshole! Anything was better than being totally blind. Now at least he had a fighting chance.

To walk out of this pit of vipers.

But to do that he had to get back into some sort of shape. He was a fucking wreck. He didn't know what the hell had happened to him back when he was captured, but it had been bad enough to knock him flat on his back for what felt like centuries. He'd been extremely fit when he'd first woken up in that red haze of pain. But as he'd lain there like a vegetable, he'd had to feel his muscles slowly dissolve from starvation, neglect, and the constant torture and abuse.

But hell, even after all this time he was still bigger than most of the skinny-ass freaks holding him prisoner.

He could do it. It might take time, but all he had was time. And a whole lot of fury. That would carry him through the pain. Pain he was used to.

His head spun like a helo going down hard, and every muscle in his body felt like soggy spaghetti, but he forced himself up to his hands and knees. He lowered himself into a push-up and started counting. By five, his arms were shaking, his knees wobbling dangerously. He gritted his teeth and ignored the pain in his fingers and stabbing behind his eyes, and the nausea lurching in his stomach. He held out until twenty. Then he collapsed.

Jesus. Pathetic. He used to be able to do ten times that many push-ups using only his fingers and toes, and not even break a sweat.

Shit. He didn't know how he knew that, but there wasn't a doubt in his mind. He'd been buff and ripped and . . .

And now he was trembling like a baby and sweating like a pig.

A pig. *Ha.* How fucking appropriate.

He squeezed his eyes shut and struggled to keep from bawling like a baby, too.

He had to get out of here.

He fucking *had* to get out of here. And he would. He had to.

Or, for real, he'd fucking kill himself.

GINA glanced nervously at the front door of the hospital. What in the world had *possessed* her to agree to this meeting?

Just because Gregg van Halen's voice was low and soothing, his phone manners warm and affable, was no reason to put herself in jeopardy. Rainie was gone. *Vanished.*

What if the same thing happened to Gina? He was from the CIA, but what assurance was *that*? So was Rainie's kidnapper. Van Halen might have been sent to shut Gina up because she was making such an unholy fuss looking for that Forsythe character Rainie had asked her to find out about. Hoping against hope Forsythe could tell her what had happened to her friend.

For the past half hour she'd been a porcupine of nerves and indecision. Should she really go? Or should she run as fast as she could in the opposite direction?

Except she couldn't do that. She couldn't.

Rainie had been gone almost three days. Gina wanted her friend back safe and sound. And she'd do anything to make that happen. *Anything.*

Including getting all dressed up and meeting this alleged agent Gregg van Halen for dinner.

She'd pulled out all stops and put on the slinky red dress she kept hanging in her hospital staff locker for last-minute dates, along with a pair of strappy heels she could barely walk in. Usually she didn't do much walking after her date saw the dress. She hoped it would have a similar brain-numbing influence on van Halen.

Tonight she planned to dazzle him with her killer body and outmaneuver him with her brilliant mind. The man didn't stand a chance.

She hoped.

Smoothing the dress over her hips, she regarded the double glass-front doors of the hospital with a tingle of apprehension.

"Dr. Cappozi?"

She nearly jumped out of her skin. The voice had come from right behind her.

She whirled. "My God!"

"Not exactly. But I appreciate the confidence." She was still wobbling on her heels and he stuck out a hand to steady her. "Gregg van Halen."

She jerked away from him. And almost fell on her butt.

Okay, wow.

She didn't know quite what she'd expected a CIA agent to look like, but this definitely wasn't it.

He was about a hundred feet tall with short cropped blond hair and muscles out the wazoo. She couldn't help but notice because he was wearing a white T-shirt that fit him better than a latex glove on a surgeon, along with low-slung jeans that hugged his package like a lover. *Ho. Lee. Cow.* Wasn't it some kind of federal law that CIA agents were supposed to wear cheap black suits and reflector sunglasses?

Of course, maybe he *wasn't* a CIA agent.

The way his eyes were taking her in from head to toe—slowly, thoroughly, like he was contemplating . . . yeah, exactly what she'd wanted him contemplating—was very un-CIA-like.

He towered over her; his shoulders were unreasonably broad, the sheer power of his very male frame . . . *um,* somewhat intimidating. Suddenly she questioned her strategy.

"Dr. Cappozi?" he repeated.

She took another step backward. "Yes, I, *um*— You know, this wasn't a very good idea after all, Mr. van Halen—"

"Please. Call me Gregg."

"—so, *um,* I think I'll just keep calling the office for Jason Forsythe—"

"Mr. Forsythe is currently out of the country," he said, and that yanked her attention back. "But he should be returning by the end of next week if you—"

"Next *week?*"

"Or . . ." Van Halen shrugged. "You could talk to me."

He stood there, his angular, shadowed face carefully neutral, like he wasn't backing her into a corner. Which of course he was. Which meant he was maneuvering her. Which meant he had ulterior motives. *Okay, not good.*

But God help her, she had to find out about Rainie.

First things first. "Do you have any identification?"

Wordlessly, he fished a thin wallet out of his jeans pocket—Jesus, how did it fit?—and flipped it open.

In the picture he had a golden mustache and was wearing some kind of uniform. Lots of stripes and medals on his chest. *Holy moley.*

Okay, so Wade was right; she really didn't go for older men these days—yeah, yeah, go ahead and call her a cradle-robber, but youth was uncomplicated and older meant expectations, which she didn't want to deal with—and this guy had at least a decade and more on the twenty-five years she preferred in a date. But damn. I mean, the man looked *good.* If you didn't look too closely at his weathered face and seen-too-much eyes, you'd never know he was pushing forty.

Not that she hadn't already noticed his extreme hunkiness. In the flesh. As it were. *So* not good.

He flipped the wallet closed again before she had a chance to read the fine print. Not that she would have. She'd been too distracted by his drool-worthy picture.

"Where would you like to go?" he politely asked.

My place?

Okay, wow. Totally inappropriate thought.

Focus on Rainie, girl.

"How about that new Italian bistro over on Seventh?" she suggested.

"Sure," he said. "Let's grab a cab."

She was a bundle of nerves anyway, and now she also had this crazy insane attraction to contend with, which made her even more nervous as she slid into the taxi ahead of him. How could you outmaneuver someone if all you could think about was jumping his delectable body?

Damn, that was *her* strategy, distracting him with thoughts of sex. Obviously not working. Or rather, working too well . . . but on the wrong party. Somehow she had to take back control.

"So how long have you worked for CIA?" she asked after he'd told the driver the address.

He gave her the shadow of a smile. "Long enough to know we don't kidnap innocent American citizens."

She bristled. "Look, if all you're interested in is telling me I'm wrong, I might as well get out right here."

The shadow flickered. "Don't worry, that's definitely not all I'm interested in."

Hello! Was he *flirting* with her? Maybe it *was* working on the right party.

But the man had yet to crack a smile. He seemed so rigid he was in danger of snapping in a stiff wind. And yet, the undercurrent was unmistakable. At least she thought it was. . . .

God, she was so confused she didn't say another word until they arrived and were seated at a small table at the back of the restaurant. Very dark and private.

He ordered a bottle of Chianti and breadsticks while they looked at the menu, and when the waiter came back, he poured as they ordered their entrees. Wine. *So* not a good idea. Handsome-as-sin men and good wine together had an alarming tendency to lower her IQ by about fifteen points per glass. Possibly twenty. And she needed all her wits about her with this one.

When the waiter left, she started in, "Mr. van Halen—"

"Please, call me Gregg."

She grabbed a breadstick just to have something to do with her hands that didn't involve drinking alcohol. *Geez.* Turnabout was definitely not fair play.

"Okay. *Gregg.* Tell me where Jason Forsythe is and why he can't talk to me personally."

Gregg's square-jawed face remained somber. "I'm afraid I'm not at liberty to say where he is. I can, however, assure you I'll do everything in my power to resolve this problem for you. Now, Gina—may I call you Gina?" He raised a perfect brow. Thank *God* he didn't smile.

"No," she cut him off at the knees. Far better to keep the distance intact. "You may call me Dr. Cappozi."

"Yes, ma'am," he said without missing a beat. *Bastard.* "Why don't you tell me exactly what has happened to cause these suspicions in your mind?"

Interesting phrasing. Nonetheless she complied. The whole time she spoke he regarded her impassively, but she could practically see the gears turning behind those hard blue eyes. Spectacular eyes, really. Like brilliant blue diamonds. Way more than two carats' worth.

"And that's when my ex-fiancé gave me Forsythe's phone number. Special Agent Wade Montana with the FBI," she added pointedly. So van Halen would know if she disappeared, there was someone important who'd be looking for her. Just as she was doing for Rainie.

He nodded, taking a sip of his Chianti. "Well, it's an interesting story. I'll look into it and call you tomorrow."

"That's it?"

"Not much I can do tonight." He tipped his head ever-so-slightly. "Unless . . . you can think of something?"

Okay. That was definitely a come-on. Wasn't it? And yet, he didn't seem the least bit distracted.

"No, you're right," she replied, looking down at her plate of barely touched lasagna. "First thing tomorrow will have to do."

God help her. This guy was so far out of her league it wasn't funny. She'd graduated summa cum laude, top of her class at Columbia, but Gregg van Halen had *skills.*

He didn't bat an eyelash at her rejection. "Tell me about your job," he said. "I understand you're a medical research scientist."

And for the next half hour he pretended to be fascinated by the details of her past and current projects in the field of immunology, where she was perfecting a controversial new live-attenuated vaccine for the RSV, or respiratory syncitial virus, delivered via the intranasal route. Controversial because it involved gene splicing and genetic alteration. A political hot topic because of the interest terrorists had in using the same method for purposes of bioterrorism.

"So you're telling me someday when I go overseas I'll be able to skip those nasty smallpox and yellow fever shots and just get a spray in the nose?" he asked.

"That's the idea." She couldn't help being flattered by his interest, even if she knew it was only his way of getting her mind off Rainie. Or possibly getting her into bed. Most men's eyes glazed over after the first two sentences of explaining what she did in her job, let alone ask a million questions and actually get it. Another reason she preferred younger men. They never asked what she did. Why pretend to care when all you were after was sex?

Van Halen had managed to appear interested for an entire half hour. He must *really* think he was getting lucky tonight.

She deliberately checked her watch. "Well, it's getting late."

Immediately he rose and pulled out her chair for her, putting a hand to the small of her back as they threaded their way through the tables to the exit.

"I'll get a cab," he said once they were out on the sidewalk.

"No need. I can—"

"I insist."

Before she could protest he'd flagged down a taxi and herded her into the back. He slid in beside her.

Against everything she was telling herself, her pulse began to pound.

Sleeping with this man would be really, really stupid. Gregg van Halen was completely inappropriate as a lover. Maybe not quite the enemy, but certainly the opposition. Possibly even dangerous. Wasn't that what had gotten Rainie into this terrible situation in the first place? Sleeping with a dangerous, inappropriate man? And now Rainie had disappeared. . . .

He told the driver the address. *Her* address. Which he knew by heart. And then he slid even closer. So her knee touched his firm, muscular thigh. His leg shifted and suddenly they were touching from hip to ankle.

Oh, God. Her pulse went off the chart.

He didn't say a word, and she didn't dare look at him.

Hell, the problem wasn't that she didn't want to sleep with him. The problem was that she *did*. With a desire that took her breath away. Talk about insane.

Rainie always said when it came to men Gina's intelligence deserted her. This was no exception. *Boy*, was it no exception.

All too soon, they rolled up to the door of her building. Van Halen got out and extended a strong hand to help her climb out of the cab.

She took a deep breath. "Thanks for dinner. I really appreciate you looking into this for me. I'm so worried about my friend. It's just not like her, and I—" She stopped abruptly. She was babbling. She felt her cheeks heat. God, when was the last time she'd blushed? "Anyway." She turned.

Her cheeks heated even more, along with the whole rest of her, when he suddenly stepped behind her. *Right* behind her. And again they were touching, this time from their heads all the way down to their feet. His broad chest caressed her shoulder blades; his muscular thighs pressed into the backs of hers. The corded muscles of his arms brushed over her bare skin as his strong, blunt fingers glided down the sides of her body and gently grasped her hips. With a subtle motion he pulled her against him. What she felt was *not* subtle. *Jesus, God.* It was long and hard, thick and ready, and the feel of it pressing against her bottom sent a rash of goose bumps careening over her entire body.

This was not the tentative arousal of a twenty-five-year-old looking for some action. This was the hungry cock of a mature man who knew what he wanted and would take it mercilessly without a second thought. He'd do her so hard and so well she wouldn't be able to stop smiling for a week.

"Gina," he whispered. His warm breath stirred through her hair and down the column of her throat.

Oh, merciful Lord. This was it.

"Shall I walk you upstairs?"

TEN

AFTER three hours, Kick deemed it safe enough to stir within his hot, sightless cocoon. He hadn't heard voices for a long time—not real ones, anyway—and the sound of the Jeep driving back and forth on the ridge above him had faded for good. By the cooling sand above him, he figured the sun had finally gone down, and the tangos had decided to call it a night.

Of course, if the situation were reversed, he'd sure as hell be sitting still as a stone Buddha on top of that cliff cradling his rifle and waiting for the enemy to emerge, no matter how long it took.

But that was just him.

He hoped to hell these guys weren't as patient—some might call it obstinate—as he was.

He supposed he should be grateful for that obstinate streak. It was only thanks to it he'd survived the past three hours of hell, hiding motionless under the burning sand, keeping perfectly still. Every minute had been pure torture. Cramps, heart palpitations, sweats, shakes. As long as he was moving, running from the enemy, keeping Rainie safe, he didn't have time to think about the drugs he was missing.

The endless craving sitting square on his chest like a sharp-toothed monster gnawing viciously at his entrails. Now that he was clearheaded he could feel every goddamned bite, magnified a thousandfold from what they had been under the influence. A double-edged sword, that razor-sharpness. The yen was terrible. But for the first time in sixteen months, his thought process was lucid and rational. Undistorted except for the clean, sharp pain. That alone was worth all the rest.

He stuck his thumb on the end of the rifle barrel he'd been using as a breathing tube and powered his arm up through the couple feet of sand that enveloped him to the surface. Jack-knifing to a sitting position, he wiggled from the parachute he'd wrapped around himself, the field pack and the duffel, like a butterfly emerging from its cocoon.

Outside, it was totally dark. Quiet as a tomb.

He glanced up at the cliffs opposite. Sketched only in the light of a billion glittering stars, the sepia rock face looked eerie and ethereal. He couldn't see the low horizontal crevice where he'd hidden Rainie. Good. Because if he couldn't see her, no one else could, either.

He'd listened carefully for the first hour after deliberately causing the avalanche of sand that had concealed him from the tangos, fearing they would retrace his path searching for him, and find her instead. But he'd left a convincing trail for them to follow. They'd never gone back.

After shaking out the parachute and stuffing it in the duffel with the other one, he quickly reversed his steps through the darkness, running back across the wadi and up the gap in the cliff. Impatiently he eased his body and the awkward pack around the jut and onto the narrow ledge, one swift step at a time, so he wouldn't stumble and fall onto the rocks below.

"Rainie?" he quietly called. Didn't want to surprise her. Getting shot by friendly fire would be a hell of an ending to this gig.

There was a scuffle and a thump, then the distinctive metallic sound of a gun bolt.

Please, God, let it be her. "Rainie, it's me," he called a little louder, his heart pounding. "Are you there?"

He heard a gasp. "Kick? Oh, my God, Kick!" An instant later, her silhouette appeared, crawling out from the black recesses of the cave into the starlight.

He closed the last few feet, threw the pack into the corner, and went to his knees to scoop her up, dizzy with relief. "Jesus," he breathed into her hair, trying to tame his galloping heartbeat. "Jesus."

"You came back," she choked out.

"Damn straight," he said, easing the gun from her clenched fingers. He was about to say, "I always keep my promises," but the words wouldn't go past his dry tongue. Instead, he whispered, "Jesus, girl, you're shaking like a leaf."

Never had he been held so tightly or desperately. Not that there'd been a lot of nonsexual holding in his past. He avoided such things, didn't do touchy-feely. Needy women in particular made him run for the hills. Probably because he didn't have the emotion to spare.

But this was different. This was—

"Thank God," she cried, voice ragged with tears. Or was that something else in her half sobbed, half moaned, "*Kick?*"

"I'm here, baby. I'm here."

Her mouth found his and she kissed him. A desperate, whole-body, tongue-down-the-throat, take-me-now kind of kiss.

Fuck. All the pent-up fear for her he'd had bottled up inside him, all the physical hell he'd gone through for three interminable hours came pouring out as voracious need. *For her.* An urgent, primal need to touch her, meet her flesh on flesh. To celebrate them both being alive in the most primitive, basic way. He opened up and urged her on.

Before she could say no, he pushed her T-shirt up over her breasts. They spilled out, plump, beautiful, and bare, nipples peaked and offering themselves to him. The ultimate symbol of life.

With a strangled groan, he lifted her up and cushioned his face against her soft bounty, sucked a crown hard into his mouth. She cried out, instantly pebbling against his tongue.

Grappling for control, he switched to the other breast,

tonguing and suckling until he couldn't stand it any longer. He had to have her. Bury himself deep inside her. Thrust into her over and over and over, or he'd explode.

"Don't move," he said, and pulled the parachute from the duffel, whipping it out onto the ground. Then he was all over her again.

"I want you naked," he rasped, whisking the T-shirt over her head and throwing it aside.

His hunger for her was like a feral thing. Wild, unstoppable. And thank God, hers was the same.

Jerking down the zipper of her jeans he yanked them over her hips as he rolled her onto the parachute. By the time she was on her back she'd toed off her sneakers and together they dragged her pants the last few desperate inches over her feet.

"You are so fucking beautiful," he growled, savoring the sight of her starlit body and the desire for him in her eyes.

"You— *Ohhh . . .*"

He swallowed her words as he canted over her and took her mouth in a greedy, devouring kiss, then thrust his hand between her thighs, spreading them, opening her to his questing fingers.

She whimpered and shuddered as he touched her there, her hands faltering in their attempt to pull off his T-shirt.

He pushed a finger into her and came out wet. *Sweet Jesus.* Her nails dug into his flesh. He circled her honeyed need.

"Give it to me, girl," he urged, wanting her total surrender. Wanting to know she was helpless for him. "I want it all. Everything you have to give."

He worked her to a frenzy with his fingers, pinching, sliding, probing, while he drove his tongue into her mouth, in and out, in and out, mimicking the motion of what would come next. Compelling her to forget where she was. Demanding she forget her fears. Making her forget her own name if he could.

Her nails scored their way down his chest and dipped under his waistband. Her fingertips met the head of his cock.

He bucked away with a warning growl. "No."

If she touched him there, it was all over. And it was way too soon to be over. He wanted this to be good for her. So damn good she'd never forget this night, or this windswept cave, and not because of the terror she'd lived through in it. But because of this. Him. Now.

Her small, feminine cries of pleasure blended with her quick, panting breaths. He loved the way she sounded in the throes of passion. He'd forgotten what a turn-on it was to have a woman in his complete power, using only his touch to bring her to helpless bliss.

Or maybe it had just never felt this good for him before. Ever.

She felt exquisite. *And she was so close.* Hot as he'd ever felt a woman.

"You want me, don't you, Rainie?" he murmured.

"Yes!" She inhaled sharply as he pierced her with two fingers. "Please, Kick."

He swirled around her clit and it swelled to bursting.

So close he could taste it.

"Show me, sweetheart," he urged, low and rough like gravel. "Show me how much you want me. Come for me, baby. Come for me *now.*"

And she did. A throaty moan hitched, then she sucked in a breath and convulsed under his hand. She cried out his name, throwing her arms around his neck as a shuddering orgasm quaked through her.

He was ready to crawl out of his skin, but he kept going until he'd massaged every last arousing quiver from her body.

Instead of going slack, her arms tightened. "You," she demanded breathlessly, leaving no doubt as to her meaning. "*You.*"

He tore at his shirt to get it off, then wrestled with his DCUs, powering them down his thighs. He was still wearing his boots. *Screw it.* He fell onto his back, and her hands were on him.

"Damn it!" Furiously he dug through his pockets until he found the trio of condoms he'd put there in an optimistic moment last night. She snatched one from his fingers and tore into the wrapper.

He groaned deep as she rolled it on.

"You on top," he ordered, lifting her so she straddled him.

Then he fisted his cock, positioned her over it, and in a sharp, swift move impaled her from below.

She met him halfway and followed him down, sheathing him to the hilt in her wet heat.

Oh, yeah. Holy mother of God, yes.

He drilled his fingers in her hair and gritted his teeth, thrusting hard into her once, twice, three times. Battling not to go off like a heat-seeking missile.

But he did anyway.

He came in a starburst of power, the sounds of his release roaring through the cave. And he could only pray that the target he decimated with this endless, exquisite pleasure, this incredible rush, was not his own equilibrium.

Nor his resolve to do what needed to be done next.

KICK moaned long and low as he fell back down to earth. Rainie was panting hard, glued to his chest.

Good freaking grief.

Okay, of all the things he could have done, this was probably the stupidest. Not that it hadn't been great, but—

"I'm sorry," she said between pants, preempting him.

Okay, so now he was stupid *and* confused. "For what?" he asked.

"For attacking you like that."

He was pretty sure he'd been the one to do the attacking, but if she wanted to claim responsibility, that worked for him.

"Damn, woman." He closed his eyes to savor the last of the sparks going off in his cock. "Anytime you feel like attacking me like that, you go right on ahead."

"I was just so . . . relieved to see you," she said.

He knew all about being relieved. For that half second after calling her name, thinking the bad guys might have gotten to her after all, he'd nearly had a stroke. Then she'd crawled out of there looking at him like he was some kind of goddamn savior . . . and it had just felt . . . so damn right. He'd wanted to *be* her savior.

How insane was that?

He *hated* feeling protective. He was no fucking good at it.

Which was just as well. Because he was no damn good at protecting, either. That was a matter of record.

She sat up, still straddling him, and traced her hand down his chest where she'd raked him with her fingernails. It stung a little, bringing him around. He was still inside her, half aroused. He should—

"I was sure they must have caught you," she softly interrupted his internal lecture. "I was so scared for you."

For him?

"How in the world did you escape?"

He cleared his throat. "Buried myself in the sand. An old trick a Paiute buddy of mine once taught me."

"More cowboys and Indians?"

"Sort of." Except the cowboys had been a cutthroat gang of Mexican drug dealers and the Indians a team of ZU commandos sent to quietly put an end to their bloody border crossings.

Had she really been scared for him?

The Milky Way reflected back from the forest green of her eyes. As she gazed down at him, something deep inside his chest twisted painfully.

"I was more scared for you," he said, wrapped his hand around her jaw, and gently kissed her. Her lips were . . . papery smooth and starting to crack.

Abruptly, reality crashed in on him. Neither of them had had anything to drink since lunchtime. *Ah, hell.*

He groaned with self-recrimination. "Christ, what is wrong with me? You must be dying of thirst, and here I am . . ."

She smiled. "Don't worry, not quite dead yet. And in case there's any doubt, I'm glad you're here."

"Ditto." He kissed her, then lifted her off him and set her down on his discarded T-shirt. He yanked his pants up from around his ankles. "I'll get the pack." Because the ceiling was too low to stand, he started to crawl over to it.

Suddenly pain streaked like fire through his leg. "Son of a—" He grabbed his thigh, twisting his body to ease the cramp, and landed on his butt.

She reached out to catch him. "Your leg?"

"Guess it didn't like jumping out of a plane, or all that hiking," he gritted out.

"So that's why you wanted me on top," she said with a wink.

He chuckled through a groan. "Hell, no. Just honoring your request to have me under you."

She made a face, but she was still smiling. "Here, let me—"

"No." He needed to stretch out the cramped muscles. And if she touched him again he'd probably end up stretching *her* out on the floor again. He'd never met a woman who could switch off his brain like he was no more than a horny teenager. "Never mind about me. Find the water."

He deliberately looked away when she crawled over to the pack. Naked. On all fours with her delectable bottom flashing at him like a sexual homing beacon. *Damn.* She found six plastic bottles wrapped in extra DCUs and a shirt. She passed him a bottle and slipped on the T-shirt. *Thank you, Jesus.*

The water was warm and smelled like plastic, but neither of them cared. They drank greedily. But both stopped after several deep gulps.

"Who knows how long this'll have to last us," she said with obvious reluctance, recapping her bottle.

"Yeah." He was glad she was smart enough to realize that. "We could be out here for days before finding water."

Her movements halted for a second, then she took a deep breath and said, "Hungry? There are packets of food. Those MREs."

"What about the radio?" he asked. "Please tell me the SATCOM was in the pack."

She glanced into the backpack uncertainly. "I don't see it, but . . ."

"Here, let me—" His leg cramped again. "Ah, crap," he ground out, and fell back onto an elbow, woozy.

"I'll look for it again," she said. "Lie down and do a couple of leg exercises. That should help."

Exercise? He'd had more than enough of that, damn it. What he needed was the SATCOM so he could call for some goddamn help. Instead of thinking about how much he wanted her to lie down with him and start all over again with the exercise.

"And maybe a couple of aspirin?" he asked. Better yet, a freaking cold shower . . . And a bottle of— No. Not that.

"I'll see what I can do."

Crawling deeper into the cave, as far away from her as he could get, he pulled the parachute along and sprawled onto it again with a grunt. The night was still hot, but it was cooler back there. He took off his jacket as he turned over onto his back, and tucked it under his head as a pillow, stacking his hands between.

All right, fine. He lifted his leg with a grimace.

She snapped a small flashlight on and flicked the beam around. "Look what I found."

"What about the SATCOM?" He lifted it again.

"Hmm." She shook out the rest of the contents and went through them. "Tool kit, mess kit, spade, a big knife, first aid kit, looks like a roll of maps, bottle of sunblock, thank God, and . . . a space blanket." She shook her head. "Sorry. No radio."

Naturally it was the wrong pack. It had just been that kind of day.

Now what? What the hell would he do with her? He *had* to get to the training camp where abu Bakr and his terrorists were preparing their attack before it was too late. He thought about Lafayette. Prayed he'd survived. Prayed harder he'd found the other pack.

He lifted his leg again. Surprisingly, the pain was gone. He was shaky as hell, his heart still felt like a locomotive at times, and the cravings were never-ending, but the actual pain had vanished as quickly as it had struck.

He could live with that.

"What will we do?" Rainie asked. She had that look on her face again, gazing up at him like he was her savior. But the hero-worship was mixed with something else. Something that had to do with him having just been inside her.

Damn.

"I'm sure Lafayette's found the other pack." Now they just had to find Lafayette. "Did you mention a first aid kit?"

For aspirin, for his leg cramps. *Not* the strip of condoms it was ZU protocol to keep in all their kits. How many more opportunities would that make? Six? Seven? He stifled a groan.

The flashlight snapped off and she crawled over to his side and took his hand. "Here." Two pills dropped onto his palm.

He popped them and swigged down another gulp of water. "Thanks."

She was sitting on her heels, her perfect, half-nude body silhouetted against the night sky, her long pale hair in tangles from the violence of their lovemaking. *So fucking gorgeous.*

"It really hurts?" she asked.

"A bit achy," he said. But it wasn't his leg that ached. It was something deep in his chest. That had nothing to do with his drug withdrawal.

"What about . . . How are you doing with . . ." From her carefully neutral tone and eyes he knew she'd clued into his discomfort. Let her chalk it up to that. Not what it was really about.

He let out a tight sigh. The craving for the drug was still there, devouring his gut like a wolverine. But he wasn't going to let it win. Not this time. He'd managed to function despite it all day. Even entombed in the sand, the craving hadn't ever taken him over totally. Close. But not completely.

"I'll be fine."

And somehow he knew he would. About that, anyway. It was rough, but he'd make it. One day, sometimes one minute, at a time.

"I'm in awe of you, you know," she said quietly.

Surprise jolted through him. "*Me?* Why?"

She picked at a seam on the fluttering parachute, avoiding his gaze. "Because you're not afraid. Not of anything. And even with the withdrawal and your leg and all, you're so damn . . . good at what you do. Here in this horrible place, I'm barely keeping it together. But you, you're hardly even fazed."

That he was shocked by her praise was an understatement. He was so undeserving of it. Him not afraid? She couldn't be more mistaken. He was petrified. And he would be until he delivered her out of this place. Unharmed.

An unexpected wash of emotions seeped through his insides. Emotions so unfamiliar he couldn't begin to decipher them.

And he sure as hell didn't want to try.

"It's my job," he said more gruffly than he'd meant to.

She surprised him again by lying down next to him. Her body felt warm. Silky soft. So different from the hardness all around. From the hardness of his life. From . . . him.

"Besides, you've got it all wrong," he said, giving in to the desire to gather her in his arms. "You, Lorraine Martin, are the bravest person I've ever met. And I really hate myself for getting you into this mess."

"The biggest *coward*, you mean," she countered. "And if I don't hate you, you aren't allowed to."

"But you've got to hate me. If it weren't for me—"

She put her hand on his chest. "I just made love with you, didn't I?"

He gave her a wry smile. "Not what I would call it."

She poked him in the ribs.

"Besides," he said, "relief sex doesn't count. And you've made it pretty clear you don't want anything to do with me after we get back." Hell, that sounded petulant, even to him. *Great.*

"Not because of you," she said softly.

"That's not what you said back at your apartment. And again after I woke up from the detox." God, was he *whining*?

"That was before I understood what you were up against."

The weight of her hand on his chest was like a brand. Under it, his heart squeezed. She *still* didn't understand, didn't know what he really was. If she knew the real truth about him, how could she not hate him?

Better to put some distance between them. Remind her of what he'd done to her. "So you're saying you've forgiven me for trying to use you that first night?"

She toyed with a curl of his chest hair. And shocked him even more. "To be perfectly fair," she said, "I'd intended to use you, too, you know."

He raised an incredulous brow. "Is that so."

"For sex," she said. Even in the darkness he could see her naughty smile.

He laughed out loud. "Oh, yeah. And I would have given in kicking and screaming, let me tell you."

She poked him again.

Yeah, he knew that was why she'd been at that speed dating event. For sex. As soon as he'd spotted her across the crowded ballroom, he'd known instinctively what she was looking for. He also knew she'd singled him out as her desired partner the first moment she'd laid eyes on him. She'd wanted sex with *him*. No one else.

Talk about a turn-on.

"There's something I don't understand," he said, going onto his side so he could breathe in the scent of her, soak up the sight of her tempting body.

"What's that?"

He reached out to touch her hair, wound an errant lock around his finger. "Why would a smart, beautiful woman like you need to use a stranger like me for sex? You must have men lining up to ask you out. Rich doctors and such."

She pushed out a warm breath. Her fingers traced over his chest, slowly sketching circles down his abdomen. His cock thickened and reached up for her.

"I suppose I have . . . issues," she said with a self-conscious shrug. "I'm not really interested in a relationship. I was only there because my friend Gina talked me into it."

"To get you some."

The corner of her mouth curved up, almost shyly. "Her idea. Not mine. She said I should find someone safe, have a good time in a safe place."

"And look how well *that* turned out."

She let out a wry laugh. "Yeah."

Their eyes collided and held. He thought about her not wanting a relationship. That was huge. On one level it bothered him like crazy. She was so attractive in so many ways, any guy would be lucky to have her all to himself. On the other hand, that guy would never be him, so he was selfishly pleased no other man would get the chance.

His body was even more pleased. He was hard as the ground they were lying on. God, he was twisted.

And ravenous.

Why fight it?

He brushed his lips over hers. Burning.

"But you didn't want it safe," he murmured in a sudden flash of insight. "You like the danger, don't you, Rainie?"

At her protest, he pulled her into his arms and her mouth parted on an intake of breath as he slid his hand over her breast. He painted his tongue across her bottom lip. Tasted her, and let out a rumble of need.

God, how had he not understood that before? She was terrified of cars and planes and guns and violence, but she had chosen the only truly dangerous man that had shown up at the speed dating, and had practically seduced him after he'd kidnapped her at gunpoint. And now, after surviving this unholy day, in this god-awful place, she'd given him the hottest sex he'd ever had in his life.

Terrified or no, the danger turned her on.

And that turned *him* on.

"Safe isn't really an option here, Rainie," he murmured, unbuttoning his DCUs again. "Not here. Not with me." He rolled his body over hers. "So how about going for another round of danger?"

ELEVEN

"WE should get going."

Kick's body was spooned over Rainie's back, his arms around her from behind, heavy in that way a man's weight could be that made a woman not only endure it but wish he would linger forever. She loved the feel of him on her. Over her. In her. And she'd finally stopped shaking with fear. Stopped even thinking about anything outside the confines of their cozy hideaway.

So his out-of-the-blue statement was like a dash of chilly water. She blinked in alarm.

"Going? Why?" Surely, he didn't intend for them to leave the relative safety of the cave? "Where?"

"We have to find Lafayette and that other field pack, and be long gone before dawn."

He placed a kiss below her ear, his breath spilling warm and moist over her skin. He was still a little winded from their last explosive bout of lovemaking. Or sex. Or whatever you wanted to call it.

Lord have mercy. The second time he'd done her so hard they'd left a long, hollow groove in the sand under the parachute. Then he'd flipped her over and done her even harder.

She'd enjoyed every rough, erotic moment. But honestly, she didn't think she could walk, let alone hike out of here without risking collapse.

"How long until dawn?" she asked. Maybe if she got some sleep . . .

He turned his head to glance out at the night sky. "Not for several hours. Maybe three before we need to get going in earnest. We want to be a good distance away before the tangos return."

She turned to follow the direction of his gaze.

The night was dark. Relentlessly dark. She'd thought she'd seen nighttime back in the city, but she'd been wrong. She had never seen a night so completely, indelibly black as the one that hovered outside the cave. She didn't know what made her shiver more: the thought of being captured by those men, or the thought of going out there in that unremitting darkness.

"How will we find our way?" she asked, anxiety starting to creep through her already weakened limbs.

"Moon's up," Kick said matter-of-factly, "and look at all those stars. Perfect conditions for recon work."

Recon? Didn't that mean to search, and thus be able to see? She frowned and looked outside again. Okay, maybe there were a lot of stars piercing the inkiness of the sky. About a billion of them. She hadn't noticed that before. But— "I don't see the moon."

"Look at the opposite cliff. See how it almost glows?"

She hadn't noticed that, either. The burnt orange of the rock face popped out against the black sky above as though lit by muted klieg lights. And the yellow tops of the serpentine ridges of the dunes below snaked along the floor of the wide riverbed in stark relief against the black, hollow void all around.

It was actually . . . incredibly lovely.

Or maybe her senses were biased to the positive by the amazing pleasure she'd just experienced. Anything would look good in the endorphin rush of a mind-altering orgasm like Kick had just given her.

Let alone three.

He kissed her again and lifted up off her back, slapping

her on the tush. "Better put on some clothes. I don't want Lafayette getting ideas."

The reminder of the STORM agent sent another harsh dose of reality coursing through her. How could they possibly find him in the dark?

But they had to find him. With any luck he had the radio. And they could finally call someone to come rescue them. The faster she got out of this godforsaken desert, the better.

Not to mention away from the man pulling on his clothes. Lord help her. Again, the incredible sex was clouding her judgment. It was unacceptable how he was already invading her mind. Influencing her emotions. Making her think about his awesome ability to reduce her to a limp puddle of pleasure instead of how to escape this horrible situation and get back to her safe, secure life at home.

No doubt about it, Kick Jackson was walking, talking dangerous. Everything about him spelled danger. He was the last man on earth to fit into that safe, careful life she had carved for herself from the chaos and violence of New York City. Great sex or not.

"How will they rescue us, do you think?" she asked, to get her mind off it. Off *him*.

"Helicopter, probably. Either that or they'll contact the DFP refugee camp to send out a vehicle. Though that could be dicey with the tangos chasing us."

Mild shock made her glance up from putting on her sneakers. "The DFP camp? As in Doctors for Peace?"

"Yup."

"As in the DFP refugee camp *Nathan Daneby* started?"

"That's the one."

Okay, this was too weird. She could almost hear the theme from the *Twilight Zone* wafting down from outer space.

Nathan Daneby. What would it be like to come face-to-face with the legend himself? *The legend she'd decided to sleep with after knowing for all of five seconds.* Except, it hadn't been Nathan Daneby at all. It had been Kick impersonating him. And worse, she'd slept with him anyway.

"Will he be there?" she asked, uncertain if she actually wanted to meet the real thing. Talk about embarrassing.

"One can always hope." Kick's face was averted but his voice suddenly sounded angry as he shoved things into the backpack.

Hello?

"Is something wrong?" she asked.

Even in the darkness of the cave she could see his shoulders stiffen. "Nope."

Surely, he wasn't jealous—

Oh, sure. She must really be living in some fairyland to think Kick might be jealous of another man just because she admired him.

Suddenly something else hit her. "You're not leaving! Are you? You're going to stay and finish your mission."

"That's why I'm here, Rainie," he clipped out. "It's been a rough start, but nothing's changed except having to get you to safety first."

Ah. So no jealousy involved. He was just angry over having to postpone the mission while he got rid of her. That made much more sense.

Okay, then.

"In that case, I guess we'd better go find Marc," she said, which for some reason earned her a scowl.

But she didn't have time to think about that, because for the next hour she was too busy trying to keep up with Kick as he scaled the cliff to the plateau, then strode through the darkness toward the closest high outcropping in sight, all the while picking his way carefully so as to leave as little trail as possible. Then they climbed the outcropping. Which was more like a small mountain once they got up close. To be fair, he did ask if she wanted to stay behind at the bottom. But no way was she letting him leave her alone again. So she determinedly shook her head and scrambled up after him.

At the top she practically collapsed in exhaustion. *He'd* been more winded after they had sex. She definitely needed to get to the gym more often.

Pulling the flashlight out of his pocket, he blinked it on and off as he turned slowly in a half circle, facing the general direction where the other parachute had gone down.

A moment later there was an answering flash. A solitary pinpoint of light.

"There!" she said. "Is that him?"

Kick just grunted and clicked out a flurry of long and short flashes. A somewhat longer series of flashes came back.

Finally he nodded, his expression grim. "Yup. It's Lafayette. And he's hurt."

"YOU have a visitor, Dr. Cappozi."

Gina glanced up from the microscope she was working at and blinked her eyes into focus. She'd been staring into the damn thing for hours now, evaluating the fragile molecular bonding of the new strain of RSV she needed to perfect before her grant ran out. Pediatric respiratory syncitial virus wasn't one of the sexy diseases that got tons of research money, and there was a good way to go yet . . . But wouldn't it be amazing to be personally responsible for eliminating one more threat to children, once and for all?

"Hey, what are you doing here so late, Yolanda?" Gina asked, pinching the bridge of her nose. Yolanda was one of her graduate students, usually gone by dinner. It had to be after nine PM. Didn't time fly when you were having fun.

"Just finishing up some paperwork, Doc. You want I should let him into the lab?"

"Who?"

"Your visitor."

Gina jumped off her stool. "Wait. *Him?*" There was only one *him* it could possibly be.

Gregg van Halen stuck his head around the door. "Hi."

Standing behind one broad shoulder, Yolanda waggled her brows with a knowing grin. "I'll be going now, Doc. See you Thursday."

Before Gina could open her mouth to protest, Yolanda had vanished and van Halen had slipped in. A high-tech motorcycle helmet tucked under one arm, he casually leaned his back against the reinforced glass door. Which was the only way out of the lab.

"Mr. van Halen," Gina said nervously. Not because she was afraid he'd hurt her or anything. He'd had plenty of opportunity to overpower her last night as she'd scraped together the strength to turn down his outrageously tempting offer to accompany her upstairs. Lord, the back of her neck still tingled where he'd brushed his lips over her skin in parting, and she could swear the imprint of his fingers lingered hotly on her hips.

You got it. She was nervous because she was terrified he'd renew his efforts at seduction, and that this time she wouldn't be able to resist. Lord have mercy, he was everything she *didn't* like in a man—rigid of bearing, conservative in style, muscle-bound and huge in body, and at least five years older than she was. Yet, there you go. Gregg van Halen was the sexiest thing to cross her path in decades. Maybe ever.

"Don't you think we've moved beyond formal last names?" he said, something dark swirling in his deep voice.

"Definitely not."

Intellectually, she knew the only reason he wanted to have sex with her was to shut her up. He hadn't even tried to deny the accusation last night.

"No, you want me to stop asking questions," she'd said when he pulled her body tight against his and whispered roughly in her ear, "I want you." "You think if I sleep with you, it'll be easier to do damage control."

He hadn't said a word at her allegation, just exhaled and kissed the back of her neck, then let her go and went back to the waiting taxi. His easy capitulation had produced a long breath of relief.

Which now seemed to be stuck in her throat.

She frowned at him. "How did you get into the building? It's supposed to be secure."

"You forget, I have top-secret government clearance," he said, finally unpropping himself from the door. He dropped his helmet on a counter and came toward her.

Her heartbeat took off like a scared rabbit. *Whoa, hello.* What was *wrong* with her? She usually ate men for breakfast, but this Neanderthal was turning her into a frightened idiot.

"I have news," he said. "I thought you'd want to hear it right away." His handsome face turned distinctly grave.

And just like that she snapped to, forgetting all about her own problems and only thinking of Rainie. Fear blasted through her. "Please tell me you found her."

"In a manner of speaking."

She gripped the edge of the high counter littered with her experiments. "What is that supposed to mean?"

"Gina, I think you should sit down."

Alarm screamed in her head. "Just tell me."

"All right." He moved a few steps closer. She could smell the leather of his jacket. Musky. Masculine. "It seems Ms. Martin volunteered to accompany one of our officers, a certain Kyle Jackson, when he flew to join a mission. As you said, she's a nurse, and Jackson had some medical issues to deal with."

Flew? Gina's jaw dropped so far it was in danger of hitting the linoleum floor. "You can't be serious. Lorraine Martin would *never* voluntarily set foot in a car, let alone an airplane. My God, she'd be terrified the whole time and totally useless."

"Nevertheless"—he shrugged—"she did."

Gina closed her mouth and folded her arms over her abdomen. *Uh-uh.* That *so* did not happen. This only clinched that her friend really *was* in trouble. And this guy was either part of it, covering it up, or totally clueless. "Thank you. I—"

"There's more."

She glanced at him sharply. "What is it?"

"Their plane went down."

Gina's heart stuttered to a stop. "*What?* Oh, my God! Is she hurt?"

"I'm sorry." Van Halen's eyes met hers unflinchingly. "The plane blew up. Jackson and Ms. Martin are among the missing. Both are presumed dead."

IT took them another hour of hard hiking before they made it to the massive jumble of jagged rock that Marc was using for cover.

He wasn't hard to find. They just followed the sound of colorful Cajun curses.

You didn't get a lot of Cajuns in New York City, but Rainie recognized enough of the words from high school French that her ears burned.

When they saw him, she understood why he was cursing. The side of his face and head were covered in blood, and he

was grinding his teeth so hard his cheeks were chalk white.
One arm hung limp at his side. His face was wreathed in pain
as he walked unsteadily out from deep among the rocks,
dragging the backpack.

"Glad to see you made it, *mes amis*," he gritted out.

"Likewise, Lafayette," Kick said, grabbing up the backpack for him. "Jesus, you look like hell. Please tell me that's
not a bullet in your head."

"*Non*. No bullet. Just a damn haircut," Lafayette said,
swiping the blood from his eyes as he collapsed back against
a boulder. "Maybe a few broken ribs." He swallowed a groan.
"And the arm, of course."

"My God, what happened?" Rainie peered closer. Fresh
blood was seeping from a thin gash in the left side of his
head. It slashed through his hair from the temple and back
about three inches. Talk about a close shave. His right arm
was obviously broken. And the way he gripped his right side
hinted that the ribs were indeed cracked.

Hell. The man needed medical attention.

"Landed badly trying to avoid the rocks," he said, his
grimace flashing into a surprisingly convincing grin. "Didn't
quite succeed. Good thing you're a medic."

"Nurse practitioner, actually. And without supplies," she
muttered. "Unless you count aspirin." *And condoms.* But
there were at least bandages and antiseptic. That would help.

He shrugged, and let out another curse at the movement.
"Jus' do what you can, *cher*. I'm tough, me."

She could believe it. The man was nearly as tall as Kick,
and muscular in the way of a guy who liked to work out. Or
maybe he'd spent time on a Louisiana chain gang breaking
rocks. *Yikes.*

She sent Kick a look, and he gave her a nod of encour-
agement.

Right. "I'll need the first aid kit."

Kick slid the pack from his back and dropped it next to
her, then went onto a knee next to the one he'd taken from
Marc. "You've got the SATCOM, righ— Ah, *hell*, no."

Marc winced. "Yeah, we're screwed, *boug*."

She looked up from the first aid kit. Her heart stalled. The
second pack was in tatters.

"Landed even harder on the rocks than I did."

"The radio?" she asked anxiously.

"Doesn't look good."

"Maybe y'all can get it to work. I kept drippin' blood on the thing. Figured better to wait."

Kick pulled it out of the pack and swore softly. "Housing's cracked." He tried the switch. Nothing happened. "Any idea how to fix these things?"

"*Désolé*. Electronics, never my strong suit."

"Mine, either."

To her surprise, they both glanced at her. "Don't look at me," she said, and started cleaning the bloody wound on Marc's head.

Kick swore long and hard. "So much for the rescue helicopter."

"Guess we'll jus' have to hoof it," Lafayette said.

Kick swore again.

"What'sa matter, Jackson? 'Fraid you can't keep up?"

"Hell, don't relish dragging your sorry ass across half of Africa, is all."

"What are you talking about?" she asked. "You can't mean *walk*! With his ribs and arm like this?" Not to mention the terrorists in the Jeeps.

Kick handed her a roll of bandages. "No choice. For obvious reasons, our best option is to head for the DFP refugee camp in the Nile Valley."

"*Mais, non!*" Marc protested. "That's in the opposite direction from the insurgent camp."

"And your point is?"

"I'm good to complete the mission," Lafayette argued.

"The *mission*?" Rainie cut in, appalled. "Are you in*sane*?" Dedication was one thing, but this was ridiculous. "Not even counting the broken ribs that could slip and puncture a lung, you see this ugly bump here? That's a displaced fracture of the radius. In this heat, it could easily go septic. Either of those things happens and you're a very dead man."

"I let terrorists blow up our embassy," he ground out, "I may as well be dead, me."

"Not going to happen," Kick said. "I'll make sure of that."

A chill went down her spine at the steely bitterness in

Kick's voice. In his eyes the pupils had swallowed up all the blue so they were like black holes in his face.

"Wait, now," she said uneasily. "You said we're going to the DFP camp."

The two men exchanged a look. Marc said, "You go get the bads, *ami*. I'll take care of her."

She choked. "I hate to break it to you, but you're in no shape to take care of yourself, let alone anyone else."

"She's right. You can't risk those ribs by carrying a heavy pack, and your shooting arm is broken."

Even in the darkness she could see Lafayette scowl, wiping sweat from his brow. "There's a village about twenty clicks to the east. You leave me there."

"And take the woman with me? No fucking way," Kick said. "And no fucking way am I leaving her anywhere that isn't safe."

She blinked at the ferocity of the statement. She wanted to believe that fierce protectiveness was for her, Rainie. Too bad he'd said "the woman" instead of her name. She suddenly got the feeling something else was going on in his mind. That he was thinking of a different mission. One where "the woman" might not have survived.

She took a cleansing breath. *None of her business.*

"How far is it to this DFP camp?" she asked, resolving to do everything he asked and be as little trouble as possible.

"About seventy-five miles, give or take."

Whoa. "*Seventy-five?*" She was in decent shape but . . . good Lord.

"Hopefully we can pick up a camel somewhere." He frowned as he ripped off a long strip of parachute for a bandage. "You're not afraid of riding a camel, are you?" He handed it to her.

She cleared her throat. "I don't know," she said, and started wrapping Marc's ribs with the silk. "I've never ridden one."

"Work on the idea, okay?"

Sure, she would.

She stabilized the ribs as quickly as she could in the inadequate light of the moon and stars. It was like plastering a wall blindfolded and using plastic kids' tools. She could tell

Kick was impatient to get moving. He kept pacing back and forth.

"What should we do about his arm?" he asked, making her jump as she tied off the parachute strips.

"It needs a splint." What it *really* needed was a surgeon, an X-ray machine, and a solid cast.

"Want me to help realign the broken bone?" She looked at him in surprise. "I've gone on a lot of missions," he said by way of explanation. "People get hurt."

She nodded gratefully. "Thanks." It took a lot of strength to pull the ends of a bone apart and carefully maneuver them so the break went back together as it should. She'd never done it alone before. Without X-rays. Or anesthesia.

God help her.

"Don't suppose either of you are packing a bottle of vodka?" she muttered, pulling an ACE bandage from the first aid kit.

Marc gave a manly snort. "*Cher.* I don' need no stinkin' vodka. Just give me a stick to bite down on."

She shot him a dry smile. "I meant for me."

He barked out a laugh, took her hand, and brought it to his lips. "I tell you what, *jolie fille*. You fix my arm, I buy you a whole case, we get back to civilization."

Suddenly, he gave out a howling yelp and practically crushed her hand with his massive fingers.

With a gasp, she looked up to see Kick gingerly gripping Marc's wrist, the other hand smoothing gently over his now straight arm. The ugly bump was gone.

"There. That ought to do it."

Lafayette said something she was really glad she didn't understand.

Kick winked at her. "That'll teach him to flirt with my woman."

She didn't know what stunned her more, that he'd done a perfect job on the bone without her help, or that he'd called her his woman.

"You make sure the break's set right," he said. "I'll get the ruined field pack. We can use the metal frame for a makeshift splint."

"Okay," she said, still too shaken to move. "Good."

Lafayette groaned and suddenly his hand went limp in hers.

"Ah, hell," Kick said. "He's passed out."

RAINIE prayed Marc wasn't going into shock. After coaxing him awake, she'd spread the extra clothes over him that Kick had pulled out of the packs, mounded sand under his feet to keep his circulation going, and held an ammonia capsule under his nose for good measure.

"Stay with us, soldier," Kick ordered, which irritated Lafayette enough to cuss himself back to consciousness. Apparently he was a Navy man.

"*Merde, sa fait mal*," Marc said, hissing out a breath between his teeth.

After Kick bent the metal frame to fit snug up against the arm, they were able to wrap it like a mummy with strips of parachute, stabilizing the break so it couldn't move. Not perfect, but better than nothing.

In the meantime, Kick had brought out water and pouches of MREs, and they ate a hurried meal. Rainie doled out doses of aspirin and Tylenol.

"Ready?" Kick hefted the pack and helped Lafayette up. "Can you manage the duffel?" he asked her.

She nodded.

He paused, giving her a look she couldn't quite decipher. For a second she thought maybe he was going to kiss her. But he didn't. He just nodded back and started walking. "Good girl. We're oscar mike."

Going single file with Marc in the middle, they fell into a swift, steady pace.

Kick seemed to know where they were going. Rainie didn't have a clue. The men had studied the maps and SAT photos as they ate, discussing the best route to take toward the Nile Valley. To her it was all just lines and squiggles. The only map she'd ever looked at was for the New York subway system, and she'd never actually had to use it to get anywhere. She didn't ride the subway, either.

According to Kick, between where they were and the DFP camp lay a vast sea of shifting sand which they were forced to skirt around, adding another twenty or so miles to the trip. How would they ever be able to make it? They only had eight bottles of water between them, and three of them were half empty already. How many days would it take to walk seventy—no, ninety-five miles? That camel was looking better and better.

As soon as the sky began changing from black to indigo she started to look over her shoulder, checking behind them for any sign of their pursuers.

She spotted the telltale dust cloud an hour or so after sunrise.

"They're coming," she told Kick, her heartbeat taking off at a gallop.

"Keep an eye on them," he said, glanced back briefly, then kept walking. "If we're lucky, they won't come this way for quite a while."

How could he be so damn calm? "Shouldn't we try to hide?" she protested.

"If they get close, yeah. Until then we keep moving."

Panic starting to flutter in her chest. "But—"

"Rainie. Trust me."

Easy for him to say.

She battled back the rush of fear that threatened. He was the expert. If he wasn't worried, she shouldn't be, either.

Deep breath. Let it out slowly.

I will be fine.

We will be safe.

There were only two Jeeps today, she realized. One roamed back and forth along the plateau where she and Kick had landed. The other plied the other side of the big wadi, as Kick called it, where he'd left his trail of footprints in the sand for them to follow. The diversion seemed to be working.

For now.

But it wasn't her imagination that, after spotting them, Kick picked up the pace even more. She could barely keep up, and Marc was looking decidedly grim. Every hour or so she fed him another pain reliever, inadequate as they were, and Kick would make him drink nearly all of his water ration.

"He needs to rest," she quietly said to Kick during one of their breaks. "Longer than five minutes."

"Have you checked the bad guys lately?" he asked somberly.

"No, I—" She'd been too busy checking on Marc. She searched the horizon.

Except the dust trails were no longer on the horizon. The two trails had come together into one. A lot closer.

And they were heading straight for them.

TWELVE

THE blazing African sun was getting higher in the sky, nearly directly overhead by now. Heat poured down like an oven broiler. Kick felt like a chicken being slowly roasted alive. At times from the inside out.

But if he felt bad, Lafayette must really be hurting. Kick couldn't imagine having to hike nearly a hundred miles in that condition. He remembered like it was yesterday the horrific pain in his leg and shoulder from the Russian land mine in A-stan. But he hadn't had to walk. He'd radioed for help and a helicopter had been there within minutes.

He shook off the infuriating memory and wiped his face and neck with his T-shirt, long ago soaked through. Dry desert air usually felt ten degrees cooler than it really was, but ten degrees cooler than one twenty was still a hundred and ten fucking degrees. Well, at least it distracted him a bit from the cravings. Jesus, when would they stop? Unfortunately, he knew the answer to that.

Focus. Don't think about it.

Behind them, the tangos were making steady sweeps of the landscape. Looked like the two Jeeps were working a loose grid pattern. They'd had a scare a few hours ago, thinking they'd been spotted, but the Jeeps had just been heading in their direction to reach a shady outcropping and take a short break—probably time for prayers.

So far the tangos hadn't picked up their scent; but careful as Kick had been to stick to the hard-packed and rock surfaces as he'd led the trio across the moonscape, there'd been plenty of patches of barren sand to cross. A good tracker would have little trouble picking up their trail. Luckily, he seriously doubted there were any nomads in this crew of ass clowns. The fact that they drove Jeeps said these boys had money, which meant they were either part of a terrorist cell with Saudi oil connections, like abu Bakr's al Sayika, or *janjawid*— government-funded vigilantes who were no better than domestic terrorists. Worse, in some ways—because they terrorized their own countrymen . . . and women. No self-respecting nomad would have anything to do with either group. The Bedouin were far too fiercely independent to kowtow to Khartoum, and too honorable to fall for the fundamentalist doctrine of blind hate spouted by *jihadi* terrorists. Every spec operator knew a Bedouin's word was sacred; once gained, you could— and many had—trust your life to it with every confidence of coming out the other end alive. Which was why they were almost always victims of the *janjawid*, rather than allies.

"Kick," Rainie said, bringing him out of his unpleasant thoughts.

"Yup."

"The Jeeps. They're getting closer."

He slowed his grueling pace long enough to look back again. She was right. Either he was losing track of time, or the dust clouds were now advancing a lot quicker. Any minute now, the vehicles would break through the thin sliver of horizon that still hid them from view. Had the enemy found their tracks?

Suddenly Rainie gave a small cry. He whirled to see what was wrong.

She pointed breathlessly to a small cluster of dunes that lay to the northeast. "Is that what I think it is?"

He and Lafayette both looked.

Behind the far, distant dunes was a brilliant blue body of water, rippling and shimmering in the sunlight like a day at the beach.

Kick gave a tired grin. "Depends on what you think it is. What it's *not* is a lake."

Her lips parted. "Wow. A mirage? Seriously?"

"Just like in the cartoons."

Lafayette chuckled. Kick was amazed the man still had it in him. Every time Kick felt like puking from the stomach cramps, he just looked at his traveling companion. The swarthy Cajun's outdoor tan had turned positively grey, with white lines of pain bracketing his mouth and eyes.

Kick lifted Lafayette's water bottle to his lips while Rainie stared in amazement at the mirage. "Drink up, man."

"*Non*, I'm good."

He was about to argue when she interrupted uncertainly, "So, in a mirage . . . are there usually real palm trees around the unreal lake?"

"What?" He jerked his gaze back. Sure enough, he could just make out the waving fronds of a clump of palm trees peeking out from behind one of the low dunes at the edge of the blue illusion. Well, hell. Where there were date palms, there was real water. And where there was water—

"Damn," he exclaimed low. "That's a goddamn village."

"Isn't on the map," Lafayette said, his voice scratchy and his breathing rattly. "Maybe it's a seasonal oasis."

Rainie came up behind them. "A village is good, isn't it? They'll help us, won't they?"

She sounded so optimistic, Kick hated to dash her hopes. "Depends," he said.

Her face fell. "On what?"

He didn't want to scare her more than she already was, so he let the question hang as he struggled for a good answer.

Lafayette helped him out. "Lotta different tribes and such in the Sudan. Most are good, ordinary people. But like everywhere, there some *bien mauvais drigaille*—very bad apples. Problem is, the bads up here have guns. Bads with guns are bads with power. Power they use to turn good people into more bads."

As she digested that rather subtle way of saying they could easily be murdered or betrayed by the good, ordinary people in the village beyond the dunes, she shifted the duffel she was carrying to her other shoulder. The duffel holding the sniper rifle that gave *him* the power of life and death, too. A power he was planning to use in just a few days.

Was there a difference between him and the villagers, or even the bads? Was he *bien mauvais drigaille*, too, because of what he did? Even if it was in a good cause?

He guessed he'd have to find out on judgment day, because God only knew.

"But surely, if they see that one of us is hurt and needs help . . ."

She was also carrying Kick's SIG. He'd fashioned her a shoulder harness out of his ankle holster and some strips of parachute fabric so it sat snug against her rib cage. Ready in case she needed it. She'd tried to tell him she didn't want it. That she hated guns. Abhorred violence. But he'd given her such a quelling look she hadn't dared argue.

He gave her the same look now. "The tangos are heading in this direction. It might not be because of us."

The poison of reality finally flowed into her eyes. "Oh," she said. "You mean . . . they could live here?"

"I hope not. I'd like to trade for some water and that camel I mentioned. But we need to find cover until we know exactly what's going down here."

Lafayette nodded. "Sounds good." He swallowed slowly, like his throat was parched dry. "I could use a rest, me."

"Find cover where?" she asked, glancing around. The landscape was a flat, undulating plain that bled into a sea of yellow dunes on one side and a line of rocky, purple hills on the other.

Kick looked back to gauge the dust cloud's progress, locked his jaw, then turned and jerked his chin at the dunes at the edge of the palm grove. "If we walk double time, we can make it before they get here." He looked at Lafayette with concern. "You up for it, buddy?"

Lafayette gave him a half smile that was hard as steel. "*Allonsez*," he said. "I can rest when I'm dead."

And Kick hoped like hell the words weren't prophetic.

SHE was touching him.

Merciful Jesus, thank you Lord God Almighty, she was

finally touching him. The redhead. His Angel with an *H. Oh, yeah*. Her hand was on his thigh. His groin. Her fingers probed.

He moaned, caught between intense pleasure and even more intense pain. *Damn*. It shouldn't hurt this much.

The fingers switched to the other side, missing the most important bits in between. He wanted to scream in frustration. Instead he screamed from the white-hot pain that exploded beneath her pressing fingertips.

A man's voice said something in bad Arabic. *"Antibiotics. He to need."*

Shit. Not the redhead. A man. Some fucking asshole doctor.

Pig roused himself from the remnants of slumber. Not a dream. This was real. A rare visit by an outside asshole. One who was playing doctor.

He frowned, playing back the words in his head. Hell. A *foreign* outside asshole playing doctor. As in a *non-Arab Westerner helping these asshole terrorists* asshole doctor.

What the hell?

He tried to concentrate on the voice. But the foreigner had moved away from his pallet, conversing in clipped, hushed tones by the bright, square-ish opening to his filthy hovel. Conversing, no doubt, with the chief tango jerk-off asshole.

Damn, he had to find out who it was.

He dared to crack open his eyelids, covering the movement with a thrash of his head and a sickened groan. Desperately, he attempted to focus his barely there eyesight, trying like hell to get a visual so he could ID the scumbag traitor's fuckface when he got out of this hellhole.

But all he saw was a shadowed profile silhouetted against the brighter square of outside sunlight. Definitely a foreigner—no beard, no girly dresslike *gellabeya*. And the man wore real shoes, not sandals.

But shit. Shit. Shit. Why couldn't he see more? He wanted to nail this fucker to the wall.

When he escaped—

Suddenly, rough hands grabbed his aching body, surprising him into a feeble yell of protest. "Get your fucking hands off me, you goddamn motherhumpers," he growled.

A fist crashed into his jaw, shooting off rockets in his

head like the Fourth of July. And what little sight he had spun
into an ever-smaller pinpoint of light.

Fuck.

Ah, well. Consciousness was overrated anyway.

THIS was going to get ugly.

Kick could feel it with the certainty of sixteen years' experience, down to his very bones.

He'd left Lafayette and Rainie hiding in a deep *V* between
two huge dunes and, armed with the H&K, he'd climbed up
the razorback of the dune closest to the village so he could
observe the action below. Lafayette hadn't been too pleased
about being left behind. He'd get over it.

Kick moved quickly and silently. His Paiute friend had
also taught him how to tread just above the bottom of a
dune's *V*, and just under its top crest, so as he crouch-ran a
small wave of sand was displaced and slid down, covering
his footprints. If you were really looking, in places you could
still see the depressions left by his boots, but for the most
part they blended.

He belly-crawled just up under the crest and poked his
binoculars over the top. As the two Jeeps approached the
village, it erupted in chaos. Women and girls ran for the
safety of stone and mud huts, boys took off for the date palm
grove growing by the patch of watery sludge that was the
source of the oasis. The men gathered agitatedly in a cleared
area in front of the largest hut. The poor fucks didn't have a
weapon between them. At least not that Kick saw. But . . .
what was that glint in the window . . . ?

The Jeeps drove smack into the middle of the group of
men and came to a sand-slinging, man-scattering halt. There
were three tangos in each vehicle. Leaving a spot open in
both for a prisoner. Or a conscript.

The tangos jumped out of the vehicles, yelling and waving guns in the air to round up the village men into a tight
clutch, then made them squat in the dirt. Disgust sent bile up
Kick's throat.

Two of the tangos broke off to conduct a search of the village. But at least no one was shooting. Yet.

Kick's Arabic wasn't all that great but he understood enough to know the guy who seemed to be in charge was interrogating the village men about the crashed FedEx plane. Asking about pieces of the wreckage. Threatening to kill anyone who helped survivors. The usual bullshit.

Instinctively, Kick checked the H&K's magazine and silently chambered a round. Too bad he couldn't shoot the bastards. He could not blow his cover, no matter what they did. Even if not acting ate at his stomach like acid going through metal.

At least that answered one question. The bad guys didn't live here, or even know these people.

He ground his jaw as he watched the überdirtbag raise his rifle and strike a villager's head. The sickening crack of the impact and the man's cry echoed sharply off the walls of the huts. The bastard laughed.

Kick's trigger finger literally itched.

Suddenly, he heard another cry. From a woman. Quieter. Close by.

Instantly he was on his feet and running toward it. He heard it again. Muffled. More frantic.

He ran faster.

The third cry was right around the next dune. He rolled to a halt, crab-crawled the last few feet to the edge. Peered around. And saw her.

God*damn* it.

He shook his head, slinging sweat like a roundhouse sprinkler. Fighting the urge to break cover. Grappling to get hold of his twitching body.

One of the tangos had a young girl by the hair and was dragging her behind the dunes where no one could see what he was doing. She was crying, trying to scream, but the asshole's hand was clamped hard over her mouth. *God, so young.* She couldn't be more than fourteen, her struggles useless against the much older and stronger man.

The fucking bastard.

Then he had her on the ground, yanking up her long, homespun dress.

No. Kick was moving even before the decision was made in his head. No way. No goddamn way.

The girl's terrified eyes went even wilder when she saw him barreling down on them. She shook her head, silently screaming and screaming under the man's brutal grip over her mouth. Kick wished he could call to her not to worry. But she'd understand soon enough he meant no harm. To *her* anyway.

At the last second he flipped his rifle around to his back, and in one swift movement leapt on the man, caught him in a headlock, and with a vicious twist snapped the fucker's neck.

The girl's scream stopped abruptly, as abruptly as her assailant's movements. Her eyes were still wide with fear as he lifted the body off her. He allowed himself a millisecond's glance downward.

Thank God. He'd been in time.

She pulled down her dress and scrambled away. But not too far. She stopped on her hands and knees a few yards from him, staring back at him in terrified, tearful confusion. A wave of nausea had him taking large, quelling gulps of air as he waved his hand in the direction of her home. Not for what he'd done. But for what had almost happened to her.

"Go on," he said quietly. "I'll take care of this piece of garbage."

He'd deliberately not left a visible mark on the man. If he worked fast, he could make it look like natural causes.

Well. Unless you did an autopsy. Not likely to happen out here.

He swung the body over his shoulder and retraced the rapist's steps to the edge of the dune closest to the village. He held him upright and checked his pants. *Thank you, Jesus.* He wouldn't have to touch the fuck. The fly was open and he was already exposed. Kick let the scum fall onto the sand as though he'd just collapsed while standing there. Then he opened his own fly and made a nice little puddle next to the body.

There. They'd think the creep had a heart attack taking a piss.

He turned and was about to hightail it out of there when he remembered the trail of footprints leading back into the dunes.

Shit. Following them would lead to the site of the girl's struggle, and tell an altogether different story.

Suddenly she appeared next to him, holding a thick bunch of palm fronds. She said something in Arabic he didn't get. But he understood when she made a shooing motion with the fronds, then started to wipe away the prints from the sand.

He gave her a somber smile, and thanked her. "*Shukran.*"

Then he turned and took off at a run. Around and back to the top of his dune. To wait with pulse pounding in his throat to see if the ruse worked.

Or if they'd come after him with guns blazing.

"I don't like it," Marc said for the dozenth time. "I'm going after him."

Rainie put an anxious hand on his arm. "No. Kick said to wait here. You're in no shape to help, anyway."

The STORM agent liked that pronouncement even less, judging by the dark look he gave her. Too bad. She was scared enough as it was. If he went, she'd have to go with him. And she didn't want to be anywhere near those guys in the Jeeps.

Not that she liked the idea of Kick out there facing them alone. A shiver traveled down her spine just thinking about it. He'd been gone forever. What was he doing?

Waiting was like torture. The sun and heat were relentless, with no shade to be found in the smooth rise and fall of the dunes where they were hiding. They were nearly out of water, too.

Marc had insisted she give him Kick's handgun, which she'd gladly relinquished. But despite his macho bravado, he was getting weaker by the hour. Even his uninjured hand shook as he held the gun. She feared an infection might be taking hold in his broken arm. He needed medical help. Gangrene was a real possibility, especially in this heat.

What the *hell* was going on with Kick? Why didn't he come back?

All at once the air was split by the *pop! pop! pop!* of gunfire.

Her heart leapt into her throat. "My God!"

"*Merde*," Marc growled.

They both jumped to their feet. He swayed against her. She grabbed him, but he shook her off with a grimace, lifted the SIG, and took off at a stumbling lope toward the gunfire. "Stay there!" he called over his shoulder.

Panic seared through her. A thousand conflicting responses kept her rooted to the spot. *Fight? Flee? Help? Stay?*

Then another burst of gunfire exploded beyond the dunes. And suddenly she knew only one thing mattered.

"*Kick!*"

God, no, please no*!*

"Marc, wait!" she screamed. And ran full tilt toward the danger.

THIRTEEN

RAINIE tripped and fell as she sprinted through the unwieldy dunes to catch up to Marc. She clawed at the sand, fighting to get to her feet. *Was she already too late?* She scrambled up and kept running. Terrible images streaked through her head. Images of a bloody Kick lying dead and—

She ran flat into Marc's back.

They would have both gone sprawling, but this time he whirled and caught her with his good arm, banding her against his side as they spun to a halt.

She let out a sob. "Please, let me—"

"Shhh. Rainie, hush, *fille*," he urged in a strange voice. Subdued, but intense. His hand cupped her head, trying to turn her face into his shoulder. She fought him. Jerked herself free. Whirled back around.

She was not prepared for the sight that greeted her.

Bodies littered the ground.

Blood. Bodies. Bloody bodies.

She gasped in horror.

People screaming.

"Nooo!"

A man rushing toward her.

Everything went red.

A child screaming. A girl screaming at the feel of huge hands grabbing for her. At the sight of her parents' bodies, lifeless and—

"Rainie!"

She struggled harder. She had to get away. Had to—

"*Rainie!*"

Against her will, her eyes flew open. And she saw—

Something was wrong. Something was different. It wasn't the carjacker coming for her; it was—

"Kick?" she sobbed.

One set of arms released her and another set pulled her to a hard, warm chest. Strong fingers stroked her back and a voice choked out, "Damn it, Rainie, I told you to stay put."

Kick's voice.

Thank God.

She'd had a flashback. Only a flashback.

She was shaking so hard her teeth chattered. She didn't even try to speak. She just stood there and let him hold her as the shakes subsided. Lord, she wanted to stay there forever and soak up his strength like she was a dry sponge. It felt so good to have someone to lean on, like she was six again and "It's going to be fine, honey" still had a shot at being true. How long had *that* been?

Lord, she hadn't had a flashback in years. Seeing dozens of injuries every day in the ER had long since inured her to the sight of blood. She'd thought, anyway. So what had set it off?

"Let's get you away from here," Kick said, something ugly coloring his tone. He pushed her back toward the dunes.

But . . . if it was just a flashback, why was he herding her away from . . . what? She turned her head and made herself look again.

"Rainie, don't—"

The bodies were still there. And the blood.

"Sweet Jesus."

His arm tightened around her. "You don't need to be here. Go with—"

"No." She dug in her heels. This time she was prepared. *She could do this.* She took a deep breath and pulled away from his comforting warmth. Forced herself into nurse mode. "What can I do to help?"

"Nothing."

"But—"

"They're all dead," Kick said evenly.

Okay. She was okay. "How do you know?"

"Because they were animals and deserved to die."

Stunned, she gaped at him as his bitter words razored through her gut. All the way to her soul. God, she'd been right about him. "You *approve* of this slaughter?"

He made a humorless noise. "Approve? Baby, I was part of it."

She knew the horror must have shown on her face because his mouth thinned and his eyes went as dead as the people lying on the ground.

"Those bastards were threatening their homes, Rainie. Threatening innocent women and children. I didn't start the shooting, and neither did the villagers, but I sure as hell helped when they started fighting back."

That's when she noticed them, the villagers. Standing in a semicircle and staring wide-eyed at the three of them. The men held guns. All aimed at them. Well, her and Marc.

But these were real people, simple villagers, not hardened, hooded thugs, or even trained special ops guys. Somehow, that was worse. How could *normal* people have done this awful thing, committed the atrocity surrounding her?

Some of the villagers studied them suspiciously, some with amazement, a few like they were aliens from another planet. Which she supposed they were to them. As their world seemed to her. And suddenly, the lover who held her with one arm and a deadly rifle with the other seemed just as alien.

But blood was blood. *Nurse mode.* She scanned the bodies on the ground. "I should still check pulses," she said, taking a step away from the man she realized—big surprise—she didn't know at all. "Someone could have survived."

He grabbed her wrist to prevent her from going. "Even if there were survivors," he said sharply, "you're a woman, a foreigner, and they'll think you're my wife. They'd never let you near those men, let alone treat them."

But she was stuck back at the first part. "Your *wife*? Why would they think that?" Especially with those flat eyes he was watching her with.

"Because that's what I'll tell them." Before she could ask why again, he leaned his face down close to hers. "Because you're a woman traveling alone with two men. In this culture, if you're not wife to one of us, you're a whore. Fair game for any man in the village. Which option would you prefer?"

Fire flamed through her face and hurt through her chest. At his sudden anger at her. At the massive confusion in her heart. At this whole hellish situation.

She couldn't help her belief in the sanctity of life. *Any* life. Even that of a lowlife scum who had no such qualms about hers. Was it so strange she might be the teensiest bit upset that a man she'd made love to was capable of the very violence that had given her nightmares for most of her life?

But goddamn it, she would not cry. She'd done enough of that to last ten lifetimes. Didn't help. Never had.

She drew herself up. Lifted her chin. "Maybe I'd prefer to be *Marc's* wife," she responded coolly.

Kick flinched. Like she'd slapped him. He gave her a death-ray glare and for one thunderous second she thought he might strike back. But his hand didn't even twitch. Instead, his voice became dangerously soft. "You want to share Lafayette's blanket tonight, fine."

With that, he turned on a heel, held his rifle above his head surrender-style, and strode toward the clutch of village men, oblivious to the guns suddenly whipping around to point at him.

"*Ah, 'tite fille.*" Marc sighed, startling her from her dismay. "*Dans in coup de colere, cet homme.*"

"Excuse me?"

"Hope you don't mind if I step out from the middle of it," he said, shook his head, and followed Kick, his good hand raised in the air.

And once again—what a shock—she was left standing apart, all by herself.

RAINIE was very proud of herself. She didn't lose it. She didn't burst into tears. Didn't stamp her feet. Didn't have a panic attack, or go running after her two "protectors." Didn't even curse. Aloud, anyway.

All she did was snap her mouth closed, turn oh-so-calmly, and walk toward a grove of palm trees at the far edge of the pathetic clutch of mud huts passing itself off as civilization. God, was she tired. So damn tired.

"Rainie?" Marc called after her. "Where you goin', *'tite*?"

She toodled her fingers over her shoulder and kept walking.

"Rainie!" This time it was Kick yelling. "Get the hell back here, woman!"

Ah, well. So much for not cursing.

"Fuck you," she yelled back.

God, that felt good on so many levels.

She'd already picked out a big patch of shade with her name on it. Let the dickhead surrender, or trade for camels, or get himself tortured, or commiserate with the murderous village men on the maddening irrationality of women. Whatever the hell floated his boat.

She was getting some sleep. If anyone wanted to shoot her over that, let them. She was so far beyond caring it wasn't funny.

Sinking down in the shade of a thick palm frond, she closed her eyes gratefully. The warm sand welcomed and embraced her into its grainy arms; a hot breeze stroked her cheek and kissed the sweat from her brow. She let out a long, shuddering sigh. And as she willed herself into an exhausted sleep, to her surprise an odd sort of peace stole over her.

Peace.

Spitting mad, five thousand miles from home in the middle of a savage foreign desert, surrounded by gun-toting natives, chased by terrorists, protected by men who were probably even more dangerous than the ones chasing them, and on top of it all, actually falling for one of the macho jerks. Talk about insanity.

And yet, there it was. For the first time in a long, long while, she didn't feel like she was teetering on the verge of terror, or balancing on the edge of blind panic.

Wow.

If that didn't beat all.

KICK was having a hard time concentrating on what the village sheikh was saying. He and Lafayette were sitting cross-legged on the ground facing the stern old bugger. The side of the old man's face was crusted with blood—the first victim of the tangos' brutality. The other village men sat around them in a circle, some holding rifles that had probably been around since Chinese Gordon marched through on his way to Khartoum. Lafayette looked like he might fall over any second.

Kick was red-hot furious, worried as hell, hurting like the dickens, and running on fumes. He was sure the only reason the two of them hadn't been shot on sight, despite the help he'd given them picking off the bads, was that the villagers were too stunned by the crazy woman sleeping under a palm tree as though she didn't have a care in the world.

Well, except for him. She'd taken great care to shine *him* on. That had been patently obvious even to the villagers. The women peeking out from behind the houses had actually giggled at him when he'd gotten the bird from Rainie. *Giggled.*

Females! Pure trouble from beginning to end. Why did he never *listen* to himself?

Jesus, the maddening woman must have ice in her veins to lie down for a snooze while he and Lafayette were being held at gunpoint.

Or maybe she was just fall-down, done-in tired. Like he was. When was the last time he'd slept? Except for a few stolen minutes on the plane . . . hell, not since he'd been unconscious detoxing. If he could just get some sleep, maybe the constant buzzing in his body would calm down, his stomach would settle, the cramps would stop, the never-ending reminders of the physical need would go away.

If only he could—

Suddenly, he realized the villagers were glowering at him. Getting agitated. Lafayette gave him an owlish look.

"Sorry," he told the sheikh in respectful Arabic. "I didn't understand. Could you repeat that?"

The old man looked annoyed. And very suspicious. "Why are you here? What do you want?"

Beyond the circle, the broken bodies of the tangos were being loaded into the backs of the Jeeps.

"Where are you taking them?" Kick asked instead of answering the question.

"Far away," the old sheikh said. "So the others won't come back for revenge. Give me one good reason we shouldn't add your bodies to theirs."

Several men shouted in agreement. Rifles rattled threateningly.

Kick cleared his throat, doing his best to look small and harmless. And not shake. *Yeah, sure.* "Because I helped you, and you are honorable men. My friend and I wish only to buy water and food."

"You are the American spies from the plane!" he accused loudly. He pointed at the dead. "The ones they were looking for."

Kick shook his head. "Not spies. We are headed for the refugee camp on the Nile. I'm sorry your village was made to suffer. I assure you—"

"Who is the woman?" the sheikh interrupted with furrowed brow.

Kick pulled in a deep breath and let it out slowly, darting a glance at Lafayette. He'd realized a while back that the STORM agent spoke Arabic and understood every word of the exchange, though he hadn't opened his mouth.

"She is a nurse."

At his prevarication, the Cajun's brow flicked up. A challenge?

No fucking way was he letting Lafayette touch her. She was *his.* "She is also my wife," Kick said returning the look.

The sheikh digested that for a moment, glancing from him to Rainie and back again. "She is willful. She does not obey her husband."

"The temper of a camel," he agreed with enough honest chagrin to raise a rumble of laughter among the men. The old man's lips finally curved in acknowledgment of a universal male dilemma.

Kick's shoulders notched down just a tad. *Whatever.* He so did not feel like bonding. He just wanted to get the hell out of there. Get Rainie to the DFP camp and safety. Christ, when she'd stalked off like that he'd nearly had a stroke, terrified some trigger-happy villager would stop her with a bullet in the back.

What was *wrong* with her?

Other than thinking he was some kind of homicidal monster, of course. Which, oh, yeah. He was.

"So you wish to buy water and food?" the sheikh asked, finally motioning his men to lower their weapons, and for the women to bring the trays of tea they'd already prepared.

"*In shah allah*," Kick said, putting on his best poker face. "And God willing, I'd also like one of those Jeeps."

SOMEONE was shaking her. *Again.*

"Go away," Rainie groused, groped for the blanket, and ended up with a handful of sand. *Crap.*

A jet of warm, mint-scented breath hit her in the face. "We have to go." Kick. He sounded irritated.

He wasn't the only one. "Be my guest."

There was a pause, then, "All right. Have a nice walk home. Or maybe the sheikh will take you for his third wife." The grinding sound of boots scrunched in sand. "Though I doubt it," he added in a muttered growl.

"I heard that."

She pried her eyelids open and watched Kick's straight back and stiff shoulders march away. He'd taken off his cammie jacket so his ripped muscles were clearly visible under his formfitting khaki T-shirt. How could someone so bad and so damn infuriating look so ridiculously good to her?

Sunstroke maybe.

She got up and trailed after him. She was *so* not wanting to— *Whoa.*

He hopped into a Jeep. Marc had already collapsed in the passenger seat. They had a ride? Her feet practically jumped for joy. Her mind started to panic.

"If you're coming with us, get in," Kick ordered her gruffly.

In.

The Jeep.

Her mind and her feet screamed at her to run—in opposite directions.

"Preferably sometime *this century*."

She told her mind to go to hell.

Gingerly, she approached the open-topped vehicle, and with her heart pounding, touched its ancient fender. A big clump of dirt and rust fell off, landing at her feet. She jumped and let out a squeak.

"You going to be okay?" Kick asked, bringing the engine to life.

"Yes," she said confidently, far more to convince herself than him. She tamed her careening heartbeat. She would be okay if it killed her.

No deep breaths necessary.

He swung his door open and leaned forward so she could squeeze past to the hard, narrow bench that laughingly called itself a backseat. It was filthy. It was cramped. It stunk like dead goat.

But it beat the hell out of walking.

And . . . the most amazing thing happened. When Kick slammed the door, ground the thing into gear, and the wheels lurched forward, panic *didn't* swamp over her.

"Here," he said, holding up the GPS unit she'd found in the pack last night. "Make yourself useful."

She grabbed the instrument and the back of the driver's seat, and hung on to both as they jounced between the mud huts, then burst out into the rocky desert beyond.

"I don't know how to work it."

"I need a navigator. Learn."

They practically flew across the landscape, which suddenly didn't seem barren at all. The dunes and hills were beautiful, the few plants that clung to the dry ground exotic and inspiring. The sky was brilliant blue overhead. Wind whipped through her hair. Even the oppressive heat didn't seem so bad.

Kick's eyes met hers in the cracked rearview mirror, holding a distinct challenge. He didn't think she could do it. *Ha. As if.* She worked every day with instruments a hundred times more complicated than following a stupid arrow across a bunch of squiggly lines. This would be a piece of cake.

"Okay," she said.

She smiled. He didn't smile back. But he did manage to look relieved as he clipped out the instructions.

Fine. Let him be surly. She wanted to laugh out loud.

For the first time since she was twelve years old she was not terrified of being in a moving vehicle. *And* she was in charge of finding their way through the wilderness. It was a pure miracle.

Almost made her wonder what other irrational fears she might be able to conquer, if given the chance.

Like maybe her fear of falling in love.

She met his eyes again and they narrowed. Almost as if he could read her thoughts, and didn't care for what he was reading. She raised her chin. *Dream on, baby.* If she ever fell in love, it sure as hell wouldn't be with a man like Kick Jackson. Dangerous, uncivilized. Able to do things without a second thought that went against everything she believed.

Too bad he was also able to do things to *her* that made dangerous and uncivilized feel alarmingly close to virtues.

Like the caveman way he swept her off her feet and took control of her. The heart-pounding thrill of his body sliding between her thighs. The sweet, savage thrust of his arousal as it scythed deep into her.

Damn.

Was falling in lust the same as falling in love?

No. No way.

Love was so much more than physical attraction and sex. It was respect and admiration and trust and security and . . .

God. Everything she was feeling about Kick.

But how could she possibly feel *any* of those things for a man who so willingly condoned violence, who so easily killed? Who, if she allowed herself to read all the ample clues he'd thrown at her, had no doubt killed a lot more than this once?

Impossible. She simply couldn't know that about him and still feel respect and admiration, let alone trust the man.

And yet . . . she did.

Rainie let out a long sigh.

Jesus. How scary was *that*.

FOURTEEN

GINA couldn't believe Rainie was dead.

No. She *didn't* believe it.

Not a chance. Gregg van Halen was handing her a big fat load of CIA BS, and that was the God's honest truth. It had to be.

At home in her Upper East Side brownstone, Gina had watched CNN the whole night, crying her eyes out and waiting for some mention of the terrible incident that had claimed her best friend's life.

Nothing had appeared.

That's when she'd started getting suspicious. *Hello?* Government agents and innocent woman killed in a fiery plane crash? When was the last time the news media had missed such a juicy, sensational story?

So as dawn slipped over the city, she searched the Internet while tuning in to every TV network and cable newscast she could find, including the BBC World News. Still nothing.

No plane crash anywhere in the country.

No plane crash at *all*. In the whole damn world.

Something just wasn't right. No, sir.

She debated calling CNN in Atlanta and asking outright if

they were sitting on the story due to government pressure. That was possible. After all, they were dealing with the mother of all Big Brothers, the C-freaking-IA.

But before she had a chance to pick up the phone, it rang.

She pounced on the receiver. "Hello?"

"How are you holding up?"

Van Halen. Anger *whooshed* through her. The nerve of the man to call her sounding all concerned, as if he were actually a friend!

"How do you *think* I'm holding up, being fed a pack of lies?" she snapped.

He was silent for a moment. "What lies are you referring to, Gina?"

Oh, right. Mr. Innocent. "There was *no* plane crash. Anywhere. What have you bastards done with Rainie?"

More silence, then he said, "I have a satellite photo showing the wreckage, if you'd like to see it." At his calm assertion her heart squeezed painfully. "We also have reason to believe there may have been a survivor," he added.

Hope swelled anew. "Rainie?"

"No way of knowing. Whoever it is, they're hiding well out of sight."

"Where?" she demanded.

"Can't tell you that." The voice brooked no argument.

She battled back her anger. "I want to see that photo." Maybe the surroundings would give her a clue as to where this alleged crash had happened. Then at least she'd know where to start her search.

"All right," he said. "Stay where you are. I'll be there in a few minutes."

She glanced at the clock. "I have to be at work in—"

"You've been up all night. You're tired. Call in sick."

Then there was a click. He'd hung up.

My God. How had he known she'd been up all night? She glanced uneasily at the drapes she hadn't bothered closing last night. Had he been watching her the whole time?

In which case the *last* thing she should do was call in sick. What she should do was get the hell out of there before he—

There was a loud knock on the door.

Hell. A few *minutes*? That had been more like *seconds*. He must have been calling from the sidewalk out front.

"Gina, it's me. Open up."

His voice sounded so neutral. So harmless. So . . . deep and reassuring. *More lies.* Lies, lies, lies. This guy was harmless like a yawning cobra.

He knocked again. "Gina!"

Should she run? She probably would have, but she really needed to see that satellite photo.

She unlocked the two dead bolts, slid off the heavy chain, and swung open her door. He stood there on the landing in the early-morning light, bigger than life and just as serious. Today, under the black leather jacket, he was wearing urban cammie BDUs and black combat boots. Trying to blend into the surrounding buildings? His silver aviator shades hung casually from the collar of a snug black T-shirt. She could see the imprint of his compact male nipples poking provocatively at the fabric.

Good grief, what had made her notice *that*?

"I thought you might have bolted out the back way," he said, regarding her with an expression she couldn't decipher.

"Don't be absurd. Come in."

Too late she remembered she hadn't gotten dressed yet.

He was perusing the crop-top and plaid boxers she used as pajamas, his eyes lingering on *her* nipples . . . and her bare legs. His gaze eased back up again and met hers. Damn, she must be a sight, her eyes puffy and face blotchy from hours of crying, and not a speck of makeup on.

Not that it mattered. She didn't care one bit if she looked like death warmed—

"I'm sorry about your friend," he said, moving past her into the foyer. Setting down his motorcycle helmet on the hall table. "I really am." Without comment, he extended an eight-by-ten black-and-white aerial photo to her.

"I still don't believe it," she countered stubbornly. Maybe if she refused to believe it, it wouldn't be true.

She took the photo and walked into the dining room, setting it on the table to examine under the light of the chandelier. Behind her, she heard the front door close, the chain slide back on, and the dead bolts click home.

"I'm afraid there's no doubt," he said, coming into the dining room. "There were witnesses to her going onboard that plane."

She shot him a look, but his face was as impassive as ever. Did the man never crack? Or let his thoughts and feelings slip past that unreadable façade?

Meanwhile . . . he had locked himself in with her.

She was proud of her brownstone. She had rehabbed the three-level town house as a fixer-upper, doing a lot of the work herself. It was beautiful. But not particularly large. As in, nowhere to hide. Not from a man like him, a trained hunter of human prey. Not if he was determined to—

To what?

Don't be ridiculous, she admonished herself silently. He was *not* out to get her. That was just paranoid thinking.

Or was it *wishful* thinking?

Hell, no!

Suddenly he was there, standing next to her. His arm brushed hers. When had he taken off his jacket? She swallowed and stayed very still.

He handed her a magnifying glass. "Here. It's easier to see with this."

Oh, Jesus. She let out a breath. What was *wrong* with her?

"Thanks," she said unsteadily, taming her thundering heart. She gave herself a mental shake and bent over the photo, peering through the glass.

He brushed closer, pointing. "See the debris, here? And here?"

Her throat closed at what she was seeing. A small plane scattered in bits on the ground in a desolate landscape.

"Dear God."

So it was true. But she still didn't understand how a woman who was even afraid to ride in a car would have willingly flown in an airplane, especially a small one like this. Rainie had just *met* that dangerous-looking man. Gina should have stopped her from leaving the speed dating with that character. This was all her fault. If Rainie had really been on the plane.

"Why would she have gone with him?" she whispered. "To this place? On an *airplane*?"

"As a favor," van Halen said. "She was helping him get clean. Apparently he was addicted to some kind of pain medication and going through withdrawal. She wasn't supposed to be on that flight, but he started having symptoms and she went with him just in case they got worse."

Gina took a shuddering breath. Yeah, that sounded like Rainie. Always the first to volunteer to help someone in need. Still . . . *this* didn't make sense. This *place*. Gina studied the landscape on the photo. Some kind of harsh desert. It looked like a different planet. Even if they survived the crash, how could anyone live for more than a day in that environment?

"What makes you think there are survivors?" she asked, her optimism waning.

"Maybe just one." His body pressed against her side and he grasped her hand, guiding the magnifying glass past a section of burned, crumpled fuselage with 'Ex' . . . something . . . painted on it, and over to a jumble of what appeared to be giant rocks. "Here. See that?"

"It looks like . . . a sheet or something flapping in the wind."

"A parachute. And see here." He pointed to an odd-shaped shadow.

"What is that?"

"The better question would be *who is it?* Unfortunately, we don't know which of the team it is. Or Ms. Martin."

Gina sucked in a shaky breath as she straightened and looked up into his eyes. "But you'll send someone, won't you? To rescue that person."

"Trust me. If your friend is still alive, we'll get her."

Gina closed her eyes against the stinging in them. Trust him?

Did she have a choice?

Gently, he pulled her against his chest. "*Shhh.* It's okay."

Ohgod. No, it *wasn't* okay. This whole thing was crazy. Rainie gone. A man she barely knew and couldn't possibly trust holding her like it was the most natural thing in the world. This insane attraction she was feeling for him, an inscrutable stranger, despite her grief. Or maybe because of it. . . .

Life was always more precious when something like this showed you how very fragile this world was. Made you want to feel, *really feel*, that you were still alive.

Would it be a mistake to trust him? Or would it be safe to let him comfort her with his tall, powerful frame; envelope her in his strong, persuasive arms?

Safe? Hardly. But Lord, it felt good.

The thing about younger men, they were enthusiastic. But they didn't know how to simply stand still and let a woman's feelings overwhelm her.

Who'd have thought this stoic, emotionless man would know how to do that so damn well?

Except . . . his heart was beating nearly as fast as hers. . . .

She grew acutely aware of his body pressed tight against her, curve to hollow, hard to soft. And his smell. Masculine, spicy. Tempting. God, she loved the way he smelled.

His fingers tunneled into her hair and he urged her head against his shoulder. She tried to let herself relax into his embrace. But she just couldn't.

Relax? She was far too aware of him physically. Of her reckless attraction to him.

His hand glided comfortingly down her back and up again as he murmured soothing words.

She'd long ago stopped being shy of wanting sex. Gina loved getting naked with a man. She knew marriage was most likely not in her future, but why forgo the best parts of life just because you didn't have a steady partner?

But this, this was different. This wasn't some innocuous intern or research fellow carefully selected to spend a few nights of harmless mutual pleasure with. No, there was something else going on here with Gregg van Halen, and throwing sex into the mix would complicate things wildly.

But Lord, she didn't know what to do with her hands.

Everywhere she touched him, he felt warm and solid and God so incredibly enticing. Did she dare put her arms around him? Or would he misinterpret . . .

Down and up went his soothing hand. Down and up. Then it slid under her top. His fingers caressed her bare skin.

Her eyes flew open. She tried to pull away. He didn't let her.

"*Shhh*. It's okay." He held her firmly against his unyielding, muscular body as his hand crept upward.

Oh, God. She clutched at his T-shirt. *Was* it okay? Was this really what she wanted?

Such a bad idea. Terrible idea. The worst—

He turned and backed her up against the dining table. His stance spread just wide enough that her legs were caught between his, her bare feet captured between his boots, her hips cradled against his. He was aroused. *Very* aroused. Hard and thick and long beneath his BDUs.

Ohgod, ohgod, oh, God help her.

Because she was aroused, too.

His hand slowly smoothed up her bare back, over her ribs, around to her breast. And he touched her there.

She gasped, her whole body reacting with a deep shiver of unwilling pleasure.

"*Shhh*," he murmured in her ear, his hot breath whispering over her cheek. "It's okay."

His hand covered her breast and squeezed. She whimpered, unable to move. Unable to pull away. What was he doing? What was *she* doing letting him?

His other fingers moved up and tightened in her hair, grasping the strands and winding them around his palm so she was forced to look up at his face. His eyes were on fire, like blue opals, burning with a million colors and the heat of hell.

"Gregg—"

"*Shhh*. It's okay. Let it happen."

His thumb and fingers raked over her breast and found her nipple. He pinched it, and she cried out. Then he rolled it between his thumb and forefinger, hard, and she cried out again in a storm of pleasure-pain. The fire in his eyes jumped and burned hotter still.

Then his mouth covered hers and she forgot completely why this was such a terrible idea.

His tongue was supple, ruthless, demanding. He tasted of coffee and barely leashed desire, and she could no more stop him than she could a ravaging virus that had infected her, making her weak and pliable in his hands.

She didn't *want* to stop him.

God, no.

She felt her boxers slide off her hips and hit the floor. He lifted her as though she weighed nothing, and kicked the boxers away, then slid her erotically back down the front of his body with a guttural moan.

"Undo my pants," he ordered, seeking her mouth again. "I want to be inside you."

Excitement zinged through her like an electric shock. She reached for his web belt, her fingers shaking so hard the buckle jingled crazily as she unfastened it. Finally she got it loose and went for the zipper, and found . . . buttons.

"Hurry," he urged roughly.

She fumbled while he kissed her senseless. She popped one, then the next. He pushed her hand aside, impatient. Whipped open his fly. And he sprang free.

Huge. Thick. *Hungry.*

He lifted her onto the edge of the table, caught her knees, and wrenched them apart.

Pinioning her with his gaze, he fisted his cock and fit it to her center. She was trembling, slick and hot with need. *God, she wanted him.* The tip breached her.

"Say it," he growled. "Say what you want."

"You know what I want," she moaned, arching toward him. Wanting him so bad she couldn't wait one second more.

"Say it."

"Fuck me," she pleaded. "Fuck me hard and fast."

With a grunt, he grabbed her hair and held her immobile. Then rammed into her. Deep and sure, filling her like nothing ever had before. *So damn good.*

She cried out. And he groaned.

Then he stopped dead. He stared at her with those fiery devil's eyes. And kept staring, and staring. Until she realized why.

She was a doctor. A medical researcher who dealt with deadly diseases every day.

And she'd forgotten all about protection.

She sucked down a breath. "Oh, sweet God."

He didn't look particularly concerned. In fact, he looked . . . smug, his unsheathed member buried deep within her. She blinked. Had he done it on purpose?

He moved slowly, grinding deeper still. In total control.

She, on the other hand, was near panic.

"Please," she whispered with a shiver. "Don't do this."

He chose that moment to smile. Just a slight curve of his sculpted lips. "Trust me," he said, his voice gravelly low.

She begged with her eyes. "I can't. I'm too vulnerable."

The curve deepened. "Yes," he agreed. "That's what makes it so exciting." He leaned in and kissed her, slow and deep, languid and thorough, until the panic subsided, until she was trembling and boneless and completely empty of her own will. Then he whispered again, "Trust me."

She tried to shake her head as he slowly drew his cock out, almost all the way, then thrust back in to the hilt. Her body clenched in impossible pleasure. She moaned, electric with need, torn between sense and sensation.

A noise of satisfaction rumbled in his chest. "Lie back," he ordered, pulling her hair so she had no choice but to follow his command and lower her bare back onto the cool wood of the table. "Grab the edge," he told her, and she did that, raising her arms above her head to reach.

His large hands wrapped around her thighs and splayed her even wider. He ground into her, making her cry out at the sharp spurt of pleasure.

He seemed to know exactly what to do to light her body on fire. To empty her mind of everything but him, and what he was doing to her. He drew out, thrust in, drew himself out again. Thrust. Over and over until she was groaning and panting, shaking like an autumn leaf with want for him.

Then he pulled out all the way.

She gave a cry of protest. But he dropped to his knees and his mouth was on her. She moaned and thrashed, helpless, as his tongue and teeth played over her, circling, probing, teasing. Making her frantic, reaching, reaching . . .

Climax ripped through her, bowing her back and tearing a scream from her throat. She came harder than she ever had before, convulsing, shuddering, and gasping as he drew the incredible sensation out forever.

Oh, sweet heavenly God.

As she struggled to come back to earth she felt him slide her body farther back on the table. And suddenly he was on top of her. Driving into her. This time with a condom. His shirt was off and they were skin to skin. Crisp hair scraped against her breasts. Oh, sweet Lord, he felt so good.

"Jesus, woman," he ground out, and held her hips in an iron grip.

He rode her hard—hard and rough, just as she liked it. She wrapped herself around him and clung. She'd be bruised and battered. She didn't care. His back would be scored by her nails. He didn't care, either. It was feral, out of control. She came twice more to the tune of his guttural whispered obscenities in her ear. And then he gave three final, feral thrusts, and roared out his orgasm, lifting her off the table with the crushing force of his grip.

She was utterly filled, and utterly drained. And so terrified of what had just happened between them that she started to shake and shake, and suddenly felt like bursting into tears.

Because it wasn't supposed to be like this. Not in these circumstances. Not with this man.

Definitely not with this man.

And all she could think, all she could feel, was . . .

Dear God, what have I done?

KICK would never get used to the abject poverty, the rank filth, and the complete hopelessness that pervaded refugee camps the world over. Even well-run ones like the Doctors for Peace camp, which, as the Jeep approached the Nile Valley, oozed across the eastern horizon like a pus-filled open sore.

Already he could smell it, even miles away, the stench of human refuse and garbage. His stomach roiled.

Mile upon mile of ragged olive drab tents littered the brown desert, flapping in the hot breeze, crowding the edge of the green cultivation zone. In the diffuse orange light of the setting sun, he could see thousands of homeless people milling about, from dozens of different tribes and cultures. All Sudanese. All victims of the thirty years of civil strife their country had suffered through, with no real end in sight.

Kick took a deep breath while it was still the relatively clean air of the open desert, and flexed his stiff fingers on the steering wheel. The drive had taken most of the afternoon and he'd been worried they wouldn't make it before dark. But they'd squeaked it, and the tension rolled off him in waves now that they'd finally made it safely. Relief was in sight.

Next to him, Lafayette's eyes fluttered open for a few seconds, then drooped closed again. The man was in crap shape, going in and out of consciousness for the past three hours. Kick'd had to choose, drive slowly and spare the man's ribs the jarring punishment, or damn the ribs and drive quickly, maybe saving his arm. Gangrene was a bitch once it set in.

Throwing the STORM agent a worried glance, he slowed the Jeep to avoid hitting a scatter of skeletal refugees shuffling barefoot along the road carrying glassy-eyed children and ragged belongings on their backs.

"My God," he heard Rainie breathe from the backseat.

"Depressing, isn't it?" he said softly.

"Who are these people? Where did they all come from?"

He glanced at her in the rearview. Her eyes were already filled with heartbreak and they hadn't even gotten to the camp yet.

"Refugees from the southern wars," he said evenly, "refugees from the reign of rape and terror in Darfur, refugees from the escalating fundamentalist pogroms in towns all up and down the Nile. People starving from the drought, people dying of malaria, yellow fever, and AIDS. Name the reason for suffering, the Sudan has it."

"Merciful God," she whispered.

Kick wasn't so sure.

He'd joined the military in order to escape the oppression of his own life. At seventeen, he'd been severely damaged goods, with few options. He'd wisely grabbed the one choice open to him where he could vent the most rage. The Marines. Channeling that rage had made him good at his job. Very good. Cold. Ruthless. Without pity. So good the CIA had recruited him for its nonofficial cover commando operation, Zero Unit, and sent him to countries like this, to silently and invisibly clean up the worst filth imaginable. Hell, he'd thought his own early years had been bad until he'd seen what the children in these camps had to live through. His life had been a fucking picnic by comparison.

And that had filled him with even more rage.

Why should *anyone* in the world have to live this way? What kind of a God would let that happen? Merciful? *Not.*

The DFP hospital compound and staff quarters were separate from the rest of the camp, surrounded by a high chain-link fence with razor wire on top and two armed UN guards at the gate. The DFP didn't believe in weapons, but after several violent robberies, the Red Cross had insisted medical supplies and personnel be guarded 24/7 or they would no longer send aid shipments. It was one of the few battles Nathan Daneby had lost.

As Kick pulled the Jeep up to the front gate, he thought again about Forsythe's covert photos of Nate accepting something—money?—from abu Bakr's right-hand man. And suddenly Nate's vehement opposition to armed guards took on a new, ugly meaning.

Fuck. Was he selling government secrets *and* the medicines sent to help these people? Kick let out the clutch so fast the Jeep stalled.

The engine backfired and the guards came running, guns drawn.

No time to think about Nathan Daneby now.

"Someone get a doctor!" he shouted at them, bringing his mind back to more immediate worries. "I've got a dying man here!"

FIFTEEN

EVERYTHING happened at once. The guards started shouting, and at the commotion someone popped his head out of a prefab Quonset hut a bit farther inside the compound. The guy disappeared for a second, then came out running toward the Jeep along with two others and carrying a stretcher. All Westerners. One wore a long white lab coat.

Kick closed his eyes briefly and allowed himself a moment of profound relief. They'd made it. *Alive.* Marc would get medical help now; Rainie would be safe. Kick could finally grab some desperately needed sleep.

And then get on with his mission.

He leaned his head against the seat back and let the people do their jobs, getting Lafayette onto the stretcher and carting him off to a building Kick assumed was the hospital. Rainie took charge and ran with them, sounding like an episode of some TV hospital show as she gave them the rundown on Marc's condition. She was in her element, that was clear.

"*Tutto bene?*" someone asked Kick. "You okay?"

He opened his eyes and saw one of the UN guards standing by the Jeep, peering worriedly at him. The blue uniform made the soldier look older, but the kid couldn't have been much out of high school. Jesus, where did they get these guys? Didn't they have anything better to do with their lives? Or maybe this kid's childhood had been just as fucked-up as Kick's.

"Sure. I'm fine. Just beat. Tired." Kick smiled wearily at him. "Any chance of finding a bed and shower in this joint?"

The kid grinned. "*Sì, sì!*" He waved a hand at a small cluster of vehicles. "You park Jeep and give passports. Then we find you sleep."

Passports. Yeah, that could be a problem.

How to explain their presence in the country, in dire straits and without proper travel documents? *Shit.* Kick drove the Jeep over to the parking area and slid out. This should be good.

He staggered on his cramped leg and the guard grabbed his arm. "You are hurt. You should go hospital, too."

"Nah." Kick stretched out his leg with a grimace and wiped the sweat with his sleeve. "Old football injury. I'm all right."

The guard shrugged in that European way, clearly doubting him. "Okay. You come, we find bed. Will lady sleep, too? Or maybe she stay with husband in hospital?"

"Not her husband. Miss Martin is with me," Kick clarified before thinking.

"Ah, *scusa*! She *your* woman. Very pretty." The guard's eyes danced as he led Kick toward the Quonset hut the others had emerged from. The dusty windows mirrored a light show of deep reds and yellows from the last vestiges of the setting sun. "I am Eduardo, by the way. From Italia."

Kick shook his hand as they walked. "Kick Jackson." He thought about where he might say he was from, but came up empty. The longest he'd ever stayed in one place after escaping home at age fourteen was being in the hospital last year, and the months hiding out afterward. *What the hell.* "Recently of New York City," he said.

As he'd figured, the magical name triggered an immediate outpouring of exclamations and explanations of distant relatives and hopes to visit by the young Italian.

"Yes, it's a great city," Kick agreed. "Listen, about—"

But they'd reached the building and Eduardo flung open

the metal door and said to him in a hushed voice, "Very lucky today. You meet important boss to take care of you." He grinned and ushered Kick inside.

The hut had been partitioned into two rooms, and the outside door opened onto a dingy office space filled with desks, chairs, bookshelves, and filing cabinets. A lone man sat at a desk squeezed into the far corner, his head bent over a stack of files.

"*Signore dottore*," Eduardo addressed him respectfully. "We have visitors. Americans."

The doctor looked up. And Kick froze where he stood.

Now, wasn't that convenient?

The man was Nathan Daneby.

ONCE again his redheaded Angel eluded him.

The night had dragged on interminably and the maggot-spiced supper they'd given him that tasted like fermented dog shit made multiple reappearances on his taste buds. His jaw throbbed like a son of a bitch.

With a groan, he opened his eyes. Everything around him was black, black, black.

For a second he panicked. *Please, God, no.* Don't let him have lost what little sight he'd regained over the past few days. Please don't let that be gone, his only hope, along with everything else he'd lost. That would be too cruel.

Taking a fortifying breath, he lifted his hand in front of his face and peered closely at it.

And almost wept. *Thank you, Jesus.* There it was, a faint blob of grey, and five fingers moving in the blackness.

He could still see. A little. It was just night.

He squeezed his eyes shut, refusing to allow the threatening tears to break loose. *Jesus, what a fucking pansy crybaby.*

He shuddered out a breath and slowly made himself sit up on his pallet. He desperately needed to use the bucket. He must have been out cold all afternoon. Thank God the dysentery hadn't left him a stinking mess before he awoke. That was always fun, to endure the added ordeal of the stench and embarrassment along with the disgusted torment of his asshole guards.

Crawling inch by inch to the corner of the room, he took care of his needs as best he could. Sweating and shaking, Mother of God, he wanted nothing more than to collapse back on his pallet when he was finally done.

Instead he forced himself up on his treacherously wobbly hands and knees and crawled to the center of the room. The rough, gravelly dirt of the floor scraped off another layer of bruised and battered skin, but he barely felt it. He took another deep breath. Lowered himself into a push-up. And began counting.

"One-thousand-one," he said aloud between gritted teeth as he raised himself up again.

And did another.

"One-thousand-two," he panted out, already exhausted.

He wanted to quit. Fuck, he'd sell his own mother to the devil to be able to quit and give up now.

But he didn't. Not when the pain screamed through his arms and legs like lethal poison. Not when rockets' red glare burst behind his burning eyelids.

Not until he counted to twenty-eight.

And after he collapsed onto the hard, unyielding ground, he managed a smile through the buzzing haze of fatigue and watery eyes.

Eight more than last time.

Hoo-yah.

He'd escape this fucking dung heap yet.

Now if he could only remember who he was, and where he should go.

NATHAN *Daneby!*

Kick was having a real hard time controlling his roiling emotions.

The last person he'd expected to find in this part of the country was Nate. Last he'd heard he was down south, setting up several new camps. Kick was unprepared to face him. And he hated being unprepared. For anything.

"Christ, Kick! What the hell are you doing in the Sudan?" Grinning, Nate held up a palm as he sprang to his feet. "No, don't tell me. Because then you'd have to kill me. But damn, am I glad to see you!"

Somehow Kick produced a smile. After all, he'd been with ZU. He had a long history of shutting down his emotions, disguising his suspicions. Lying like a dog.

But never before with this man. God, it hurt.

Especially since there was no way he could confront him. Not with his mission in the balance. If Nate was involved with terrorists, with abu Bakr, and found out about Kick's mission, he'd betray him again without blinking.

No, their confrontation would have to wait. But not bursting out with accusations was the hardest thing Kick had ever had to do.

He made a quick decision. "Haven't you heard?" he said. "I'm no longer with the Company. I'm guiding tours now."

Nate's face fell in obvious shock. "You're shitting me."

Kick gave a wry smile, doing his best not to bare his teeth. Slapped his bum leg. "Not much use for me in this condition. Besides, lots of money in specialty tours these days. Seems my particular knowledge of out-of-the-way places is in big demand."

Nate seemed nonplussed. Almost like he was upset. "Sure. Yeah, I suppose it would be. Although, somehow I can't . . . Hell, I never thought I'd live to see the day." He shook it off and opened his arms. "Anyway, it's great to see you, buddy."

He returned his friend's—former friend's?—quick hug and masculine back-pounding. "Likewise. It's been a while."

"You ain't kidding. Haven't seen you since . . ." Nate cringed visibly and swept his gaze over Kick from head to toe, this time more carefully. Was that true regret in his eyes, or only regret that Kick wasn't dead like the others on his team in Afghanistan? "Anyway. Glad to see you're back on your feet, man. We've got a lot to talk about."

He sounded so fucking sincere. If Nate was the traitor, he definitely had a set of big brass ones. Which would make sense. If underneath it all, Saint Nathan really was just another greedy bastard, he'd played his role of world savior to perfection.

"Thanks," Kick said stiffly, inner conflict and confusion desperately trying to break free in his mind and heart.

"Can't say I'm sorry you've changed employers. You know I never approved of your former occupation."

"Yup." Which only added fuel to Kick's mental fire, depressing him even more.

He so wanted his friend to be innocent. And after all, why should he trust a thing Jason Forsythe said? Or anyone else at Zero Unit, or the whole damned CIA for that matter? Kick was convinced someone in the government was a traitor working for al Sayika. Hell, maybe *Forsythe* was the traitor—no, wait, he was dead; that would be a clue to his innocence. Forsythe's boss, then, or someone working with him. But then, how to explain that photo of Nate . . .

"I was lucky," he forced himself to say conversationally. "It was touch and go for a while whether I'd keep the leg, let alone the job. Still limping a bit. But I'll take it over the alternative." He used the excuse to limp over to a chair and sit down.

"Jesus, of course. Sit. What am I thinking? Are you hungry? Thirsty?"

"All of the above," Kick admitted, rubbing a hand through his gritty hair. "And I could use about a week's worth of sleep. But first, could you find out for me how Lafayette is doing? He was pretty bad off."

Anything to get Nate out of the room for a few minutes so Kick could regain his equilibrium. Stop the shakes and armor himself against the stinging hurt and suspicion, so he could pull off this distasteful charade.

"Sure." For a second Nate looked uncertain, as though he detected the undercurrent of fury and betrayal in Kick's jerky movements and avoidance of his gaze. "You relax here. I'll just, *um* . . ." He took a couple of steps toward the door. "Kick? Is something wrong? Something I should know about?"

He always had been a perceptive bastard. Kick shook his head, producing another weary smile. "Nope."

Nate nodded somewhat reluctantly. "Well, we should talk. But I guess it'll wait," he said, then went out of the door.

Shit. No fucking kidding.

Shit, shit, shit.

Kick put his elbows on his knees and his head in his hands. He had to get hold of himself. Calm down. Push himself to a place where he could function normally and not want to wrap his hands around the man's throat and squeeze. Demand the truth from him. They'd have a talk, all right. But *after* his mission had been carried out and there was no longer an imminent threat to—

Except, crap. If Nate really was somehow involved with the terrorists, he might even now be warning abu Bakr. Regardless of Kick's cover story, a former CIA operator's sudden appearance in the Sudan would trigger grave suspicions in anyone's mind. A real traitor would definitely be paranoid enough to alert the terrorists to a possible coming attack. And no doubt set up another ambush to forestall it. Kick would be as good as dead.

Fucking A.

When he'd decided the A-stan massacre had been due to an inside traitor, he'd never in a million years suspected it could be Nate. He'd always assumed it was an al Sayika mole, someone inside CIA itself, or Zero Unit, with some secret agenda to push. But Forsythe's photo had been more than damning. Nate had been at the nearby Afghan DFP camp at the time. And he'd taken money from Abbas Tawhid, one of the two top al Sayika leaders and abu Bakr's right-hand man. Kick's mind told him it had to be true. Nate had sold him out, along with his team. How else could that photo be explained?

But his heart still refused to be convinced. Which was the only reason he wouldn't take out his knife tonight, creep into the man's tent, and slit his fucking throat.

Kick wanted revenge in the worst way for the deaths of his men, and especially that of his best friend, Alex Zane. God, he craved revenge with every fiber of his being.

One day he would get it. *Soon.*

But not today.

Today he had to think of his mission. Killing abu Bakr would be the first step to clearing away the worst detritus of his troubled past. Then he'd come back for Nate. Oh, yeah.

He'd find out the truth. Good or bad. And justice would be done.

That was a goddamn promise.

MARC was going to be okay.

Rainie watched from behind a glass partition as two amazing doctors—one from Denmark and one from India—worked miracles on Marc's injuries while a Sudanese nurse stuck him with IV needles and adjusted the oxygen mask over his nose. It was obvious they'd done this before.

Rainie was very relieved she didn't have to help. She was so dead tired she probably would have made mistakes.

"How is he?" someone asked.

She turned to see a handsome man smiling down at her. His face was tan and his eyes sparkled with European charm. His brown hair was stylishly slicked back and he was dressed in khaki shorts, a periwinkle polo shirt, and expensive leather desert boots.

"He's going to make it," she said, smiling back. "Thanks to your brilliant colleagues. I'm assuming you're a doctor, too?"

He made a courtly bow over her hand. "Count Girard Virreau, at your service. And, yes, I am a doctor."

"I'm Lorraine Martin. Rainie. Pleased to meet you." She raised her brows. "A real count? Honest?"

His smile grew wider. "You Americans are so easily impressed. I assure you, being a count in my country is not so noteworthy."

"If you say so. But being here in the Sudan as a volunteer with Doctors for Peace, that *is* impressive." The man looked more like he should be playing tennis in Saint Tropez. It spoke volumes that he'd chosen to be in this dirty, depressing camp, helping people instead.

He inclined his head. "For that I thank you. But now, my dear, you must follow this doctor's orders. I fear you are in grave need of treatment, Mademoiselle Martin."

Her free hand flew to her hair. She made a face. "I must look even worse than I feel. Honestly, I'm just—"

"Starving, thirsty, and in need of a good night's sleep.

Plus, I think a glass or two of fine French wine would not go amiss, *non?*"

Non, indeed. "That does sound wonderful."

He was still holding her hand. He took it now and tucked it into the crook of his elbow. "Excellent. Why don't we go to my—"

Two men came through a door and strode down the hall toward them.

"Ah, there is Signorina Martin," one of them exclaimed. He was young and wore a blue uniform, staying one step behind the other man, who walked tall and sure, like a man in complete authority. That one must be the director of the camp.

The tall man gave her a pleasant once-over before peering through the glass partition in at Marc. "I understand your friend is injured," he said. "Will he be okay?"

"Yes. Thank you," she said with heartfelt gratitude. "I'm certain your doctors saved his life. There was nothing we could do for him out in the desert. I felt so hopeless."

He looked back at her. "In that case I'm glad you got him here in time. Please allow me to introduce myself. I'm Dr. Nathan Daneby." He stuck out his hand.

Her shock was sudden and complete. Too rooted to the spot to react, she opened her mouth but nothing would come out. She just stood there like an idiot. *Oh, jeez.* The *real* Nathan Daneby. This was just as weird as she'd feared. The *Twilight Zone* music danced in her head.

Count Virreau stepped forward with her hand still clutching his arm. "May I present Mademoiselle Lorraine Martin."

That snapped her out of her paralysis. Embarrassed, she dropped the count's arm and grabbed Daneby's outstretched hand. "Dr. Daneby, I am truly thrilled to meet you. I've followed your work for years and am a huge admirer. I had no idea you'd be here. Please pardon my bad manners. I never expected . . ." Her words jumbled on her tongue.

Daneby's lips curved wryly. "Apparently my presence surprised more than you. Your guide practically had a stroke when he saw me."

"My guide?" She blinked. "Oh! You mean Kick." Suddenly heat rushed into her face. He *would* have a stroke, considering how he'd taken advantage of the good doctor's name—while he took advantage of her. "You *know* each other?" she asked incredulously. "For real?"

"Oh, yes. Kick and I go way back. Over the years we've often seemed to end up in the same poor backwaters of civilization. For very different reasons, of course," he added with a bland smile.

"Yes," she said, her mind awhirl. "I would imagine so."

"*Alors*, if you will excuse us," Count Virreau said. "I've just asked Mademoiselle Martin to share a bottle of—"

Suddenly the younger man in uniform interrupted, talking to Virreau in a rapid patois of French and Italian. But she was sure she heard her name mentioned in the mix. What was going on?

The young man stopped speaking and grinned at her. The two older men's eyes met, then swung to her. Virreau looked annoyed. Daneby looked intrigued.

"Ah," Virreau said with a small bow. "I am sorry. I did not realize you are with the other man, this guide."

Her face heated even more. By now she was sure it must be as red as the sunset. "Kick? Yes, well . . . Is that what he said?" She slammed her eyes shut then opened them. "I mean, yeah, we are, *um*, kind of . . ." *Ho-boy.*

The young man bailed her out in his singsong Italian lilt. "I have found a free tent so you both to sleep. Come, I show."

"Thanks Eduardo," Daneby said. "But first we must allow our guests to clean up and have something to eat." He gestured down the hall toward the outside door. "Virreau, I hope you'll contribute that contraband bottle of wine to our impromptu welcome feast. I for one could go for something stronger than mint tea."

KICK was acting even stranger and more tight-lipped than he had since the massacre at the oasis village, which was saying a lot. Rainie didn't know what to make of it. He was still hurting physically from the withdrawal, and no doubt the cravings were eating at his concentration. She knew that. But it was no excuse for avoiding *her*. Which he was most definitely doing.

Okay, maybe he was still smarting from that remark she'd made back in the village about preferring to be Marc's wife. He hadn't said more than two words to her since then, other than answering her many questions about the GPS unit. But that hardly counted. And he had to realize she hadn't actually meant it about Marc. Really, were men's egos so delicate?

She sighed. *Apparently.*

He'd been visibly relieved to hear Marc would make it, but other than with the young guard whose name was Eduardo, Kick responded only in monosyllables to most of the conversation around the dinner table. Afterward, since alcohol was technically illegal in the Sudan, the small group of foreign doctors and staff gathered for discreet drinks in the small hut belonging to the UN guards, which was the most secure from prying eyes. Still, though he never said word one to her, Kick deliberately sat next to Rainie and kept his arm draped proprietarily across the back of her chair the whole time, as he also had at dinner . . . much to Virreau's visible displeasure.

The poor count must not get any action at all in these parts to be so interested in her in her present less-than-glamorous state. Even after a welcome shower, shampoo, and change into clothes borrowed from one of the female doctors, she must look like a real train wreck. Sunburn, no makeup, and no sleep for four days will do that to a girl.

So why would Kick pretend they were an item? Even before the wife remark, he'd made it known he did not want to actually *be* an item with her. Beyond sharing a bed, of course. That, he'd made no secret of. Was he so anxious to get laid again before they parted ways? She really couldn't see any other reason for the sham.

He had also spun some story to account for their presence south of the Egyptian border. Something about an aborted tour to the Cave of the Swimmers on the Egyptian/Libyan/Sudanese frontier, an accidental fall from a cliff by Marc, and getting lost in the desert trying to find help. Thank goodness she'd heard of the famous Saharan cave filled with strangely incongruous Stone Age drawings of people swimming in a watery paradise, and was able to play along with his scenario and not blow it out of the water through sheer ignorance. So to speak.

God, she hated lying. But she understood that his mission was top secret and needed to be protected. And there was also that confidentiality agreement Forsythe had made her sign, with its not-so-implied threats if she opened her mouth. She just wondered what would happen when Kick had taken off again, and she was left to fend off Nathan Daneby and his staff's prying questions on her own. Would she be able to maintain the story?

A sobering thought.

Not just because of the legal repercussions, or even because she hated lying. Which she did, vehemently. But because this time Kick really would be leaving her behind. And for good.

Damn, that sucked.

He was a dangerous, arrogant bastard. But against every inner warning and instinct for self-preservation, she had to admit . . . she was falling hard for the man. Falling hard enough that she didn't just tell him to go straight to hell with his pretense of their being involved.

Because she, too, wanted to share his bed one last time before they parted ways.

And not just for the great sex.

But to feel his arms around her, smell his comforting scent, lay her head on his strong, broad shoulder. And one last time feel what it was to be loved by a man who'd rocked her world and changed her profoundly, from the inside out. Even if he was a goddamn bastard.

She sighed inwardly. So much for keeping her emotions out of this crazy relationship.

Too bad he was so good at keeping his locked up as tight as his heart.

SIXTEEN

"SO what on earth made you choose to visit the Sahara Desert for your vacation, of all places?"

Kick's arm stiffened on the seat back behind her as Rainie looked up from her second glass of excellent French wine. He'd told everyone about their cover: tourists and guide, lost from their bigger group. Yeah, like anyone would believe a man with those muscles and deadly eyes could be a simple tour guide.

But the friendly question had come from Margit, the plain and very sweet Danish doctor she'd borrowed clothes from, and everyone was curiously awaiting Rainie's answer. She had to work not to let the truth show on her face—that it wasn't by choice she was here, and it sure as hell wasn't a vacation.

"Well. *Um*," she wavered, "you probably wouldn't believe it if I told you."

Naturally, that just made them all the more curious.

"Oh, no. Now you *have* to tell us," Nathan Daneby said. He'd been acting squirrelly all evening. Like he had something on his mind. He'd also been trying to draw out Kick, but to no avail, either. "That's far too intriguing a statement to leave us hanging like that."

Kick turned to bore holes in her with his sharp gaze. "Yes, do tell," he said in a tone that she knew really meant, "Tell, and your career as a nurse is toast."

Okay, now what? She cleared her throat. And went with the angle she'd been thinking a lot about today. "The truth is . . . my therapist recommended it."

Everyone's eyes widened. Including Kick's.

Okay, so she hadn't had a therapist in years, but when she'd had one, he *had* suggested she should take a road trip in order to work on some of her bigger fears. Like riding in cars and going outside a one-mile-square safe zone. She hadn't heeded his advice, of course. She'd dealt with the grinding fear in other, easier, ways. Instead of challenging them, she'd organized her life to avoid them altogether. It hadn't been until she'd landed—literally—in this unbelievable situation that she'd been forced to deal with her well-hidden but all-too-real neuroses in earnest. God, she hated when she ignored advice and it turned out to be right.

"Your *therapist*?" someone asked.

She cleared her throat again. "Yeah, I, *um,* suffered a trauma when I was young, the consequences of which have somewhat . . . limited my life. He encouraged me to overcome my irrational fears."

Margit grinned with incredulity. "By driving around the Sahara looking at caves?"

"Well, actually, that was Kick's idea," Rainie said, glancing at him. Well, it *was* the truth. She could tell he really wanted to scowl at that, but didn't dare. "Wasn't it, sweetie?" she asked innocently. *Ha. Take that and smoke it.*

Nathan Daneby gave a dry bark of laughter. "Figures you'd come up with something so bizarre, Jackson."

"You two knew each other before the trip, then?" Virreau asked, refilling her wine. Kick put a hand over his glass when it was his turn.

"Sure," she said, sending her lover an I-dare-you-to-disagree smile. "We met speed dating."

"Speed dating?" Margit asked in her delightful accent. "What is that?"

Rainie explained, which had all the Europeans shaking their heads over the pathetic love lives of Americans. "Kick was the most interesting man there by a mile," she said with a wink.

The two female doctors giggled appreciatively. Virreau snorted under his breath.

"So you let him sweep you away to the Sahara." Margit sighed. "How romantic."

Nathan Daneby got the strangest expression on his face. Alert, almost hopeful.

"Well, as it turned out," Kick said gruffly, "not so much."

Everyone sobered at the reminder of their supposed "accident" and the emergency that had brought them to the DFP camp.

"Speaking of which, I should go and check on Marc," Rainie said, stifling a yawn. The company was convivial, but she was about to fall over from exhaustion. The wine hadn't helped any, either. She rose to her feet. "See you all tomorrow."

Kick quickly followed suit. "I'll go with you." He paused and turned back to the others. "I'll be leaving very early in the morning, so in case I don't see you again, thanks for helping us. Especially for saving Lafayette's life. I can't thank you enough."

"What? You're leaving?" Daneby said, obviously shocked. "So soon?"

"Have to. The tour must go on." Kick gave a wry smile. "My company will be in touch to arrange for Marc's evacuation back to the States, and—"

Nathan gave his head a shake. "Yes, of course, but I thought we could catch up before you—"

"What about Mademoiselle Martin?" Virreau interrupted. "Will she be leaving with you?"

Kick sent him a dark look. "No, she has graciously volunteered to accompany Lafayette home."

"Oh! What a shame," Margit said. "To come all this way and miss seeing the cave, and all the other wonders of Egypt."

"Yes, I really wish I could stay, but . . ."

"Nonsense," Margit said. "Then you must. In a few days Mr. Lafayette will be well enough to travel alone. And just think what your therapist will say if you abandon the trip now." She looked positively Machiavellian as she said it.

Rainie pursed her lips. And thought about all those travel posters tacked up on her apartment walls. This trip was a far cry from those glamorous images. But still . . . By leaving, she really was wimping out. On levels she didn't even want to think about.

Maybe the other woman had tickled her inner imp. Or the three glasses of wine had robbed her of her good sense. Or maybe it was the thought of never seeing Kick again . . . or the way he had studiously avoided speaking to her, or barely even looking at her, all evening. The man was truly insufferable, and she dearly wanted him to be as tormented as she was.

"Maybe you're right, Margit," she said. "I *should* stick it out and rejoin the tour with Kick."

"No," he said emphatically. So emphatically, everyone turned to stare at him. He shifted defensively. "Maybe your phobias aren't so far off the mark," he said brusquely. "We're in the Sudan now, and the Sudan is a dangerous country, nothing like Egypt. Plan a trip to see the wonders of Yosemite instead."

"And will you be my guide there, too?" she asked, batting her lashes. Baiting him.

His eyes narrowed. "We can talk about that," he said, herding her not-so-gently toward the door, "later."

Eduardo jumped up and hurried after them. "I go with and show where you to sleep."

After saying their good-byes to everyone, they dutifully followed the young UN guard to a small cluster of canvas tents on the far side of the compound. The night was still warm, but a breeze had kicked up, stirring the dust and rippling the tent roofs like a school of olive green stingrays. Luckily it was coming off the desert, putting the refugee camp with its ripe smells downwind.

"I'm sorry it not so fancy," he said in cheerful apology when he lifted their tent's flap to reveal the inside, which was big enough but bare of anything within its drab canvas walls save two cots under mosquito nets, a few blankets, and a rickety stand with a pitcher of water and two chipped glasses.

But to Rainie, anything resembling a bed looked like paradise. "No, it's great," she assured him.

It was only when she and Kick were making their way to
the hospital building to look in on Marc a few minutes later
that it occurred to her how narrow those cots were. Kick
would barely fit on one, let alone have room for company.

Well, damn.

"I hope you weren't serious about coming with me when I
leave here," he said, breaking the somewhat tense silence.
"Because it's out of the question."

"I know," she said. "You've made that quite clear."

He shot her an exasperated glance. "I've got a job to do,
Rainie. This is hard enough. There's no room for—" He cut
off abruptly with a jetted breath. What had he been about to
say? *Distractions? Meaningless sex? Her? All of the above?*

What. Ever.

Maybe the narrow cots were a good thing.

And as for her imagined fantasy vacation, that's all it was.
A total, foolish fantasy. The reality of this nightmare trip
didn't even come close. It was scary, dirty, and awful, and
her supposed guide was being a pill.

"I could have sworn you were desperate to get back to
New York," he said with more than a touch of aggravation.

"Oh, I am," she assured him. And she was. Very desperate.

"Then what's the problem?"

"No problem. No problem at all."

She had no clue why she was reacting this way, pushing
it—him—like this. It was almost as though, now that she'd
overcome her first big fear, some inner demon had been set
loose, urging her to go all the way. To take them all down
while she had the chance, every last one of the debilitating
suckers, so she could finally live a normal life. A life without
any limits on what she could do or where she could go or
whom she could trust, due to her own irrational panics. Most
of all, a life without Kick freaking Jackson and his heart-
crushing emotional indifference.

"Good," he said. "Because you've got no freaking
chance."

Didn't she *freaking* know it. She halted and turned to
glare up at him.

"What?"

"Let me make this as clear as I can, Kick. I have no interest in going anywhere with you. None. In fact, I wouldn't go with you if you were the last man on earth and *begged* me to."

With that, she spun and kept marching toward the hospital, leaving him trailing in her dust.

She didn't look back and he didn't call after her. Big surprise *there*. But she heard his crisp bootfalls follow in her wake all the way to Marc's bedside.

To her relief, Marc was awake.

"Hey, you," she said with a big smile. "How are you feeling?"

She sensed the heat of Kick's presence behind her.

"Like crap warmed over," Marc said with a valiant attempt at a smile back. "But it's good to be alive. For a while there I thought . . ." His words trailed off and his eyelids dropped for a moment.

"We would never have let that happen," she assured him, taking his good hand and giving it a gentle squeeze.

He opened his eyes and they softened. "I believe you." His gaze shifted behind her. "So what's the plan, *mon ami*? When do we get going?"

Kick moved forward to stand next to Rainie. He surprised her by saying, "I've already contacted STORM Corps and alerted them to the situation."

When had he done that? He must have borrowed the camp radio and called them while Rainie was helping with Marc. Or maybe when she took a shower earlier.

"As soon as you're fit to travel, they'll send a helo in for you and Rainie."

The other man's brows shot up. "*Mais, non!* I can't be pulled out! You need me to—"

"You're in no shape for a mission, my friend," Kick interrupted. "You've been officially recalled."

"But who will be your backup?" His eyes flicked to her. "Rainie?"

"Hell, no!" Kick said.

Marc frowned. "Have you forgotten this was designed as a three-man operation? How the devil will you, one man alone—"

"I'll manage," Kick interrupted. "You just concentrate on getting better, for the next mission."

Marc shook his head. "Going in alone will be suicide. You know that."

Kick shrugged. "Yeah, well."

Rainie whirled around to face him, aghast. "*What?* You're *still* planning to *die* out there?" He'd said that before, in New York, but since then, to her relief, he'd seemed to change his mind and to be determined to survive. Why had he changed his mind back again?

He looked at her indulgently. "I take that chance on every mission I go on, sweetheart. It's what I do."

Swiftly, her horror turned to fury. She pressed her lips together. "No. Not anymore. You *quit* that job. They're *forcing* you to do this, and—"

He grasped her upper arms. "No. They're not. I could have gotten away from them before taking off, if I'd really wanted to. Admittedly, you were—are—a complication. But now you're safe." He took a deep breath. "I *have* to do this, Rainie. Not for them. For me."

"But—"

"Hell, you've seen how I live. Looking over my shoulder, angry at the world, killing myself slowly with pain pills."

He didn't say it, but she could see it in his eyes. And all at once, she understood. The real pain wasn't out here in the world; it was on the inside. In his heart. His soul. Her own heart broke at what she saw in the depths of his haunted eyes.

"What's the fucking point of it all?" he muttered.

She put her hands on his arms as he held her. "The point is to be *alive*. If you're alive, there's always hope, Kick. Hope for something better."

He shook his head but avoided her gaze. "Not always."

She stared at him and her soul filled with a sudden, blinding anguish. *Jesus.* And she'd thought *she* had hang-ups. Her fear of life was *nothing* compared with this man's. What the hell had happened in his past to make him this way?

But he was wrong. So very wrong. Life was always worth living, in spite of the nightmares. Because with a little courage and a lot of help from your friends, you could conquer those nightmares. You really could. She was living proof.

She drew herself up and gathered her courage. How much worse could it get than it already had been?

"Well, I disagree," she said determinedly. "And I'm going with you. To make sure you *don't* die."

His lips turned down. "You can't possibly mean that."

"Hell, yeah, I mean it." There was no way she could let him face his formidable demons alone—because she was sure that's what this was for him, a way to prove to himself he was worthy of life. Not a chance she'd leave him, not when he'd always been there for her when she'd been forced to face hers. Not a chance she would let him choose death. Besides . . . he needed her. He might not see it, but he truly did.

Sure, she was terrified. *Heck, yeah.* But for the first time in her life, she didn't care. Fear would *not* stop her from doing the right thing. Not *this* time.

She turned back to Marc. "What do I have to do? What do I need to learn?"

Kick grabbed her shoulders and spun her back. "What part of *no way in fucking hell* don't you get?"

"Well, apparently not the fucking part," she said tartly, and wrenched out of his surprised grip to turn back to Marc. "Now. If you'll just tell me—"

"Baby, anytime you want to fuck, just say the word," Kick growled behind her. "But you are *not*—"

"She's right, you know," Marc broke in quietly.

Kick pointed a finger at him. "*You* I don't need help from."

"*Donc*, yeah. Listen to me."

She took a step away. Kick looked like he was about to have an apoplectic fit. "Have you lost your mind completely? She is an *untrained civilian*. One with major head issues, at that. I don't care if these tangos blow me up or slice me to ribbons. But *not her*."

"Think about it, Kick," she argued. "I can—"

"No!" he roared, then glanced around and lowered his voice to an intense growl. "You are *not coming on the mission.* Not if you're the last person on earth and you beg me," he added with a cutting glare at her.

Okay, ouch.

"What about your tour guide cover?" Marc asked, his hushed voice a sea of calm in the storm of wills raging between her and Kick. "I saw that photo in Forsythe's file. What happens to Rainie after you leave the camp without her?"

Her attention pricked at the mention of Forsythe. *Photo? What file?*

"I've already taken care of that," Kick gritted out. "She volunteered to accompany you home."

Marc slowly shook his head. "And when they—when *he*—starts asking her questions? Hell, he's already suspicious. How long do you think it'll take him to figure out what's really going on? You honestly think that I—that *we*—will live long enough to get on that transport home?"

She straightened. *Huh?* What was going on? "Wait. We're in *danger* here? At the DFP camp?" She blinked at them in disbelief. "From who?"

Kick ignored her questions, his face twisting into a portrait of hostility as he regarded Marc like a thundercloud.

"*Alors*," Marc said, lowering his voice further yet, "surely, he already suspects us. If I keep pretending to slip in and out of consciousness so I'm not a threat, I have a fifty-fifty chance of getting on that STORM helo intact. But if you leave her here, the odds go down dramatically. For *both* of us."

Her alarm was growing by the second. "What the hell are you two talking about?" She spoke in a loud whisper, matching the cue of the men.

Kick paced away and then back, hands on hips, glaring at Marc. "You're assuming he *is* the traitor. But what if he isn't? That FedEx plane wasn't shot down by accident, you know. *And* he was genuinely surprised to see us."

"*Who?*"

"Did you contact STORM directly to request extraction, or through Zero Unit?" Marc asked.

"Directly. I don't trust anyone at ZU."

"Then we've all still got a fighting chance. But only if you get her out of here."

Locked in a staring match, they were deliberately shutting her out of their plans. *God*, she hated that. Just like the flipping male doctors in the ER. She thrust her fingers into her hair and pulled at it in frustration. "Will you two *please* stop talking in riddles and tell me what the *hell* is going on?" It came out louder than she'd intended, causing the men to glance around worriedly.

Then they exchanged another look.

Kick blew out a breath. "Before the—" His jaw twitched. "On the plane, Forsythe showed me a CIA file he had on the Afghanistan incident where I was injured. I'd always believed someone on the inside had betrayed us, but I was never in a position to figure out who. Apparently Forsythe did. He had a photo of Nate taking money, or something, from a notorious terrorist. He said it was Nate who betrayed our mission and got my men killed."

Rainie suddenly couldn't breathe. "Nathan Daneby?" The man she'd admired for years? A *traitor*, working for terrorists? It was too much to fathom. He was in contention for a Nobel Peace Prize, for crying out loud! "Impossible. How could an idealist like Nathan be a traitor to his country?"

"He could be trading in conflict diamonds," Marc suggested. "Lot of money in that."

"Blood diamonds?" She'd heard about the trade, of course. Seen the movie. Knew about the connection between them and terrorism. But . . . *"Nathan?"*

"Doctors for Peace routinely cross national borders that are closed to most people, with relief shipments of food and medicines. Smuggling diamonds would be very easy, and very lucrative, for anyone willing to take the risk."

"The profits would help a whole lot of refugees," Kick agreed gravely.

"But you said he betrayed your mission."

"Anyone involved with terrorists would have to protect himself," Marc said. "From *both* sides."

Kick looked ill. "Nate's always been opposed to military solutions to the world's problems. Especially CIA and its covert operations. Maybe the thought of sabotaging the Agency, along with receiving a whole lot of money to help his own cause, maybe it was too much to resist."

"But he's your friend!"

"That's what I thought." Kick's expression was deadly.

Rainie's heart went out to him. "There must be another explanation. Have you asked him?"

Kick's head shook once, like he was afraid to speak for fear his voice would betray him.

"Then how can you believe a friend could do such a terrible thing?"

"Yes, how *could* you believe that?" someone said from the doorway.

She spun. It was Nathan.

Before she could react, Kick swooped down, pulled the SIG from its holster on his ankle, and trained it on the tall man in the door. At the same time Marc slid a deadly black automatic from under his pillow and did the same.

She yelped when Kick grabbed her arm and yanked her behind his back.

Nathan sighed, leaning a hip on the doorframe. "So much for the DFP's 'no weapons allowed' rule."

"How much of our conversation did you hear?" Kick asked, his voice soft but deadly.

"Enough."

His eyes narrowed. "Got anything to say to me?"

Nathan's expression was tired, almost sad. "Would you believe me if I said I was innocent?"

"That photo says otherwise."

Nathan's lip curled wryly. "Then I won't bother to deny it."

Kick stared at him for a long moment, finally asking, "Nate, did you take money—or anything—from abu Bakr's right-hand man, Abbas Tawhid?"

There was an even longer moment before Nathan answered.

"Yes. I did. And I'd do it again."

GINA came awake with a gasp.

She shot to a sitting position in bed. What had awakened her? A sound? A draft of air that didn't belong? A dream?

She was alone, the other side of her bed empty and cold. Disoriented, she looked at the clock on the nightstand. The amber digits glowed three fourteen. But AM or PM? She couldn't remember how she'd gotten there.

Her body reminded her. She felt sore, bruised, violated. And incredibly, mind-blowingly replete and satisfied.

She took a deep breath, and smelled him on her skin, on the sheets. The smell of his sex surrounded her.

Gregg.

Memories rushed back.

Omigod. The things they'd done.

Heated embarrassment streaked through her whole body, even as her nipples hardened in aching desire at those memories.

The man liked it rough and dirty.

And mother of God, she had, too.

He'd made her come and come, then called her bad names until she'd come some more, and then as punishment he'd put her over his knee and spanked her with his large, strong hand until she'd come again and begged him to take her with his enormous cock, and *then* he'd tied her to the bed and put that enormous cock and his talented fingers and tongue in places they had no business being until she'd screamed herself hoarse with excitement and pleasure.

Jesus, she'd never been so turned on and insatiable in her life.

Then after he'd wrung every last bit of sensation from her limp body, and had spent every last drop of seed he had in her and on her, they'd fallen asleep, exhausted, in each other's arms, him collapsing on top of her, covering her body with his like a heavy blanket of pure male muscle.

But now he was gone. And she ached for that body to cover her again.

The phone rang, startling her badly.

She grabbed it. "Gregg?" she blurted into the receiver.

There was a pause, then, "Sorry to disappoint you."

Not Gregg. *Wade.*

"But then, it seems I always did," her ex-fiancé said dryly.

She struggled to switch mental gears. "Self-pity is so unbecoming in a man, Wade. Don't start. I'm not in the mood."

Amazingly, he let it drop. "Still no word from Rainie?" he asked.

"No." The image of the wreckage on the satellite photo swam through her mind, bringing a different kind of bruising to her heart. Before he could sidetrack her, she asked, "Wade, have you heard any reports of a small plane crash anywhere, somewhere in a remote desert?"

There was a long silence on the other end. It scared her.

My God, he knew something! "Tell me," she ordered past the lump in her throat. "Tell me what you know."

"That information is classified."

She wanted to scream. She carefully modulated her irritation to a soft pleading. "Wade Montana, if I ever meant anything to you, anything at all, please *tell* me."

He hesitated again.

She wasn't above begging. "*Please.*"

"What will you give me for it?" he asked, his voice low.

Shock permeated her. In all the years she'd known him and his work with the FBI, she had never, not once, sensed a wavering of ethics on his part. Despite their personal problems, she would never have believed him capable of blackmail or taking bribes, or any kind of exploitation of his position as a law enforcement officer.

Could she be misinterpreting what he meant?

"What do you *want*?" she carefully asked. Just to be sure.

"I want you to come down here, to D.C. Be with me for a few days. No, a full week."

Stunned even further, she felt her jaw drop. "Why?"

"Why do you think?"

She almost choked. *Whoa.* "Let me get this straight. You'll tell me what you know about that plane crash in exchange for a week of sex?"

He actually chuckled. "Hell, Gina, that would be soliciting prostitution. Which is illegal, last I heard."

"No shit."

She waited for him to say something. Like deny it.

After a moment he exhaled. "I just want you to come down for a visit, okay? That's all. See where it goes. I miss you," he said, sounding like he really meant it. *Wow.*

Her resolve to stay far, far away from him faltered.

Talk about laughable. She'd just come off the most amazing, incredible night—morning?—of sex in her entire life, super-agent Wade Montana included, and she was actually beginning to wax nostalgic for the little prick. Unbelievable.

Not that it was so little—his prick, that was. No, *that* was nice and big. Kind of like his ego.

Which jerked her back to reality. She could visit him all he wanted. It would never work between them because his big, fat male ego wouldn't let it.

"Fine," she agreed easily. "Now tell me everything you know."

"Really?"

"Really."

"Swear?"

"Yes, I fucking swear! Now, what have you heard?"

"All right. Supposedly, there was an unauthorized intrusion of Sudanese airspace by a FedEx plane yesterday. Paramilitary border guards suspected it of being a drug transport and shot it down."

Confusion swam in her brain. "*Sudanese?* You mean as in the country? In *Africa*?" And what the heck? "A *FedEx* plane carrying drugs?"

She suddenly remembered the big "Ex" painted on the crumpled fuselage she'd seen in the SAT photo. And the desert landscape. It all fit. Everything except . . .

Oh, please. She started to laugh. Relief poured through her. *Africa?* She might have gone along with her friend somehow braving a flight to D.C. Or even Atlanta. But freaking *Africa*? Rainie couldn't *possibly* have been on a plane for that long without having a serious breakdown. Which meant Gregg really had been lying to her all along.

God. She was so damned gullible.

But it didn't matter. Because that could only mean one thing. Rainie was still alive and safe. Not crashed and dead in goddamn *Africa*!

"Gina? What's going on?" Wade now sounded as confused as she'd felt earlier. "I thought you were worried about her."

"Not anymore," she said unable to stop the smile from spreading across her face. "You met Rainie and all her phobias, Wade. She couldn't possibly have been on that plane."

Still . . . a tiny ripple of uneasiness suddenly went through her. Okay, he must have had a reason for putting her vague description together with a report from such a distant location and coming up with Rainie. "Why in the world did you think that crash had anything to do with her?"

"Other than you asking about a plane that went down in the desert?" he snipped.

"Yeah. Other than that."

"Because," he said with an insufferable edge of superiority, "according to my sources, that was no ordinary FedEx plane. It was a covert transport owned by a private spec ops outfit called STORM Corps. But there's a clincher. You'll never guess who was onboard."

Gina's smile and laughter vanished. "Who?" she asked, cold dread seeping into her anew.

"The same guy you originally called me about. That CIA officer you said kidnapped Rainie. Jason Forsythe. *He* went down in that plane."

SEVENTEEN

"GO," Lafayette urged, waving his MEU 45 at them. "I'm good."

Kick hesitated, glancing down at Nate, whom he had trussed up like a Thanksgiving turkey and who now sat on the floor staring back up at him from above his gag. Surprisingly, there was no recrimination in his eyes. Just disappointment. It was almost enough to make Kick believe in his innocence.

Well. Except for the part where he'd admitted taking a bribe from one of the world's most notorious terrorists. That sort of trumped the innocent thing.

"How the fuck are you going to explain this to the other doctors and the UN guards?" Kick asked Marc for the fourth time. "They'll never believe Nate is in league with al Sayika. Not in a million years."

As soon as someone came in to check on him in the morning, all hell would break loose. Along with Nate. They'd think Marc had lost it completely, and section-eight him so fast his head would spin. Leaving Nate free to find a way to contact his terrorist buddies and warn them of the coming shit-storm.

Fucking hell.

"I'll think of something," Marc said, seemingly unperturbed. But Kick knew damned well what the odds were of Lafayette making it out of the DFP camp alive, now that they'd shown their hand. Down from fifty-fifty to slim-to-none.

"Get the hell out of here," Marc ordered. He pointed to the SATCOM in Kick's hand that he'd liberated from Nate's office. "Hopefully without the satellite radio he can't get in touch with them, but there's no guarantee. You gotta take every minute of lead time you've got."

Which they could only pray was enough to do the job.

Kick gave a short nod, so damn reluctant to leave him. This was likely the last time they'd see each other alive.

Fuck. Fuck. *Fuck.*

Marc's gaze flicked to Rainie, who was standing nervously next to the door, looking shell-shocked but determined. "Take care of him, *cher*," Marc told her. "He's gonna want to play hero, that one. Don't you let him."

Her mouth quavered into an attempt at a smile. "I won't. You be careful, too."

"*Toujours.*"

Kick cleared his throat of a sudden tickle, turned, and strode toward the door. He grabbed Rainie's arm and just before hustling her out, looked over his shoulder. "Semper fi, *mon ami*," he said softly.

Marc's lip curved. "To hell and back, man."

KICK'S mind was going a million miles an hour, trying to figure a way out of this mess. He felt like hell leaving Lafayette in that position, but under the circumstances there was little choice. He didn't even want to *think* about Nate. He should have slit the man's throat there and then, saved everyone the trouble and anxiety of keeping him alive. But Kick just couldn't do it. He needed an explanation first. A reason for his friend's betrayal.

But nothing had changed his mind about Rainie. He had no intention of taking her along to watch him eliminate his mission target in cold blood and then call in an air strike to cook the rest of abu Bakr's fledgling martyrs, praying the mothers didn't find and kill him first. Which was all too likely.

She wouldn't understand the need for their deaths, even though they were vicious terrorists actively planning to blow up hundreds of innocent people within the week and would end her life in a heartbeat without an inkling of remorse or guilt. And if he got dead, that's what surely would happen. All of it.

Rainie was too good a person to be involved in this no-win situation. And it was all his doing. Hell, he might not deserve to live, but she damn well did.

"Tell me," she said, prying her fingers off the dashboard, which she'd been white-knuckling since rousing Eduardo to unlock the gate so they could exit the camp in their hastily stocked-up Jeep. Ever since, she'd been watching Kick like a hawk.

He stifled a series of yawns. *Damn*, he was tired. The good news was, that blended in with all his other miserable physical issues so it was impossible to distinguish one symptom from the other. "Tell you what?"

"Tell me what I need to do to help you."

He jetted out a breath. "You need to get the hell out of this goddamn country and go back home," he muttered, bringing the Jeep to a stop at the edge of the cultivation and trying to decide whether to go north or south along the Nile road. North would take them to Wadi Halfa and the Egyptian border. South would take them down to Dongola and the closest airport.

"For once we're in agreement," she said grimly. "Unfortunately that's not possible until this mission is over and done. So just fucking tell me what I need to know so we can get on with it."

Right. Like *that* was going to happen.

North or south. North or south. Either direction put another two-day delay in his already diminished op timetable. And either way she'd run into trouble because of her lack of passport and travel docs. Sudanese prison was no place for a foreigner. Especially a woman, who would be considered a whore for traveling alone, or worse, having been with a man who just dropped her off with a wave, to face her fate on her own.

Sweet fucking hell.

"Hello?"

He turned a sour face to her. "You still don't get it. I'm *not* taking you with me."

"Oh, yeah?"

It was the middle of the night and dark as Hades, but he didn't need to see her face to recognize the pressed-lipped stubborn tone he'd grown so familiar with.

"Yeah."

Hell, she didn't know from stubborn. You looked *stubborn* up in the dictionary, his picture was right there under the word.

"So, where are you taking me?"

'Course, it was right there under *clueless*, too.

"I'm working on it."

"I can see that," she muttered sardonically, and he realized the Jeep had been stopped at the same goddamn fork in the dirt road for the last five minutes.

"Smart ass," he muttered back. But it lacked real heat.

"Look, Kick. I understand what you're trying to do. And I appreciate it. More than you'll ever know. But just forget about trying to protect me. I know what's at stake. For real." She turned to him, her face deadly serious. "Trust me, I'll never forgive myself if those embassies get blown up and even one person dies because I kept you from doing your job in time to save them."

He ground his teeth in anger. "Lafayette had no right to tell you about that."

"He didn't. Not on purpose. He mumbled some things while under anesthesia. Don't worry," she added when he shot her a horrified look. "No one else heard. And even if they had, it didn't make sense by itself. But with what I already knew, I could put two and two together."

He didn't respond. It was a little late for denials, but he sure as hell wasn't about to add fuel to her fire.

"Anyway, it's my life," she said resolutely, "and my decision. I won't deny I'm scared to death. And believe me, I'll do everything you say, follow your orders to the letter, so we can both come out of this alive. But I *am* going with you."

He gave her his special narrow-eyed I'm-in-command-here look, the one that had scared full-grown Marines into obedience. It didn't even make a dent.

"If you try to leave me behind, I'll just start walking," she quietly warned. "Or steal one of those camels you've been threatening me with. I'll come after you, Kick. I swear I will."

And the hell if he didn't believe her.

God*damn it*.

With a furious exhale, he jammed the Jeep into gear and lurched it into a U-turn, heading back the way they came. West. Past the DFP camp and out into the waiting arms of the desert. Toward abu Bakr's insurgent training camp.

To wreak revenge on the bastard once and for all. And possibly to die doing it.

Except if Kick died, so would Rainie.

There was no way he would let that happen. So he had only one option open to him. Somehow, some way, he'd have to figure out a way for them both to survive the coming ordeal.

For both their sakes, he had to live.

HIS heavenly Angel came to him that night. *Thank you, Jesus.* It had been so damn long. Days that had felt like years.

He was so happy he wept all over her. Big, clumsy tears fell from his eyes and plopped onto her sweet, pure, naked flesh, running down between her soft curves to soak into the putrid mattress below.

She sat up on his pallet, her red hair gleaming like a halo, and ran her finger delicately through the moisture on her body, touching it, rubbing it between her finger and thumb. Catching his gaze and holding it, she gathered another of his tears and placed it on the tip of her tongue, visibly savoring the taste.

It wasn't fair. It so wasn't fucking fair.

He dry-swallowed down his thick throat, parched and swollen, wanting so badly to taste her, too, as she was tasting him.

Not *fair*.

"So, Nick"—tonight he was Nick—"what would you like to talk about?"

He let out a long, frustrated breath. "How about how much I want to suck your gorgeous tits?" Not to mention her tempting pussy. But baby steps.

She smiled in amusement, as she always did when he suggested they get down and dirty. Not that he blamed her. He was a filthy mess, in both the physical and the mental. What woman in her right mind would want to fuck him? Or even let him touch her soft, pristine skin, or caress a lock of her beautiful red hair?

"You really want to?" she asked, eyes sparkling.

"Oh, yeah."

She tipped her head. "What if I gave you a choice?"

God, he hated these games. "What kind of a choice?"

"Either you could touch me all you want—"

"Touch how?" he interrupted. He didn't want to be tricked. She was beautiful, but she lived to torment him.

"Any way you like."

"*Any* way?"

She nodded.

"With any body part?" The one he meant started saluting.

She smiled as she nodded again. "Anything you like."

Merciful hallelujah. Before she changed her mind, he opened his mouth to say, "I'll take it," but she cut him off.

"Or," she said, silencing him with a raised finger.

"Or?" he asked impatiently.

"Or you can get out of this prison. Escape."

He fucking *knew* there'd be a catch.

He regarded her, fury boiling up in his chest. "Bitch!" he growled. Then instantly regretted it. She'd been his only companion for all this time. He didn't want to lose her.

Hell, he didn't believe her anyway.

"That's bullshit," he said, his anger fizzling to despondency. "You don't have the power to let me escape."

"Don't I?" she asked, her green eyes wide and clear and holding all the secrets to the universe.

"No," he cried in despair. "So I choose to touch you. I choose to fuck you raw every single fucking night until I die in this fucking place!"

She tilted her head the other way. "Are you sure?"

"Yes, I'm fucking sure! Come here." He grabbed for her.

"Give me your fucking breasts." He opened his mouth, already watering in anticipation. Between his legs he was hard as the rocks the guards amused themselves by throwing at him.

She slid her hands under her breasts and cupped them, offering them up in invitation. "Take them. They're yours."

He almost came. He opened his mouth wider and extended his tongue, reaching for her nipple. He groaned. Finally. *Finally* he would taste her.

"Pig!" a guttural voice shouted in his ear.

No!

But the dream had already shattered.

IN a straight line, it wasn't that far from the DFP refugee camp to the al Sayika training camp where abu Bakr was spreading his perverted lessons of hate. About a hundred thirty-five miles or so. An easy two-hour trip by paved road. But of course, there were no paved roads in the Saharan desert. And on top of that, Kick had to drive around deep, plunging wadis and towering rock formations, skirt rugged hills, and go around vast rolling seas of deadly shifting sand.

Oh, and they had to avoid being spotted in the process by the bad guys.

The men in Jeeps who'd been pursuing them after the crash were dead, but more would undoubtedly have taken their place. The Sudan seemed to have an endless supply of brutal men willing to terrorize one group or another for fun and profit, some scumbags from within the country, like the *janjawid*, and some from without, like the Saudi abu Bakr and his gang of international terrorists. Whoever had gone to the trouble of shooting down the FedEx plane would not have given up the search for survivors. Not this soon.

A yawn shuddered through Kick. He was totally exhausted. Couldn't remember the last time he'd slept. His hands had started shaking badly, and despite the cool night air, sweat had long since soaked through the T-shirt Eduardo had scrounged for him. Every few minutes the inside of his head spun like a top.

But when that happened, all he had to do was think of the

men who'd lost their lives in that plane, and those in A-stan, and his anger focused and sustained him for another few miles.

"You need to stop and sleep," Rainie said, startling him so badly the Jeep swerved, almost hitting a jagged boulder. He stomped on the brake and shifted to neutral, lurching to an abrupt stop.

"Jesus," he swore.

"I rest my case," she said, but had the grace not to look smug. She actually looked worried.

"I'm fine," he said.

"Yeah. And I'm the next American Idol," she retorted.

Did he detect a touch of sarcasm? He couldn't recall ever hearing her sing.

Shit. He was losing it.

He leaned his head back on the seat. "Okay, you're right. I'm not fine. Give me twenty minutes with my eyes closed and I will be."

She snorted.

"You got a better idea?"

"Yeah."

He rolled his head, cracked an eyelid and peered at her.

"I'll drive," she said. With a straight face, yet.

This time *he* snorted, closing his eye again. "Uh-huh. In which parallel universe?"

"You are so fucking amusing."

He smiled. "I've told you already. Anytime, baby."

"Okay. Now."

Huh? He must have lost the conversational thread. "What?"

"I assume your little invitation referred to fucking. Well, I want to. Now."

He forced both eyes open and frowned at her. "You're joking, right?"

"Nope. Out of the Jeep, lover boy, and make good on your braggadocio." She popped open her door, raising her brows at him expectantly.

It finally dawned on him what she was doing. He let his eyes drift shut again. "I take it back. Anytime but now."

"Can't get it up, eh?"

His smile returned. "Nope. Sorry."

She hit him in the arm.

He grinned and started to drift off.

"How 'bout if I give you a blow job?"

His eyes sprang open. He regarded her with suspicion as his nether regions also woke up and surprised him by starting to stir. She pointedly followed its progress with her gaze. Suddenly he wasn't nearly as tired.

Hell, two could play this game. "If you insist, who am I to say no?"

He smiled, but she smiled back even wider, making him think maybe he'd missed a vital clue somewhere.

Or maybe she just liked giving him blow jobs.

Worked for him. It had been forever since she'd last taken him in her mouth and turned him into a quivering mass of Jell-O. Well, at least a day. Or had it been two? So hard to remember . . .

To his annoyance, his hands began shaking even harder when she reached for the buttons of his DCUs. Damn, she was really going to do it. Leaning across the gearshift, she laid a kiss on him as she unbuttoned his fly, sticking her tongue deep into his mouth. He moaned in mindless pleasure as her velvet, wet tongue slicked over his and her wicked fingers brushed his straining cock.

She lifted from the kiss and gave him a sultry, knowing look. *Oh, baby, baby, baby.* Then she bent down to—

"Ow!"

His eyes shot open to see her rub her head. She'd hit it on the steering wheel trying to reach him.

She did it again. "Ow!"

To hell with that.

"Switch places," he ordered, sliding her over his body as he took her spot on the passenger seat. "There. Now you— *Ahhhhh!*"

The seat back lowered behind him so he was half reclining. His hips arched as she took him all the way into her hot, sexy mouth, all sweet liquid suction and pale golden hair tumbling over his belly.

His mind went completely blank and pure pleasure took over his whole body and consciousness. He shook with it. He cried out with it. He gave it its head and didn't even try to rein in the orgasm as it swiftly stretched and thickened him, filled him to the bursting point, and exploded like a heat-guided missile.

He moaned like a dying man, wasted in the aftermath, helpless to do anything but lie there with his eyes closed as she milked him dry, then came up to let him taste himself on her lips and tongue.

"Give me a second," he murmured, savoring the throbbing, light-headed bliss.

Oh, man. He was going to return the favor, then flip her over the seat back and fuck her till they both passed out from the pleasure.

In just a minute.

Or maybe two.

Yup, that's definitely what he was going to do.

RAINIE looked down at the sleeping man she loved so much her heart could barely stand it. She'd denied her feelings as long as she'd been able. Twisted the fact that he wanted so badly to protect her, to be the lone wolf macho commando to her damsel in distress. To push himself until he dropped, ordering her around and railing against her, rather than put her in a moment's danger. She'd called it obstinate chauvinism and emotional bankruptcy. But seeing him so helpless and vulnerable, finally having given in to both his need for her and his total exhaustion, her heart could deny the truth no longer. Everything he'd done was to keep her safe. From the bad guys. But also from himself.

And somewhere along the thousands of miles they'd traveled together, she'd fallen completely and utterly in love with the man.

God, she loved him.

Smiling, she reached out to smooth her fingers along his slightly drooping jaw.

And God, was he ever easy.

She leaned over and pressed a kiss to his stubbled cheek. Poor guy. Didn't stand a chance.

Gingerly she fished the two ends of the old-fashioned seat

belt up from the tangle of exposed metal springs poking out of the passenger seat cushion and fitted them together over Kick's expanding and contracting abdomen with a snap. She froze at the noise, darting a glance at his face, but he didn't wake. Good thing. If he woke at a seat belt click, he was sure to wake when she started the Jeep's engine.

If she managed it.

Deep breath. Let it out.

Deep breath.

After buckling her own belt, she turned her attention to the vehicle's controls, going over them one by one in her mind. *Ignition. Gearshift. Gas. Brake. Clutch.* Those were the main players. She'd been carefully studying Kick as he drove today, especially when he'd stopped and started, so she'd be able to do it herself if need be.

Well, the need was screaming at her. *She* was fine. In addition to back at the palm grove, she had also managed a couple hours of sleep as Kick carefully navigated through the desert after leaving the DFP camp. He, on the other hand, had been running on nothing but adrenaline for over two days now . . . or was it three? She was amazed he hadn't fallen over in a dazed stupor long before this. She also hadn't missed how the symptoms of his drug withdrawal had been giving him trouble, even though he'd done his damndest to hide them from her. The trembling. The sweats. The dizziness and elevated heartbeat. It hadn't all been because of her skills as a fellatrice.

She stole a look at him. So peaceful in slumber. It did her heart good to see him this way. Awake he always looked so . . . haunted.

She could do this.

For him.

She turned back to the controls. Reached for the ignition, brushing back the panic.

Deep breath. Let it out.

Deep breath. Let it out.

With her left foot she pushed down on the clutch pedal. It barely moved. Wow. It took a lot more strength than she'd thought. She pushed harder. It sank to the floor. Her heart thundered. What now?

Deep breath.

She pulled the gearshift into the slot for neutral and wiggled it, as she'd seen Kick do before starting the Jeep.

Then she turned the key.

Her heart jumped to her throat as the engine caught. She wouldn't exactly call it a purr, but it didn't die, either. *Thank God.*

She risked a glance at Kick. His head shifted to the other side and he made a soft noise, but he didn't wake up.

Let it out.

Luckily, one of the first things he'd taught her when they'd left the village yesterday—God, had it only been twenty-four hours ago?—was how to use the handheld GPS locator and coordinate its display with the map and SAT photos from the field pack, which were now spread out on the dashboard along with a flashlight. Being familiar with digital readouts in the ER, she'd caught on quickly. And once she'd gotten over her blind fear of the huge open desert, she'd earned his trust enough to take over navigation duties completely.

Therefore, she knew pretty much exactly where they were now. And thanks to the big red circle around the tango training camp on the SAT photo, she also knew exactly where they needed to go. And it was time.

Deep breath.

It took her three tries to wrestle the gearshift into first. She was certain the unholy grinding of the gears would wake Kick. But after muttering a grumble of protest, he settled back to sleep. She'd made the right decision. The man was totally zonked.

Let it out.

Along with her breath, she slowly eased out the clutch. It coughed and sputtered, reminding her to press on the gas. Which she quickly did.

And miracle of miracles, the Jeep started to roll.

A grin broke out, ear to ear.

Oh. My. God.

She was actually driving!

EIGHTEEN

"KICK."

A hand clapped his arm and Kick came awake in an instant. Lightning-fast, he whipped his SIG from its makeshift holster and aimed it at the voice.

The voice screamed. *She* screamed.

Oh, hell. *Rainie!*

By the time he'd reacted, lowered the SIG, and reached for her, she was curled in a tight ball in the seat under the Jeep's steering wheel.

"*No!* Don't touch me!" she screamed.

Oh, hell. "Baby, it's me. I'm awake now. Please, honey. I'm not going to hurt you." Shit, shit, shit.

With eyes squeezed tight, she pulled in a deep, halting breath and slowly exhaled. Good girl. He let out his own pent-up breath, and dared to gently rub his hand up and down her back.

"God, I'm so sorry. I must really have been out of it. I didn't mean to scare you."

She gave him a tentative look, and her eyes gradually emptied of fear.

"I know," she said, shuddering out a sigh. "I should have known better than to wake you like that, with no warning."

"You okay?"

She nodded.

"Come up out of there." He helped her to uncurl and scootch back up, then gave her a hug and held her until her heartbeat slowed from hyperspace down to just warp speed.

That's when he noticed their positions. She was in the driver's seat, and he the passenger. He frowned. *What the hell?*

He tried to remember. And suddenly, he did. Why, the little . . .

He didn't know whether to laugh out loud or be really, really angry. Except . . . Holy hell.

She'd been—

"Damn, woman," he said, drawing back to gaze at her in serious admiration. "You *drove?*"

"Yeah." Her smile was shy but unbelievably proud.

"You are one amazing lady, you know that?"

"You think?"

"Oh, yeah." To top it all off, the sun was peeking over the horizon behind them. Jesus, she'd been driving for *hours*.

"Any idea where we are?" he asked, glancing around. He wasn't worried. She'd been good with the GPS.

"That's why I woke you," she said, and pointed to something in the distance. Some kind of structure. "What is that? I couldn't figure it out from the map and didn't want to get any closer if . . ." Her words trailed off nervously.

"Let's take a look."

He turned to dig the night vision goggles from the field pack in the backseat. He slid them on and peered at the silhouetted buildings, which popped into an orderly complex he easily recognized. "It's a refinery. Probably close to the Egyptian border. Are we that far north?"

She looked apologetic. "There was this huge area of sand dunes. I didn't think I should chance going through them."

"Definitely the right choice." He adjusted the NVGs and looked closer at the refinery. "Hmm. Weird. No spotlights on the perimeter."

"Is that bad?"

"Security's usually pretty tight at these places, lights on 24/7." He flipped up the goggles and eyeballed the silhouetted compound. Sure enough, except for the leap of fire spurting from one of the chimneys, the structure was completely dark against the dim rays of the dawn sky.

They watched silently for several moments, then she said, "What should we do?"

What he'd *like* to do was check it out. He suddenly had a bad feeling about it. Something was wrong up there. He felt it instinctively.

But if there really was trouble, he didn't want Rainie within a hundred miles of it.

"Maybe it's been abandoned," she ventured. "Because of all the unrest in the country."

He shook his head. "Doubtful. If the foreign owners jump ship, the facility is fair game for the Sudanese government to take over."

"So then it must be . . . Oh." Comprehension seeped into her eyes. Along with a trickle of fear, and a whole lot of determination. "It shouldn't be all dark like that, should it." Not a question.

"Probably not," he conceded.

She digested that. "Kick?"

"Yup."

"I think it's time you tell me exactly what your mission is. Why you're here."

She already knew about the terrorist plans to bomb the Western embassies, thanks to Marc. She had to figure they'd been sent to somehow stop those attacks. It didn't take a mind reader to know where she was going now. Like, were terrorists possibly connected to this, too?

The hell of it was, they just might be. Kick wasn't aware of any reports of local incidents involving a refinery, but in this part of the world things happened fast, and intel was slow in coming. Could this be abu Bakr and his band of merry fuckers setting up a diversion in preparation for the Khartoum bombings? In which case, this could get really ugly.

She gazed at him expectantly. *Right. The mission.* Leaning back in the seat, he ran his palms over his eyes, pulling off the NVGs and tossing them into the back. Buying time. So he could decide how much to tell her.

Yeah, because that strategy had worked so well last time he'd tried to keep her out of harm's way.

And yup, he'd really been delusional when he'd thought there might be a chance of keeping her from knowing exactly what he did. What he was. Especially after the bloody scene in that village. That had to have been a big clue.

She'd thought that was bad; she was *really* going to hate him when she found out that's what he did for a living. Even if he was working for the side of right and good, a sniper's sole function was to kill people. Period.

When he'd first been recruited by Zero Unit from the Marines, that hadn't bothered him. In fact, he'd sought out the specialty. He'd been one angry young man. He'd wanted to kill the whole world back then, and one person at a time would do just fine. Especially if he could slap the label of patriotism on and not have to go to jail for doing it.

It was a sick kind of therapy, but it must have worked. After a while it *did* start bothering him. More and more. Until he finally started to wonder who was worse, his targets or himself. But when the good guys had started dying instead of the bad guys, that's when he'd finally had enough, and got out. Or rather, he'd tried.

And he'd gotten *that* close to escaping that life. One last job to set things right. One last job, which, once he was clean, he would have done for free, even if Forsythe hadn't promised to rip up his contract and expunge his CIA file. But Forsythe's promise had undoubtedly died with him. Along with Kick's chances of escaping his past while he still had a future. Hell, while he was still breathing.

A normal life with a sweet woman like Rainie in it? Sure. Maybe when hell froze over.

She was about to learn her lover was a paid assassin. And wouldn't *that* go over well.

As in *ex*-lover well.

"Yeah, I guess you should know," he said, resigned to his fucked-up fate. Hell, why should this be any different, just because he was stone in love with the woman?

Jesus.

He let out a weary sigh and raked his hair back with his

fingers. Some days he felt as old and broken-down as those wind-worn statues of ancient kings littering the ground up in Egypt. Today he felt even older.

"My designated target is Jallil abu Bakr," he told her. "The leader of the al Sayika terrorist cell planning the attacks on the embassies in Khartoum." He figured he didn't need to explain what *target* meant in practical terms. She was a smart girl.

"Just the leader? Not the whole cell?"

Okay, smart but possibly a bit naïve.

He gave her a wry curve of the lips. "Your faith in my abilities is flattering. But no, others will take care of that task once abu Bakr is eliminated."

The word *eliminated* did it. She swallowed. Glanced away. To her credit, she met his eyes again. "Others? What others? There's just you, now. Us," she quickly corrected.

But she was oh, so wrong about that. There was no "us." Not now. Certainly not her and him. Hell, there would probably never be an "us" for him. But he let it go.

"STORM Corps," he explained. Lest there be any misunderstandings, any delusions left in her mind, he said, "I'm to personally take out abu Bakr, then call in an air strike. Disguised to look like the Sudanese government cracking down on terrorism, a STORM bomber will completely destroy the insurgent camp and everyone in it."

She blinked owlishly. Swallowed more heavily. "I see."

Yeah. He figured she did. Finally. *Hi, honey, how was your day at the office? Great. Killed twenty people today . . .*

"But—" She cleared her throat. "But why make you come all the way over here and . . ." She cleared her throat again. "I mean, wouldn't the air strike . . . If everyone . . . It would accomplish the same thing without putting you in such danger."

Jesus. She was *still* worried about him? Trying not to get tangled up in the pathetic hope *that* spurred, he shook his head. "Abu Bakr is one very intelligent, very evil dude. He and his al Sayika coleader Abbas Tawhid have been eluding us for years, just like Bin Laden. Until the Afghanistan op, no one had even seen abu Bakr's picture. But I managed to get a look at him in the flesh once before—" He flexed his leg at the onslaught of bitter memories, and wiped sweat from his brow. "Anyway, this time we need to be sure he's dead. One-hundred-percent no-doubt-about-it certain. So he doesn't get away from us again."

The sun had climbed higher by now and the pink sky was melting to azure blue. As she turned to face him, golden rays lit up her golden hair and dusted her golden skin, making her even more perfect and beautiful. Ethereal. She'd probably be worshipped as a fucking goddess if she were transported back in time four thousand years. Sort of how he worshipped her now.

She slowly nodded. "I understand. So where do I come in?"

Was she *kidding*? She obviously hadn't been listening. "Baby, you don't."

Her meadow green eyes snapped back at him, goddesslike in their vehemence. "I thought we'd been through this. I'm here to help you, and I have no intention of hiding under a rock while you take all the risks."

"Rainie—"

She glared out at the desert, toward the structure in the distance. "We should see what's going on at that refinery. I can tell you want to."

"Yeah, but—"

"So let's get going." She reached for the gearshift.

Holy hell. "Whoa! Let's take a pit stop first. Get ourselves organized. A plan. And you'll need a weapon."

And *he* needed to wait until his head stopped spinning. Probably from the fact that he'd told her what he was, and she hadn't run screaming for the hills. Yet, anyway.

So what the hell was that supposed to mean? For him?

For *them*?

Surely, it didn't mean he actually had a chance?

OKAY. She was officially terrified.

Rainie held the handle of the long KA-BAR knife Kick had insisted she carry—like she'd ever actually use it— gripping it so hard her fingers cramped.

Deep breath. Let it out.

Deep breath. Let it out.

Crouching behind a prickly, scraggly bush growing just outside the refinery's perimeter fence, she watched Kick efficiently snip the chain links so they could slip through. Inside. Where he was convinced something bad was happening. He didn't even look worried, but she was about to pee her pants.

Her own fault. When he'd parked the Jeep half a mile back and said he was going into the seemingly deserted compound to have a look around, fool that she was she'd insisted on going with him. At the time she couldn't imagine anything scarier than being left behind at the Jeep all by herself.

In the past few minutes her imagination had gotten a whole lot better.

Deep breath. Let it out.

I will be fine.

I can do this.

She *had* to do this. It was either that or die of a heart attack before she could prove to Kick—and herself—that she really wasn't a big scaredy-cat, candy-ass wimp.

Even though that's exactly how she felt.

"I'm in," he said low, and glanced back at her. "Wait there. I'll be right back."

What? Alarmed, she stoop-ran over and dropped to her knees beside him. "Oh, no, you don't. I'm going—"

He grabbed her wrist and took the knife from her, slapping his gun in its place. "If Marc were along, he'd stay right here covering my six. I expect you to do the same."

She was definitely going to hyperventilate. "If Marc were here, he'd actually know how to do that. What the hell's a six?"

Kick gave her a lopsided smile. "My ass." He wrapped her fingers around the butt of the pistol. "If a bad guy tries to hurt you, point this at him and pull the trigger."

Her eyes started to sting. She didn't know if she could do that. "How will I know if it's a bad guy?"

Something shifted in his smile. "You'll know. Just don't point it at me, okay?" She made a noise intended as a laugh, but it sounded half hysterical even to her. He handed her a

Roman flare he'd dug out of the field pack earlier. "You remember the plan, right?"

The plan. Sure. If she saw anything suspicious, she was to set off the flare.

She really wished she knew what he meant by *suspicious*.

He took hold of her shoulders. "If anyone—like a patrol or guard—comes along the fence, run like hell back to the Jeep before they find you. If they see you, shoot them. Don't hesitate. Just pull the damn trigger. Okay?"

She nodded.

Her palm was sweating, making the metal of the gun slick and unwieldy in her hand. Before she could make him stay and give up this idiocy, he gave her a firm but quick kiss. And then he was gone.

She wanted to scream in protest as he belly-crawled through the hole in the fence then got up and ran to the nearest building. With his back to the wall he took a few long breaths, gave her a shooing motion with his hand, then disappeared around the corner.

Oh, sweet Lord. *Please let him be all right.*

After closing up the fence gap as best she could, she retreated to a shallow gully several yards back to wait for him, lying on her stomach with just her eyes peering over the top. She gripped the pistol hard.

Would she be able to use it on a human being? She'd always worked to *save* lives. She didn't know if she could take one.

She thought with dismay about what Kick had told her. That he'd been sent here to kill a man. Apparently that was his job. Killing people. Or it had been when he'd worked for Zero Unit. She wondered how many people he'd killed in his life.

Gooseflesh rose on her arms. But to be honest, she wasn't sure if it was from pure revulsion or a perverse kind of attraction. Because it had to be perverse to be attracted to a man who could kill another human being. Didn't it?

Or maybe her attraction was understandable, because of her past. Knowing a man could protect her, would not hesitate to kill to protect her, if need be . . . that was a mighty powerful thing. Was she a sicko for being relieved to know that about Kick? To be so drawn to him even though he was . . . or maybe just *because* he was . . . so downright dangerous?

She knew the answer even before she'd asked herself the question. She'd answered it the first moment she'd seen him across that crowded speed dating ballroom. She'd taken one look into his eyes and known she'd go anywhere he asked, do anything he wanted. Let him do anything he wished with her. To her. *Because* he was dangerous.

Even when things had gone so terribly wrong, when he'd turned out to be someone completely different from the man he said he was, when he'd kidnapped her at gunpoint, Jesus, she'd *still* been attracted to him. No, she'd been *more* attracted to him. Because of those eyes. Those flint-hard, seen-it-all, done-it-all eyes.

She'd known instinctively that he was the only man she'd ever met who could kill to protect her. Who *would* kill to protect her. She'd been an instant goner.

And wasn't *that* an eye-opening self-realization.

Along with the next one. The realization that it didn't matter what he'd done in the past, or what he was about to do. Nothing could make her change the way she felt about him. She'd love him anyway.

NINETEEN

IT took Kick less than fifteen minutes to return.

Rainie almost wept with relief when she saw him run across the open ground between the nearest building and the fence. He was carrying something that made his gait uneven. Or maybe his leg was bothering him again. It had been getting quite a workout the past few days. She knew he'd been hurting. But he hadn't complained, not once.

She met him at the fence and he pushed a big red jerry can into the opening.

"Got us a few more gallons of petrol. Figured we might need it."

She grabbed the top handle of the square container and dragged it through, landing on her butt in the dirt because it was so darn heavy. No wonder he'd been limping.

"What'd you find out?" she asked as he crawled under, picked up the jerry can with one hand and helped her up with the other.

"First let's get the hell out of here."

His expression lay somewhere between murderous and . . . Okay, maybe just murderous. Fear lanced through her. This couldn't be good news.

She ran to keep up with his long strides. "You okay?"

"No."

"What happened?"

"We just need to get out of here, all right?"

She shut up. And threw a nervous glance over her shoulder as she ran, half expecting armed "tangos" to be sprinting after them, guns blazing. But the place appeared as deserted as ever.

By the time they reached the Jeep and he threw the gas can in the back, she was out of breath and scared to death.

"Please," she said as they jumped in and he started the engine with a roar. "Tell me."

"You really don't want to know."

"Probably not, but I need to know."

His eyes sought hers, bored holes into her gaze. "They've killed everyone. The Europeans *and* the Sudanese who worked there. Killed them all and stuffed them into a storage shed to rot."

Her heart stalled. "Oh, dear God."

"I was afraid it might be something like this."

"I don't understand. Why?"

"I told you abu Bakr is one smart mother. My guess? It's a diversion in the making. When he leaks a report on this to the press, it'll draw the world's attention away from Khartoum long enough to launch his real attack."

She stared at Kick, appalled. "You mean this abu Bakr killed these innocent people just so the CIA or whoever will think *this* is his primary attack, let down their guard, and be unprepared for the embassy bombings? Like those sick first-responder traps?" Working in the ER, she was familiar with the horrifying phenomenon.

"Exactly."

"You're right. He is evil. We have to stop him."

"I need to call STORM. Let them know what's going on."

Kick drove for a few miles, then pulled to a stop in the shelter of some low hills, and got out the SATCOM. She listened as he swiftly called in and described what he'd found. She felt sick to her stomach and tuned out the rest of the conversation. How could people *do* these things to other human beings?

When he put the radio away, she asked, "What can we do about this?"

"Nothing. Not yet." His jaw worked. "It's too late to save those refinery workers. So we let abu Bakr think his plan is working. Right up until I put a bullet between his eyes."

She bit her lip to keep from wincing at the vehemence of his hatred. Not that it wasn't justified. This abu Bakr was a true monster. She didn't doubt that he deserved a death sentence. What she wasn't sure about was her own government acting as judge and Kick playing executioner, with no jury involved. Even monsters deserved a fair trial.

Didn't they?

Or were some crimes so heinous that the perpetrators gave up that right when caught in the act?

She didn't get a chance to ponder it. Suddenly, a vehicle roared up right behind them, scaring her to death. It had bounced up out of nowhere.

"God*damn* it. Hang on!" Kick yelled, and jammed down the accelerator. It leapt forward.

Bang!

The Jeep spun crazily.

Rainie screamed while Kick swore a blue streak, struggling to keep the Jeep from rolling. "Down!" he yelled. "Keep your head down!"

Another shot exploded through the air, followed by an ear-shattering *pop!* The Jeep slammed to a stop, wrenching her against the seat belt.

"Get on the floor!" Kick ordered.

Terror ripped through her. She started to shake. *Please God, don't let this be happening.*

He whipped off his seat belt, positioned himself between the seats, and started shooting back. *Bang! Bang! Bang!* She slammed her hands over her ears.

Between shots she could see him shouting at her. But she was too terrified to understand his words. Her ears rang like church bells. Her heart thundered so hard she was sure it would burst into pieces.

All at once, men swarmed around the Jeep.

The world stopped turning. Fear literally paralyzed her where she sat.

Oh, God. She'd been so wrong before. She'd thought being kidnapped by hooded agents and forced onto a plane to

some unknown country had been her worst nightmare. Or
being left alone in a deserted cave. But, no. This was her worst
nightmare. This!

Being attacked. In a car. To be slaughtered.

Just like her parents.

Repressed memories of that day blindsided her. Memories
of raw-throated screams and the evil faces of drug-crazed
strangers. Of her mother shoving her out of the car and telling her to run. Of her father's chest exploding in a shower of
crimson. Her mother's face as it ran with his blood. The comforting neck she'd cried against so often, splitting hideously
and blooming scarlet. Oh, God, so much blood. And she herself cowering in a doorway, not doing anything to help them.
Unable to move for fear and horror.

Like now.

These men were going to kill her. She was going to die!
And Kick along with her. Because she couldn't move.

It barely registered when two of the assailants went flying
backward, spurting blood.

So much blood. Blood everywhere!

"Rainie!"

Kick was yelling at her again. Something about a knife.
She tried to hear. But couldn't peel her hands from her ringing ears. *Help! Please help!*

He leaped out of the Jeep and launched himself at one of
the attackers. Where was his gun?

Suddenly, a big, ugly brute reached over her door and
grabbed her.

She screamed. He raised his meaty fist. Kick shouted
again. Urgently. Something . . . "—*knife*!"

The world tunneled down to a slow crawl as she watched
the iron fist come slowly around to smash her face in.

And something inside her snapped.

No.

This was *not* going to happen.

This was *not* how she would die. *Not today, goddamn it.*

Kick needed her. He couldn't fight them alone. And she
would not be a victim.

Never again!

At the last second, she dodged the fist. She dove for

Kick's long knife—*that's* what he'd been yelling about!—hidden under the seat. *There!* She wrapped her fingers solidly around the metal handle. And brought it up.

All the pent-up rage of her whole life surfaced in one mass of adrenaline and fury.

She slashed the knife hard across the groping fist. Her assailant screamed in pain.

"*This is for my father, you goddamn asshole!*"

She sliced the blade up his arm and stabbed it deep into his shoulder.

"And *this*. Is for my *mother!*"

She brought the knife around again. His eyes bugged out. She gritted her teeth. Plunged it into his neck. And again. Severing the artery.

He spun away. Dropped to his knees. Then fell to the ground on his face. Dead.

"Jesus God," Kick murmured behind her, breathing heavily.

She clutched the door with red-drenched, slippery fingers. Her breath came in ragged, staccato bursts. "Is he—"

"Yeah." Kick put his hands tentatively on her shoulders. They were shaking. "He's dead."

"Are w-we s-safe?" she croaked, closing her eyes as they swamped with tears. Willing her breath to slow. Her heart to stop pounding like a jackhammer. They didn't listen.

Kick's fingers squeezed her, but he didn't answer. After several moments she managed to turn. She searched his face. His jaw was set, his eyes burning with concern.

No, they *weren't* safe.

"For now," he said. His voice sounded far, far away. "You all right?"

She swallowed. Tested her insides.

A drowning mix of emotions swept through her in a whirlpool. Abject horror at what she'd done . . . My God, she'd killed a man! But also . . . immeasurable relief.

She'd fought back.

Sweet God, she'd fought back.

And *won*.

"Yeah," she said, eyes brimming over. "I'm all right." And suddenly a huge weight lifted from her soul. For the first time in twenty years, she meant it. She *was* all right.

The fear was gone. Vanished. In its place . . . she wasn't sure yet.

"I'm good," she said, wiping her eyes with a shaky smile.

The concern didn't leave his gaze, but he gave a curt nod. "Okay. Here's what we do." And she fell in love with him even more for giving her the respect the moment deserved. For not insisting she *wasn't* all right. Even if they both knew she wasn't.

"The Jeep's tires are trashed," he said. "So we'll take their vehicle. Gather your stuff, okay?" His voice was calm, modulated, like he expected her to fall apart any second, despite the pretense that she wouldn't.

Except, she really wouldn't. Not ever again.

She slid out of the Jeep and went over to the body of the man she'd killed. She picked up his headcloth, which was fluttering next to him. And wiped his blood off her face and hands. Then she tossed the cloth back on the ground.

Stalled in midmotion as he grabbed the field pack, Kick watched her, the look in his eyes unreadable. He didn't say a word.

"I'm okay," she repeated, and gathered her stuff. "Really."

Because amazingly, she'd never felt more okay in her life.

She approached the other vehicle. A newer model Toyota Land Cruiser, no doubt stolen from the refinery. Tossing her things in back, she climbed into the passenger seat and buckled up.

"Hey," she said with a wobbly smile, already memorizing the controls so she'd know where they were when it was her turn to drive. "It's got air-conditioning."

"THERE you are."

Gina whirled, nearly fumbling the specimen slide she was trying to secure under the portable scanning electron microscope. "Gregg!"

"I waited at your place."

She stared in disbelief. It was late. Almost midnight. She'd totally given up on hearing from him. Ever again. Last night had just been too mind-blowing—in an extremely scary way—

to expect a repeat. Sex like that didn't happen to her. Probably a good thing. She'd never get any work done.

Her latest and greatest lover moved toward her, all killer jawline and black T-shirt panther-man. "From now on let me know where you are."

From now on? Obviously delusional. He hadn't even *called* her today, and—

She peered at his face. Good Lord, he was *serious.*

God, she hated men like that. All cocky and arrogant and God's gift. Like a woman had nothing better to do than to wait around until His Royal Dickhead deigned to make contact the morning after.

Oh, yeah, *now* she remembered. *That's* why she only dated young, worshipful interns and residents. They knew how to show a woman she was appreciated, after a night of life-altering sex.

Report her movements to Rambo here, like a two-year-old to mommy? She didn't *think* so.

"What makes you think I *want* you to know where I am?" she asked incredulously.

Besides, she wasn't speaking to him. She'd been stewing all day about what Wade had told her this morning. About that ill-fated FedEx plane. In freaking *Africa.* And Jason Forsythe going down with it. There was definitely a whole lot Gregg wasn't telling her. He was playing her, and she couldn't figure out why. She wanted no damn part of it.

She turned back to the SEM, dismissing him. A second later she felt him behind her. When she'd found him gone this morning, no note, no fresh coffee in the carafe, not even a damn phone message, she'd deliberately dressed in her I-don't-give-a-damn clothes: short lab coat over plain khaki pants and a washed-out baggy T-shirt, white Keds, and her hair pulled back in a severe ponytail. Because she *so* didn't care if he saw her without makeup. Not that he'd show up, she'd figured.

Wrong.

His warm breath tickled her bare neck. His boots brushed up against her sneaks. She made herself ignore the fluttering low in her belly.

"What's the matter, sweet thing?" he murmured in her ear.

He didn't press his body into her, but kept himself just a shade apart. Not that she *wanted* him to press it into her. "Didn't I satisfy you last night?"

Something disturbed her ponytail and she realized he was stroking it. Almost imperceptibly running his fingers down the strands.

She covered a shiver with a tossed-off laugh. "Couldn't you tell?"

"Yeah," he said. "I could tell. Which makes me wonder why the leper greeting."

She snapped the slide into place on the digital scope. "What's the matter, van Halen? You can dish it but you can't take it?"

The fingers in her ponytail got more obvious in their stroking. Was that supposed to be some kind of *threat*?

"You expected flowers maybe?"

Nice. She made a derisive noise. "That's the *last* thing I'd expect from you. Look, I'm kind of busy right—"

The chains on his leather jacket jingled. "No, you're not." Her head suddenly went back in what would have been a jerk if it hadn't been so smooth and controlled. She gasped, groping for the counter.

A glass beaker next to the scope hit the floor and splintered in a million pieces. "What—"

He spun her around and suddenly his tongue was in her mouth. He was hot and muscular and, oh, *God*, why did he have to taste so good, feel so arousing? She forgot all about his macho arrogance and just gave in. Melted into him and his amazing tongue.

Bastard. *Damn* him, he knew exactly how easy she'd be.

Except, wait—

She wrenched away from him, bits of glass crunching under her Keds. The man was truly a menace on every front. "Stop it. You *lied* to me."

He just stood there, a vein pulsing below blue eyes that were as hard and unreadable as those cat's-eye marbles kids used to play with before Sony and Steve Wozniak changed the games of childhood forever.

"You lied about Rainie," she accused. "You said she went on that plane voluntarily."

He continued to watch her silently. Not denying the lie, she noted.

"That plane crash was in *Africa*," she bit out. "Rainie would *never* willingly get on a plane to goddamn Africa."

Something flashed through his eyes. Fleeting. Barely there. Like he was surprised she knew where the plane had crashed. *Miracles. Finally, a reaction.* Okay, a micro-reaction. But the tell was big. She was right.

"Rainie was kidnapped and forced to go against her will. Wasn't she?" Gina demanded. "Forsythe's dead, and she's dead, too. *Isn't* she?"

Moisture from her own tongue glistened on the commando's lips as he regarded her evenly, his stony façade firmly back in place. Not answering. Not moving an eyelash.

Jesus, the man was as scary as he was sexy.

She took a crunching step backward. "I'd like you to leave now."

His head tilted. Just a little.

And that's when she knew she was in big, big trouble.

RAINIE was whistling the theme from *Lawrence of Arabia*.

Kick glanced at her and, despite the grinding tension in his stomach, couldn't help smiling. She wasn't just riding on top of a camel; she was riding on top of the world.

God knew it wouldn't last. That brief feeling of invincibility. The unbelievable but temporary high from beating the living crap out of the biggest, nastiest, most soul-defeating nightmare in your entire life, the one that had been snarling and snapping at you from the inside out and bringing you down since before you could remember. You'd finally won, and all because you'd killed a man who'd been hands down certain he'd be killing you.

That first win, it was powerful medicine.

Kick was happy for Rainie. Hell, if he could miraculously transport her back to her job and apartment in New York City right this minute, she'd be fine for the rest of her life. At least about the irrational fears that had plagued her. She'd never get another panic attack, or feel she had to circumscribe her actions because of her inner demons. The ZU psych had

preached at Kick hard and long enough about somatic therapy to know she had just slain those demons, every last one
of them, along with the tango she'd left dead on the desert
sand. He also knew because he'd slain his own childhood
demons the same way. It had just taken him a lot longer. Well
okay, he'd probably started out with a whole lot more demons than she had.

Anyway. She was sitting there on her camel like a cross
between Joe Cool and T. E. Lawrence, wearing Kick's gold-
lensed aviator shades and the off-white Bedouin clothes that
he'd bartered for along with the camels, including a *kaffiyeh*
that she'd wound around her head covering all but her face.
She must have sensed his gaze, because she turned and
grinned at him. Damn, that New York girl was enjoying the
shit out of riding that camel. Who'da guessed?

Kick, not so much. But not because of his leg, which,
miraculously, hadn't been hurting him at all today, leading
him to suspect the psych had been right all along—the pain
really *was* in his head, not his leg. Damn, he hated that. Not
only the wasted months spent wasted on painkillers, nor the
money wasted to procure them, but also because it only
confirmed he was a total head case.

Not that he hadn't known it all along. Just add one more
fucked-up thing to the list.

Of course, who could tell if one measly leg was hurting
when his entire body felt like it was going through a constant
wringer?

Wiping the sweat from his brow—*damn*, it was hot—he
shifted on the hard, wooden instrument of torture the Bedouin he'd traded the dead giveaway Land Cruiser for clothes,
two camels, and three skins of fresh water had actually called
a saddle. What a joke. And yet Rainie was perched cross-
legged on hers like she'd been a freaking Bedouin princess in
a previous lifetime. If there was such a thing.

She was scanning the desert rim above and the narrow
wadi channel behind them for any sign of being pursued. They
weren't. He'd been damn careful in plotting their hundred-
mile route to the insurgent camp. Camels were fast when
they got their steam on. Didn't have to take all the detours a
wheeled vehicle did; those big saucerlike feet could eat up

pretty much any kind of terrain you threw at them. She should be more concerned about what lay ahead. . . .

Kick pulled out the GPS and checked it. They'd been hugging the bottom of the wadi for a while now, using it for cover as they approached their target. Wouldn't want to overshoot and end up in the middle of the enemy camp. *Oops. Sorry, Osama, just out lookin' for General Gordon's lost candlestick . . .*

When she saw his jaw tense, the humming stopped and her smile faded. "Are we getting close?"

"Should be just past those next hills." About five miles away, the hilltops were just visible above the wadi wall.

Definitely close enough. His pulse was already pounding in his ears. He scanned the dry riverbed. Saw a large covelike area just ahead that would give her a bit of shelter.

He urged his mount over to hers. "Let's stop here. The cover is good and we're far enough away that the camels can't be heard." Nor would enemy patrols stumble across her. "We'll set you up over there in that hollow."

Naturally she picked up on the one word he didn't want her to.

"Set *me* up? What's that supposed to mean?"

He met her gaze head-on. "You didn't really expect to go with me," he said. Not a question, but the answer was obvious in her face.

"Why did you bring me this far, if you never intended to let me help you?"

She was actually pissed off. He couldn't believe it.

No, what he couldn't believe was that he'd brought her along in the first place. All day he'd been reaming himself a new one, thinking about the danger he was about to put her in. *Christ.* The woman he loved might *die* because of his colossally bad judgment. He should be lined up against a wall and shot for—

The woman he loved.

He slammed his eyes shut. *Ah, hell.* He couldn't deny it any longer, could he?

He loved Lorraine Martin.

It was the second time in one day he'd heard the same fateful word echo in his head. *Love.*

The first time he hadn't had time to think about it. The thought had just sort of crept up and leapt out at him suddenly, and retreated just as fast.

But this time . . .

Yeah, he'd really done it. He'd gone and uttered the dreaded words, if only in his mind. He'd actually formed the thought and admitted it to himself.

And wasn't this a fine time for *that* conversation with his conscience.

He loved Lorraine Martin.

He *loved* her.

He loved every obstinate, admirable, frustratingly wonderful and achingly touchable inch of her.

And he'd just put her in mortal danger.

Shit.

Double shit. Because not only was that unforgivable, but he couldn't have her anyway. He could never have her.

Even if they managed to live through the next twenty-four hours, and even if he somehow miraculously managed to get them both out of this goddamn country alive, with Forsythe dead, that promise to release Kick from his contract had about a snowball's chance in hell of being honored. Forsythe had never signed anything. Kick had no proof.

Therefore so much for a normal life.

And so much for being in love with Rainie.

Shit, shit, shit, *shit.*

"Well?"

They were still staring at each other; it was obvious she actually expected an answer.

Why *did* he bring her? If only he hadn't. . . .

His frustration boiled over. "You *want* to die? Is that it? Maybe I should have taken you into that refinery so you could see what's in store for you if we're caught." He slapped his forehead. "Except—no, wait, you're a woman! It'll be a *thousand* times worse for you than for those men, because first they'll brutally rape you and subject you to every kind of humiliation known to man, and only after they've had their sadistic fun will they put you out of your misery. Probably by stoning. A quaint little method of execution. Have you ever seen a woman stoned? Because *I* have and it's—"

The look on her face made him stop abruptly. It had drained of all color. Horror bled through her eyes.

Her bottom lip trembled. "It doesn't matter. I can't let you do this by yourself," she said hoarsely.

Oh, God.

"They'll make me watch," he ground out. "If I close my eyes, they'll probably cut off my eyelids. And when they finally kill me, my last thought on earth will be that *I* let them do that to you."

A sob caught in her throat. "No!" He saw her sink in on herself in defeat. "All right! You win."

"I need you to be safe, Rainie, so I can do my job without worrying about you. And if the worst happens, I need you to find your way back to the Bedouin we traded with. I made a deal with them to take you over the border to Egypt, to deliver you to an American embassy official there."

"And you really think they'll keep a deal to smuggle some Westerner across a closed border?"

"Absolutely. A Bedouin will keep his word to his dying breath. You can trust them with your life, Rainie. *I* trust them with your life. They're expecting you."

Her skepticism turned to consternation. "Wait. What?"

"I've been saying this all along, Rainie. There's a damn good chance I'll be caught or killed tomorrow. I needed you to have a safe way out of here when I'm not around to help."

Tears filled her eyes. "You won't be killed! You *can't* be."

He reached out to put his arms around her but his camel chose that exact moment to sidestep over to nibble on a green bush. He cursed as the tears tracked down her cheek.

Giving the harsh throat-hiss command for the camel to lower himself to the ground, Kick dismounted and got her camel down, as well. Then he pulled her off and finally was able to put his arms around her.

"I deserve to rot in hell for getting you into this. I'm so sorry, Rainie."

She sniffled against his chest. "Stop *saying* that. Because I'm not. I'm *not* sorry." She looked up into his eyes. "I was living in a nightmare of my own making when you found me, Kick. You showed me it doesn't have to be that way. And you've also shown me there are far worse nightmares in the world, *real* nightmares, that are much more deserving of fear. And you know what? For the first time in my life I find I truly *am* afraid of dying. Not because I fear death itself. But because, finally, I have something to *live* for!"

Sweet, holy God.

He did not want to hear this. He was plain terrified of what she might say next. Because it was impossible. Whatever she was thinking, if it had *any*thing to do with him, it was impossible. She *had* to know that.

"Baby—" But no words would come out. They got stopped by the giant lump of choked-up emotion that was firmly lodged in his throat.

She reached up and sweetly kissed his lips. "You are *not* going to die, Kick," she whispered.

Which caused the worst possible thing ever to happen.

It gave him hope. Hope that he might have something to live for, too. That a normal life was possible, after all. *With Rainie.*

She made him dare to hope.

When there was none.

TWENTY

HE made love to her so sweetly.

In a wedge of shade from the waning afternoon sun, lying on parachute silk over hot sand, Kick kissed and touched Rainie with a gentle passion that took her breath away. He filled her with his body and his seed as though she were more precious and cherished than a remembered childhood dream.

If she hadn't already fallen completely in love with the man long ago, this would have done it for sure.

Now, afterward, as he ran his desert-roughened hands worshipfully over her nakedness, there were actually tears in his eyes. And he didn't even try to hide them.

Moved beyond words, Rainie gave in and wept in his strong, sheltering arms. For what they had shared. For all they might not.

"*Shhh*. Baby, it's okay."

Tomorrow, those strong, sheltering arms could be cold and still, forever, in a bloody grave.

The thought made her weep all the more. "No, it's *not* okay. Oh, Kick, let's just get out of here. Call STORM and tell them abu Bakr is dead and to send in the air strike. No one will know the difference. He'll be just as dead. Then we can escape and run somewhere far, far away and forget all about—"

"Sweetheart, you know I can't do that."

"But why?" she demanded tearfully, pulling back to look up into his face. His dusty, sunburned, beard-stubbled, exhausted, adored face. The face she loved more than life itself. She would do anything in her power to keep its owner from being harmed.

His hand continued to stroke over her bare skin. His blue eyes gazed back at her, clear and brimming bright like a mountain stream. Filled with pain. And guilt.

"It's not your fault," she said. "Whatever you think you did, it's not your fault."

His fingers combed gently through her hair. "But it is." His gaze moved away and he inhaled a shuddering breath. "It is my fault."

He was so wrong. He had to be. "Even if that were true, you mustn't throw away your life because of it. Whatever is haunting you, you have to forgive yourself."

"That's not why I'm doing this."

"No? Then why?"

The warm mood evaporated. "Drop it, Rainie. I don't want to talk about it."

She peered up at him. "Why? Are you afraid if you tell me the truth, I might accidentally talk some sense into that thick head of yours?"

The muscles of his body went still and his hand stopped stroking her. "*Rainie . . .*" he warned.

She lay her head back down on his chest. "Okay, fine. Play the wounded hero. But is this really what the friends who died in Afghanistan would want you to do? To throw your life away on some suicide mission for revenge?"

"Says the woman who just threw away everything she believes in and killed a man because of what happened fifteen years ago," he murmured.

Okay, yeah, nice try. She pressed her lips together. "*Fourteen* years ago. And if you recall, that scumbag tried to kill me first. And you. But if you want to pretend it's the same thing, great. Whatever."

She felt him exhale. "Anyone ever tell you you're the most irritating woman alive?"

That's right, deflection might really work. *Not.* "Not usually after making love," she said with honey in her voice.

He swore softly. Under her cheek, his heartbeat kicked up. "I've never talked about this to anyone before. I don't know if I can."

She blinked in surprise. "Not even when you were debriefed by your commanders back home?"

"When I first woke up in the hospital, I couldn't remember a thing. I kept letting them think that."

Ah. "But you did eventually? Remember?"

He nodded. "Unfortunately."

Hidden, guilty secrets. That explained a lot. No wonder it was eating at him. Damn it, he *needed* the catharsis of talking about it, getting it all out in the open. Especially now. So he could concentrate on staying alive and coming back to her.

Anger twisted through her heart when she thought about a childhood that he'd hinted was beyond awful, and all the bad stuff he'd been forced to endure since. He so didn't deserve it. He was such a good man. Kind and sympathetic and intelligent. Given half a chance, he could have been anything he chose, a doctor or a judge or a teacher, anything at all. Instead he'd felt compelled to kill people for a living just to survive on the right side of the law. And then to witness . . . whatever it was that drove him on this mission now . . .

It was *so* damned unfair he was still paying for the sins of his parents, even today. God*damn*, if he died . . .

"I want to understand, Kick. If you're really going to do this, maybe sacrifice your life and leave me all alone here, I deserve to know why."

He sighed. At length, he said, "All right," sounding even more guilt-ridden than before. "I suppose you do."

He was silent again for a very long time. She held him close, soaking up the feel of his muscular body against hers, skin to skin. So vibrant and alive. *For now.* And waited.

When he began, his voice was low and tentative. "Abu Bakr had been on everyone's Most Wanted list since 9/11.

CIA, FBI, MI-6, Interpol, and every country in the West were hunting him."

"And you found him?" she prompted when he seemed to falter. "In Afghanistan?"

He cleared his throat. "Yup. Through an informant." She could feel his body tense as he slipped into the memories. "It was a village like any other. High up in the mountains, poor as dirt, villagers with dead eyes that wouldn't meet yours. Except this one young girl who kept crying and looking at us like we'd been sent by the devil. It sent up a red flag, but I wasn't about to call off the mission because of it. I mean, we'd been tracking this fucker for six years. She was a girl. Girls were always crying over there. And everyone hates us in these places, so being the devil wasn't anything new."

"That must be hard," she couldn't help saying. "Doing something you believe in, and being so hated for it." But he was too deep in the moment, and didn't hear her.

"We'd had information that abu Bakr was spending the night there, on his way to some bigwig meeting with the other al Sayika leaders. We almost didn't believe it. But sure enough, we overheard them call him by name, this arrogant man walking to the mosque for evening prayers surrounded by an entourage, like he was some kind of holy saint." Kick exhaled slowly. "That night, we took up positions for an ambush a few miles up the road. Two of the team stayed behind to watch the village, so he wouldn't slip away from us. One of them was a woman, Sheila. We thought she'd be safer—" Kick halted for a moment. Gathered himself. When he continued, his hands trembled as they held her. "Anyway, abu Bakr still hadn't shown up by noon the next day, so this other guy, Drew, and I went back to investigate." He swallowed heavily.

Rainie braced herself for what would come next.

"Sheila and Tyrone had been tied to two wooden posts. She was covered in blood, had obviously been—" He cleared his throat, wetted his lips. "Both their stomachs were slit open, spilling guts onto the ground. The bastards had lit a fire and—" His fingers dug into her. "Christ, Rainie, they were still alive. Sheila and Tyrone were still *alive*." His voice broke on the last word.

Baby Jesus and Mother Mary.

Rainie could barely speak, but managed, "My God. I hope you . . ." No. She couldn't finish it. But she did't have to. He understood.

"Hardest thing I've ever done," he whispered in a rough rasp. He took a shaky breath. "That's when we heard gunfire coming from the team's position up the road, and I knew I'd led my men into a trap."

"Oh, Kick."

Her tears pooled on his chest. At last she understood the depth of his guilt and his fury. If only tears could wash away the anguish that permeated every pore of his body, every syllable of his words as he continued.

"I knew there was a regular army unit stationed about twenty minutes out. So I used my radio to call for support." He shook his head. "Cardinal sin. We were spec ops. Officially, my team wasn't there, didn't even exist. But I wasn't thinking too clearly at the time. Obviously. Or I would have tackled Drew before he could take off like a jackrabbit up the road to get to the others. The tangos must have laid out land mines overnight. He stepped on one. Blew him to bits right in front of me. A wall of shrapnel caught me in the back and leg pretty bad. I couldn't walk, so I figured, yeah, this is it. I was done for."

Couldn't walk. She traced her fingers gently along the angry raised scars on his thigh. Understatement of the year.

By now his voice had lost all emotion. "But you know, they didn't even bother to kill me. Abu Bakr himself came over and stared down at me, sprawled there in the dirt like a broken, bleeding dog. 'You'll never win,' he said in this fucking perfect American English. And then he left me lying there to bleed out. A few minutes later an old truck came barreling down the road from the mountain." He squeezed his eyes shut, as though trying to shut out one last horrible vision.

Oh, God. Could this get any worse?

"They'd tied a rope around my best friend Alex's ankles, and were dragging his body behind it. I couldn't even see his skin for all the blood. I just prayed he'd died before that truck started moving."

Oh, dear God.

Dear merciful God.

She'd barely managed to keep it together so far. That last part tipped the scales. She scrambled up off Kick, dove for a nearby thorny bush, and lost the meager contents of her stomach.

"Jesus, Rainie." In an instant his sturdy arms came around her from behind, his demeanor changed. He was back from the dark place. On his knees, he held her steady as the world spun around her. "Christ, I should never have told you all that. I—"

"Yes. You should. It's okay. *I'm* okay. I understand now. I totally understand, and—"

God, who was she kidding? She groped for the edge of the parachute and wiped her tears and mouth on it, turned to him. There was such misery in his beautiful face that it broke her heart clean in half. Misery because he was the only one who had survived that day, was therefore the only Westerner who could identify abu Bakr by sight. It was pure guilt that had driven him finally to embrace this mission that Zero Unit had heartlessly sent him on.

She threw her arms around him. "Oh, Kick, I know you feel guilty about not dying that day, too, but I'm so glad you didn't. I love you so much. God, how I love you."

In her embrace, he froze. Didn't move as much as an eyelash.

Oh, hell. Had she really said that out loud?

She swallowed, dropped her arms, and pulled back. Squirmed under the total disbelief in his eyes as he stared at her.

"I mean . . ."

He shook his head.

Oh, *crap*.

"Rainie, even if I thought you really meant that, you have to know I can never . . . We can never . . ."

"Yeah." Plastering a brittle smile on her face, she shook her head and climbed to her feet. "I know. It's all right. Thank you for telling me what happened. I know it couldn't have been easy, and—"

"Rain, stop. We need to talk about—"

"No. Seriously. We don't. I know we're not a match made in heaven. I just, like, wanted you to know, you know, just in case . . ." She caught her bottom lip between her teeth. Bit hard so she wouldn't burst out in tears.

He was on his feet now, too. He pulled her back into his arms. "Baby, if there were any way—"

"But there isn't. I get that. Like I said, no biggie." She tasted blood.

"It is to me," he said softly, and began to lower his mouth to hers.

She jerked away with a forced laugh. Rather than howling with anguish. "*Ew.* I've got barf breath." She grabbed up her Bedouin robe and escaped over to where they had stashed the waterskins in a shady crevice. After slipping the robe over her head, she rinsed her mouth with a stream of lovely goat-flavored water.

He watched her, looking, if possible, even bleaker. She could totally relate. Why was it, when he showed his vulnerability so starkly, she loved him even more?

Not that it mattered how she felt.

No future, remember?

"I wish things could be different," he said.

"Yeah," she agreed shakily. "Me, too."

IT was moving day.

Callooh callay.

Every ten years or so . . . or was it a hundred . . . or maybe every month, who could tell? . . . they moved him. To a new pigsty, they said. *Haha.* The fuckers should be on Comedy Central.

He still hurt like hell. Could barely walk as they impatiently herded him barefooted over sharp rocks and pokey shrubs to his new luxury accommodations. Last week's torture and the beating yesterday—the day before?—hadn't helped his physical condition. Nor did his putrid mattress, which they forced him to drag behind himself to his new quarters. If he dropped it, he'd sleep on bare dirt until next time he was moved. A barrel of laughs, he knew from plenty of previous experience. And if he fell down they'd just drag

him by what was left of his tattered clothes. He had nightmares of being dragged. His skin was raw and scabbed, evidence of when they'd dragged him across the ground before.
His back . . . Well, someday maybe the skin would stay put.
If he lived that long. The mattress helped. Couldn't lose his
grip.

He stumbled along following the asshole guard du jour,
careful to give the other bastards the fun show they expected
from the blind infidel. They deliberately let him run into
walls and crap, and step on disgusting shit on the ground, and
then guffawed uproariously. Motherfuckers. One of these
days . . .

Okay, *focus*.

For the first time, he could actually see things besides four
walls. Granted, not much. But the dim outlines of decrepit
shacks, piles of refuse, dark shadows—human or animal he
wasn't sure—moving about on the fringes of his hazy vision
were actually somewhat recognizable by now.

Let's see. Mud shack, mud shack, trash heap, big cement
block hut, what was that, an outhouse? Whoa! A Jeep! *No
reaction. Don't give yourself away.* More ghetto shacks. He
strained to clear out the cobwebs of his brain and remember
it all. So by the time he got his body back in shape he could
have this whole fucking prison memorized.

Providing they didn't kill him first.

Not that he'd ever get so lucky. He was like a freaking bug
on a string for them. There for apparently no other reason
than their daily amusement. If he died on his own, tough shit.
But the scumbags weren't going to help him along. Too
many fun beatings and good entertaining torment left in him
to brighten their days. Which, going by the little he could see
of this rancid hellhole, must be the highlight of camp life.

He smacked into the rough wall of a dried mud shack to
the sound of Arabic laughter. He ground his teeth mercilessly
so he wouldn't mouth off and get himself another beating. A
hand shoved him in through a yawning black hole and he
landed on his face. The mattress was kicked in after him and
the door slammed, almost clipping his feet.

For a long time he lay in excruciating pain on the dirt
floor and struggled to keep it together.

When he was sure he wouldn't cry out, or worse, just cry, he forced himself up to his treacherously wobbly hands and knees. Straightened out the mattress. Crawled to the center of the room. Took a deep breath.

Shaking like a baby, he slowly pushed himself down on his feet and hands, and then up.

"One."

IT was pretty clear to Gina that Gregg van Halen really liked tying her up. He enjoyed having that edge of power over her and was especially turned on when she walked a mental tightrope of uncertainty—would he go too far? Would he let her go if she asked? Would he ever actually hurt her . . . ? He was so big . . . so strong . . . so comfortable with his own barely leashed violence. She had to wonder if she was truly safe.

Especially when she was naked and spread-eagled, blindfolded, and tied wrist and ankle to the sturdy black ironwork of his specially designed bed.

She couldn't believe she had consented to this.

She tested the strength of the velvet ropes binding her. She wasn't getting away unless he let her go. Her heart pounded like mad.

"Comfortable?" he softly asked, the huskiness of excitement in his voice subtle, but definitely there.

"Gregg, you're scaring me," she admitted.

"Kinda the idea," he murmured. "Being afraid arouses you."

"No. It doesn't."

His deep chuckle told her he knew better. "You've been wet since the first time you saw me, babe. Because I scare the living crap out of you."

The bed dipped and she turned toward the movement, listening carefully, trying to figure out what he was planning. She pulled harder at her bonds, wishing belatedly she had said no to the blindfold. "You're a sexy man, Gregg. I'm attracted to sexy men. Not scary men."

A stream of warm breath spilled down her body, leaving a shivering trail of goose bumps in its wake. Her back bowed up. Something made of soft, buttery leather touched between her breasts.

A needy, desperate sound vibrated in her throat. "What are you going to do to me?" she asked, barely able to get the words past her sudden shaking.

"Sweet thing," he whispered, a barely there rumble in her ear. "I'm gonna do anything and everything I want."

RAINIE was obviously one unhappy camper.

Well, too bad. There was no fucking way Kick was going to bring her along on this recon expedition.

Period. Done. Finito.

To her credit she didn't yell, or break down and beg. She just watched him with those big unhappy eyes in her how-can-you-do-this-to-me-after-all-we've-gone-through-together? face. Which was bad enough.

Well, guess what? One thing he *didn't* want to go through together was *dying*. At least not yet. Maybe in sixty or seventy years, in a big fluffy bed, in their sleep.

Yeah, dream on, buddy.

Well, *she* could dream on about coming with him now. He could very well be walking into an even bigger trap than in A-stan, if Nathan Daneby had warned the tangos they were coming. Kick was stressed out enough about this little foray without having to worry about Rainie tied to some post—No, not going there.

"You remember what to do, right?" he quizzed her.

"Same as the last twenty times you asked," she answered testily.

"Tell me again," he ordered, double-checking the SIG and tucking it back into its ankle holster.

She crossed her arms and recited impatiently, "If you're not back by midnight, I'm to pack up and get as far away from here as fast as I can. Back to the Bedouin."

He swung the H&K sniper around from his back and checked that, too. "And?"

"If a patrol comes by, I'm to hide, then pack up and get as far away from here as fast as I can. Back to the Bedouin."

He did not want to think about patrols finding her.

He swung the rifle back, then touched the KA-BAR Mule folding knife strapped to his wrist, the water bottle and ammo clips in his DCU pockets, and the compass around his neck. He was leaving the NVGs with Rainie, and the GPS. Just in case. "And?"

She rolled her eyes. "And under no circumstances do I go back to the DFP camp. But Kick," she protested, breaking out of their well-worn script, "I still don't believe Nate would—"

"Which is exactly what he'd want you to believe," Kick interrupted, "if he's guilty." Hell, he didn't want to believe his friend was a traitor either, but until someone came up with an alternate explanation, that's the theory he was going with. "And . . . ?"

She jetted out a curse, then, "And I find the Bedouins, who'll help me over the border to Egypt. Though why I'd need their help to get to the goddamn border if I can manage to find *them* in the first place, I'll never—"

"I told you. They'll keep you safe. You need someone trustworthy to smuggle you over into Egypt. There are all sorts of—"

"Whatever. Kick, *please*—"

Okay, scratch that about not begging. He gave her a look. She shut her mouth and didn't say another thing. Right. All set. Time to go. He felt the full measure of her discontent as he gazed at her, for maybe the last time ever. The silence stretched.

Ah, well. Had he really expected a repeat of her unexpected and emotional declaration of love? *Tcha.* Not after he'd rejected her so soundly the first time, he didn't.

But damn, how he longed to hear those words again. Just once, before he—

Fuck it.

He wrapped his hand around her jaw and kissed her whether she wanted him to or not. But with a soft noise, she melted into his embrace, clinging to him like a burr. *Thank God.*

"Please be careful," she pleaded when he finally lifted his

lips from hers. So maybe he could get used to the begging thing. The look of naked worry in her eyes was almost as good as her declaration. Almost.

He nearly broke down and made one of his own. Telling her how much he loved her, and how he wished to God that—

Yeah, nearly.

But instead, he said, "I'll be back in a few hours. I promise."

As he strode off toward the setting sun, all he could do was hope like hell that was one promise he'd be able to keep.

KICK fully expected to be attacked any second by a swarm of angry fanatics out for his blood.

His heart was pounding like an M-3 the whole time he belly-crawled across the open desert surrounding the training camp, keeping to the shallow dry creek beds and using the ever-lengthening sunset shadows as cover.

He had to get close enough to see the details he'd need to know to complete his mission. Like how many tangos were being trained. How many were in charge. Where they slept. Where they ate. Defenses. Weapons. Transpo. Etc. But not get close enough to be spotted by one of the two dozen or so scruffy men wandering around the conglomeration of mud-walled, tin-roofed Quonset huts. The tangos were all armed to the teeth. *Naturally.* What terrorist-in-training worth his salt didn't walk around in gazillion-degree heat draped with an assortment of MP-5s, Remingtons, and AK-47s as fashion accessories?

However, to Kick's immense relief, not one of them paid the slightest bit of attention to anything outside the camp perimeter. Which was not fenced. Or even guarded.

Un-fucking-believable. Either these bozos really sucked at security, or no one had warned them he might be showing up. Hopefully both.

Thank you, Lord. He might actually survive this gig.

With palpable relief, he shook off the sweat and the roiling tension that had been cramping his muscles ever since leaving Rainie, and pulled out his binoculars.

He lifted them to his eyes. And that's when he saw it.

What the *fuck*! He almost dropped the nocs in shock.

A Westerner. Limping badly and obviously hurt. Unkempt, dressed in rags, beaten black-and-blue, and thin as a rail, the man was being mercilessly pushed through the camp with a gun to his back.

Holy shit.

The fuckers had a prisoner.

Shit, shit, fucking shit.

Kick's stomach zinged in dismay.

And just that fast, everything changed.

TWENTY-ONE

A hostage?

Goddamn it. Kick drilled his hands in his hair and pulled it back so hard it hurt. So what the hell did he do now?

When the poor fuck was shoved unceremoniously into one of the smaller, more squalid huts—not that there was a huge difference between squalid and merely disgusting—Kick lowered his field glasses, rolled onto his back in the shelter of a low dry creek bed, and stared up at the darkening sky. He was trembling all over. And not from drug withdrawal.

Hell.

That guy was one of *ours*. Under all that filthy blond hair and beard, his features were unmistakably Northern European. Odds were, American.

God only knew how long the poor slob had been held and tortured in this pile of shit camp. Kick dredged his memory for any hint of a newspaper story or CNN report of a Western soldier or businessman or diplomat having disappeared in the region. There'd been several abductions over the past five or so years in the Sudan, but the victims were all accounted for. Rescued or dead. Gruesomely executed or scooped from the jaws. He knew for a fact that STORM had been involved in at least one of those invisible rescues.

Jesus H. Christ.

He wiped his hands down his face. Okay. Okay. So. Stick to the plan for now. Watch the tangos for a few hours to see if anything noteworthy happened, keep his eyes peeled for the head motherfucker himself, then get the hell back to Rainie. Call STORM. Figure out how to extract that prisoner without compromising the mission. Because one thing was for damn certain, he was not going to call in an air strike until the guy was safely out of there.

Daaamn.

And he'd thought it was going to be tough to escape this clusterfuck in one piece with Rainie in tow. Now he had a goddamn crippled POW to contend with.

Things just got better and better.

"SO basically, what you're saying is, we're screwed."

Kick nodded wearily. He'd wracked his brain, but he simply hadn't been able to come up with an easy out, or even one with a fifty-fifty chance of success. "That about sums it up."

Rainie bit her lip. "That poor man. What he must have gone through."

Kick had just pretty much outlined a death sentence for at least two of the three of them. Leave it to her to be concerned about the wounded prisoner and not herself.

"Poor all of us," he corrected. "If I take out abu Bakr, the hostage will be executed instantly. If we go in and liberate him, abu Bakr will be gone so fast we saw his dust yesterday, *and* his buddies will be on us like F.O.S. We can't lift the prisoner without alerting the whole camp to an attack. STORM can't air strike without killing the hostage. Any which way, someone dies. Probably us."

"F.O.S.?"

He grimaced. "Flies on shit."

She grimaced back. "Charming. So what are we going to do about it?" Her eyes filled with angry determination.

Hell. Once she'd gotten past that whole terrified-of-life thing, she'd turned into some kind of big-time, kick-ass ninja-wannabe.

He held up his hands. "Whoa, there, sweetheart. There's no 'we' involved here. You can help me brainstorm ideas, sure, but that's it."

"But I—"

"Nonnegotiable." He gave her a smile to soften his uncompromising edict. "Unless it involves sex."

"You are so not funny."

"Hell, I'm *serious*. If I'm going to die in the next twenty-four hours, I'd—" She gave him a withering look. "Okay, fine. Ideas?"

As she pondered, she took the bottle of tea he was holding and sipped. The Bedouin had thrown in a small packet of China oolong along with the camels and waterskins, and Rainie had made sun tea in one of the plastic water bottles she'd saved, hanging it from her saddle. The brew was tepid, with a slight note of *eau de goat*, and they had to strain the leaves out through their teeth, but all things considered it tasted damn good.

She passed the bottle back to him. "All right. Let's take a page from their own book. Create a diversion. Were there any explosives in that field pack?"

The first thing he'd thought of, too. "Yeah, but what do we blow up? And how do they not think it's an attack on the camp so they don't kill the prisoner?"

Her lips turned down. "True. Okay, how about we stampede the camels through the camp and create a panic."

"With two camels?"

"Well, *I'd* be panicked."

He couldn't help chuckling. "Yeeeah."

She stuck her tongue out at him. "Okay. So, we, *um* . . . We take one of *them* hostage and make a trade." She glanced at him hopefully.

The moon had risen, painting a silvery glow over the brown of the desert, and reflected bright twin crescents in her eyes. She was so beautiful it almost hurt to look at her.

"Uh-huh," he said, swallowing away the pain of knowing she would never be his. "I was thinking along those same lines." *Sort of.*

She perked up. "Really? So who do we snatch? And how do we—"

"I was thinking more of using *me* as a hostage. Trade myself for the prisoner." Well actually, more like turn himself into a prisoner. Your basic Trojan Horse bang-and-grab scenario. The only thing he could think of that had a prayer of succeeding. Maybe not exactly fifty-fifty odds, but definitely in the double digits. Possibly. If things went down perfectly.

She blinked, surprised. Clearly undecided as to whether or not he was serious. She nibbled her lip. "Okay," she said, "that sex thing is sounding pretty good about now. You're obviously delusional and need a break from the strain."

She did not, however, start taking off her clothes.

"Look—"

"Are you *insane*?" she demanded, cutting off the explanation—okay, rationalization—he was formulating. "There is no flipping *way* you are doing that."

"Rainie—"

"No."

"Just hear me—"

"*No!*" She jumped to her feet and started to pace across the wadi. "How can you even *think*—"

"Get the hell *down!*" He grabbed her arm and yanked her onto her butt.

"*Oof.*"

"Goddamn it, for any of this to work, *you*, at least, need to stay alive."

"No one's out there patrolling. You said we're too far awa—"

"I don't care what I said. You are not to take chances with your safety!"

"Oh, oh, but it's okay for *you* to just walk into that nest of terrorists with your hands on your head and expect me to—"

"Damn it, Rainie, we don't have a choice here! Besides—"

"There's always a goddamn choice!" Her eyes were shooting flames now, and her fingers held onto his arms so hard it would take the jaws of life to pry them off.

Hello? Who are you and what have you done with the timorous Miss Martin?

This woman was a warrior.

A strong, sexy, amazing, confident warrior queen.

God, if she turned him on before, this version of Rainie made him want to get down on his knees and howl like a caveman.

Daaamn.

He slid his hand behind her neck and pulled her to him. Before either of them knew what he was doing, he'd covered her mouth with his and rolled her under him. In a motion he had her Bedouin robe over her head and—there was a God— she hadn't put her clothes back on after last time they made love. She was soft and lush and desperately welcoming, and completely, soul-permeatingly naked.

This time the buttons on his DCUs didn't give her warrior fingers the least bit of trouble. They were down around his ankles in record time.

And then he was inside her.

Oh. My. Sweet. Lord. This was where he wanted to be. Forever and always. Not tortured and dead in some—

Not going there. Not now.

He kissed her and kissed her, thrusting his cock in so deep he was momentarily afraid he'd hurt her. But she just moaned low and wrapped her legs even tighter around his waist. "Oh, Kick."

It sounded so sweet on her lips. But suddenly he needed more. "My real name's Kyle," he told her, almost hesitantly.

She looked up at him, her face a portrait of exquisite pleasure. She smiled.

"Kyle," she whispered into his mouth, and for a second he couldn't move, hung in suspended animation. No one had ever called him by his real name before while making love. It felt . . .

He broke through his emotional paralysis, pulled out of her and thrust back in. "Say it again," he wanted.

Wanted to test it. Roll it around on his senses. The sound of his real name wrapped in a moan of need. Test the way it made him feel. The unbelievable reality of someone truly wanting Kyle Jackson, of someone calling it out loud, not with hate or disgust, but with love.

"Kyle," she breathed, that love so obvious in her beautiful green eyes that it almost made him believe in miracles. Except if this truly were a miracle, he wouldn't have to go out there tomorrow and sacrifice his life for a man he didn't even know.

Or maybe . . . Maybe this was the punishment and penance demanded of Kick to redeem all the bad he had done in his lifetime. Maybe if he did this one noble, unthinkable deed, sacrificed the only good thing that had ever come to him, gave up the only woman he'd ever loved, maybe then his sins would truly be forgiven.

"I love you, Kyle," she whispered.

And his heart bled.

I love you, too, Lorraine Martin, he wanted to say to her. Over and over. But didn't dare. Instead, he bit his tongue and held her tight, tight, tight. Wishing he didn't know for certain what he must do. Tonight. Before she woke up and stopped him. *More than you'll ever know.*

KICK moved.

Rainie awoke abruptly. One nanosecond she was asleep, dreaming of making sweet, wonderful love to Kick—Kyle— and the next nanosecond she was awake, filled with the certain knowledge that he was slowly, gingerly, trying to extricate his protective arm from around her body.

Goddamn it.

He was actually planning to do it. To go to the insurgent camp to exchange himself for that damn prisoner he'd probably hallucinated to begin with. Honest to God, what did he think those terrorists would do when he showed up and asked them to let their prisoner go and he'd take his place?

Laugh in his face, and then shoot him in the head. That's what they'd do.

Worse, he'd planned to do it without telling her.

Before he'd moved five inches, she grabbed his arm. "I don't *think* so."

"Baby—"

"Don't you *dare* 'baby' me, Kyle Jackson." Even in the moonlit darkness she saw him wince.

She couldn't *believe* he would do this. After last night. After they'd both let their emotions tumble out and light up the night with more sparks than the meteor shower that had rained over them in the magical lull between two amazing sessions of lovemaking. He hadn't said the words she longed to hear, but his feelings had shone through in living color.

But now this. She didn't know whether to cry, or shake him in frustration until his teeth rattled.

"You were going to leave me here, weren't you? While you go off and sacrifice yourself in some kind of PTSD-induced guilt-fest."

"Wow, that was harsh," he said, looking wounded. "And no, I wasn't leaving. Not for good, anyway. Not yet."

"Oh, great. You aren't killing yourself until tonight. That makes me feel *so* much better."

He let out a huff. "I have no intention of killing myself, Rain. I've been thinking. About your idea with the explosives. About a diversion."

She glared at him for a long second. "You really think they'd fall for it? I mean, you said yourself, it's the oldest trick in the book."

"Then we better pray they don't know how to read."

She backpedaled. "I know it was my suggestion, but there has to be another way." How could a desperate Hail Mary like that possibly work? Especially with only two of them to execute it? Two dozen against two weren't great odds. Especially when it was really more like two dozen against one and a half because of Rainie's total lack of training.

"If there is another way, I can't think of it," he said. "And it's hard enough leaving you unprotected out here without you making me feel even more guilty about it. So please, enough with the recriminations, okay?"

She sighed. "I'm sorry," she said, and she was. That crack about PTSD was uncalled for. However . . . the fear behind it was all too real. She knew him. He'd play the hero and end up dead. *Deep breath. Let it out.* "But you have to promise to take me with you this morning."

"Rainie, there's no need to—"

She *knew* it. "I swear to God, Kick, if you don't let me help you set this up, I will shoot you myself." At his expression of incredulity, she added, "Dude. You seriously don't want to test me. I'm an ER nurse and know exactly where to place a bullet to incapacitate but not kill, and I'm getting damn good at tying stuff to camels."

He actually choked out a laugh. She narrowed her eyes but he held up a hand, sobering. "Fine. You win. This is going to take both of us to succeed, so you should probably be in from the start."

She sagged in relief. "Good. I really wasn't looking forward to shooting you."

His gaze softened. "Yeah, like you could have done that."

Then he kissed her, and with his lips on hers so warm and loving, she knew without doubt that . . . yeah, she could. She'd do anything in the world, anything at all, to keep him from dying.

Because *he* would do anything in the world, anything at all, to keep that hostage from dying.

He was a better man than she would ever be.

And she wanted him. In her life.

Yeah, for always.

THEY ate a fortifying if fairly yucky breakfast of MREs and lukewarm sun tea, then Kick gathered the supplies he needed and stowed them carefully in his DCU pockets. Today he was wearing cammies head to ankle, looking handsome and dangerous as all get-out. He'd made Rainie wear one of his extra cammie T-shirts with her jeans, and today she covered her hair and arms with the khaki parachute-silk *kaffiyeh* he'd made for her after the crash, rather than the brightly visible white Bedouin head shawl.

"We'll only take one of the camels, to save time," he told her, "and leave it hidden while we nail down the plan details and place the explosives."

They'd talked it out, and the idea was to rig up a diversionary explosion which Rainie would set off tonight, creating an opening for Kick to rush into the chaos and grab the prisoner. Meanwhile, she'd circle around to the other side with the camels and pick up Kick and the hostage there, then all three would ride hell-bent for the Egyptian border. STORM would already have been radioed beforehand and the air strike coordinated. With any luck that would catch the insurgents before they lit out in pursuit of them.

Pretty standard—and predictable—strategy. Unfortunately, they didn't have the time, supplies, or numbers to get more creative. It was their only shot.

When they reached the hills, Kick hobbled the camel and they climbed up to the top of the ridge to study the camp below. She was nervous as hell being this close. She still remembered the mouth-drying terror she'd felt that first day hiding in the cave after the plane crash, and those awful men nearly finding her. Not to mention Kick's horrific story.

The good news was that this time she wasn't on the verge of a panic attack. She really was better.

Kick passed her a bottle of water.

"If we do this, what about abu Bakr?" she asked.

Kick grimaced, pulling out his binoculars. "With any luck I'll run into the bastard during the rescue and can nail him then."

Despite her continued ambivalence on the subject, she knew he would hate not completing his real mission. She'd come a long way on this journey, not just in mileage, but in mind-set. She'd killed a man herself. And come to accept that sometimes there's no choice. It's you or them. How could she condemn Kick for his past sins? Or agonize over what they were about to do? Killing these terrorists would save hundreds of lives, possibly thousands.

But for Kick, killing abu Bakr was highly personal. Revenge for his friends' terrible deaths. And yet, here he was, willing to forsake that mission in order to save the life of one unknown prisoner. Her respect for him was definitely off the charts.

"I have to trust the air strike will take care of him if I can't. The most important thing now is saving that prisoner's life, and preventing the attacks on the Khartoum embassies." He raised the field glasses again. "One thing . . . whatever abu Bakr's planning, I have a sneaking suspicion it involves something inside that cement hut in the center of camp."

She peered down at it. "Why do you say that?"

"It's the only substantial structure in the whole camp, and

the only thing besides the prisoner that has a constant guard. Something important's in there. I can smell it."

She recognized that stubborn tone of voice. "Don't even think about trying to check it out, Kick. There isn't time."

"I know. I just wish—"

"Yeah, there are a lot of things I wish, too." He glanced over and she met his eyes, allowing the full extent of her worry for him to show in hers. "Please don't take any chances. I can't make it without you."

"Sure, you can," he responded quietly. "If you haven't learned that much over the past week, I sure as hell have. You can do anything you put your mind to, Rainie. There's no doubt about that."

She wondered if he'd deliberately interpreted her words in the narrower context of her making it out of the Sudan alive. Or if it had even occurred to him that she might mean it in a bigger sense. A whole-life sense.

But before she could say anything more, he rolled over, dug in his pocket, and handed her the funny-looking goggles he'd used briefly at the refinery. "Here. Better start getting used to these."

"Now, what are they again . . . ?"

"NVGs. Night vision goggles. They'll let you keep track of me in the dark tonight. I'll have a marker in my pocket that will blink hot and cold so you can tell it's me." He adjusted a knob.

She slid them on and winced at the bright green images. "Yikes."

"The daylight messes up the optics so I've stopped them down, but you get the general idea. When you're done, put them somewhere safe until tonight. I'll rig the explosives now. And for God's sake, stay down and well out of sight."

She watched anxiously as he went a few yards further along the top of the ridge, hunkering down and cutting off small chunks from what looked like a brick of grey clay, which he then placed around several sandstone boulders, and connected the chunks with stiff string. Then he pulled a box out of his pocket and carefully unwrapped its contents.

"Detonator cap," he explained. "Without this, no bang."

Gingerly he measured and attached a long piece of a different type of string to it and stepped away.

"That's the fuse I'm supposed to light?" she asked nervously.

"Det cord, yeah. It's super-slow-burning so you'll have plenty of time to get clear to the other side of the camp after lighting it."

"You're sure?" she asked, grim visions of Wile E. Coyote blowing himself up while lighting endless sticks of dynamite dancing through her head.

"I'm sure," he said, handing her a disposable lighter. "Keep this safe, too."

She slid it into her pocket.

Movement down in the camp snagged their attention. The men were gathering in an open area in front of the cement hut, laying down little rugs on the dirt.

Stricken, she stared. *Oh, Lord.* "They're praying."

"Don't," Kick said, taking hold of her shoulders and spinning her away from the sight. "Don't do that to yourself."

"But how can we—"

"Remember why those men are here, Rainie. They're here to learn how to bomb and kill and maim. Think of the innocent people in the embassies who'll die, and the workers in the refinery, how easily and brutally they killed them. And never, ever forget what they would do to *you* if they found you."

She bit down on her lip. "I know you're right. It just feels . . ."

"Believe me, I know. But if they were truly spiritual men, they would not be here." He pulled her close. "I'm sorry, I have to get going or I'll miss my window. Will you be all right?"

She sucked down a breath and nodded.

He gave her a kiss. "Be safe. And if anything happens to me down there, you know what to do."

Her heart squeezed. "Yeah. Come in after you, guns blazing."

He scowled. "Don't even joke."

How well he knew her. And yet, how little. If he were captured, did he really expect her to run off to the Bedouin and leave him here to be tortured and killed? *Yeah. Snowball's chance.*

"Please don't let anything happen to you," she pleaded, throwing her arms around him. She was so afraid to let him go, even just to quickly set things up on the fringes of the camp. How much worse would it be tonight, to watch him charge right into the midst of the enemy and try to drag a wounded prisoner out of there?

Oh, God. This plan was never going to work.

Deep breath. Let it out slowly.

He will be fine.

We will both be fine.

One final kiss and he stepped out of her arms.

Yes. Yes, it *would* work. It had to.

Because there was no other way to get out of this whole situation alive.

For any of them.

He disappeared over the top of the ridge, and for a long time she sat hidden and watched like a hawk for him to appear somewhere below.

The weird, melodic chanting of the terrorists' prayers drifted across the desert, creating a surreal soundtrack to her jangling nerves. The sun was high over the horizon now and the temperature hotter than Hades. Sweat ran down her temples and slowly soaked through her T-shirt.

But there was no sign of Kick. That was good, right? If she couldn't see him, and she even knew he was down there, the bad guys couldn't see him, either.

Wait! What was that? A disembodied shadow moved across the back of a mud hut, then blended into a pile of debris next to an old Jeep. He'd said he planned to disable it. And also to try and find where they stored the petrol and their extra ammo, then wire it all to blow, in order to lay down a second layer of cover.

With her heart lodged firmly in her throat, she waited for him to reappear. And waited. And waited.

There! For a split second he was a blur crossing a bare section of desert just beyond the camp perimeter, making tracks for a nearby wash. Thank God! He must be finished and heading back to her.

But all of a sudden, there was a loud shout. One of the terrorists, the one who'd been guarding that damned cement
hut, yelled and pointed, then took off running after Kick.

"No!" she cried, then slapped her hand over her mouth.

Instantly, every man in the camp was on his feet giving
chase.

Run, Kick! Run!

She bit down hard on her tongue, wanting to explode in
rage and scream in pain, and keep screaming and screaming
for him to keep running and running, until she couldn't make
another sound.

Suddenly, he just stopped in his tracks. And with a quick
look up at the ridge where she was hiding, he turned, and
raised his hands high.

No. *No, no, no!* What was he *doing*?

Don't surrender!

The terrorists were on him like a pack of angry dogs.
Shaking their fists and shooting off their guns, they savagely
dragged him into the camp. He didn't even resist.

Oh, dear God.

Please, God, no!

He'd given himself up! But *why*? Why not run? Run and
hide, as he'd done on that very first day?

Because he didn't have any way of tricking them this
time, she realized with a sinking heart. He knew they wouldn't
give up hunting him until they'd found him. And . . . *Oh,
God*. It suddenly hit her like a two-by-four what must have
driven his decision to surrender so quickly. They'd find *her*,
too.

Oh, dear Lord. Kick had deliberately let himself be captured by those monsters.

In order to protect *her*.

TWENTY-TWO

MACHINE guns were going off. Shooting wildly.

Shouting.

Outside the four walls of his pigsty, mayhem reigned.

What the fuck was going on?

Pig swallowed heavily. Possibilities burned through his head.

Was this it?

Had his captors finally decided to put on the Big Finale? Would they come for him now and drag his ass out into the middle of the camp and slice off his head as the video cameras rolled, amid much joy, celebration, and merriment?

Shit.

Every day for as long as he could remember he'd expected to die. Just not, like, right now this minute.

Fuck. He wasn't ready. He still hadn't gotten down with his redheaded Angel. Hell, he still didn't even know her damn name. Or his own, for that matter. He couldn't die. Not yet. He wasn't—

Suddenly, the door swung wide. Sunlight streamed through the opening, lighting up his dark, confined world. Great. Why couldn't he have stayed blind for just a few more weeks?

Now he'd be able to see their laughing eyes as they killed him, see the glint of the curved sword they'd use to—

Someone was tossed into the small space, slamming into the back wall with a bone-crunching crash.

"Yeah! Fuck you, too, Osama!" the guy yelled, along with a string of other curses as he slid down the mud wall onto his ass.

Holy Christ, that was English! American English.

Pig gripped the edge of his tattered mattress in disbelief. The door smacked shut, cutting off the light like a switch.

"Jesus." The single word whispered through the hut like a breeze in the tall pines back home. Back home . . . Home had pines?

And that voice . . .

His pulse shot through his veins like neutrons in a superconductor. Impossible. No. *This had to be a dream. Another of the redhead's cruel games.* He couldn't even remember what a pine tree looked like. If there was such a thing. And that voice probably only seemed familiar because it sounded like the voice in his own head. He knew he was American. They'd told him often enough. *American Pig!*

"Hey," he attempted to say aloud, but it came out more like a croak.

The American voice didn't answer.

He squinted and peered but couldn't see shit. Maybe he really was dreaming . . . He crawled closer, on unsteady hands and knees across the packed dirt floor, desperately trying to clear his fuzzy vision and wade through the dimness to see—

A man really was sitting there where he'd dropped, staring back at him. Probably in horror. Yeah, well, they didn't call him Pig for nothing.

"My God," the man whispered in the darkness.

"Are you real?" he asked the dim vision, hardly daring to hope. He wanted to wish—for the other man's sake—he was only hallucinating. But he couldn't. He was too starved for friendly human company to do anything but pray like hell the guy was for real. And friendly.

Again no answer.

He picked his way closer still. Slowly, warily, ready to

roll into a ball at the least sign of violence. The guards had tricked him before. But this man didn't move. And the guy wasn't dressed like a guard. Were those Army DCUs and boots?

He lifted his hand and touched . . . a real face. Warm flesh and bone. Not an illusion . . .

Real fingers reached out to touch his face in return. He flinched away.

"Jesus God," that familiar voice breathed. "It can't be. I must be losing it. . . ." Infinitely slowly the fingers kept coming.

He couldn't help his instinctive reaction; he squeezed his eyes shut, shrank back, and started to shake violently. Waiting for the slap, or the punch, or the grab and twist. But instead a gentle touch pushed aside his long, rat-nest hair and faintly traced the outline of his bruised cheek.

"Jesus. Jesus God, Alex. It's really you."

RAINIE had to get out of there. Fast.

The ugly bastard that seemed to be in command had tossed Kick into one of the shacks, then started shouting loudly. As she watched, just as she'd feared, a swarm of gun-wielding men came pouring out of the terrorist camp. To search for Kick's hideaway, to confiscate his belongings. The hideaway where they'd foolishly left evidence of *two* people, not just one. Once the terrorists found it, they'd know there was a second infidel lurking around somewhere. And go after her.

Crap. This could get very ugly, as Kick would say.

She had to get down there first, and remove all her belongings. Anything that would give away her presence. Kick's life depended on her staying alive and free.

She managed to rush down the hill without killing herself or leaving too obvious tracks, then clamber up onto the camel and get the recalcitrant beast moving. For a moment she was so terrified she debated with herself if she really should go back to camp to gather up any signs of a second person . . . or just take her chances.

Except she also needed water. She only had a half bottle

left. And no food. Heck, no sunscreen, either. Oh, yeah, or
weapons, other than a cigarette lighter. She *had* to risk going
back. All of Kick's guns were still at camp—except for the
SIG, which he'd had with him—along with everything else
she'd need to survive in this desolate country.

Let alone rescue him.

Just thinking about the man she loved in the clutches of
those maniacs made her heart sick with pain. And bolstered
her courage.

Pack up and get as far away from here as fast as you can.

Nope. Not gonna happen, baby.

Either *both* of them got out of this godforsaken place
alive, or neither of them did.

Make that all three of them.

She turned the camel and urged it forward, heading to the
wadi.

Failure wasn't an option. She had plans for Kick. He
might think he could never . . . whatever . . . but last night
he'd shown her he loved her, even if he couldn't say the
words. Hell, she didn't care about the past. His past, *or* hers.
For the first time ever, she was more concerned about the
future. As in, she *wanted* a future. A future with him.

It was up to her to make sure they both got that chance.

All she needed was a plan. And water, sunscreen, and
anything in the field pack that went bang.

GINA gazed at Gregg over the rim of her wineglass. Yep, it
was official. She was a total weenie.

The jerk hadn't even asked her out to dinner. Again. And
yet, for some mysterious, incomprehensible total-insanity
reason, she'd let him into her apartment anyway when he'd
shown up at her doorstep at a quarter till the middle of the
night.

Again.

So granted, he *was* the hottest thing she'd ever seen in a
pair of pants, or those black T-shirts and leather jacket he
always wore. Or that lickable bronze tan that left white crin-
kle marks at the corners of his eyes and thin white lines

shooting back into his military-short haircut from wearing those sexy aviator sunglasses all day.

Never mind when he took *off* those pants, T-shirts, and shades.

Okay, so he was one killer hunky man.

But sorry. No excuse. Gregg van Halen was a Neanderthal of the first degree.

Because not only all that, but now he wanted to know why she hadn't told him she'd be working the afternoon shift at the hospital. And insisting she detail for him exactly what she had planned for tomorrow. Like it was his God-given right to know.

So unattractive in a man.

The worst part was, she was seriously considering giving in and telling him. Just so he'd stop with the annoying Sphinx imitation.

She gave a silent eye roll. More like *sphincter*.

She took a big sip of wine. "You have real control issues, you know," she told him, irritated as hell.

He gazed back at her impassively. "So do you, sweet thing."

Okay. Yeah. So sue her. She liked being in charge of every aspect of her life. Who didn't? She hated it when she wasn't in control.

Like with him, for instance.

Except, wait. *He* seemed to control every damn thing that went on between the two of them. Especially in bed.

And God help her if *that* part didn't arouse her like nothing else ever had. She, who had been a tireless women's advocate all her life, all but swooning over a man who dominated her sexually.

How freaking nauseating was that?

And he'd completely spoiled her for all those harmless young interns and research assistants forever.

Damn him, the bastard. Because this guy was *so* not the type to stick around. Not even to feed her sudden and über-mortifying appetite for being tied up and helpless when she was naked.

Lord.

She took another fortifying chug of wine. "Look. I'll admit I enjoy the things you do in bed. I'm a strong woman, and it's a huge turn-on to meet a man who"—*ho-boy*—"has a strong hand sexually. But—"

His brow rose as he interrupted. "Is that what this is about? You want me to spank the information out of you?"

"No!" she said, appalled that he would think that. And the heat that shot through her limbs was from anger, *not* excitement. "*No*. Let's just say there's a big difference between what I like in bed and what I'll allow outside the bedroom. I don't need a man, don't *want* a man running my life. So don't even *try* that caveman bullshit with me. Okay?"

Tilting back in his chair, he gazed at her for a while, hands laced over his abdomen, his pale blue eyes unreadable. Then he said, "What if I told you someone has been following you for the past few days?"

Wait. What? Her wineglass sloshed. "Who? Why would they be doing that?"

He lifted a shoulder. "Gina, you've been asking a lot of indiscriminate questions about a CIA black op. Your best friend is suspected of stealing drugs from a hospital. You work in a controversial field known to be of interest to terrorists. Your ex-fiancé is an FBI agent. Hell, take your pick."

Her jaw dropped. Indiscriminate? *Terrorists?* That was an awful lot right off the tip of his tongue. Did he really think—

"How do you know about Wade?" she asked warily, concentrating on the easy one. She was pretty certain she hadn't mentioned her former lover to her current one, who just regarded her evenly. "Right. Silly me. You're a goddamn secret agent. You know everything. *Except*, apparently, who is following me." She lifted her glass in a salute.

"Not my job," he said, unperturbed. "Just happened to notice."

Not his job.

A frisson of suspicion sifted through her. Someone was following her, but it wasn't her secret agent boyfriend's job to find out who. Then . . . "What exactly *is* your job, Gregg?"

The corners of his mouth curled. "Whatever it is you're thinking, it's not that."

His gaze didn't waver as she drilled him with hers. Total

innocence. Yeah, right. More like really, really good at his job. As a secret frigging agent.

She leaned forward. "I *think* I must have been asking too many *indiscriminate* questions about Rainie. The CIA sent you to placate me. Didn't they," she demanded, with a sudden sinking feeling it might actually be true.

Jeez, why hadn't she put two and two together before this? He'd been sent to keep tabs on her and shut her up! To deflect her persistent digging for the truth about Rainie's disappearance. Using whatever means necessary. Like false information and doctored photos. And mind-blowing, no-strings-wanted sex.

Wow.

And hadn't *that* worked like a damn charm. She hadn't made a single irate phone call since the first time they'd—

Oy.

"Placate," he echoed. "Cute." The front legs of his chair hit the carpet with a soft thud. "All this from being a gentleman."

This time she laughed aloud. "You're kidding, right?"

"Giving the lady what she wants," he said mildly, getting to his feet and coming around the table. *Damn*, he was big. And strong. *Whoops*. And angry. "That *is* the definition of a gentleman, isn't it?"

Okay, now he was scaring her.

So what was new?

She scrambled up from her chair, knocking over her wine. "No. The definition of a gentleman is someone who always tells the truth."

He loomed over her, his smile both amused and intimidating. "The truth? Hell. That wouldn't be any fun, now, would it?"

TEN minutes later, Rainie tied her camel just outside the sheltered hollow where she and Kick had hidden their belongings. She had to leave it close by, where it would be found. Carefully, she crept along the outcropping that obscured the hideaway from the wadi, hugging the stone wall.

At the edge of their encampment, she halted, scanning the

floor of the deep riverbed. No sign that their secret place had been disturbed . . . None of their things had been moved.

She tilted her head to listen. All quiet on the terrorist front. No shouting. No gunshots.

So far, so good.

Setting to work, she swiftly gathered the parachute they'd slept on, only to pause in frozen anguish when she caught the lingering scent of their intimacy. Oh, God. *Kick. I'm coming for you, baby.* Forcing herself back into action, she swiped up the long duffel bag with his knives and sniper rifle and stuffed the chute into it, along with her jeans and T-shirt, which she'd left spread on a boulder last night to air out. A waterskin quickly joined them, though reluctantly she left the other behind, or the searchers would be suspicious. She hesitated over which field pack to grab. Settled on the one containing the SATCOM, and threw the first aid kit and a handful of MREs on top of the extra DCUs and miscellaneous things still in the pack.

All at once she heard yelling. In Arabic. Echoing down the wadi from the other direction. The direction of the terrorists.

Crap. Out of time.

Slinging the field pack over one shoulder and the duffel over the other, she started backing up, scanning for anything she shouldn't have left. Her heart was pounding out of control. Terrified, she prepared to turn and run like hell back to where the second camel was still hidden.

When suddenly she was grabbed from behind.

Panic exploded through her. She tried to scream. But a hand slapped over her mouth. Hard.

Please, God, no!

She kicked and fought, trying to tear herself from her captor's unrelenting hold.

But the man was as strong and impervious as the Terminator. Despite her struggles, he easily dragged her and the heavy packs back along the wadi.

Please, please, please. This could not be happening. She couldn't believe they'd caught her! And so soon.

Tears of desperation sprang to her eyes. From the pain of

Terminator Man's merciless grip. But more from the thought of letting down the man she loved. So completely.

Oh, Kick, I am so, so sorry.

Now he really *was* going to die.

And surely she would, too.

"ALEX!"

Kick was still reeling with shock. His fingers stalled on his friend's grizzled cheek, unable to break the contact even though he knew better than to touch a man as feral as Alex Zane had obviously become. Kick had to literally hold himself back from grabbing his friend into his arms and hugging him hard.

Holy fucking shit, Alex was alive! But how?

God he needed a fix. Bad.

The man Kick had thought dead these sixteen months opened his tightly shut eyes. "Alex?" He repeated his own name uncertainly, as if . . .

"Oh, man, you're alive," Kick said, nearly choking on emotion—happiness and dismay and stunning shock. His head spun with dizziness. "Don't you recognize—" His words cut off as he realized to his horror . . .

Aw, God. Alex *didn't* recognize him!

Behind the matted mop of hair and beard that mostly hid his face, those green eyes filled with a volatile mix of hope and suspicion. "You know me?" Alex's voice was cracked and rusty with disuse. "You know my name?"

"Yeah, of course I do. It's Kick, man. We've been"—he swallowed—"friends for years."

"Kick? But . . . you said Alex."

Ah, shit. Kick felt like there was a giant stone sitting on his chest. Even bigger than for the past week. "I'm Kick, buddy. You're Alex. Don't you . . . You really don't know who you are?"

"Alex," he whispered, as though hearing the name for the first time.

"Christopher Alexander Zane. You were . . . lost in Afghanistan. We thought—I thought—you were dead."

"Dead."

Very gingerly, Alex sat back on his mattress. It was unnerving how those familiar yet unbearably distant eyes peered back at him through that curtain of wild-man hair. Jesus, how he must have suffered. To survive being skinned alive by dragging behind that truck, then somehow to be transported to this armpit of the world only to be treated worse than an animal. Kick couldn't even imagine the hardships the man had endured. No wonder his mind had shut down. Or maybe it had been irreparably damaged. God, he didn't even want to think about that possibility.

Alex leaned forward and beckoned with blackened fingers. Kick scooted closer. Tears glistened on his friend's cheekbones as he whispered, "Have you come to rescue me from the dead?"

Kick felt his own eyes sting as he swallowed again, more heavily. "Yeah, buddy," he promised him. "I've come to get you. Gonna take you home."

And he would. If it was the last thing he ever did.

"**SSST!** Stop struggling! Ay *merde*!"

At the low command, muttered in French-accented English from behind, Rainie did stop. Stunned.

"Mademoiselle Martin, it's me, Girard Virreau."

Surprise nearly knocked the wind from her lungs. She turned her head and she relaxed his grip on her enough to confirm his identity. *Omigod!* It really was him, the charming French count from the Doctors for Peace camp!

"No screams, *non*?" he whispered.

She shook her head, trying to quell the shaking in her limbs. *Lord* he'd scared her. He let go and put a finger to his lips to keep her from speaking. The angry voices of the terrorists were getting closer and closer. Any second now they would discover her and Kick's hideaway and belongings. At least those she'd left there.

He took the backpack from her and waggled his head for her to follow, which she did, even though her legs still felt like two leaden noodles. As swiftly and quietly as possible they made their way along the rocks at the base of the wadi wall, until they came to a large boulder. Virreau disappeared behind it. She followed. There was a shallow natural cave behind the boulder, where he now crouched, waving for her to join him. They might actually have a chance of escaping detection.

Terror pounded through her veins with every heartbeat. Along with a thousand questions. But she let him put his arm around her, and buried her face against his shoulder as, mere yards away, the terrorists triumphantly found her former encampment and tore through Kick's belongings.

A few minutes later the tangos left, carrying away every last thing, as well as the camel, which they'd also found.

When they were sure the search party had gone for good, she let out a shuddering breath. "That was close," she whispered. Drawing away from him, she hugged herself around the middle, relief nearly bending her in half. "Oh, my God, I can't believe they didn't find us." She couldn't stop the tears that trickled down her cheeks.

He gave her a crooked smile and handed her an embroidered handkerchief. "Do not worry, you are safe now, *chérie*."

She straightened, dabbing at her eyes. "Not that I'm ungrateful for the company, but, Girard, what are you doing here?"

He gave a shrug. "When Marc told me you had gone with Monsieur Jackson, well, I simply must come after you. Make sure you are all right. It is a very foolish thing to do, Rainie. These men are not to trifle with."

"Marc told you where we were going?" That surprised her even more than the count's sudden appearance.

"But of course. When he woke up, he was very worried about you, *chérie*."

Strange. Marc had been the one to talk Kick into taking her with him in the first place. Something must have made Marc change his mind. And what about Nate? Didn't he say anything?

"You see," Virreau interrupted her thoughts, "as a doctor I have had dealings with the fanatics in these insurgent camps. God forbid you should fall into their hands."

She crumpled the handkerchief in her fist. "That's what

Kick kept saying. But now they have *him* and I'm scared to death they'll hurt him."

Virreau let out a low sigh. "Yes, I am sure they will."

"I can't let that happen. I've got to get him out of there!" She shut her eyes for a moment to keep from breaking down completely. *Breathe in. Let it out slowly. Breathe in.*

She opened them to Virreau giving her a look of sympathy. Although . . . for a split second it seemed more like pity.

"I understand," he said, his expression smoothing out. "But as I said, I have had dealings with these men. Let me see what I can do."

Hope *whooshed* through her. But also disbelief. "You mean, like, go in and *talk* to those people? You really think you can get them free?"

His eyes sharpened. "Them?"

"They have another prisoner, too. Besides Kick. Another Westerner."

Concern whipped across Virreau's face. "You have *seen* this man?"

She shook her head. "No. But Kick did. That's why he went down there, to—"

"*Mon dieu.*" Virreau suddenly became furious. "This is very bad."

"I know. I have to do something—"

"*Non!*" His vehemence shocked her to silence. But his face immediately smoothed in apology. "You must not risk your life, *chérie*, attempting anything foolish."

Where had she heard *that* before? "But I can't just sit here and—"

"Yes. You can. You must." He gripped her arms fervently. "Let *me* go instead."

"But—"

"They know I am a doctor. I have met them. They wouldn't dare hurt me."

She wasn't so sure about that. Not after they'd found Kick on their doorstep. But if Girard was willing, she had to let him try. Still . . . "What do I do if they take you prisoner, too?"

"They won't." He smiled so confidently, her desperate

heart chose to believe him, even though her head told her this plan of his could only end in disaster. As Kick's had.

Out of options, she exhaled. "All right."

"But you absolutely must promise me to stay here. Exactly here. Do not move, not for anything. Do you promise me?"

She nodded. Another order she was used to. "I will. How do you—"

But before she could ask him what, exactly, he planned to do, he kissed her on both cheeks and slipped out from behind the boulder.

And once again she was left behind. Which was really, really starting to annoy her. She could have helped him. Done something. At least told him about the—

Oh, my God! She *definitely* should have told him about the explosives rigged to blow. In case he needed to use them, or—

She jumped up and went after him.

She scrambled up the shallow wadi slope and started to climb over the rocky rim.

To her surprise, Virreau was hurrying toward a Jeep that was parked in plain sight, in a shallow ravine several yards away. It was dirty white, with a large red cross painted on the hood. How could the terrorists possibly have missed it?

To her even bigger surprise, suddenly the tail of Virreau's shirt flapped up in a gust of wind. Under it, the unmistakable shape of a large black gun stuck out of the waistband of his khaki shorts. It looked just like the one Marc had had hidden under his pillow. Okay, well, at least Virreau was armed.

But then it hit her. With just as much impact as it had the first time she'd seen Kick pull out a gun in New York.

Doctors for Peace didn't allow their volunteers to carry guns.

Ever.

She stopped dead in her tracks. So what did its presence mean about Virreau? Surely, not . . .

Pulse pounding, she ducked back down under the protective rim of the wadi to think.

Okay. This *couldn't* be what it seemed. It just couldn't.

Could it?

The thought that Virreau was somehow in league with the terrorists . . .

Kick and Marc had been totally convinced that Nathan Daneby was also working with them. Some kind of photographic evidence had been mentioned. When confronted right before she and Kick had left the DFP hospital, Daneby hadn't denied the allegation, either. Which was why they'd left him tied up.

Maybe he and Virreau were working together. *And* with the terrorists.

That would explain the lie about Marc. . . .

Marc! Oh, God. What if Virreau had freed Nate and they'd hurt Marc!

The Jeep's engine coughed and sputtered to life and she heard it take off with a spin of tires in the sand.

Virreau was on his way to the insurgent camp, and God knew what he was planning to do once he got there.

She didn't even want to imagine what would happen to Kick.

She had to do something. And quickly.

TWENTY-THREE

"CAN you walk?" Kick asked Alex after they'd both recovered their composure. Well, Kick had. Mostly anyway. Alex was still shaking like a Chihuahua, clinging to the edges of that disgusting pile of filth pallet of his, peering at Kick in unfocused anguish, as though he expected him to disappear any second.

He also didn't answer the question.

Kick hesitated to touch the man for fear of losing him completely. "Alex!" he repeated. The sound of his name snapped his friend's attention up.

"Are you real?" Alex asked for at least the tenth time.

Kick gave him what he hoped was another reassuring smile. Not that he'd be able to see it in this dark hovel. "Yes. I'm real. Do you think you can walk, buddy?"

Alex slowly nodded. "Home."

"Yup. We'll get there, but—"

All at once the door banged open, blinding Kick with sunlight that poured in like a klieg light.

"Pigs!" someone yelled.

Alex covered his head and ducked. *Holy fuck.* What the hell had they been doing to him to make him constantly react like that?

A handful of gravel pelted through the air, catching Kick painfully in the neck and shoulder, answering his question.

"God*damn* it, you sons of bitches!" he yelled, batting the stinging rocks off his cheek. One of his captors lunged in and clipped him in the temple with a rifle butt. Stars burst through his head as he toppled over. He sensed more than saw Alex roll next to him, shielding Kick's head with his body.

The next blow landed on Alex's back. He screamed.

Fuck.

Kick untangled his limbs and shook the stars from his eyes, then threw himself at the asshole with the rifle. Two more assholes were on him in a flash.

Damn. This was going to hurt.

He was right. His head felt like it exploded.

Then blissfully, everything went black.

RAINIE couldn't believe what she was seeing.

She'd run to fetch the hidden camel and ridden as fast as she could back to this morning's observation post on the ridge overlooking the terrorists' training camp.

She was so appalled she could barely see straight. Girard Virreau had driven right into the middle of the camp and was now being greeted like an old friend.

She told herself to calm down. This might not be what it seemed. It could be just as Virreau said—they trusted him because he belonged to Doctors for Peace.

The ugly terrorist leader guy came striding out of the mysterious cement hut, went straight to him, and shook his hand.

Or because he was a goddamn traitor.

Her heart literally stopped when two guards came around the corner of the shack, hauling Kick between them. His seemingly lifeless body hung limp, his boots plowing uneven furrows in the dirt as they dragged him along. Another man limped after them, prodded by a third guard with a bayoneted rifle. At least she thought he was a man. He looked more like a feral creature, dirty, tattered, crazy-haired and wild-eyed. *The prisoner.*

The two men turned to watch. Ugly Guy jerked his thumb at the hostages, said something, and Virreau laughed.

Fury burned through Rainie's insides like a firestorm.

Oh. My. God.

The motherfucker had lied through his teeth.

Okay. Now she was *really* mad.

Not only would she save Kick and the other hostage. That pompous frog was going to pay.

ALEX winced as Kick—his friend, Kick—was thrown onto the floor and his head bounced off the bare cement.

Damn. Even a blind man could tell that had to be painful.

Although, much to Alex's surprise, this time he could actually see inside this hut. More than fuzzy shadows. Jesus, there were electric lights! *Electric lights.* How was that even possible? He was so shocked he almost gave himself away by staring. So he deliberately walked into a table.

His guards leapt at him, yanking him backward.

A vicious slap bit across his cheek. "Pig! Do not move!"

He put his chin down and didn't move . . . as much as possible, since his legs were shaking like a newborn's and could barely hold him up.

Appropriate, he thought wryly. He *felt* like a newborn.

Finding out his name was like being given new life. *Christopher Alexander Zane.* The name didn't sound the least bit familiar to him, nor had any of the stories Kick had told of their friendship and the many dangerous jobs they'd done together for something called Zero Unit. But Kick was sure he was this Alex person. That was good enough for him. Kick wouldn't have made up all those stories. And why would he have come to take Alex home if he didn't know him?

Of course, at the moment, it didn't look like anyone was going home anytime soon. He'd been in this hut before. He recognized the foul smell. The memories of it were filled with pain and torture. But tonight it smelled like death.

God *fucking* damn it. He did not want to die. Not now. Not when he finally knew his name. When he'd at last learned he really *did* have a friend in the world. When freedom was so close he could taste it.

Two men came in behind him. One set of heavy footsteps he recognized immediately. The Sultan of Pain.

God, no! Not again, so soon!

Alex kept his head down and forced back a wave of despair clawing at his throat. *He couldn't do this. Not again.* He glanced furtively at Kick, still on the floor unconscious. There'd be no escape now, no help from that quarter.

The Sultan and his sidekick were speaking in intense undertones. In Arabic. Except . . . the sidekick couldn't speak it very well. Definitely not a native—And they were talking about . . . diamonds? Diamonds and blood? Had they invented some kind of new torture device? If so, the Sultan didn't seem pleased with it. He snapped out an impatient retort, and the other man wheedled unhappily.

Suddenly Alex remembered. That whiny, out-of-place voice. He'd heard it before, a few days ago when he'd been totally delirious with fever—aftereffects of his injuries or some disgusting malady. Or the constant abuse. Take your pick.

But there was something else about the scumbag. Other than being a spineless traitor. Alex studied the cracks in the floor, straining to think. A pair of brown leather boots walked across his field of vision.

That was it.

Boots, not sandals.

It *was* the same man. A Westerner. A doctor, or someone acting like a doctor.

And now Alex was close enough to see his face.

Excitement made him light-headed. He staggered against one of his guards, earning him another backhand. But just before he crumpled, he saw the traitor's face. Hitting the floor, he made a ball and rolled up against the closest wall.

Brown Boots and the Sultan continued past him, and Alex pressed himself tighter into the wall. His pulse took off. This was where the fun and games would start.

But they paid him no mind. Instead, they stopped in front of Kick. And were joined by a third man who had apparently been sitting quietly behind the desk at the back of the hut. All three stared down at Alex's would-be savior.

Oh, shit.

No. No, no, no.

What were they planning? He couldn't let them hurt Kick. Kick was his only way out of this hell.

"Hey!" he called, to distract them. It came out little more than a croak. "Leave him alone!" he yelled. Whispered.

The evil triumvirate turned to stare down at him cowering there on the floor like a wounded bird. Then they all smiled. Evil smiles.

The third man, who was older, with white hair and a dark, wrinkled face, opened one of two small metal briefcases sitting on the table Alex had collided with earlier. From it the man carefully lifted a vial, and then a hypodermic needle. He stuck the needle in the top of the vial and expertly filled the tube part with a brownish liquid. Then he turned back to Alex with eyes that twinkled.

"Do not worry, infidel," he said quietly in English, in a strange accent Alex didn't recognize. "You won't die alone. You will just be the first. The first of millions."

THE sun was going down.

Finally.

God help her.

Rainie attempted to tame her nerves by rolling onto her back on the rocky ridge and gazing up at the stars that were just beginning to emerge in the darkening sky. The same stars she and Kick had watched together just a few short nights ago, when he'd shown her a handful of constellations and taught her how to find the North Star. The same stars they'd made love under, exchanging silent vows that neither dared voice aloud. Could he see the stars now? Was he watching them, too, thinking of her?

Oh, Kick. *Kyle.*

She squeezed her eyes shut. What did she think was she doing?

Just last week she'd been a simple ER nurse, unwilling to stray from her safe, circumscribed, ten-block world. Shunning love because she didn't want to be hurt so badly again. Afraid to really live because she was afraid of dying like her parents. And now here she was, running around a dangerous foreign country, riding camels without a second thought, desperately in love with a man she knew very well she could never have, about to gamble her very life to save him from merciless terrorists.

This was *insane*.

She had no flipping idea how to do this stuff. She could *die* tonight if she messed up, even a little. They could *all* die.

But what choice did she have?

Visions of that other prisoner haunted her. He'd been so gaunt, so filthy, so feeble. And yet for all that, it was obvious he'd once been a tall, robust warrior like Kick. The agonizing thought of her lover ending up in that same awful condition gave her the motivation she needed to break her paralysis.

She'd spent the whole morning watching the camp, helpless, terrified the entire time that she'd be forced to witness Kick's summary execution. Thank God it hadn't happened. And when the sun was at its zenith, that's when she'd made up her mind. She wouldn't be able to live with herself if she didn't at least *try* to free him. *Them*.

The first thing she did was don Kick's extra DCUs and khaki T-shirt from the pack, wrapped her head in the parachute silk *kaffiyeh* he'd made for her, and strapped his KA-BAR knife to her side. Completing the transition from nurse to commando. Physically . . . but also mentally. All afternoon she'd prepared, most of that time spent crawling on her belly through the sand just outside the training camp, heart in her throat, retracing Kick's movements to see what he'd done with the rest of the explosives, making a few prayer-filled modifications. Then she'd loaded Kick's weapons onto the remaining camel, filled her DCU pockets with the NVGs, the rest of the water bottles, and food, and hiked up the ridge to watch and wait for sunset.

Which had arrived at last. Everything was set. The diversion ready to launch.

Lord give her strength.

She took a deep, steadying breath. Checked the camp below. In a few minutes the tangos would start their evening prayers.

Just one more thing to do. She reached for the field pack and took out the SATCOM. Pressing the same buttons and repeating the same words she'd heard Kick use, she made the call.

"STORMdog six come in. This is STORMsix kilo, over."

After a short burst of static, there was an answering, "STORMdog six actual, here. Identify yourself, over."

"This is STORMsix kilo," she said again. She had no idea what any of that meant, but it's what Kick had said both times she'd heard him use the SATCOM. *Oh, hell.* "Please, this is Lorraine Martin," she said, jettisoning the military-speak and trying not to sound panicked and desperate. "Am I talking to STORM Corps?"

Another burst of static. Then, "STORM lima mike, we read you. Do you need assistance, over?"

"Yes! No. I mean, oh, God, they've got Kick. I just want you to know, I'm going in after him. Tonight."

"Negative, STORM lima mike," whoever it was said emphatically. "Do *not* attempt a rescue on your own. Do you read me, over?"

"Did you hear what I said? They've *captured* him. There's another hostage, too. Kick said he's one of ours. And there's a traitor. A doctor named Girard Virreau. He's in the camp with the terrorists now. I don't have time to wait for help."

"Please stand by, STORM lima mike. Do you read? Keep the COM open, over."

"There's no *time!*" she repeated impatiently. "Evening prayers are about to start. Just send in the air strike if you don't hear from me within fifteen minutes." That should be enough time for the plan to work. Or not, as the case might be. Either way, it should all be over by then. "Can you do that? Please? Over."

"Miss Martin, this is STORM commander Kurt Bridger," the guy came back, also abandoning the double-talk. "You need to listen to me very carefully. You must extract yourself immediately from—"

Why did no one ever *listen* to her? She glanced down the ridge. The tangos below were starting to come outside and spread their mats for prayers.

Time was up.

She used the old trick from the movies, pressing the COM call button to produce several seconds of static. "Breaking up," she said, then pressed it a few more times for good measure. "Fifteen minutes. Send in the air strike." Then she switched off the radio. And prayed STORM would actually do it. Their lives depended on the chaos to cover their get-away. Not to mention the need to eliminate abu Bakr and the rest of the tangos.

Swallowing heavily, she fished in her pocket for the lighter Kick had given her this morning, before he'd been captured. Make that before he'd surrendered himself to the enemy rather than endangering her.

This was it. Now or never.

Before she could change her mind, she strapped on the backpack, flicked the lighter, and touched the flame to the end of the fuse. It took with a spark and a hiss and the acrid smell of sulfur.

Allahu akhbar, the terrorists prayed below.

Sending up a silent prayer herself, she turned to launch herself down the ridge.

And ran straight into Nathan Daneby.

GINA tried to ignore the nervousness that spilled through her as she put on the extra helmet he handed her, and slung her leg over the back of Gregg van Halen's motorcycle.

She wasn't nervous about the bike. God knew, she'd ridden her share of Harleys growing up in the rough neighborhoods across the river in Jersey. No, it was the meeting they were on their way to that had her wondering if she'd lost her mind.

Last night, after taking her to places she hadn't known existed in the dark recesses of her sexual fantasies, Gregg had informed her as he'd released her from bondage that his commander wanted to see her in the morning. About Rainie.

She'd been instantly terrified. "Have they found her?" she asked. "Is she . . . ?"

He'd hesitated. Then, "I'm not sure."

This morning, she'd tried everything to pry out of him what was going on, but he kept insisting he didn't know.

She didn't believe him.

He was lying about something. She could feel it in the way he avoided her gaze and her questions.

Rainie had disappeared. Was she about to, as well?

He kicked the bike to life and pulled out into the bumper-to-bumper noonday New York traffic. She wrapped her arms around his rock-hard abs, wondering what had prompted him to take his bike today. Up until now, they'd always travelled by taxi when she was with him. In fact, she'd never actually seen his bike before now. Was it so a cab driver wouldn't be able to identify him later? A motorcycle helmet totally obscured one's features. . . .

No. That was crazy thinking. Gregg would never hurt her. Or let her be hurt. He might walk the line sexually, but under that controlling façade he was a good person. Sure, at times he scared the crap out of her. But at other times he'd held her so lovingly, kissed her so tenderly, her heart had simply melted in her chest.

She was half in love with the man. She was sure he felt the same about her. How could he not?

Oh, jeez. Had she really *thought* that?

Suddenly, she noticed they were heading in the opposite direction of downtown from her Upper East Side brownstone. In fact, they'd just passed the north end of Central Park and he showed no sign of slowing.

"Where are we going?" she shouted to be heard over the noise of the traffic. "I thought we were meeting your boss."

"We are."

"Isn't the CIA office downtown?"

"There's more than one."

Okay.

Fifteen minutes later they were driving through an area that looked like a war zone. Burned-out buildings, vacant lots; derelicts and druggies camped out in cardboard shacks. Would the government really have an office here?

"Gregg, I don't like this. I want to go back," she shouted.

He just shook his head.

Nervousness swamped back over her, more powerful than it ever had before. But there was nothing she could do. Jumping off the bike in this neighborhood would be nuts, just asking to be mugged. Or worse.

Suddenly, he turned into an alley. Trash littered the pot-holed pavement and graffiti covered the dirty brick on either side. Straight ahead the solid wall of an abandoned building blocked their path.

"Gregg?"

He didn't reply, but pressed the bike's horn in a short pattern. All at once a square section of the wall went up like a garage door, exposing the gaping black expanse of an empty warehouse bay. The motorcycle shot forward into it.

Two men with machine guns came running toward them from either side as he spun the bike around to a halt. They were dressed just like Gregg, black T-shirts, BDUs, and combat boots. She clung tight to him, burying her face in the soft leather of his jacket. It smelled like him, and she desperately needed the reassurance that he was there with her. That this armed greeting was normal in his profession, that she'd be fine, and that they'd both be laughing at her silly fears over dinner tonight. If he finally asked her out.

"Gina," he said, pulling off his helmet, turning to her. "We're here. You need to get off."

Reluctantly, she dismounted the bike, took off her own helmet and handed it to him as he got off, too.

He indicated a door on the far side and started for it. "This way."

No kiss. No reassuring hug. Not even a smile. It was like he'd become a different person.

She walked next to him with a growing sense of wild unease, down a long hall and into a small, bare room furnished only with a table flanked by two chairs. The guards marched behind them, posting themselves at the door.

"Sit," Gregg said, indicating one of the chairs.

"Please," she said, reaching out to touch him. "Tell me what's going on. Why am I here?"

He didn't take her hand, letting her fingers slide off his leather-clad arm. "I'm sorry. Colonel Blair will have to tell you that, ma'am."

Her lips parted. *Ma'am?*

Pain razored through her heart as another man strode into the room. Posture straight as an arrow, with iron-colored hair and a stern, leathery face that had seen a lot of outdoor action, the man looked like he hadn't smiled for the five decades since he got his first toy rifle.

"Dr. Cappozi?" he asked.

Obviously Gregg van Traitor wasn't going to be any help. She was on her own here. *Oh, what a shock.*

She lifted her chin. "Who wants to know?"

Colonel Dour scrutinized her for a moment with a calculating stare. Then he turned to Gregg, thrusting him a manila envelope. "Van Halen, your team has been mobilized. You'll join them immediately. Wheels-up in two hours."

Gregg took the envelope and came to attention. "Yes, sir." Without another glance at her, he turned to leave.

"Oh, and van Halen?"

"Yes, sir?"

"Good job."

"Thank you, sir."

Then he was gone.

Shell-shocked, Gina stared after him. *Oh, God.* What had he done?

Worse, what had *she* done?

"Now, then, Dr. Cappozi," the colonel said with his deep, abrasive voice, no doubt made so from a lifetime of yelling at his men. "I understand you're the head researcher on Columbia University's respiratory syncitial virus project. Is that correct?"

She was still so stunned by Gregg's cold turnabout she didn't think before answering, "Yes. Why?"

If possible, the colonel's expression shuttered even more. "I'm afraid there has been a slight change in plan."

"What plan?" Her alarm heightened even more, bringing her around. She put on her best I-take-no-crap college professor face. "I was told you wanted to see me regarding the kidnapping of my friend, Lorraine Martin."

He folded his arms behind his back. "I'm afraid Miss Martin is dead, along with the man who kidnapped her."

Gina swallowed an instinctive gasp. And reminded herself this wasn't the first time she'd received that same bad news.

"Can you prove it?"

The scrutinizing stare was back. "As a matter of fact," he said, "I was hoping you would identify the body."

She grabbed the back of the metal chair for support. So it really was true. *Oh, Rainie.* She couldn't believe it.

"Yes," she said, sadness gripping her. "I can do that." This could still be a mistake. Misidentifications happened all the time. The whole situation had been so surreal from the outset, who knew what was real and what wasn't.

"Good." The colonel gave a signal to the two men at the door. "Gentlemen, you know what to do."

At his clipped order, a shiver went down her spine. For some reason it sounded . . . sinister.

"Ma'am," one of the men said. "If you'll follow me."

With little choice, she did so, noting that the second man fell in behind them. As they marched her single file down the long corridor back to the warehouse bay where they'd arrived, every nerve in her body screamed at her to get out of there.

This was *so* not good. How could Gregg have just left her with these awful people, in the awful place? And without a word, or even a look good-bye?

They reached the door and went through it to where a black SUV was parked idling.

Suddenly she was surrounded by six men in ski masks, wielding even bigger machine guns than her two escorts. The barrel of one was thrust under her chin, and in the next second her arms were yanked behind her back and her wrists handcuffed.

She tried to scream, but a hand slammed brutally over her mouth, pinching her nose at the same time. She couldn't breathe. Hands grabbed her arms and held like iron claws. She couldn't struggle. There were too many of them. They were too strong.

Duct tape replaced the hand, and she sucked in a deep lungful of air. A hood was slipped over her head. And an accented voice growled in her ear.

"Get in the vehicle or you die."

TWENTY-FOUR

NATE grabbed Rainie and clung fast to regain their balance, sending a shower of stones and pebbles careening down the hill to the wadi. She clapped both her hands over her mouth to keep from screaming and giving away their position.

"What are you doing?" Nate demanded, glancing behind her at the hissing explosives fuse.

Her pulse had gone off the charts. Oh, hell. *Friend or foe?* She had to choose quickly. But how?

"You first," she answered, then grasped his arm and started down the hill. "But talk fast because we have to move."

"Where?"

"Wrong answer," she said, whipping the KA-BAR from its sheath. She jammed it into his ribs. "Walk. Fast."

"Jesus, Rainie! I thought you were on my side! I could have sworn you were the one voice of reason in that argument. Innocent until proven guilty? Ring a bell?"

"Yeah, well, that was before Girard Virreau pulled a gun and turned traitor. I'm a bit more suspicious now."

"Girard?" Nate seemed honestly shocked. "What are you talking about?"

They reached the bottom of the hill where the camel was

hobbled. She pointed toward the insurgent camp while raising the KA-BAR so close to his throat that a drop of blood trickled down it. "Virreau's in league with the terrorists over there. They're holding Kick prisoner, along with another man. Give me one good reason I shouldn't tie you up right now and leave you for the jackals."

His Adam's apple bobbed past the knife blade, producing another scarlet trickle. "Because I'm *not* a traitor. I didn't betray Kick and his team in Afghanistan, and if he's a prisoner, I'll do anything you tell me, to help get him out of there."

She narrowed her eyes. "What about that photo Kick was talking about? The one showing you taking money from abu Bakr."

"Abbas Tawhid, you mean. Abu Bakr's right-hand man."

"So you admit it."

"It wasn't money in that packet. It was photos, and a list of names and places."

"Explain," she said impatiently. Time was literally ticking away.

"Tawhid's mother came to the DFP camp with a raging infection. I saved her life. He let me name my reward. I asked for the lives of a group of aid workers who'd been kidnapped a few months earlier. He came through. I turned the information over to STORM Corps, and they were rescued."

"Why didn't Kick know about this?"

"Kick doesn't work for STORM."

"But Marc does."

"Not every operator knows about every rescue mission. You have the SATCOM. Radio STORM and confirm my story."

She pinioned his gaze with hers, searching for any sign of deception. She wasn't a cop, but in the ER you had to develop a pretty good lie-radar. People were often stupid, preferring to hide the truth about an injury or condition and risk misdiagnosis rather than tell how they really got it.

All she saw in Nathan Daneby's clear blue eyes was open sincerity.

"No time," she said, hoping to hell she was right about

him. She withdrew the knife and hurried over to the camel. "All right, then. Get on. We've got about eight minutes before this whole place blows."

THE boom of a massive explosion hurled Kick back to consciousness.

At the blast, chaos erupted all around him, tangos running and shouting in staccato Arabic. A nearby gunshot battered his eardrums, dialing down the sounds around him like a dimmer switch.

Kick's head was spinning and his limbs weaker than they'd been since detox, but he'd been an operator long enough to know when action was needed. *Immediately.*

Where the hell was he?

He shook his head to clear it, spraying sweat and blood, and realized he was lying down, inside a neat room. Brightly lit. *The cement hut.*

He tried to sit up. But was jerked to a halt by restraints on his wrists and ankles. *WTF.* He bit down on a groan. His whole body felt terrible.

A low moan drew his attention. From the floor.

"Alex!" he called. "You all right, man?"

Another moan. "Is . . . this . . ." The words were tinny but at least the gunshot hadn't taken out Kick's hearing completely, thank God.

He had no idea what was happening, but they definitely needed to move. Now, in the first flush of confusion. "Can you get free?" he called.

"Not . . . tied," Alex returned tightly. He sounded in worse pain than Kick.

No time to find out why. "Come get me loose. We gotta go."

Alex lurched up and nearly collapsed on top of him. Ah, *Jesus.* Blood was all over his friend's rag of a shirt, his arm hanging useless. Yet somehow he managed to untie one of Kick's wrist restraints.

"What the hell did they do to you?" Kick asked as he frantically undid his other wrist and eased out from under Alex's panting body. By that time he was panting himself.

"Shot," Alex gasped.

Fuck.

Kick scooted down to free his ankles. "Where? Can you still walk?" Could *he*?

"Arm. I'm okay."

A second explosion ripped the air outside, much closer, lifting one of the corrugated metal sheets off the roof and sending it sailing. The sound of the generator sputtered off, and the hut plunged into darkness.

Kick scowled. *Please, no.* This was feeling *way* too familiar.

This was *his* plan being executed. Which meant—

Rainie.

She hadn't left to go find the Bedouin as he'd made her *swear* she would do if anything happened to him.

God *fucking* damn it! What in the freaking *hell* did she think she was doing?

He had to get to her, and now.

Gritting his teeth, he banded a supportive arm around Alex's waist and made straight for the door. No guard was there to stop them, so he kept right on plunging on. Muscles screaming, he half carried Alex across the camp and away from the inferno of the burning munitions dump that Rainie— he assumed furiously—had somehow managed to blow up. At the last second he remembered to stumble past their prison hovel and grab the SIG from where, in anticipation, he'd hidden it this morning under a flat rock along the outside wall before his surrender.

"You doin' okay?" he asked Alex, who mumbled something indecipherable back.

Hell, the man was doing well just to stay on his feet. As was Kick. He was light-headed and it felt like there were a million insects crawling through his veins. They were both stumbling every two or three steps, Alex's breath coming in sharp gasps of pain and exhaustion. Luckily he didn't weigh more than a child, so Kick was able to support him as they ducked and zigzagged between the various huts of the training camp, avoiding the tangos. He was making for the opposite side, and the rendezvous spot beyond that, which he and Rainie had decided on yesterday.

He prayed with everything in him that she'd be there, waiting.

They rounded a corner and suddenly crashed headlong into a familiar figure. In his foggy state it took Kick a second to recognize the smarmy count from the DFP camp. "Virreau!" he said, steadying himself and Alex. "Which way out?"

The count backed up a few steps and made the mistake of thinking about it. His second mistake was to raise the pistol clutched in his hand. The pistol a DFP doctor was forbidden to carry.

Suddenly the puzzle pieces clicked into place in Kick's mind. *Holy hell.*

Nate wasn't the traitor; *this* man was.

"I've seen those boots before!" Alex accused in a halting rasp, staring down at them. Confirming Kick's deduction.

Kick managed to beat Virreau to the draw, drilling the SIG into the skeet-shooting Eurotrash bastard's forehead. "You've got *one* chance. Tell me who you work for and I'll let you live," he growled.

Virreau just laughed. Kick's arm was so weak it was obvious to both of them he could barely hold up the gun. "You have no idea who you're dealing with, Jackson. Kill me, and they'll just find someone else to take my place."

"I guess we'll see about that," Kick muttered. Debated whether or not just to shoot him and be done with it.

"You can't stop these people," Virreau said. "Besides, you're already a dead man." To Kick's shock, he turned and started running back into the burning camp, toward what was left of the cement hut. What the hell—

The SIG wobbled and he let it drop to his side in disgust.

"So are you, buddy," he mumbled. He hoped whatever it was the bogus count was going back into the camp for was worth dying over.

Shielding his eyes, Kick turned and started hurrying straight into the eye-stabbing glow of the setting sun. Earlier, he'd deliberately picked this angle for their escape, to make it harder for the enemy to spot them in the glare. Thank God it seemed to be working. They had no more cover, no rocks or bushes to hide behind. Totally exposed.

With one last surge of energy, he threw Alex over his shoulder, ignoring the man's cry of pain and his own weakness and woozy head, and ran like hell toward the shelter of a shallow gully that would lead them to the rendezvous spot in a deeper wadi further out in the desert. No time to lose. The diversion had worked, but their captors would soon realize the ruse and discover their prisoners had escaped. Then it would only be a matter of minutes before they'd be on them.

He shot a quick glance up at the sky, hoping to see or hear a STORM aircraft swooping in from the north.

So far, nothing.

Sliding on his backside down into the ravine, he forced himself back to his feet, adjusted Alex, and struggled through the sand. Around one curve, then another, then they were clambering down the steep rocky trail into the wadi.

"Rainie!" he risked calling out. "Baby, where are—"

The words lodged in his throat at the sight that greeted them.

Oh, sweet fucking Jesus.

He lurched to a wobbly halt and let Alex slide down to his unsteady feet. They were both breathing hard, in pain and sweating profusely in the residual heat from the scorcher of a day. Alex landed next to the unconscious body of Nathan Daneby.

Kick slashed his gaze up, meeting Rainie's pleading eyes.

No!

Abu Bakr had an arm around her throat. And a gun pressed to the pulsing vein in her temple. She looked . . . damn, he couldn't read her expression.

Kick's entire being burned with fury. This was *not* happening.

No. Way. He'd come too far to lose her now. Not like this. Not to this animal.

Abu Bakr looked perfectly calm, standing there with a small metal case hanging from one hand, his gun in the other, threatening the woman Kick loved more than life. For one horrible moment he was transported back to that time in A-stan. The fucker had been just as calm then, after tearing Kick's world to tiny shreds, brutally slaughtering the closest thing he had to family. He glanced down at Alex, who had rolled himself up in a ball, cowering on the ground next to Nathan. Was he remembering, too, the hideous fate he'd suffered at this man's hands?

It would not happen again. To any of them.

It. Would. *Not*.

He dragged up the SIG, aiming it between the snake's flat eyes. But to his dismay, even holding it with two hands, it wavered like a mirage. He couldn't keep his hands steady.

Abu Bakr didn't even seem to notice. "So close," he said almost approvingly, in that perfect American English that had haunted Kick's nightmares for sixteen months. "You nearly got me. I couldn't have done better myself." The motherfucker smiled with false modesty. "Except, well, yes, I *did* do better. Didn't I, Mr. Jackson." It wasn't a question. More like a gloating observation.

And the fucker knew his name. How? Surely, he didn't remember that long-ago night . . . ? No, it must have been Virreau who'd told him.

Abu Bakr caressed Rainie's temple with the barrel of the gun so she whimpered. "And I always will," he said. "Because you're a fool. Unlike you pathetic Westerners, I don't let my emotions rule my actions."

He was right. Kick was so angry black spots shot across his field of vision like falling stars. He swallowed down the urge to charge the bastard and rip his fucking head off with his bare hands. "Easy for you. Sociopaths don't have emotions," he gritted out.

The fucker actually smiled. The man was a sick, perverted agent, through and through, and that was for damned sure.

On the ground, Nate moaned. His eyes fluttered open and he grimaced in pain.

I'm so sorry, buddy. Sorry I doubted you for a single moment.

"You may be right about that," abu Bakr said as he casually watched Nate rise on his elbow, blink, touch the back of his head, and try to figure out why he was sprawled on the sand, then struggle to sit up.

Alex clutched Nate's arm and yanked frantically at it, trying to pull him back down on the ground.

Abu Bakr gestured at Kick with his gun. "You, I've already killed." Then he waved it in annoyance at Alex. "And the pathetic Mr. Pig, as well." He looked down and studied Nate like a kid might study a dung beetle. "But that one, no." His finger moved, and his gun jerked to the sound of a shot blasting through the wadi.

Nate's body gave a sickening shudder, and blossomed in a spray of scarlet.

"Nate!" Rainie screamed. Alex let out a yowl and scuttled over to Kick's feet, babbling something he couldn't understand.

Nate's eyes met Kick's in surprise, then grim understanding. Then they rolled back in his head and he fell back to the ground. And didn't move again.

"*Nate!*"

Christ Almighty. Kick desperately reined in the red-hot rage seething within him, and struggled to hold the SIG steady enough to take a shot at abu Bakr. But it was no use. He was too shaky. He couldn't risk hitting Rainie.

Somehow he had to get her out of this. *Please, God. Please.*

Alex continued to clutch at his leg, muttering.

"Let the woman go," Kick demanded, battling to hold it together. "She's done nothing. She's innocent in this."

The bastard chuckled. "Not *exactly* true. But in any case, the innocent are precisely who I'm after. It is the innocent who must die, in order to punish the guilty. She must die to punish *you*."

The man was insane. He had to—

Suddenly, Kick heard a low buzzing sound in the distance. A plane?

STORM!

But Jesus, no. This wadi was too close to the insurgent camp. If they didn't move, they'd all be injured or killed in the air strike. The one consolation being that abu Bakr would be, as well.

The terrorist's cocky smile widened. "Right on time. So predictable." He started to drag Rainie toward the camel— *their* camel, loaded with *their* belongings, including his sniper rifle—waiting at the ready nearby. "We'll be going now."

Alex tugged at Kick's leg. "You've got to get," he said in a gritty croak, "the metal case."

What? "Forget the briefcase," Kick snapped.

Rainie fought against abu Bakr's hold, bending and squirming. Kick was terrified he'd use the gun pointed at her head if she didn't stop.

"Wait!" Kick shouted, trying to shake off Alex, who was tenaciously hanging onto his ankle. "Leave her. Take me instead," he pleaded, knowing in his heart it was useless.

In his peripheral vision, a green aircraft flying low over the northern horizon was getting closer by the second.

His nemesis glanced up at it as he tried to control Rainie, then shook her angrily by the hair. "You try my patience, whore!" They'd reached the camel now. He pulled back her head savagely, exposing her white throat. "Throw down your weapon, Mr. Jackson. You'll never make it out of here alive, but you can assure she lives." His grin was evil. "For a while, anyway. Put down your gun or I kill her now. Your choice."

Rainie's wildly frightened eyes pleaded with him. But he didn't know which choice she was pleading for. He thought of Sheila, and her horrible fate. And knew he would never let that happen to Rainie. He lowered the gun, but held on to it with all the strength he had left. Kick's insides, his entire being, churned with the need to kill the bastard. But if anything, his body was even less steady now. He felt sick. Helpless.

"Like I said, a fool," abu Bakr said with a sadistic smile. He moved the gun under her chin and started to pull the trigger.

"*No!*"

"No!" she yelled at the same time, and came to life. She twisted wildly in the bastard's arms. The shot exploded. But missed her. She bent, and twisted the other way. This time his KA-BAR was in her hand. It slashed out, scoring the bastard's face. Abu Bakr grabbed for his bloody cheek, and she wrenched away from him.

The furious terrorist shot at her, but she rolled to the side, taking cover behind a boulder. Kick squeezed off three shots, but the world was tilting like a seesaw and they all went off target. Abu Bakr ran around the camel, throwing himself onto its back as he urged it to its feet.

With a feral growl, Kick started to lunge after the bastard, but Alex still clung to his leg like a leech, preventing him from going more than a couple of steps. "Let me go!" Kick yelled.

"Metal case," Alex cried, then fell to his knees with a gasp of pain.

Abu Bakr shot again. But at the loud bang so close to his head, the panicked camel lurched up and took off like a frightened jackrabbit, with abu Bakr on its back.

Kick roared in fury. Desperate. With every ounce of will-power and every lesson he'd ever learned as a sniper, Kick focused his concentration on the swiftly receding back of his enemy. He steadied his arm. Became the gun. And took the shot.

In a spray of red, abu Bakr crumpled and tumbled to the ground, his body landing at a crazy angle. Dead.

A *whoosh* of nauseous relief swept through Kick. *Thank God.* But there was no time to savor the moment of triumph.

"Rainie!" he shouted, stumbling over to her, grabbing her up into his arms. "Are you hurt?"

She flung her arms around his neck. "Oh, Kick. I thought we were all dead for sure."

"My love." He kissed her, looked back at Nate's lifeless body, then buried his face in her hair, his eyes filling. "We need to move fast," he said, already urging her down the wadi. Fighting the weird dizziness that spun the world around him. "The air strike."

Her eyes widened as she darted a glance at the sky. "Oh, God! I'd forgotten!"

"Help me with Alex."

"What about Nate?" she protested. "What if he's not dead? We can't just leave him!"

He nodded. "Of course not. I'll get him."

While he clumsily hoisted Nate's inert body over his shoulder, she got Alex to his feet, exclaiming, "You've been shot!"

Alex waved it off. "I'm okay."

They took off as fast as they could up the wadi—hardly more than a crawl. The plane was getting closer and closer. The insurgents at the camp started firing on it with everything they had left in their arsenal, which thankfully wasn't much more than sidearms. Rainie had done a thorough job of blowing the ammo dump.

They stumble-ran, Kick clenching his jaw, desperately battling the weakness and black void threatening to overtake him. The growling plane *whooshed* overhead, so close they could practically touch the bottom of it. The sound of gears ground above them. It was about to drop its payload.

At the last second, he hustled them under the shelter of a large rock outcropping.

Far too close by, the pounding boom of munitions suddenly thundered from the camp. Seconds later, the air around them whistled with debris whizzing past; it crashed into the walls of the wadi and splintered over the rock above their heads. An avalanche of sand and stone began to bury them. They huddled together, hugging each other tight.

Thoughts bombarded Kick along with the pelting rubble.

Abu Bakr was dead.

His reign of terror was finally over. At long last Kick had gotten his revenge. And the sweetest revenge was that Alex was alive. They were *all* alive.

Except . . .

Kick started to shake uncontrollably. He just couldn't fight his body any longer. He was burning up from the inside out. Sweat streamed into his eyes and his vision started to pinwheel.

"Rainie," he managed, suddenly terrified of what was happening to him physically, on the inside. Something definitely wasn't . . .

"Kick! What's wrong?" Alarm colored her voice.

What did that goddamn abu Bakr do to me? Even after death, he was still controlling Kick's fate.

He should have known. The man had said it himself. *You, I've already killed.*

"Talk to me, please! Kick!"

All around, bombs went off, obliterating the terrorist camp and raining destruction, even as his own body closed down on him.

Sweet Jesus. He was *dying*.

The bastard had won, after all.

"*Kyle!*"

He strained to squeeze out one last thought. "Rainie, I lo . . ." The words slurred on his thickening tongue, and in despair he felt his eyes roll back in his head.

Rainie's beautiful face clouded with anguish.

And that was the last thing he saw.

SOMEHOW, Rainie managed not to be knocked out by flying debris or buried alive by falling rock. The men were not so lucky. Kick had collapsed with his large body covering hers as a human shield, and the rescued prisoner, cradling one arm which appeared badly injured, was curled in a skinny ball under them both. Poor Nate, possibly beyond caring, now lay sprawled over their legs.

Desperately, she wriggled to extract herself from the suffocating pile of bodies and the dust-cloud of sand and grit surrounding them.

"Kick!" she called into the sudden, odd silence, attempting to rouse him while gingerly rolling him over. She ran her hands over his body, searching for anything broken. He appeared to be in one piece, thank God. But his skin was hot as a fry griddle. "Baby, wake up. Please, Kick. *Kyle*. Talk to me, sweetheart."

He moaned, and swallowed thickly. "You . . . okay?" he asked hoarsely, surfacing to consciousness, but just barely. His lashes fluttered with the effort.

"I'm fine," she said, relief swamping through her that he was lucid. But the relief was fleeting. "You feel like you're on fire. What's wrong?"

He grunted. "Don't know. Alex? Nate?"

"They're here," she said, and turned her attention to the other men. The sun was sinking below the horizon and the sky going black, making it hard to see. She put her fingers to the side of Nate's throat. The pulse was barely there. She swallowed down a renewed spurt of despair. Okay. Shot was better than dead. She could deal with shot.

Forcing herself to focus, she examined his gaping wound. Dabbed out the worst debris. Then quickly unwound her silk *kaffiyeh* and tied it tight around his torso, wadding up the cloth of his T-shirt to stop the bleeding as best she could, until she could fetch the antiseptic and bandages from—

Next to her, the hostage—had Kick called him Alex?—let out a soft moan. She turned to bend over him. "Alex, can you hear me?"

She carefully put her hands on his emaciated, badly bruised body, testing for breaks. He flinched at her touch. He moaned again.

"You're safe now," she told him reassuringly. "With friends. Kick got you out of that awful place."

Slowly the poor man opened his eyes. The expression in them nearly broke her heart. So much pain and suffering in those blue depths, and yet so much hope.

Tears blurred her vision. "I'm Rainie," she whispered with a vain attempt at a smile. "I'm a nurse. Are you hurt anywhere?"

He looked up at her, gazing at her tangled hair for a long moment. "Just my arm," he finally said in a rasping whisper.

Lord. Another gunshot. The arm was in bad shape. But then, so was the rest of him.

"Okay. I'm going to fix you up," she promised. But she really had to get back to the camel first to fetch the first aid kit from their pack. Only—

Her heart stalled. *Damn.* She jumped to her feet and looked around for the animal. As she feared, the camel was long gone, together with all their belongings.

Now what?

She still had a water bottle in her DCU pocket, and maybe she could tear a strip from Nate's *kaffiyeh* tourniquet to use as a bandage for Alex. That would have to do until she got them back to—

Where?

Yeah, she'd worry about *that* bridge when she got to it.

With the aid of Kick's KA-BAR, she gingerly cut the strip of silk. "This might hurt a little," she warned Alex as she helped him uncurl his body to get to the arm. She didn't allow herself to look at the angry cuts and bruises and half-healed pus-filled wounds that covered his exposed skin—

which was a lot of area, because of the ragged state of his clothes. There was nothing she could do for those. He needed a surgeon. So did Nate. They needed a hospital. Hell, they both needed a lot of things she couldn't help them with right now.

She firmly quelled the panic that threatened. *One thing at a time.*

When she'd done what she could to staunch the flow of blood and stabilize Alex's arm, he looked up at her with heartfelt gratitude. "Thank you."

She smiled back. "You're more than welcome."

Next to her, Kick tried to sit, but let out a groan, and flopped right back down.

"Oh, honey," she whispered, turning to feed him a few sips of their precious water. "What on earth is going on with you?"

"Metal briefcase," Alex said, his ragged whisper barely audible above Kick's labored breathing.

"What?" She frowned with a glance, trying to understand.

"*Needle*. In . . . metal case. Gave him . . . something . . . bad."

Needle . . . Fear rushed through Rainie like a cold wind. "You mean a *hypodermic* needle?"

Alex closed his eyes with a slight nod. "Very bad shit."

She pressed her fingers to her mouth. *Oh, God.* Did they inject poison into Kick? Or some kind of horrible biological agent? What kind of monsters *were* they?

But she'd seen firsthand the kind of psychopath Jallil abu Bakr was. She wouldn't put anything past him.

She also knew because of the tight security surrounding genetic research, even Gina's harmless pediatric flu project, that Homeland Security and the CDC feared a medically based terrorist attack almost more than bombs and hijackings. A lot of really nasty stuff occurred naturally in Africa. Anthrax. Ebola. Avian flu. Strains of deadly diseases that could be modified to spread like wildfire. Could this remote training camp also be some kind of experimental laboratory to create a biological weapon of mass destruction?

Abu Bakr had been holding on to that small metal case like his life had depended on it. A bio agent made sense. And suddenly, so did Alex's concern over that briefcase. Where had it gone?

She looked back at Kick. Despair clawed at her throat. And if it were true that Kick was infected . . . what could she possibly do to save him out here? What could she do to save *any* of them?

Nothing, that's what.

She muffled the sob that threatened to escape at the help-lessness of it all.

No! There had to be something. Some way.

She could not watch Kick die of some terrible disease out here in the desert, helpless, unable to do a damn thing to help him. Or watch Nathan Daneby slowly bleed to death. Or look into the eyes of poor, tortured Alex and tell him he'd come this far only to die out here in this desolate wilderness. No. That she *couldn't* deal with.

She pressed a firm palm to Nate's bloody wound. Some-how, she'd—

"*Shhh.*" Alex's weak admonishment sifted through the night air, seeping into her tormented determination. "*Shhh.*"

"What?"

"Listen!"

She held her breath.

Far in the distance she heard a sound. Like a tiny mos-quito.

"What is it?" she whispered.

"Incoming," he said. "It's . . . a helo."

TWENTY-FIVE

FOR about thirty-five years now, whenever Kick awoke, he'd lie completely motionless and take a few seconds' cautious sit-rep. Just in case. In the past, he'd woken up in some pretty bad places.

But today he felt purely surrounded by good. A soft bed under him, the temperature perfect, the pungent smell of coffee in the air; all that was missing was a warm woman nestled in his arms. A very specific woman.

He heard someone take a sip from a paper cup.

"Rainie?" he croaked through a throat dry as the Sahara. Since when did they have beds this nice in the desert?

"Welcome back to the living, Jackson. Weren't sure you'd make it."

Concerned but uninvolved. Male. Not Rainie.

He kept his eyes closed. And tried to remember . . . "Where is she?"

"Checking on Mr. Zane, I believe. Right down the hall. She'll be back in a few minutes."

Relief zinged through him. A hospital of some sort, then. "They're both safe? Alex and Rainie?"

"Both doing fine. Your woman has been driving the doctors here crazy taking care of the two of you. Making sure you're everyone's top priority. Helping Alex reacclimatize to the civilized world. Sleeping next to you tangled up in all those wires every night, in case you woke up from your coma."

Coma? Hell . . . No wonder he couldn't remember anything except Rainie's worried face fading from sight. She *would* be a spitfire taking care of her wounded charges. For the first time in as long as he could remember, Kick smiled, and felt it through his entire being. *His woman*, the guy had called her. Damn, how great did *that* sound?

God, he loved her.

Bits and pieces were coming back to him. Escaping capture . . . The air strike . . . Killing abu Bakr . . . But not how he'd gotten here, wherever *here* was. "I was in a coma?"

"Oh, far worse." The man sounded completely serious when he said, "I'm very sorry to inform you of your tragic death from injuries sustained during your heroic rescue of Mr. Zane."

Wait . . . Ah! Kick cracked an eyelid, enjoying a wry moment of relief. "I can live with that."

The other man gave him a ghost of a smile. Took a sip of coffee.

He'd never seen the guy before. Midforties with shortcropped hair. Sitting in a chair by the bedside, one ankle carelessly resting on a knee, one hand holding a coffee cup, the other a silver envelope. He was dressed in jeans and a blue polo shirt. Too casual for Company. But the man's watchful eyes were smart, cool, and assessing. Behind the relaxed façade, Kick recognized a man who'd seen action. And plenty of it.

"I'm Kurt Bridger. STORM Corps," he said, forestalling Kick's query. "If you were wondering, you've been admitted to Haven Oaks, a sanatorium in upstate New York. We own it and run it, but only a few of the staff know of the connection to STORM. Safer for our operatives who come here to be treated. I'd appreciate it if you kept it that way."

"Of course." Kick digested what the man was telling him. *He was back in the States*. Must have been some damn coma.

He glanced around at the array of instruments lining the wall, and the catheter line along his collar bone. It felt all too familiar. "What the hell happened to me? Did I have a relapse or something?"

"Not exactly," Bridger said. "Abu Bakr injected you with a very nasty genetic hybrid of what appears to be avian flu virus vectored with anthrax. Luckily the mutation has some problems, so although the incubation period is alarmingly short, with treatment it's survivable. We were able to get you to a hospital in time."

"Jesus," Kick breathed. Avian flu and anthrax? Talk about a lethal combination.

"You were in and out of consciousness for nearly a week. Some of it induced, but mostly just sick as a dog."

He believed it. He still felt like shit. A whole week . . . "Who else knows I'm here . . . alive?"

"Miss Martin, Mr. Zane, Marc Lafayette, and STORM Command," Bridger listed succinctly.

"Marc? He's here, too?"

Bridger shook his head. "He's recuperating down South. Wanted to see his family. He's doing fine, though."

"I'm glad. And Nate?" Kick asked, hoping against hope his friend had survived. He needed to apologize in a big way.

"Dr. Daneby is still in critical condition, taken to a private hospital in Paris as per DFP instructions. I can request an update if you like. I understand you two are friends."

"We are." At least he hoped so. If Nate could find it in his heart to forgive him. Kick sighed heavily. "I'd appreciate that." He paused for a second, thinking of the bad start to the mission. "I'm sorry about the others—the guys who went down with the plane. Losing men really sucks."

"Yeah," Bridger said. A look of grim sadness snaked across his features. "It does. And it makes STORM all the more determined to find those responsible."

"I killed abu Bakr," Kick said, feeling a potent brew of satisfaction and relief. Then he frowned. "That's been verified, right?"

"Mr. Zane did make a preliminary ID," Bridger told him. "But the body was pretty badly torn up during the air strike. We're waiting for your confirmation of the photos, to be 100 percent sure."

"Shit," Kick muttered. "I suppose DNA is too much to ask for?"

"We took samples, but there's nothing to compare it with.

Meanwhile, one of the other al Sayika leaders from the camp is unaccounted for. Abbas Tawhid."

"*He* was there?" Kick strained to remember, but came up blank.

"Yes, according to Mr. Zane. You didn't see him?"

"No . . . but I was unconscious a lot." Unwillingly, he thought about the photo of Nate and Tawhid that Forsythe had shown him.

As though reading his thoughts, Bridger quickly explained about Nate saving Tawhid's mother's life and the subsequent deal they'd made over the kidnapped aid workers. It sounded exactly like something Nate would do. Why hadn't he just said so?

Why hadn't Kick just trusted him?

Hell.

The same reason he hadn't trusted his feelings for Rainie. Or hers for him. Trust issues? Just a bit.

"Anyway," Bridger continued, "Tawhid escaped with a briefcase which Mr. Zane believes contained vials of the bio weapon they were developing there at the camp. The same virus they injected you with."

Alarm zinged through Kick. "Abu Bakr had a briefcase on him. But, surely it was destroyed in the air strike."

Bridger pursed his lips. "We recovered traces of the case abu Bakr was carrying, and the vials. The heat of the attack obliterated any trace of the virus itself. But according to Mr. Zane, there were two cases. We have to assume Tawhid took the other with him."

Kick stared. The implications hit him hard. "*Je*sus! Al Sayika is already planning their next attack."

"That's STORM's assessment, too."

He swore harshly. "We have to find that briefcase."

"Already looking," Bridger concurred. He set the coffee aside and leaned forward. "Mr. Zane seems pretty sure al Sayika has turned someone on the inside. CIA, FBI, maybe the military. Someone highly placed."

It was unsettling to hear Kick's own conspiracy theory spoken aloud. "You've questioned Alex?" he asked, buying time to think.

Bridger nodded. "Every day since you arrived. Mr. Zane

has one hell of a story. It's a goddamn miracle he's still alive."

"Shocked the hell out of me," Kick admitted. Never in a million years would he forget that split second when time stood still and he realized that his emaciated fellow prisoner was his best friend. He let out a shaky breath.

Bridger gave him a moment, slowly spinning the silver envelope in his hand, then said, "He told us there was a Western doctor who was working with abu Bakr."

Kick nodded. "Count Girard Virreau. Ran into him during the air strike. Pretty damning."

The other man darted him an assessing look. "He's dead. They searched his belongings at the DFP refugee camp. It appears he was smuggling blood diamonds for al Sayika."

"Marc and I surmised as much." Kick thought about the mysterious warning the count had given him. *You don't know who you're dealing with. Kill me and they'll just find someone else to take my place.* "A lot of terrorists get their funding through the illegal diamond trade. But Virreau was only a pawn in the bigger scheme. The real traitor is closer to home."

"So you agree with Zane's theory about the mole in our government."

Kick met the other man's eyes. "Yeah."

"Sure you're not both being—understandably, mind you— paranoid?"

He wondered how much more he should say. One word to the wrong person and he was as good as dead. He was pretty sure he'd only stayed alive these past sixteen months because he'd quit Zero Unit and kept his mouth shut about his dark suspicions. Which, admittedly, had eaten at his soul the entire time like a cancer. But with his injuries it had been impossible to do anything about it. Then—with the help of his addiction—he'd convinced himself it wasn't his problem.

But now he could. Bridger and STORM could ferret out the bigger scumbags and expose them. Being dead to the world was great, but Kick wanted that normal life with Rainie. He wanted to be able to walk down the street without fear, wanted Rainie to be able to pursue her career without worrying that some bad guy would find her and use her against Kick.

This man Bridger could do that. Kick just had to level with him. Give him all the information he had. Share his theories. "Yeah. I've been convinced there's a traitor on the inside ever since A-stan," he told him. "It's why I went off-grid for so long. There's definitely a connection here in the States. I'm sure that's how we were ambushed in A-stan, and hit going into the Sudan. Abu Bakr was warned."

Bridger smiled. But it wasn't a nice kind of smile. "STORM Command agrees. Which is why we'd like to offer you a job."

Whoa. Wait. "*Me?*"

"Marc Lafayette has already requested this mission. And highly recommended we recruit you for it, too."

Not exactly what he had in mind for his immediate future. Or the long-term. He'd wanted to get out of the sniper business for good.

On the other hand . . . what else did he know how to do, really? And what kind of a future could he enjoy if he didn't do everything possible to stop this threat to his country . . . and himself?

Damn.

But he had to talk to Rainie. Work out a few important things first. "Give me a couple of days to think about it," he told Bridger.

The older man stood. "No problem. It's the kind of work that could easily get a man killed. For real this time."

Nothing new in that. "If I accept," Kick said, "I'd want complete protection for Rainie."

"We've already offered her a job, too. Here at the sanatorium, taking care of Alex. Secure facility, twenty-four-hour guards." Bridger held up a business card, then set it on the nightstand along with the silver envelope he'd been holding the whole time. "When you're ready, give me a call. Meanwhile"—he winked—"enjoy being a dead man."

"THIRTY-three."

Alex collapsed on the soft carpet of his room at Shady Acres—No, Haven Oaks. Apparently it was a small, private sanatorium—no doubt very expensive. He didn't know why

STORM Corps was footing the bill, but he wasn't about to complain. He was just grateful they'd been able to keep his return to the States top secret and need-to-know, so the press hadn't gotten wind of the story. Just what he'd need— his face to be splashed across every damned newspaper and TV news show in the country:

LOST HERO RETURNS FROM THE DEAD!

Nothing like handing his ass to the enemy on a platter. The Sultan of Pain might be dead—thank you, God and Kick Jackson—but al Sayika was alive and well, no doubt determined to tie up a talkative loose end in the form of one Christopher Alex Zane.

Cheek to the carpet, Alex gulped down several stinging lungfuls of air. He wasn't supposed to be out of bed yet. Doctor's orders. Rainie was being a real Nurse Ratched about it, too. He'd had to sneak behind her back. But if he could fucking do push-ups back in his old prison hellhole, he sure as fuck could do them now, too . . . even if they were of the one-armed sissy variety. And not take a shower? Just try and stop him. So he'd carefully watched how she attached the IV leads so he could unhook himself, and had confined his covert infractions to naptime.

After tortuously climbing to his feet again, he hurried across the room—if by hurry you meant shuffling like a hundred-year-old geezer—to the bathroom. He peered into the mirror in disgust. Some damn hero. Body like a skeleton and could barely see an inch of skin between all the bandages. Hell, could barely see, period. His eyes were so inflamed the doc was amazed his sight was slowly coming back at all. Thank God for modern medicine.

He swiped a fluffy towel from the rack and pressed it to his sweaty face. And thank God for civilization. For a moment he just stood there, holding the towel against his cheeks, absorbing the miraculous softness and breathing in the clean, flowery scent. Trembling like a baby but counting all of his goddamn blessings.

He was doing well with his exercise regime. Up to thirty-three one-armed push-ups, and twice that number of sit-ups today. A record, for sure. The gunshot arm was healing nicely. And all the torture wounds. They'd grafted skin from where he still had some. Shaved him and given him a fly haircut. Finally able to keep food down, he'd gained eight pounds in the past week. Good progress, his doctor said.

But the memory? Not so much.

Give it time, his doctor said. Baby steps.

Every morning his bed was wheeled to the video conferencing room, where a whole string of military and intelligence people took turns interviewing him, his old bosses from Zero Unit included. They'd been pretty furious that STORM wouldn't tell them where they had him stashed. But that was the deal—the only way he'd agree to talk to them. Kick was convinced, and he agreed, one of the bastards was a traitor and surely out to kill them both. Alex didn't want to push his luck. He'd probably used up all his come-back-from-the-dead tokens over the previous year.

He peered into the mirror, studying his own unfamiliar face. And wondered which of the faces on the video monitor was that of an enemy whore. . . . He was keeping careful notes on everyone who questioned him. He'd bet anything the bastard who had sent him to die was one of those flag-waving hypocrites who were interrogating him like *he'd* done something wrong. Too bad he hadn't recognized a damned one of their faces. Not even his old commanding officers.

Fucking scary as hell. And fucking depressing, too. Almost made him miss the cruel but brutal honesty of his late tormentors.

Okay, that was a fucking lie.

One by one, he started peeling off his bandages. Wincing at what he found beneath the hospital white. Wishing *those* memories would disappear, instead of the ones before the torture had started. It would be nice to have a good memory or two to dwell on.

Hell, even his naked redheaded Angel with an *H* had deserted him. No teasing erotic dreams had appeared since they'd started him on the meds. Not one. Just long nights of dreamless sleep. He missed *her* like fucking crazy.

He'd asked his doctor about her, of course. Another delusion? The doctor had smiled broadly and told him he'd been engaged before going missing. Engaged! To a Helena Middleton.

Helena. With an *H*.

Hallelujah! He'd found his Angel!

Maybe a visit from her would jog his memory. Would he like to try?

Ya *think*?

So today he'd have something far better than dreams. He was getting the real thing. They were transporting her up in a private jet. Blindfolded, he presumed, so as not to give away his supersecret location. Whatever it took.

With excruciating slowness, he gingerly showered—how great was *that*?—carefully combed his hair, laboriously plastered on new bandages, put on a fresh arm sling, and dressed himself in his most masculine scrubs—the cammie ones Rainie had bought for him. Yeah, they wouldn't let him wear real clothes just yet. Still too messed up.

He hooked himself back up to the IV catheter. But he couldn't make himself get back in that bed. So he stood facing the window, staring out at the carefully manicured sanatorium gardens, waiting to meet the woman who had given him the most precious thing possible through sixteen months of hell—hope.

He waited. And waited. And then finally—

"Alex?"

He spun away from the lush view, his heart pounding out of control.

From the door, Rainie smiled excitedly. She knew. "You have visitors."

Visitors? More than one? "But—"

"Your fiancée, Helena, is here, and, *um*, a liaison from the FBI."

"FBI?" Alarm zinged through him. "No. I don't want to see—"

But then she was standing there. In his doorway. *His Angel.* Alive, in person! Looking as radiant and gorgeous and stunning and oh-so-tempting as in any of his dreams. Oh, my fucking God, she was beautiful. Even in that awful brown suit, with her wild red hair wound tight into a bun at the back of her neck.

"Zane?" she whispered, her eyes glistening.

Helena. He took a step forward, suddenly tongue-tied. "Christ," he murmured past the lump in his throat. "Do you have any idea how fucking many times you saved my life in that hellhole?"

Her eyes softened along with her watery smile. "Language, Zane."

He gave a wobbly grin, and somehow knew she'd said that to him many, many times in the past. He reached for her. "Please—"

"Alex!"

Suddenly, another woman burst into the room like a whirlwind. A striking brunette. "Rebel, you *promised* to wait! Oh, *Alex!*" she squealed, and flung herself straight into his arms—well, arm—her silky sundress whirling about them like a colorful cloud, knocking down a monitor so Rainie had to save it while he winced and grabbed the edge of the bed to keep them from falling over onto that. She smelled like . . . fresh cucumber. "I cannot *believe* you're alive! This is just so amazing!" She kissed him on his bandaged cheek, beaming.

Alex blinked. An FBI liaison, Rainie had said? She acted more like a high school cheerleader.

He looked over at his Angel in abject confusion. "Helena?"

Rainie's smile was ear to ear, but his redheaded Angel's faltered.

"No, silly," Rainie said, "that's your friend with the FBI, Rebel Haywood."

Rebel . . . Wait, *who* did she mean? "What?"

Rainie pointed to the woman clinging to him, the cute brunette in the sundress smelling of cucumber, laughing as if nothing in the world was back-asswards, and beaming at him like he should be the happiest man in the world.

"*That* is Helena Middleton, Alex. *She* is your fiancée."

KICK didn't have to open his eyes to know it was Rainie. He just knew. By her quiet, sure footsteps; by the way she lovingly adjusted the sheet over his body, her hand lingering on his chest to feel it rise and fall. The way she bent to brush a tender kiss onto his forehead with a sigh, the soft tickle of her silky blond hair on his cheek. The uniquely compelling scent of her filling every one of his senses.

Rainie. The woman he loved.

Yes, loved. Loved with every cell of his body and every breath of his soul.

Being that close to death had taught Kick one big, important lesson about life.

Live for today. Grab love with both hands and hang on as long as you possibly can. Trust that it's real.

Don't punish yourself for past actions. Don't anesthetize your heart because of past hurts. And don't assume others can't love you just because you find it hard to love yourself. Forgive. Others, but most of all, yourself. Move on.

He wanted a normal life. But what was normal? For anyone? Fuck that. Life was what you made of it. Today. The past was just that. Over and done. Gone forever. What he wanted was a future.

With Rainie.

Damn it, he needed her in his todays and tomorrows. Needed her badly. In every one of them. Every minute of every one of them. And he wasn't going to deny himself the opportunity to have her there just because he was too big of a coward to ask her.

Not that he had to. She'd already told him how she felt about him.

I love you. She'd said it so sweetly. So honestly. Twice.

She trusted. *He* was the one who hadn't been able to say it back. Or do anything other than make lame excuses.

Idiot.

But he planned to remedy that mistake. For the rest of his life. For every today he was given with her. For every minute of every one of them.

I love you.

He needed to say it back.

He opened his eyes. "God, Rainie, I—"

She gasped in shock. "You're awake! Finally! Oh, thank God." She plopped on the bed and hugged him fiercely. Then gave him a long kiss . . . ending with her hand on his forehead. Ever the nurturing caretaker. "How are you feeling? Oh, you're hot!"

"So I've been told," he said with a wink. He felt like crap, feverish, with the mother of all headaches, but he wasn't about to tell her that. There were more important things to talk about. He held her face in his hands and kissed her back. "You look pretty hot yourself."

She rolled her eyes, but the warm glow in them didn't diminish, and her smile just grew. "In a coma for a week, almost dead, but some things never change."

He pulled her close and held her tight. Never wanted to let her go. "I can't believe we made it back alive. No thanks to me."

"You are so wrong. You taught me so much. I wouldn't have lasted a day over there without you."

He drew back. Stroked her face. "But how on earth did you get us out of the Sudan? With the three of us in that condition?" Not that anything about this woman would surprise him any longer. Her bravery and resourcefulness were unending.

"It wasn't me. STORM sent a helicopter."

He raised his eyebrows. Bridger hadn't mentioned that. "But you must have radioed for help. How? Did the camel come back with our packs?"

She got an impish look. "Not exactly. I'd called in for the air strike earlier, like we were supposed to, but when they learned you'd been captured and I was going to try and rescue you and Alex, they sent backup."

"Across the border? That was risky."

"Thank goodness," she said, "because without immediate medical intervention, most likely neither you, Alex, nor Nathan would have made it."

A sobering thought.

STORM really did take care of their operatives. What a contrast from Zero Unit.

He pulled her down to lie on the bed next to him, tugging her close. He wanted to feel her warm breath on his skin, feel the flutter of her heart against his chest. "Were you okay? With the plane ride and everything?"

She smiled up at him. "Other than the part where you were dying?"

He kissed the tip of her nose. "Yeah, other than that."

"Actually, I enjoyed it. Seeing all those clouds below was

unreal. And the little fields and houses and cars. An amazing sight."

He chuckled. "They just offered me a job, you know." When she gave him a puzzled look, he added, "STORM Corps."

For a nanosecond her face froze. Then her smile was back. "Yeah? Wow. That's . . . Are you going to take it?"

He cupped his hand around her cheek. "Hell, we did our part. Let someone else have a turn at saving the world. Besides, there are one or two things I'd much rather do."

Her gaze warmed. "Yeah? Like what?"

It was obvious what she was thinking. But she was wrong. Well. Okay, she was right, but that wasn't what he meant. Not this time.

He reached over for the silver envelope Bridger had left on the table and handed it to her. *Rainie* was written on the front of it.

"This, for starters."

She tilted her head, confused.

"Compliments of STORM." He hadn't peeked inside, but he had a pretty good idea what it contained. Which would play into his plans perfectly. "Open it."

She ripped open the flap curiously, and pulled out a key on an elaborate chain. The tag said *Penthouse*. She hesitated. "Okaaay."

Kick smiled. He'd heard stories about STORM Command's generosity to its operators and consultants. Huge bonuses. Lavish digs, safe houses, and vacation paradises—all with flawless security, like here at Haven Oaks. If STORM had arranged for the penthouse, an entire army wouldn't be able to get to them. And it would be a whole lot more private than a hospital room for what he had in mind.

"Their way of saying thank you for salvaging a disastrous mission," he explained. He winked. "But I figure they'll let me go along, too."

She made a face, then pulled out the only other thing in the envelope—a calling card. Engraved on it was the address of a venerable Park Avenue hotel.

She gasped softly. "The hotel where we met! But . . . how did they know?"

"Zero Unit aren't the only ones good at tracking people down."

He tugged her close for a lingering kiss. "How long do you think before I'm discharged?" he asked, his voice husky with a sudden voracious need for her. And a whole lot more.

"Not tonight, so don't get your hopes up, mister."

He groaned softly. "Shame to waste that penthouse . . ."

"It'll wait." She frowned down at the card. "I hope."

"*Mmm*. Probably just as well." He nuzzled her neck. "You'll probably need a few days to arrange things, anyway."

She snuggled against his chest. "Not a problem. I doubt I'll have to pack much." Her lips teased his neck.

"Why pack at all?" he suggested as she drew her moist tongue erotically over his Adam's apple.

She made a sexy noise in her throat. "You are so bad."

"That's why you love me, baby."

She glanced up and the look of loving tenderness in her eyes took his breath away. "Yeah. I do," she murmured sweetly.

And he'd never get tired of hearing it. "*Mmm*. Let's not forget the license," he murmured back.

"Can't. I don't drive. Remember?" She chuckled softly. "Though, I s'pose I could get one now."

"Different kind of license," he corrected, smiling down at her.

"Oh? For what?"

"The kind that will make an honest man of me. I was hoping this could be . . . kind of like"—he took a deep breath and crossed his fingers she wouldn't run screaming from the room—"our honeymoon."

She stared up at him in stunned disbelief.

Oh, hell. "Unless you didn't mean what you said about loving me . . ."

"No. I mean yes! Of course I do. But . . . I thought you weren't interested in anything long-term, relationship-wise . . . ?"

"A guy can change his mind, can't he?" He slid his fingers into her hair, brushed a thumb over her cheekbone. "I love you, sweetheart. So very much."

She looked up at him, her gorgeous green eyes filled with

tears of joyful surprise. And pooled with undisguised hope.
"Yeah?"

"Yeah." He drew in a deep, cleansing breath, filling his
soul with the scent of her, the nearness of her. "You are all I
live for, Rainie. All I'll ever want. I want to be with you, now
and always."

"Really?" she whispered.

He swallowed. He couldn't believe he was doing this. But
it felt so right. So incredibly right. "Marry me, Rainie. Make
me the happiest man in the world. I know I'm probably the
worst risk on the planet, and you could do so much better,
but . . ."

Her eyes softened and glowed with joy. "I disagree. And
I'll take that risk, if only you'll let me prove you wrong."

"Let you? I'll get down on my knees and beg if I have to.
I love you with all my heart, Rainie. Please say you'll marry
me. Or at least move in together or—"

"Yes," she breathed, pressing her lips to his. "Oh, yes. To
all of the above."

He sent up a prayer of profound thanks. At long last, he'd
found what he'd been shooting for all his life. To find his
own true love, someone to cherish and be with. His own
place in the world.

And the thrilling promise of a future overflowing with
warmth and happiness.

EPILOGUE

Haven Oaks Sanatorium, NY
Two weeks later

"THANK you so much for doing this," Rainie said to Alex's fiancée, Helena.

She, Helena, and Alex and Helena's FBI friend, Rebel, were standing outside Alex's room at Haven Oaks, where Rainie was about to become Mrs. Kyle Jackson. She and Kick had decided to hold the small wedding ceremony here because the doctors still wouldn't let the best man out of bed.

"Oh, Rainie, please. It's an honor! Truly." Helena beamed. "It'll give me practice for when Alex and I get married!" She gave her an air-kiss on the cheek and disappeared into the room.

Rainie wished she could beam, too. This should be the happiest, most amazing day of her life. And it would be, if only her best friend were here. It should be Gina standing at her side, holding the bouquet of pink roses and orange blossoms that Kick had bought for her, and dabbing tears and sharing hugs afterward, not a virtual stranger.

But Gina had disappeared.

Rebel squeezed Rainie's hand. "Don't worry, the FBI will find your friend," she said. "It's what we do."

"Thank you," she whispered, blinking back a wellspring of emotion. The woman had no idea what was involved.

Gina'd told neighbors she was visiting relatives, but Rainie had called every one of them, and no one knew where she was. She was terrified that by originally calling Gina for help while talking with Jason Forsythe, she'd somehow put her friend in danger. She couldn't imagine what kind, but look what had happened to Rainie when she just flirted with the wrong man.

Yes, okay, she was about to marry that man . . . but still. The thought that Gina could be in some kind of awful trouble because of her filled Rainie with a sick, gnawing fear.

Where *was* she?

"Are you sure you don't want to postpone the wedding?" Rebel asked sympathetically. "I'm sure Kick would wait for you no matter how long it took."

Rebel was sweet, pretty, and a bit more perceptive than her friend Helena. For a split second, Rainie wondered about Alex's choice of fiancée.

She took a deep breath. "I know he would. Believe me, I've wrestled with the decision all week. But Kick may be leaving on an assignment any day now, and we don't want to chance waiting."

Kick had insisted he didn't want to take the job with STORM, but Rainie knew better. Abu Bakr might be dead and his attacks on the Western embassies prevented—this time. But his organization was still out there, planning its next reign of terror with the horrible virus that had nearly killed Kick. She knew he would never forgive himself if even a single person died because he'd decided to take the easy way out, letting others finish the job he'd started. Not to mention the fact that he'd have to stay "dead" until the threat from al Sayika was neutralized for good.

Rainie wanted him alive . . . in every possible way.

So she had insisted right back. And they'd both accepted the jobs with STORM—effective as soon as they returned from their penthouse honeymoon.

Honeymoon . . .

Just the sound of it brought a smile to her face, despite everything. The thought of finally having Kick all to herself was almost as enticing as the thought of being Mrs. Kyle

Jackson. *Almost*. It had been a very long two weeks, with barely a minute alone together.

"Okay, then," Rebel said encouragingly. "Ready?"

"Ready." Rainie straightened her shoulders, raised her bouquet, and turned to Alex's door, at last allowing joy and excitement to flow through her. "I can't believe I'm getting married."

"You look stunning," Rebel said, and smiled as she opened the door for her. "Good luck."

Rainie stepped over the threshold to a collective sigh from the small crush of friends and staff who'd gathered in the room for the wedding. As soon as she saw the dazzled look of love in Kick's eyes, everything else flew from her mind.

Oh, my God. She was really doing this. Marrying the most dangerous man she'd ever met in her life—no, make that the most *amazing* man she'd ever met in her life. The most wounded and needful. But also the most honorable and brave, by light-years. Quite simply the most *man* she'd ever met.

And he was all hers. At least he would be, after he said, "I do."

She couldn't wait.

Kick took her hands in his and the pastor started saying the traditional words, but she didn't hear a thing save the beating of her heart, certain she would wake up any second and find this was all just an incredible dream. How could her ordinary life have changed so drastically in three short weeks? How could *she* have changed so drastically?

Finally, the pastor got her attention. "Do you, Lorraine Emily Martin, take this man, Kyle Spencer Jackson, to be your lawfully wedded husband?"

"I do," she managed to say past the sweet clot of emotion rising in her throat.

Looking into the eyes of the man she loved to distraction, joy filled her heart to the very brim. They would be so happy together. Sure, there would be bumps, but she couldn't imagine a better person to face them with. They'd already been through so much together. Their relationship had been forged in danger and shaped by passion and respect.

It was funny . . . for most of her life, she'd ached for someone like Kick to keep her safe and protect her from all the evil in the world. At last, she'd finally found him—but she was no longer terrified, no longer felt the need to be protected—and all because of what he'd taught her . . . about herself. Now, instead, she wanted to protect *him*. From the cruelty he'd hinted at in his childhood, from the violence he'd witnessed in the world, from the emptiness and desolation that had marred his life before they met. She wanted to shower him with love and warmth and affection, so he would never again feel alone or unloved.

Because, oh, how she loved him!

"Do you, Kyle Spencer Jackson, take this woman, Lorraine Emily Martin, to be your lawfully wedded wife?"

"I do."

There. Finally!

He was all hers.

"With this ring, I thee wed," he murmured, the grittiness of his voice betraying the emotion in his throat, too.

The simple gold band he slipped on her finger was the most beautiful thing Rainie had ever seen. It felt so right. Meant so much.

She slipped her ring on his finger, and breathlessly recited the words that would bind her to him for all time. Then looked up into his beautiful, passion-filled eyes.

"I love you," he whispered.

"I love you," she whispered back.

And then the smiling minister said, "I now pronounce you husband and wife."

And finally, *finally*, Kick kissed her.

A perfect kiss, filled with possibilities and promises for the years ahead.

And everyone cheered.

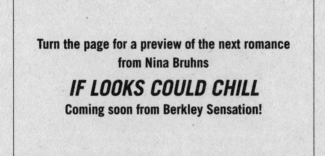

Turn the page for a preview of the next romance
from Nina Bruhns

IF LOOKS COULD CHILL

Coming soon from Berkley Sensation!

"SHE seems young."

Marc Lafayette flicked a glance over at fellow STORM operator Bobby Lee Quinn, who was lounging against a pillar in an elegantly tailored tuxedo, sipping a martini, appearing for all the world like he attended embassy parties every day of his life.

Marc knew better. Quinn was a Bama redneck with gun grease under his fingernails from all the ground ops he'd led in the past six or seven years working for STORM Corps. Still, for some obscure reason women loved him.

"Too young for you, *boug*," Marc warned. For all the good that would do. If it wore a skirt, Quinn was all over it. He returned his gaze to the newest CIA officer to hit Istanbul this summer. Darcy Zimmerman. Fresh as spring rain, and pretty as a bayou orchid in a strapless blue gown that had their Arab hosts either frowning or drooling. Her cover was assistant to the cultural attaché at the US embassy. But already she was attracting too much attention for a spook.

He gave the blond ingénue a week in this cauldron of politics, jealousy, and backstabbing. Tops.

"Wonder if she's even legal," Quinn mused.

Dieu. Less than a week, if Quinn got his hands on her. "Why? You plannin' some kind of mischief, *mon ami*?"

"You got a problem with that, friend?"

Yeah. He did. The girl looked fresh out of college, and no way was she ready to handle whatever Quinn had in mind to dish her way. But . . .

Not his business. Besides, they'd assigned her to Istanbul, so she must be able to look after herself. As long as she didn't compromise his mission or need rescuing, Marc didn't care what she looked like. He shrugged, dismissing the girl and the subject.

They weren't here at the Dumani embassy decked out in penguin suits to pick up women. They had a job to do. And Quinn was a pro. He wouldn't get distracted. If he did, *he* could do the *foutre* rescuing.

CIA had brought in STORM to help on this dash-and-grab for the deniability factor. Strategic Technical Operations and Rescue Missions Corporation—STORM Corps—was a nongovernmental spec ops outfit that hired out to private companies and individuals, mainly to recover and defend hostages and other assets. But they were often used to carry out sensitive or controversial covert ops in locations and situations where official government agencies couldn't or wouldn't go.

Such as this one.

Upstairs on the third floor of the Dumani embassy was a safe containing an envelope with new identity papers for Jallil Abu Bakr and Abbas Tawhid, the two men suspected of being the driving force behind al Sayika, one of the worst terrorist organizations to burst onto the international scene since al Qaeda. Last year alone, al Sayika cells had blown up the Dutch stock exchange, poisoned a Jordanian prince actively advocating for equal rights for women within Islam, and murdered a French National Police commander for clamping down on the race riots in the Paris *banlieux*. Just as fanatical as bin Laden, and far more sophisticated in his long-term planning, abu Bakr and Tawhid were up there on everyone's Most Wanted list, right under their fuckbuddy.

Tonight Marc and Quinn were to get to the embassy safe, open it, and photo-digitize the duo's documents without making a ripple. That last part was vital. No one could know the safe had been breached. abu Bakr was an enigma; no living Western agent had ever seen his face. Abbas Tawhid was a cruel, ruthless sociopath who had risen through the ranks through sheer brutality. His face was well known but the aliases he traveled under were not. Getting their hands on these identity papers would be huge. The information they contained would insure the two would be caught and al Say-ika's growing power in the terrorist world stopped before it gained any more momentum.

CIA Barbie—aka Darcy Zimmerman—was supposed to pass them the combination to the safe—obtained from an enterprising embassy cleaning lady who'd gotten the deal of a lifetime, compliments of the US taxpayers.

Marc wondered how Zimmerman had managed that coup, especially looking like she did. Frankly, he'd been expect-ing their contact to be a short, frumpy fortysomething old-maid type with no makeup and sensible shoes. But tall, golden blond and model-gorgeous Darcy Zimmerman broke the mold on all counts. The Company must be raising their standards.

Speak of the devil. Zimmerman was coming toward them on the arm of the Dumani agricultural attaché. She laughed at something the old roué said in her ear—he had to go prac-tically on tiptoes—just as she spotted them.

"There you are!" she called with a cheerful wave, as if they'd actually met before. "I thought you two had left with-out me!"

Without missing a beat, she answered Quinn's welcoming smile with one of her own and slid into his arms for a hug, kissing him on the cheeks, Euro style. "Darling, meet Sheikh Asood." She introduced them, using code names they'd been given for the op.

She was smooth; Marc had to give her that.

And so was Quinn. One smarmy smile and *he* ended up as the boyfriend, *le tayau*. Not that Marc was particularly inter-ested. *Bon*, she was beautiful, but definitely not his type. He preferred women who had nothing to do with the world he worked in. And unlike Quinn, he never mixed business and pleasure.

As they made meaningless chitchat with Asood, Marc studied what he could see of the embassy's structure. He knew from blueprints supplied by STORM that the building was an old converted Ottoman palace. Complex mosaic décor adorned the carved stucco walls and high ceilings; intricate marble arches and gilded scrollwork were everywhere, the perfect backdrop to the luxurious furnishings, rugs, and tapestries. Pretty impressive stuff.

The good news was because of the palace's age and historical value, very little renovation had taken place inside—including even the most rudimentary security features. No cameras, alarms, or motion detectors. The bad news was, guards had been liberally sprinkled around the main staircases. It would be tricky getting past them.

"Shall we visit the buffet?" Zimmerman suggested, looping her wrists around each of their elbows after Asood saw which way the wind blew and moved on.

"I'm Quinn, by the way," Bobby Lee said, pulling her closer to his side than was strictly necessary.

She smiled up at him. "Yeah. I know. You guys ready for this?"

"You've got the combination?" Marc asked, trying to move things along as they casually strolled from the salon toward the opulent dining room. They had to wade through three smaller rooms crushed with people to reach it. He instinctively scanned faces and body language, looking for anything suspicious. So far, so good.

"Just follow my lead," she said.

They grabbed plates and selected a few morsels from the overflowing buffet table, slowly making their way down the line. She obviously had a plan, so he and Quinn just went along, ready for anything. Marc already had a plan, but what was he going to do about it, stamp his foot and demand his was better? Besides, maybe his wasn't better. *Semper Gumby.*

"How do you like Istanbul so far?" he asked Zimmerman, to fill the silence. Ah, *merde.* She and Quinn were already making goo-goo eyes at each other over the hors de oeuvres. Marc barely resisted rolling his own. *Get a room.* Please. *After* the op.

"Amazing place," she answered, still looking at Quinn. "Gorgeous city."

"Aren't you afraid?" Quinn asked. "Being a young woman alone and all. Dangerous place, Istanbul."

She gave him a dazzling smile. "Worried about me?"

He grinned. "Wouldn't want anything untoward to happen."

Not until he got her back to his hotel room, anyway.

Bon Dieu.

She reached up and touched Quinn's chin with a finger. "Hell, no fun in that."

Marc was just about to clear his throat and suggest getting back to business when she winked at him and suddenly melted back through an arched opening he recalled seeing on the blueprints. Hidden by a beaded screen, it blended in perfectly with the line of marble arches marching along the back wall of the room. But this one opened discretely into a darkened hallway leading to the kitchens in the back.

She'd timed her exit to exactly when the guard was looking the other way, distracted by a serving spoon clattering onto the marble floor like a firecracker. A setup?

Well, damn. Not bad. Marc slipped through after her, followed by Quinn.

She deposited her plate on a cart sitting in the shadows and they quickly did the same. She beckoned, hurrying down the hall until they reached a narrow flight of stairs.

"This is the servants' staircase," she whispered. "It goes all the way up. You know where the safe is hidden, right?" She glanced between the two of them, her gaze finally landing on Marc.

"Third floor. Second office, east wing," he recited.

"Exactly. Here." From a low hall table drawer she produced a red-patterned *kaffiyeh* scarf of the type worn by the Saudi-aligned Arabs, along with the distinctive bronze knotted *agal* of the Dumani security guards to hold it in place. "You'll blend in better than Quinn," she said.

Considering Quinn had short, golden-blond hair and striking blue eyes reminiscent of an Alaskan Husky in the dead of winter, and Marc was typical Cajun dark, yeah, you think?

"I'm also lead on this one," he informed her dryly.

"Pretend you're a guard," she said, ignoring the gentle barb. "You speak Arabic, right?"

He nodded. "Some."

"Good. However, there's been a complication."

Naturellement. It wouldn't be a typical joint-CIA goat-fuck without one. And here he'd thought he'd gotten off easy, with just Quinn's flag waving in the air.

"The stairs between the second and third floors were varnished today," she said. "They're still wet."

Which meant he'd leave permanent footprints. Yeah, *mal pris.* Not good.

"*What?*" Quinn exploded under his breath, his face clouding with anger. "Why didn't you tell us this in the—"

"It'll still work," she insisted to Marc. "You'll just have to come around to the front staircase and sneak past the guards to get to the other wing. There's an old *harim* staircase that leads up to the third floor."

They already knew that, but had dismissed it as unnecessarily dangerous. The staircase spilled out into the ambassador's private quarters rather than the hallway. *Foutre.*

Quinn looked ready to strangle her. "And how the *fuck* is he supposed get by the guards without being—"

"He'll look like one of them. And you and I will create a diversion," she said impatiently, then turned back to Marc. "Just be in position and ready to roll in five, okay?"

It sounded crazy. But crazy had worked before.

"What the hell." He grabbed the *kaffiyeh* from her and wound it expertly around his head and shoulders. What was the worst that could happen? Firing squad at dawn? No big deal. Standard occupational hazard.

"Safe combination?" he asked.

She rattled it off and he committed it to memory. To his surprise, she reached up and gave him a kiss on the cheek, too. "Good luck." Then she was off, hurrying back toward the dining room.

Quinn shook his head, obviously not pleased. "Still time to call it off, buddy. Or switch back to our own plan."

"No worries, *boug.* But that diversion? Make it a good one. Anything goes wrong, see you back at the rendezvous point."

"Sure. Right after I kill that chick."

* * *

GRINDING his teeth, Robert Lee Quinn strode double-time after the CIA babe. This thing had clusterfuck written all over it.

Well, what did he expect from the Company? And here he'd had visions of trying to establish closer relations between their two organizations. . . . *Much* closer.

He snorted silently and followed her back through the beaded screen into the dining room. Darcy Zimmerman was hot as a Tuscaloosa afternoon in July, but if her lack of seasoning and preparedness got his friend killed—

Bobby Lee had worked with the Cajun Lafayette off and on over his six years at STORM, and liked him a lot. Marc was the kind of man who expected the best from people and usually got it. Like now, for instance. What planet did he live on to think this plan could actually work?

The long strands of beads clicked closed behind Bobby Lee and to his momentary surprise, Darcy Zimmerman greeted him with an "accidental" brush of her lush body as they rejoined the buffet line. He had to white-knuckle the plate in his hands so he didn't drop it. The under-the-lashes look she gave him was pure, unadulterated walking sex. She'd even managed to mess up her hair so it looked like he'd had his fingers in it just seconds ago.

Well, okay, then.

He readjusted his thinking. *This* part of her plan worked just fine for him, at least.

He'd caught on immediately, of course. They'd just slipped back from a steamy tryst in the hallway, which explained their sudden emergence from an off-limits area. The guard by the archway was shocked to see them. But at that sizzling look from Zimmerman, he gave them a salacious grin and let it go. Bobby Lee waggled his eyebrows.

Just call him Stud Lee.

His plate suddenly disappeared from his hands, and he found himself being steered through the crowd toward the front foyer with just enough casualness not to attract attention. But that full body contact had already gotten his unwavering attention.

And God, that dress.

The floor-length gown she wore was a true work of art. Blue like the Prophet's paradise, slinky like pearls running through your fingers, and without straps or any visible means of staying up, it hugged her curves like a man begging for more. And just about any man in the place *would* be begging for more, given half a chance. Including him. Hell, especially him. His breath was virtually backed up in his lungs waiting for her drapey blue bodice to come sliding down off her breasts. Her very amazing breasts. Full, ripe breasts that were pert and high and just the right size. Breasts a man could lose himself in completely.

Maybe CIA wasn't so stupid after all. Talk about Mata Hari potential.

And okay, this diversion thing might work. It could happen.

They got to the foyer and he tore his eyes off her long enough to do a quick survey. The evening was still early, but a few departing diplomats and their companions milled around to depart, waiting for limos to be fetched by chauffeurs.

He checked out the room itself. Despite having no furniture and no function beyond serving as the main entrance to the old palace, the massive octagonal gold-and-marble foyer was bigger than the whole stinkin' house Bobby Lee had grown up in. Which admittedly wasn't tough, since that had been a two-room backwoods shanty. Unlike that bad memory, this space was all done up fancier than a whore's wedding cake with a series of deep, fussy alcoves around the perimeter that contained giant potted palm trees and aromatic flowering shrubs. The place smelled like jasmine and oranges.

Or was that Darcy Zimmerman?

She looped her arm through his and tilted her head a fraction toward the centerpiece of the foyer, the grand staircase that ascended like a gilded stairway to heaven. The one Lafayette would have to get across at the second floor landing—past three armed guards—and reach the other side unseen before continuing up the *harim* stairs to the floor where the safe was located. Those guards looked big, mean, and no-nonsense, dressed in traditional Arab garb, complete with flashing scimitars hanging at their sides. Oh, yeah, and AK-47s.

This could get ugly.

"All right. Now what?" he asked under his breath, speaking into Zimmerman's cloud of golden hair.

He was six-four but he didn't even have to bend over. Man, she was tall in those heels. And she smelled damn good, he couldn't help but notice as she tipped up her face up to answer. Not jasmine and oranges, but some exotic blend of—

"You carrying a condom in any of those pockets?" she murmured, taking hold of his tux lapels and easing into him like a lover. Her fingers started to trail south.

Whoa. Hold on, there. *What?* "Um—" What the *fuck* did she just say?

Not that he wasn't all over it.

"Just in case you want to forget about the op and go back to my place," she added with an amused wink.

He felt his lips curve up. Very funny, ha-ha. Okay, she'd focused his wandering attention. But she obviously had no idea she was playing with fire here.

Far be it for him to warn her. Where there was smoke, fire wasn't far behind. And the woman was insanely smokin' hot.

Distraction? He'd give her a stinkin' distraction.

He put his hands on her waist and leisurely ran them over her hips and down onto her ass. Like her lover might. He held her gaze as he gathered her in his arms and ground her into him. Yeah, *him*. Center to center. Right where he was dying to have her.

The room's chatter suddenly dropped to whispers—some giggling, some disapproving—and he knew without a doubt that every person in the foyer was watching them.

He tilted his head down again, murmuring, "There's no 'just in case' about it, sugar. Later, you're all mine."

Her eyes widened, as though his calling her bluff caught her slightly off guard. Hardly surprising. She was a real firecracker. Probably most men she'd encountered out in the world either wilted like a linen suit in all that heat, or turned tail and ran screaming from her kind of strength and audacity.

Him, it just turned on all the more. He liked a woman to be his equal. Which she most assuredly was.

Ignoring everything and everyone around them, he leaned
down and languidly trailed hot breath over her cheek, down
to her lips. She gasped softly as he covered them with his.
And kissed her. Like he had every intention of following
through on his threat, but right then and there.

This was highly inappropriate behavior for an embassy
party, especially with a Muslim country as host. He figured
that outrageous kiss would earn him a resounding slap on the
cheek. As part of the diversion, of course.

But somewhere along the line his bold strategy backfired.
Because she kissed him back. Like she had every intention of
taking him up on that little dare.

Christ on a fuckin' cracker.

From the second his tongue touched hers he was hard as
the marble columns that surrounded them. Sweet mercy, she
tasted good.

But he couldn't. Not here. Not now. *The guards*, he reminded himself. Distract *them*, not himself.

He grasped her head in his hands and managed a glance
upward at the second floor landing as he changed the angle
of the kiss. At least it was working. The three Dumanis
were stunned by the sight of a beautiful woman's very public kiss with a man obviously not her husband.

Bobby Lee caught a glimpse of Marc taking a careful step
out from the shadows of the east wing hallway.

This was it.

He needed to be absolutely sure those guards would stay
distracted, shocked motionless, so absorbed by what he and
Zimmerman were doing that Marc could glide past their
backs in perfect safety.

And that was the only reason he spun her around and
walked her backwards one deliberate step at a time, kissing
her to within an inch of her life. Honestly it was.

He aimed for the short wall between two of those fancy
archways, and kept going until her backside hit mosaic tile.
Which finally roused her. She jerked out of his arms, took a
second to regroup, then shoved him away with an embarrassed giggle, playing the enamored junior embassy staffer
belatedly trying to salvage her job. "Darling, stop! People are
staring!"

But her eyes said, "Just wait till I get you alone, boy."

Real, or part of the charade?

Both?

One could only hope.

"Okay," she murmured, taking a deep breath. "Marc made it to the other side."

Thank you, Jesus.

Bobby Lee straightened his jacket, joining her where she leaned her back against the cool wall. He was breathing hard, his body thrumming with need. *Damn*, he wanted her.

"So, are you always this creative in your operations?" he asked, pitching his voice to barely audible. Suddenly he was insanely jealous of all the other operators she might have done this with in her short but no doubt illustrious spook career.

"Oh, you'd be surprised," she said.

Oh, he doubted it.

"But it seems to me *you're* the one who took it up a notch," she pointed out.

Possibly.

He looked at her. Wondering. *Was* this personal? "You didn't seem to object." He shrugged, playing it cool. "Got the job done."

"Yes," she agreed. "It did."

He stuck his hands in his trouser pockets so he wouldn't grab her again. "By the way, you're one hell of a kisser."

She smiled. "I know."

He barked a humorless laugh. "That mouth of yours is gonna get you in real trouble someday."

"Tell me something I *don't* know."

"Okay." He made a quarter turn to face her, dead serious. "When they fire you tomorrow, come work for me."

She blinked and stared at him. "Don't be absurd. They won't fire me."

"Maybe not tomorrow. But I'll bet you a thousand bucks that within two weeks you'll be suddenly transferred. To somewhere not nearly as glamorous as Istanbul. They're gonna ask you to do things you won't want to do." He hoped to hell she didn't want to do them. "When that happens, give me a call."

"I'll take that bet," she said. "Because you're crazy."

"Maybe. But I've been in this game a long time, sugar. I know how your bosses operate."

Her look turned incredulous. "All this because I let you kiss me?"

"Hell, no. It was the *way* you let me kiss you."

She obviously didn't understand. And he had to know.

He stepped in close, as though whispering licentious suggestions in her ear. "My kissing you had nothing to do with this job. You and I both know that. But *they* don't. They won't understand that I'm an irresistibly sexy guy and you want me naked. They'll think you'd do this with anyone they order you to."

He held his breath, waiting for her reaction.

"Oh, my God." Her mouth went crooked. "You really *are* insane."

Fuck.

"Just remember, STORM Corps. We're in the D.C. book."

"Look. I appreciate the—"

But he didn't give her the chance to finish the thought. He cut her off and in an instant was back to business.

"It's Marc. He's back on the landing, giving the signal that he has the package. We better do something quick."

DARCY banked her amazement at the sheer massive ego of the STORM operator and prepared herself to continue their mock-seduction-slash-pantomime diversion. But apparently the provocative but fairly harmless kissing she'd expected was not what Bobby Lee Quinn had in mind. Now, there was a shock. The man was simply unpredictable.

They were still leaning with shoulders against the wall, face-to-face, when he suddenly grabbed her and pushed her right into the nearest alcove.

She yelped. "What are you—"

His mouth crashed onto hers.

Taken by surprise, she didn't have the presence of mind to resist. And after about three seconds, okay, call her fickle, but resisting was the last thing on her mind.

Sometimes unpredictable was good.

Good Lord, what a kiss.

Everything about the man was hard. His body was hard against hers. His muscles were hard where they pressed into her. His lips and tongue were hard as they took her mouth in a blinding, grinding assault. His cock was huge and hard as it rocked into her belly, telling her it wanted her *now*. He practically vibrated with sexual power and virility.

Did she say *mock* seduction? If this was acting, Bobby Lee Quinn deserved a freaking Oscar.

She moaned, unable to stop her body from responding to the onslaught. Her nipples tightened. Her pulsed throbbed. Her limbs weakened—along with her mental capacity.

He might have an ego the size of Canada, but he was ridiculously, totally to-die-for sexy. In college she would have done Quinn in a hot second. She'd like to think she had more sense now, having managed to avoid men altogether since her last disastrous relationship. Talk about a train wreck. That one had actually had the audacity to propose marriage and babies while seeing someone else on the side.

But this man . . . This man made her stomach zing, and that sweet spot between her legs ache with a breathtaking need for his touch.

She might just have to let him have her.

She completely melted under his hands as they claimed her, touching her body. Caressing her breasts. Then they yanked the top of her gown down to her waist.

Sweet Jesus. "Quinn!"

"Distraction," he muttered.

She sucked in the cry of utter protest that leapt to her lips. But his fingers found her bare breasts, then her nipples, and squeezed, hard, and she cried out loud, for real.

Except it didn't sound like her. The cries sounded male. But not Quinn's. His mouth was still too busy kissing her.

She ripped her lips from his.

The guards. It was the *guards* shouting. At *them*.

For the second time that night, she forced herself to break out of Quinn's sensual web. How did he keep *doing* that to her?

Vainly she attempted to yank her top back up, but the guards were on them too fast. Yelling. Waving guns. Pulling them apart. Dragging them out into the public foyer.

"Damn it, let me go!" she screamed at them.

His expression appalled, Quinn struggled to get free, to get to her. Apparently not what he'd had in mind. *That* was a relief.

"Leave the lady alone! For chrissakes let her cover herself!" he shouted. Among other choice, anatomically difficult suggestions.

As a diversion it was pretty damn good.

She was half naked. Quinn's vocabulary was amazingly imaginative. Deadly AK-47s were pointing at their heads. Everyone in the place was mesmerized with shock.

Except the third guard.

This was the night in her fledgling career that Darcy Zimmerman learned an important lesson: There's one in every crowd—the inevitable *one* member of the enemy camp who is actually alert and good at his job.

The third guard wasn't staring at her bare breasts. Or aiming his weapon at Quinn. Even though he was standing in the middle of the melee, he was watching the stairs like he was supposed to be doing. Which was where he spotted Lafayette. Sneaking down them. She cursed under her breath. Where was Marc's *kaffiyeh* and *agal*? He must have decided to take a shortcut and try blending into the crowd.

"Halt!" the guard shouted, rushing over to intercept him before he jumped the banister and got away. "Stop or I will shoot you!"

The sound of a half-dozen guns being locked and loaded echoed like shots off the marble.

Lafayette froze. And was instantly surrounded by three more guards.

Darcy's stomach plummeted.

Oh, *fuck*.

They were so screwed.